A TASTE OF SEDUCTION

MARY CAMPISI

MARY CAMPISI BOOKS, LLC

COPYRIGHT

A Taste of Seduction was previously published in 2011 by The Wild Rose Press.

Print ISBN: 978-1-942158-64-6

INTRODUCTION

Love and Betrayal...Regency style

A young woman of noble blood, raised as a peasant girl...

An orphaned stable boy, now grown and the surrogate son of a powerful earl—the same earl who just so happens to be the young woman's father...

Francie Jordan and Alexander Bishop have nothing in common—she runs barefoot and talks to animals. He won't loosen his cravat unless the bedroom door is firmly closed. She believes in love, second chances, and happily ever after. He believes in keeping a safe distance from anything that resembles an emotion. Indeed, they have nothing in common but an undeniable desire for one another they can't ignore, and an ailing "father" who will employ any means to bring them together.

Unfortunately, not everyone wishes to see a union between Francie and Alexander, and they will stop at nothing to keep this couple apart.

An Unlikely Husband Series:

To my mother—because you believed.

THE STORY BEHIND THE STORY

Alexander Bishop came to me as I lay on the hospital bed waiting for outpatient surgery. There I was, tucked into an oversized blue-and-white print hospital issue with an IV in one arm, beeps, buzzes, and scuffing footsteps pushing me toward a migraine. Without glasses or contacts, I could see about three inches in front of me, and that's a generous estimation. I didn't even have the calming voice of my husband next to me as he'd been shuttled to the waiting room.

I did the only thing a writer can do at a moment like this—I closed my eyes and thought of my next book, or more to the point, my next hero. I love creating heroes, the wounded kind that "bleeds hurt and been done wrong"—the kind every woman wants to heal. My mind wandered, the noises quieted, and there he was, Mr. Alexander Bishop, in his proper attire and perfectly tied cravat. When he popped into my head, I didn't know the details of his painful history, the lowly beginning as a stable boy with an empty belly and grimy hands, the father who beat him, the mother who didn't love him enough to save herself. I knew none of Alexander's story, but then I began to think about what would make a man like this avoid anything that smacks of emotion and what kind of woman could change his mind and heal his heart. Enter Francie Jordan, a carefree spirit who runs barefoot, dons men's breeches, and loves animals and people with innocent abandon and boundless energy.

1

England 1797

"Promise me."

The words fell from the woman's parched, bloodless lips. "Promise...me."

Her green eyes misted, filled with pain at the sudden tightening in her belly. She would endure. She had to.

"Let me send for the doctor, Catherine. Let him help you." The urgency in her sister's usually calm demeanor filled the room.

"No!" Another pain gripped her. Fierce. Powerful. It stabbed at the thin layer of control separating her from sanity and madness. She must hold fast until she knew.

Catherine tried to squeeze her sister's hand. Eleanor's fingers were so warm compared to her own, which felt as though she'd just plunged them in a mountain of snow. Cold. Numb. Like the hands of death. She shivered. "Promise me, Eleanor."

She saw the tears in her sister's eyes and tried to offer a

smile of reassurance. Strong, capable Eleanor. Just like an older sister. Oh, how Catherine needed her strength now.

Eleanor leaned over and smoothed a damp lock from Catherine's forehead. "I promise," she whispered. "But it won't be necessary. You'll see. The child will be a healthy, black-haired babe. And he'll look just like you and Edgar."

Catherine's fingers tightened on the small gold locket in her right hand. She clutched it to her chest and pressed it against her damp nightclothes. The mere idea of the child resembling the man she loathed made her gasp for air. No matter the unbearable consequences, she did not want the child to possess even a trace of the Earl of Belmont. Rather, when she gazed at her babe, she hoped to lose herself in blue eyes the color of an early morning sky. She wanted to bury her fingers in curly, fire-red locks, shimmering with hints of gold, soft and smooth as the finest silk.

She wanted her child to look like him.

Her fingers tightened around the locket that held her lover's picture. Actually, only half a locket—he held the other half.

Pain ripped through her again, forcing a muffled cry from her lungs. Was God punishing her for one night of passion in her lover's arms? Catherine panted, blowing out short, quick breaths. How could it be wrong when she loved him so very much? Had always loved him. Her belly tightened, pulled like a board, bulging and ready to explode.

A low, keening sound escaped her lips as something warm and sticky pooled between her legs. Soon she would know.

"Eleanor," she murmured between pants, clutching her sister's fingers in one hand and the locket in the other. "Be prepared. If necessary, leave...right away." The muscles in her lower belly crested and fell like waves. "I think...it's time."

She tried not to scream, tried to keep her pain confined to the four walls, lest her husband insist on the doctor's presence.

Blackness threatened to plunge her into its abyss where nothing existed save the darkness. She fought its inky manacles, sat up and bore down, pushing through the agony.

"Now," she ground out. "Now, Eleanor." Her body grew slick with sweat, every nerve alive and throbbing with anxiety and anticipation.

Her sister hurried to the end of the bed, pushed aside the bedclothes, and lifted Catherine's nightgown to her hips. Catherine bit down on her lower lip, trying to control the horrible sensations coursing through her lower body. So much pressure. She forced another push.

"Yes," Eleanor coaxed, "just a little more." Catherine squeezed the locket, thought of him, thought of their love, and pushed. Hard. Seven more times, until the child passed through the birth chamber. Her head fell back against the pillows, perspiration dripping down her forehead, into her eyes, blurring her vision. At last, it was done.

She tried to lift her head, tried to see, but the effort proved too much. "Eleanor?" The unspoken question hung between them, as thick and heavy as a drenched Aubusson rug. Now she'd have the answer to nine months of waiting. Now she would know if the child she bore was her husband's. Or her lover's.

"All's well, Catherine," Eleanor whispered. She moved toward the head of the bed carrying a tiny bundle, swathed in white. "All's well." A whimper escaped from underneath the layers of cotton. "She's beautiful." Her voice dropped even lower. "With a full head of black hair."

A single tear trickled down Catherine's cheek. Belmont's child. Born out of duty and subservience, not passion and love. Her gaze moved to the bundle of white squirming in Eleanor's arms. "Claire," she murmured. She could still love the child, even though she hated the man. Catherine reached up to stroke the babe's cheek, her fingers white against the infant's flushed skin.

A stab of pain tore through her, stronger than any before, searing her insides, burning a path through her lower belly. She jerked her hand back in agony and clutched her stomach.

"Catherine?" Eleanor's voice drifted to her. "What is it? What's wrong?"

Catherine opened her mouth to let the torture out, but no sound came. She shook her head from side to side and fought the nightmare claiming her body. Hot, sticky wetness slipped between her legs, pooling around her thighs. Blood. Too much blood.

"Oh my God."

Something was wrong. She heard it in her sister's voice, but she was too weak to speak. Her eyes drifted shut. Too weak...

"We've got to stop the bleeding." Eleanor shoved something between Catherine's legs and repeated in a shaky voice, "Got to stop it." And then it grabbed her. A pain tearing the life from her.

"You've got to pass the afterbirth. Push, Catherine. Push."

Catherine bore down, pressed herself into the bed, and pushed. A scream surged through the room, bounding off the walls, filling her brain with its agony.

"There's another baby," Eleanor babbled. "Another baby."

"Twins," Catherine breathed, sucking air into her lungs. She was so cold. And so tired.

"A girl," Eleanor said, on a near-hysterical note.

"A red-haired little girl."

Catherine forced her eyes open and tried to focus on the bundle in her sister's arms. If she squinted, she could just make out the baby. A cap of ringlets covered the infant's head like a little bonnet. What beautiful red hair.

"Francine," she breathed. Gathering her wavering strength,

she forced out the next words. "Take her, Eleanor. Far away. Before Belmont sees her." She gasped for air. "Tell no one. When the time is right, give her this." She pressed the half-locket into her sister's hand and fell back against the pillows again, closing her eyes for the third and final time.

A short while later, the Earl of Belmont received news of the birth of his beautiful, black-haired daughter—and the death of his beautiful, black-haired wife.

2

England—1815

"Frannnncie. Oh, Francie."

He was gaining on her. She heard him rustling about in the woods, pushing through the brush, his voice closing the distance between them, taunting her with his nearness. She should never have taken the shortcut. What a foolish idea. Danger lurked in the woods. So did *he*.

Francie ran faster, her nimble body darting around trees and branches long familiar to her. She'd climbed many in her eighteen years in Amberden, knew the texture of the dense foliage surrounding her and the hidden lairs of her four-legged friends.

But she was not prepared for the two-legged monster chasing her.

"Oh, sweet Francie." His honeyed voice rippled with laughter, seeping through the hot summer air. "Come out and play."

She ducked behind a huge oak tree, crouching low, her breath slipping out in uneven gasps as she repeated the litany in her head. *I am safe.* He only took willing victims, didn't he?

Why, then, did she feel like a trapped rabbit running for her life? She peeked from behind the green leaves of a bayberry bush. The woods lay quiet, save for a few swallows chirping and a gentle breeze whispering through the trees. Where was he? She pulled her worn shawl closer and waited.

"Looking for someone?"

Francie whirled around, nearly hitting her head on the rough bark of the oak as she came face to face with her pursuer. Lord Jared Crayton, second son of the Duke of Worthington, stood not three paces from her. She sucked in a deep breath and straightened, determined not to let him see her fear.

"I am not in the habit of having men chase me through the woods," she replied, trying to keep the quiver from her voice.

He laughed, tapping his tan gloves against his breeches. "I wasn't chasing you, Francie." He cocked a golden brow. "I thought we were playing a game." His voice dropped an octave. "Just the two of us. All alone."

"You were mistaken, Lord Jared. I do not play games with strange men in the woods."

"Ah," he teased, "but that is just the problem, don't you see? If you stopped long enough, you would no longer consider me a stranger." He lifted a finger to her cheek. She flinched, took a step back. Right into the rough bark of the oak tree.

He moved closer, ignoring her rebuff. "Be my friend, Francie," he murmured.

She shook her head, looking away. "I do not think so."

"No?" His warm breath stroked her cheek. "I should very much like to be *your* friend."

Francie met his gaze and said, "Friends? Just like you were 'friends' with Sally, Gertrude, and Fanny?" The words fell out before she considered the repercussions of her boldness.

Jared's Crayton's face darkened. "What do you know of them?"

Perhaps boldness might rid her of him. "I know they're sweet girls, all of them," she said. "Barely sixteen and pregnant. With your child."

He laughed and folded his arms across his chest. "Ah, yes. Sally, Gertrude, and Fanny." He tapped his chin with long, tanned fingers. "My brother may inherit the dukedom, but I will leave behind my own legacy." The corners of his lips tilted up in a smile as he continued. "A whole village of children, if I am fortunate. All with my blood running through their veins. Even my noble brother will not be able to make that claim."

He spoke as though the women of Amberden were no better than brood mares. The fact that their families were disgraced and their lives ruined made no difference to him.

How could the son of a duke, with the mouth of a poet and the body of a Greek god, harbor such calculating coldness, such cruel intentions? It proved difficult to discern at first, because the man's golden looks outshone his true character. But scrap by scrap, truth emerged in the shape of a self - centered, cruel beast. Innocents were drawn to him by the golden hair falling just below the collar, the moss-green eyes, the quick, ready smile, and deep dimples.

But Francie guessed above all what drew them were the lies, like sonnets, whispered promises of love and protection, and of course, marriage. The young girls, dreamers and believers of fairy tales, thought their prince rode in from his grand estate on his big white horse, to marry them and whisk them away to a life of wealth and luxury.

Three girls. Three lies. Three ruined lives. When would it stop?

Francie swallowed her disgust and tried reason. "We're but simple villagers here. Why would you bother with any of us? Why not stay with your own kind?"

His heated gaze roamed her body, settled on the worn, blue fabric covering her breasts. "Do you really need to ask?"

He looked at her as though he were about to pounce, like a cat after a mouse. "I think you want to sample our wares with no obligation to make a purchase."

His full lips curved into the faintest of smiles. "You wound me with such unkind words." He stepped closer. "The young ladies I've made acquaintance with in this village did not reject my attentions."

"And so you've decided to get half the village with child?"

"Half? A bit more than that, I'd say." He grabbed her hand and searched her face. "But all I really want is you, Francie."

She tried to pull away but his fingers tightened, twisting just enough to render her immobile.

"Try to understand my duty to the others, a legacy that needs fulfillment. But even as I lay with them, you're the one I want. Just you," he whispered. "Only you."

Francie pulled at the hand holding hers. "Let me go."

He released her but did not step away. The rough bark of the oak tree dug into her shoulder blades as she tried to put distance between herself and this man whose arrogant nonchalance toward others sickened her.

Jared Crayton laughed, a deep, menacing sound that swirled around her. "Seems you can't quite get away from me." He tilted his blond head to one side. "Or perhaps you don't wish to."

Francie bit the inside of her cheek to keep her tongue still. She'd like to tell him the truth. She found his kind revolting. Loathsome. He belonged on the ground, slithering about like the viper he was. Her nails dug into the palms of her hands. She would say nothing because he was, after all, the son of a duke.

And the man knew full well how to take advantage of his position and his title.

"You haven't answered." He reached out to grasp a reddish-gold curl. "Might I be hopeful you will turn a kind smile my way? It would surely gladden my heart and lift my spirits."

He toyed with her, most likely hoping for submission. Well, she would never submit. She bit the inside of her cheek harder, not stopping until she tasted blood.

"Francie? Too shy to answer?"

"I am certain many women find your attention most flattering. I, unfortunately, am not interested in an association of any kind with a member of the opposite gender."

"I see." He paused, looking at her as if to ascertain whether she told the truth, then continued. "I am being patient with you, Francie. But there will come a time when my patience will end." He released her hair and yanked on his calfskin gloves. "You wouldn't want to displease me."

He stepped back and brushed off his buff-colored breeches with slow precision. "The old lady you live with, your aunt, I think," he said, busying himself with straightening his waistcoat. "Wouldn't it be a shame if those weeds she grows didn't make it through the summer?"

"What are you saying?" Aunt Eleanor grew enough flowers and herbs to supply half the village with sachets, wreaths, and medicinal concoctions.

He shrugged and gave her a dazzling, harmless smile. "I'm not saying anything other than accidents happen. Misfortunes occur every day. Disease. Drought." His green gaze pierced hers. "Fire. Vandals."

She didn't even attempt to hide her disgust. "You'd harm an innocent woman, ruin her livelihood, to satisfy your own selfish needs?"

"Did I say such a thing, Francie?" he asked, his tone once

again soft and persuasive. "Did I give one small indication I'd be predisposed to commit such a heinous crime? Hmm? Of course not," he answered when she remained silent. "I merely pointed out what could happen and perhaps given the proper incentives, I might be persuaded to protect your aunt from such a dire situation."

Anger drowned out the rest of his words. Nobility or no, the man was worse than the slime at the bottom of a rubbish bin. Someone must stop him. Somehow. "You disgust me."

She stepped away from the tree, hands balled into fists. "You try to prove your manliness by seducing young girls and getting them with child. You're nothing more than a coward hiding behind your father's title. Do what you will, I'll never submit to you."

Jared Crayton's eyes turned cold and hard like rough waters in the eye of a storm. He stared at her a long while, his handsome features rigid and assessing. Then, just as calm settles after a torrential rain, his countenance relaxed. And he smiled. "Never say never, my dear Francie."

He turned and waved, disappearing into the woods, his words trailing after him. A shiver raced through her as she thought of the man, his words, and the unspoken threat between them.

3

"Where were you, my dear? What took you so long?" Aunt Eleanor glanced over her wire-rimmed spectacles and smiled.

"Just out checking the roses." Francie avoided her aunt's gaze and tried to keep the emotion from her voice. Anger and fear warred with one another, each trying to smother the other like a snuffed flame. Anger told her to fight Jared Crayton, expose him to his father as the lecherous coward he was. But, in truth, she doubted the Earl of Worthington cared. Jared Crayton was after all, only a second son, and she was but a commoner.

And then there was the fear. Fear that the soft-spoken words were indeed a threat, warning of impending destruction to her aunt's livelihood should Francie continue to resist his advances. Was this how he'd lured the others?

"Francie?"

"Yes, Aunt Eleanor?"

"Is something wrong? You sound odd."

Francie shook her head. Aunt Eleanor had been the only

mother she'd ever known and understood Francie's moods, even when she herself did not.

"Francie?"

She turned and met her aunt's clear blue gaze. No use hiding from Eleanor Jordan. She might seem soft and harmless, like a round, gray teddy bear with a little extra stuffing tucked in here and there, but when it came to Francie, she was fiercer than a mother bear guarding her cub.

"It's him again, isn't it?" Her lips flattened into a straight line. "It's that miserable miscreant, tormenting you with his sugared words and evil smile."

"You know I'm much too clever for the likes of him," Francie said, forcing a smile. "He's no better than a pesky bug I intend to swat away at every turn."

Her aunt cleared her throat and folded her arms over her more-than-ample bosom. "That pesky bug is twice your size with no honor and even less scruples when it comes to a young innocent like yourself. I don't want you roaming the woods or fields alone."

"I'm not afraid of him." At least not overmuch.

"He's a rakehell and a scoundrel," she spat out. "Worse than the lowest scum on the earth."

The door opened on those last words and Francie's Uncle Bernard entered. "Who's worse than the lowest scum on the earth?"

Aunt Eleanor marched over to her husband, thrust her hands on her wide hips, and shook her head. "Something's got to be done, Bernard." Her voice broke as she murmured, "Perhaps she shouldn't stay here any longer."

"Sending her away possesses dangers of its own."

What in heaven's name were they talking about? Where would she go? Amberden was her home, had been the whole of her eighteen years. She loved this cottage with its wide windows that let in the morning light and drenched the rooms in gold. She adored the patchwork comforters and homemade curtains Aunt Eleanor helped her stitch in beautiful pinks, yellows, and greens. No one's kitchen smelled better than when she and Aunt Eleanor baked bread sprinkled with rosemary or thyme.

And then there were the stacks of books she and Uncle Bernard pored over at night. Books that challenged and entertained, brimmed with tales of explorers from the Far East, sojourning to distant lands where language and lifestyle were as diverse as the people who traveled there. Some volumes expounded on the brilliance of inventors, reconstructing and proving various theories involving everything from ropes and pulleys to stones and crystal.

Leave this slice of heaven? No. She wasn't going anywhere.

Aunt Eleanor darted a quick glance at her husband, one packed with meaning only the two of them understood. They'd done that more often these last weeks, ever since Francie's first encounter with Lord Jared Crayton.

She'd been in the far fields that morning, cutting lavender and chamomile for sachets, lost in the sweet heady scents surrounding her. She never heard the horse or its rider until they pulled up less than five feet from her.

Startled, she'd looked up into Lord Jared Crayton's moss-green eyes, wondering if the whispered tales she'd heard these past months were true. He despoiled young virgins, flashing his white smile and well-bred manners at them, casting them under his spell. For those who resisted, as Francie did that day, he dropped subtle threats with perfect diction and just the right touch of velvet in his voice, making one wonder if his words were laced with menace or mere misinterpretation.

That morning, he'd dismounted and moved toward her. "Beautiful maiden, how is it I have not seen you before today?"

Francie lowered her gaze, uncomfortable with the intimacy in his tone, and went about cutting chamomile. "I have been here."

"Then it is my great misfortune I have not met you. But..." He took a few steps closer. "'Tis a misfortune which may be quickly remedied. Allow me to introduce myself. I am Lord Jared Crayton."

She'd hazarded him a quick glance. She'd seen him twice before from a discreet distance. The sun glared behind him now, casting a brightness about his face that made it difficult to discern his features. Francie nodded, clutching the basket between her hands. "I am Francie."

"Francie," he breathed, as though it were a caress. "A beautiful name for a beautiful woman."

Heat seeped into her cheeks as she turned away once again. Tales or not, something in the man's voice sent a chill through her.

He touched her shoulder and she spun around, quickly distancing herself from him. In the next instant, a huge animal lunged out of the bushes, knocking Jared Crayton to the ground, ripping at his white neckcloth.

"George! George! Off, boy! Off!"

The mastiff's growl rumbled low in his throat.

"Get the beast off!"

"George! Off!"

The dog relaxed his grip and released the tufts of white from his jaws. Backing up from his prey, he settled on his haunches, his upper lip curling to reveal sharp teeth.

George protected his mistress above everything. Jared Crayton scrambled to his feet, brushing dirt from his breeches. "Damn the beast," he spat, his eyes burning with rage. "I should shoot him where he stands."

"No!" Francie rushed toward the animal and threw her arms

around his neck. "Don't touch him."

The man pulled at his tattered neckcloth with quick, jerky movements. "One bullet through the head," he hissed, adjusting the white cotton streaked with dirt and saliva.

"Please. Don't harm him."

Several seconds passed before Jared Crayton spoke. The trembling rage of moments ago was replaced with smooth even tones. "As you wish, Francie. The beast will live." He turned and whistled for his horse, which grazed several feet away.

Francie kept her gaze fixed on him, not trusting his soft-spoken words. He mounted his horse and flashed her a bright smile. "You should not wander unattended. There are all manner of beasts about, just waiting to send you into peril." He raised a gloved hand and pointed toward George. "Who knows what misfortune might befall such an animal in these fields with the woods so close by." His smile deepened. "A wild beast might tear him apart. Good day, Francie. Until the next time." He nodded his blond head in her direction and spurred his horse into a gallop, heading away from the village, taking with him any doubt all of the horrible tales about him were true.

Three days later, George limped home, his left hindquarter raw and bleeding. Uncle Bernard said he must have tangled with a possum or some such animal, but Francie knew in her heart the creature that injured him was two-legged and bore a royal crest.

A whimper in the far corner brought her back to the present. Poor George lay on his rug by the hearth, head between his paws, golden eyes alert, his left leg bandaged in white cotton.

"Perhaps we should have told her a long time ago," Aunt Eleanor said, gnawing on her lower lip.

Uncle Bernard shook his gray head. "She was happy. Living

the life of an innocent. How could we thrust such a revelation upon her?"

They were talking about her as though she weren't in the room.

"But perhaps we've done her an injustice." Tears welled in her aunt's blue eyes.

"Perhaps," Bernard said in a quiet voice.

They made no sense. "Would someone please tell me what you are talking about? And why all the 'perhaps'?" She smiled at Uncle Bernard. "I feel as though we're hypothesizing on a new method of germination."

Her uncle moved toward her, his tall figure bent like a sapling swaying in the wind, his bony shoulders stooped. He smelled of tobacco and a hint of peppermint and when he smiled from beneath his thick mustache and beard, his eyes brimmed with affection.

"My Francie," he said, taking her hands in his. "You always were a smart one."

"Tell me, Uncle Bernard. Tell me what you and Aunt Eleanor are talking about." She interlocked her fingers with his and whispered, "Please?"

Her uncle's gaze drifted past her, no doubt meeting Aunt Eleanor's for a brief second, before he turned back to Francie. "We fear we can no longer keep you safe here." His gray eyes misted. "It's only a matter of time before the scoundrel increases his efforts over you. And, perhaps one day, he'll tire of the game and pursue you in earnest." He drew in a deep breath and added, "Whether you're willing or not."

"I would never welcome that man's attentions," Francie spat out. There it was again. The very word that man warned her about using. *Never.*

"He might feel differently on the subject." Her uncle shrugged. "We have very little defense against a duke's son."

What a strange discussion, peppered with subtle overtones only Uncle Bernard and Aunt Eleanor understood.

"But we know someone who does," he continued. "Your father."

Father? She stumbled backwards but caught herself. "My father is dead. Why would you say such a thing?" Her father died in a hunting accident years ago. They'd both told her so.

He cleared his throat. "No, Francie. Your father is not dead."

His words made no sense. She spun around and looked at her aunt. Tears streamed down the older woman's pale face, falling from her chin onto her ample bosom. "Aunt Eleanor? He's dead," she said with great conviction, and then, "Isn't he?"

A sob escaped her aunt's lips. "No, child," she whispered. "He's very much alive."

Francie couldn't get air to her lungs. It felt like the time George toppled her over in play, all one hundred and ninety pounds of him landing on her belly.

"We've wanted to tell you for a long time," Uncle Bernard said from behind her, placing his long fingers on her shoulders. "We thought we were protecting you, but now there's a greater harm threatening you and your father might well be the only one who can help."

Father. She couldn't get past the word. She considered Uncle Bernard her father. He had raised her. And all these years another man held the title, yet he'd never sought out his daughter.

"I fail to see how this man can help us." Francie swiped at her cheek, surprised to feel wetness. "If he hasn't contacted me in eighteen years, I doubt he'll be interested in 'helping' me now."

Aunt Eleanor buried her face in her lace handkerchief.

"He doesn't know about you."

"Doesn't know?"

"He has no idea he has a child." Uncle Bernard nodded to Aunt Eleanor, who disappeared into the couple's bedroom, returning moments later with a small object.

"Here, child," she said, holding the object out to Francie. "This belonged to your mother."

Francie reached for a tarnished and scratched half-piece of locket, turned it over in her palm, and brought it nearer. Her gaze narrowed, then widened, as she stared at the tiny picture nestled inside. The man's laughing blue eyes, *her eyes*, stared back at her, and fiery curls, *her curls*, framed his handsome face. Uncle Bernard drew her into his embrace, speaking in soft, soothing tones. She was colder than a frozen pond in the dead of winter, and not even her uncle's jacket or the steady beat of his heart pounding in her ear could warm her. His words made no sense, scattering about her like errant raindrops, falling to nothingness as they touched her ears.

She blinked hard but the tears continued to fall, soft, silent, and unstoppable.

4

F rancie jostled from side to side as the rented carriage rolled down the road. She grabbed the edges of the worn seat to steady herself. Good heavens, what a contraption! It would be amazing if they reached their destination without a broken bone or some other mishap. A red curl escaped from her bonnet, springing halfway down her nose. She swiped at it, tucked it away, and straightened the bonnet for the seventh time since they'd begun their journey.

"We might as well be riding horses bareback," Francie said to her uncle, planting her feet on the floor of the carriage and leaning forward. Anything to prevent hitting her head again.

"When you're at Drakemoor, Montrose will see you ride in nothing less than a carriage bearing his crest." He gave her a gentle smile. "As you deserve."

"I'm sorry, Uncle Bernard. Please excuse my thoughtlessness."

"All will be well, child. Soon."

Francie squeezed her eyes shut and rubbed her temples. A blasted headache threatened. The third in as many days. She leaned further away from the lumpy, faded emerald squabs and wished she'd never heard of Lord Montrose or Drakemoor.

The carriage rolled on, closing in on a destiny she could no longer avoid. And she'd tried. For three days, she'd waged a firm, steady battle of wills against her aunt and uncle, posing questions she was certain would make them reconsider their insistence to send her to Drakemoor.

But to no avail. And so, with great misgivings and a multitude of questions swimming in her head, Francie packed a small satchel and readied herself. She wasn't staying, so there was no need to select more than one other gown. Not that she owned more than a handful that would be presentable in public. Most were either too short, or too tight, or too worn, and Aunt Eleanor hadn't the time to make the appropriate alterations. Dress and style never concerned Francie. She'd much rather bury her head in a book or wander the fields collecting sweet-smelling herbs and flowers.

"We should be there in just a few minutes."

Her uncle's voice brought her out of her musings. She opened her eyes and looked down at her blue muslin gown. A visiting gown, Aunt Eleanor called it. Cerulean, like the sky on a warm summer's day. It matched her eyes and the wide ribbon that bound the annoying mass of red curls at the nape of her neck.

"You look beautiful," Uncle Bernard said in a low, soft voice.

Francie smoothed her gown and picked one of George's hairs from her sleeve. "You know I've never cared about such things."

"Which makes you all the more beautiful. You are a rare find, a diamond among a heap of rocks. Montrose will need to protect you from the vultures of polite society."

She wanted to tell him Lord Montrose needn't protect her from anyone because she wasn't staying. Not for long anyway.

Her purpose for meeting Lord Montrose was twofold. First, she wanted to ask him how a man could love a woman to distraction and never know she bore him a child.

Next, she would request his assistance in her village's battle against Jared Crayton. Perhaps the Montrose wealth and power could stop the duke's son from ruining the lives of more young women. She'd take his words, and if fortune were with her, his support and promises to protect her village.

And then she would leave.

~

THE QUIET RAP on Alexander Bishop's door surprised him. No one ever interrupted him in his study. It was his rule. Not unless Philip needed him or there was a dire emergency, like a fire in the kitchen or a band of marauders in the foyer.

"Yes?" He looked toward the oak door, curious as to the nature of the intrusion.

"Excuse me, sir. So sorry to interrupt." The thin little man entered, closing the door behind him with a quiet click. He scurried across the room, halting a few feet from Alexander's massive cherry desk.

"What is it, James?"

The butler tapped his foot five times. Very fast. Tap five times. Rest. Tap five times. Rest. After the third set, Alexander drew in a sharp breath and glared at the man's bony face. James's foot arrested in mid-air.

"Well? Out with it, man."

"There's a young woman, sir," James began, his small, beak-like nose twitching as he spoke. "It's quite curious actually. Quite curious indeed," he said, nodding, his sparse brown hair separating with each movement.

Alexander cleared his throat.

"Yes, well, there's a young woman in the gold salon who insists on seeing Lord Montrose."

"And you interrupted me to tell me that?" He turned back to his ledger. "Send her away."

"But sir, she insists it's of dire importance and must speak with him at once."

"Impossible."

"But, sir—"

"Do I not pay you an adequate wage to perform the task of butler of Drakemoor?"

"Yes, sir. Indeed, sir. But—"

Alexander slashed a hand in the air. "Then earn your keep. Get rid of her."

James's foot tapped five times. "She...refuses to leave, sir."

"Refuses to leave?" The words fell off his tongue in a soft, melodic tone. Only those who knew him well, and they were few, would recognize the controlled anger in his voice.

"Says she won't leave until she's spoken to Lord Montrose," James finished, stammering on his last words.

Who in the devil would be so bold as to present herself uninvited, and demand to see the earl?

"What's her name?" Alexander asked, torn between annoyance and grudging curiosity.

"Miss Francie Jordan."

"Never heard of her."

"No, sir."

Who in the devil was Francie Jordan? Moreover, how was it she possessed the temerity to present herself to one of the wealthiest men in the countryside without invitation? Alexander rubbed his jaw. Interesting. He'd handle her himself.

"Show her in, James."

"Yes, sir," the butler replied, turning on his heel and scurrying out the door.

HOW MUCH LONGER WAS SHE going to have to wait?

Francie scanned the spacious room for the fifth time, taking in the grandeur surrounding her. So this was how nobility lived, comforted with luxuriant brocades and Aubusson rugs. She pictured George burying his nails in the tan rug. It matched his coat, almost to the exact shade.

Gold and burgundy damask draperies filtered the sun, washing the room in a warm, rose-colored glow. Not anything like the white and yellow curtains in her humble abode that welcomed the first rays of bright light through the last fading fingers of day. And the accessories. Her gaze settled once again on the three oriental vases sitting on the mantel. Brought over from a trip to the Far East, no doubt. Her home also boasted three vases on an old pine mantel, but they were simple pottery with a rose design. One even had a rather large chip in it that Francie turned toward the wall.

How could Aunt Eleanor and Uncle Bernard consider Drakemoor as a home for her? Even if Lord Montrose accepted her, she didn't belong here. Ladies in this society wore fine silks and diamonds, their delicate skin protected from the sun and wind. Francie doubted they'd ever buried their fingers in the rich soil of the earth. Or walked barefoot in a field of clover. And certainly they'd never rolled on the ground with a one-hundred-ninety-pound mastiff.

No, she didn't belong at Drakemoor and the sooner she concluded her business here, the sooner she could return to the rented carriage, rattling back to her simple life. Hopefully, minus the intrusion of one Lord Jared Crayton.

Then her life would be perfect.

A light rap at the door disturbed her thoughts. The butler, a little man with a twitching nose, entered the room.

"Follow me, Miss Jordan." He nodded and held the door for her.

Francie grabbed her bonnet and rose from the burgundy sofa. "Thank you," she murmured, watching the little man twitch his nose and tap his feet. He reminded her of one of the little mice at home who roamed in the lavender fields.

She pretended the opulence surrounding her was something she saw every day as she clicked down the black and marble hallway behind the butler: gilt-encrusted mirrors, more Chinese vases of varying sizes and shapes, a huge gold chandelier of ornate design. But in truth, she'd never seen or even read about a house as elegant as Drakemoor.

They stopped before one of the oak doors and Francie knew a moment of panic. What if Lord Montrose rejected her outright? Refused to listen to her? Refused to help her rid Amberden of Jared Crayton? She drew in a deep breath, pushing her nervousness aside. Aunt Eleanor said he loved her mother very much. Certainly, even after all these years, that should count for something, if only a few minutes of his undivided attention.

The butler opened the door, ushering her into Lord Montrose's study.

"Miss Francie Jordan, sir," he announced.

"Thank you, James," a deep voice boomed from across the room. "That will be all."

The door clicked behind her and Francie forced her gaze in the direction of the voice. A man sat behind a large desk, writing. He was somewhere in his thirties, with closely clipped black hair, save an errant cowlick above his left brow. He had rough, hard features: thick, bushy eyebrows, a straight, firm nose with a slight crook to the left, high cheekbones, and a jaw that was too square. Nothing soft about him, except perhaps his mouth, which boasted a pair of well-formed lips.

But when he looked up, the frown on his face pulled his lips into a thin straight line and Francie changed her initial opinion. There was *nothing* soft about the man. She met his stormy silver gaze, cold as a winter's chill, and just as biting.

And then there was the scar. It ran down the right side of his face in a jagged path, from the edge of his bushy brow trailing halfway down his cheekbone.

She swallowed. This man was most definitely not Lord Montrose. Besides being much too young, Uncle Bernard told her Lord Montrose loved her mother beyond reason. She doubted this man ever loved anything in his life.

"Sit down, Miss Jordan."

He spoke with such commanding presence Francie could do little else than slide into one of the deep green chairs angled in front of his desk.

"Thank you...sir," she managed. Who was this man? Lord Montrose's son, perhaps? Or nephew?

He gave a slight nod, cocked his head to one side, and stared at her as though she were a curious bug and he was trying to decide how to get rid of her.

"I've come to see Lord Montrose," she said, fingering the small locket in her pocket.

The man sat back, steepling his long fingers under his chin. "That's not possible."

"Not possible?" She thought she'd at least get an audience with the earl.

He shook his head. "No. Lord Montrose hasn't had visitors in over three months."

"He's ill?"

There was a slight hesitation before the man gave a quick, almost imperceptible nod.

"Well, I hadn't quite considered this," Francie said, as much to herself as the man seated across from her. The sharp edges of the locket bit into the flesh of her palm. "I don't mean to intrude upon Lord Montrose, but I need his help." The man raised a black brow but said nothing. "You see," she rushed on, determined to tell her story, "the village I come from, Amberden, is being assaulted by a nobleman. A duke's son. Actually, it's not the village, but rather, the young women residing in the village who are being," heat rushed to her cheeks, "taken advantage of."

"Miss Jordan." The man held up a tanned hand.

"No. Hear me out." Her voice rose with passion and desperation. "Please." When he said nothing, she continued. "This scoundrel seduces the young girls in our village, filling their heads with fairy tales, promising marriage in order to have his way with them." She leaned forward, eager to share her disgust. "Then when he gets them with child, he casts them aside, leaving them to face disgrace and humiliation on their own."

Silver eyes burned into her. "And you, Miss Jordan, are you one of those young innocents?"

"No! Absolutely not!"

Silence.

"I'm not." Heat spread to the rest of her face.

"Then I fail to see why it is your concern," he said, as though he were discussing a flock of sheep. "And I am most perplexed as to why you seek Lord Montrose's assistance."

"Don't you see?" She rose from her chair to stand before his desk. "These girls are young and innocent. They trust this man. They want to believe his lies. He's taking advantage of them. Don't you feel any responsibility, as part of the noble class, to put a stop to his incorrigible behavior?"

"That depends," he said, his voice cool and void of emotion.

"What could it possibly depend upon?" How could this man be so unfeeling? So disinterested?

"On why you seek out Lord Montrose when there is a veritable list of other earls and the like who might be more willing and able to handle this situation."

"Because he might be the only one who would help us."

"Pray tell, Miss Jordan, why should he help you?"

She pulled the locket from her pocket and thrust it at him. "Because I am his daughter."

Francie thought she saw him falter, just a slight clench of his jaw as the meaning of her words sank in, before he recovered and then retrieved the locket from her outstretched palm. It looked small and fragile in his big hand. He turned it over several times, his eyes narrowed on the tiny picture of Lord Montrose.

"I fail to see the resemblance." He thrust the locket back at her, his voice chilling her more than the wind seeping through the rented carriage had.

"But don't you see?" Her gaze darted from the red-haired man in the locket to the dark, formidable one seated before her. "We've got the same red hair, curls as well. And our eyes... they're the same blue. Surely you can see that."

She may as well have spoken to a stone statue. "I see no resemblance," he repeated.

"But—"

"None."

She hesitated a second, wondering if she should try another tactic to see the earl. Perhaps pleading or tears. No. She would not beg or cry in front of this man who watched her with such arrogance and disinterest. Francie stuffed the locket in her pocket and grabbed her bonnet. She would leave with dignity. Without saying a word, she pulled on her gloves.

"Good luck with your search for your father." Insincerity filtered his voice. He didn't believe her story. He probably thought she was trying to cheat the earl out of a piece of his vast wealth. As though money or the like mattered to her.

It had been a mistake to come. A mistake to hope the embers of a long-lost love might still flicker. If the earl were anything like the uncaring man before her, she should count herself lucky to have been spared another humiliation.

Somehow, she'd find a way to help the women of Amberden wage a battle against Jared Crayton. As for the father she never knew, well, one couldn't miss what one never had. She clutched the locket, squeezing so hard the broken hinges dug into her palm once again.

Francie squared her shoulders and met the man's hard gaze across his desk. He'd been studying her those few seconds she'd given up to thought and disappointment. Had he detected her intense dislike of him? A tiny part of her hoped he had because good breeding forced her to bid him a proper farewell, despite his rudeness toward her.

"Thank you for your time, Mr...." She floundered, searching for a name. But there was none. They hadn't even been properly introduced.

"Bishop," he supplied.

"Bishop," she repeated, nodding her head. "Good day."

And then, before she suffered any other manner of insolence or deviation from proper comportment at the hands of the man called Bishop, she turned on her heel and left.

ALEXANDER BISHOP MAINTAINED his air of assumed arrogance until the door clicked and he heard Francie Jordan's footsteps fleeing down the hall. Then he let out a deep breath and sank back in his leather chair.

What the devil! He ran his hands over his face and thought of his encounter with the red-headed stranger. She was beautiful, of that there was no doubt. With her tumbling fiery mane and brilliant blue eyes, the woman was the type who could weave truths from lies and capture the heart of any unsuspecting fool. Not him, of course. He'd never been considered a fool.

Alexander rose from his chair and turned toward the cherry sideboard. *Whiskey*. Exactly what he needed. He lifted a crystal decanter, poured two fingers in a glass, and downed the amber liquid in one swallow.

What the devil! He couldn't get the woman's face out of his mind. The red hair. The blue eyes. The light dusting of freckles on her nose. He poured another drink. Full lips. Fair skin. Not to mention the tall, slender frame.

She could not be Philip's offspring. She was probably nothing but a greedy little chit, looking to capitalize on an old man's failing health and fading memories.

No one would take advantage of Philip Cardinger. Not even a beautiful mystery woman who professed to be his daughter.

He enjoyed the burn of one more whiskey before he straightened his cravat and quit the room. He had a sudden desire to visit Philip, just for a minute or so, to be certain he was feeling well today.

And to assure himself Francie Jordan's hair was not the same shade of red as Philip's, but rather a bit lighter with a hint of gold. And her eyes, a deeper, brighter blue.

By the time he reached Philip's door, he had a dozen or so physical traits he wanted to compare. *Blast the woman!*

5

Alexander entered the master bedroom, adjusting his vision to the dim interior. The cream damask draperies shut out the afternoon's sunny greeting, lending a soothing quiet to the room. Philip slept late these past few months, ever since he'd taken ill with a severe cold that settled in his lungs. The cough persisted still, turning at times from a dull hacking to a fierce hoarseness that made his fair skin ruddy from exertion.

Philip Cardinger was a big man, thick and bulky, though in recent months his face had grown leaner, his cheeks hollowed out and pale. He'd come to rely on the ebony walking stick Alexander gave him to move about Drakemoor. When he exerted any type of energy, his tall frame leaned on the stick, his breath coming in short little puffs as he maneuvered from room to room.

He was a sick man and the last thing he needed in his life was an upset of any kind, especially one involving a possibly illegitimate daughter.

"Do you plan to stand there and watch me all day, boy, or help me get up?" a gruff voice called from the bed.

Alexander met the older man's gaze and smiled. He hadn't missed the tender familiarity when Philip called him *boy*. He was the only one who could get away with calling him that, or Alex, as he often did. Others referred to him as Alexander, but most addressed him as Mr. Bishop.

"You should be sleeping, Philip."

"Sleep. Sleep." Philip let out a big yawn and stretched his long arms over his head. "All I do is sleep." He rubbed his eyes. "Open the drapes. At least let me see light."

Alexander obliged, moving toward the draperies and fastening each one back to emit a shock of light into the room.

"Better." Philip sighed as he pushed himself up on his elbows. "Much better." He coughed twice, the hoarse sound filling the room. "Damnable cough."

"Would you like me to send Thomas in to help you dress?"

"No. I can dress myself." He pulled at the top of his night-shirt. "I'm not an invalid yet."

"You know that's not what I meant. It's perfectly acceptable for a man of your position to use a valet," Alexander said, easing into a chair near the bed. "We've gone over this countless times."

"Then you should understand my answer by now, Alex." He took a deep breath and said in a firm voice, "I can dress myself."

Ornery old cuss. "Fine." Alexander preferred the use of a valet to assist him with his wardrobe. Pristine shirts. Countless numbers of them. Shiny Hessians. Ten or more pairs. Lint-and wrinkle-free jackets. Hand-tailored, of course.

But some days, despite the refinement and luxury, he still felt the dirt under his nails, still remembered the grime clinging to his breeches. It had been years since Philip lifted him from the edges of depravity, rescued him from a hopeless existence as an orphaned stable boy and offered him a new life. Alexander had grabbed on, held tight, refusing to look back and dwell on the death of his parents as anything more than a blessing.

They had never shown him love or taught him about family or duty. Those lessons came from Philip. The only thing Alexander's father left him was the jagged scar running down the right side of his face, a remembrance from a man who spent more days drunk than sober.

Trust no one. Love no one. They will only hurt you. They will always betray you.

This was the lesson Alexander's father embedded in his brain, seared into his skin, clawed into his heart. Only Philip breached this barrier and gained his love.

"So tell me, how much money did we make today?" Philip asked, drawing Alexander out of his dark thoughts.

"Just the usual," Alexander said. "The market looks good. But it's our ships I've got my eye on." He settled back in the overstuffed chair and crossed his arms over his chest. "We should see quite a profit when they return with the French lace. The silks and satins will up the ante as well."

Philip let out a short laugh, followed by a fit of coughing. "Well done, my boy. Well done. Glad to see the Oxford education hasn't gone to waste."

A faint smile played about Alexander's lips. "Sorry to disappoint you, Philip, but you, not Oxford, taught me everything I needed to know about trade and commerce."

His words made the old man smile and puff out his large chest with pride.

"Thank you, son."

Son. It was one of the greatest compliments Philip could pay him. He'd called him that for years, but still it warmed Alexander's heart to hear it. And sometimes, if he closed his eyes and tried hard enough, he could almost imagine himself as Philip's *real* child instead of the gutter rat offspring of a drunken groomsman and his over-obsessing wife.

That thought made him think of someone else who claimed the position. *Blast the woman*. He'd clear the matter up in his mind once and for all. Then he could stop thinking about the red-haired little chit.

"Philip, do you know anyone by the name of Jordan?" He'd never heard the name himself and doubted Philip had either. After all, she was a commoner.

The blood drained from the older man's face at the mention of the name. "Bernard?" Philip whispered, leaning back against the bedpost.

"No," Alexander said, shaking his head. "It was a woman. Not much more than a girl, actually. Odd creature. Very strange."

"Where is she?" Philip asked, his blue eyes bright.

"She..." He hesitated. "She made some rather bizarre statements."

"Where is she?" the older man persisted.

All of a sudden the room grew stifling. Alexander pulled at his cravat, loosening the folds. Why was Philip so intent on the woman? "I sent her away." He shifted in his chair as his gaze darted back to the bed. "She presented herself and delivered this preposterous story. It was incredible. Totally unbelievable."

"What did she say?" The words fell out in slow, even puffs.

"Philip, she was a commoner. Dressed in rags. She was probably trying to get some coin out of you."

"What did she say?" Philip repeated, his voice more demanding.

Alexander ran a hand through his perfect hair. Blast the woman. She was lying. She had to be. Just a little money-hungry creature trying to get her greedy hands into Philip's pockets. The words didn't come easily. He had to drag them from the depths of honor and duty. "She said she was your...daughter." There. He'd said it.

Philip stared at him as though he hadn't heard or couldn't comprehend the words.

"It's all a lot of bunk. I know that. She just wants a piece of your wealth." He slashed a hand in the air and settled back in his chair. "Just because she possesses red hair and blue eyes means nothing. And that ridiculous half-broken locket with your picture in it—"

"Find her!" Philip demanded, an unnatural strength vibrating through his words. "Find her," he repeated with less force, his long, bony hands balled into white fists.

Alexander sprang from his chair and leaned over the older man. "Philip? Don't upset yourself."

"Find her, Alexander. Now." The earl's eyes grew stark, *desperate*, like frozen waters in winter. Alexander hadn't seen that look in years. Not since shortly after Philip found him in the stables and brought him into the big house. In the early days, the earl had been gentle but quiet, with a haunted look about him. As though he'd lost something very valuable. Or someone.

He had that look about him now. In all their years together, Philip had never asked Alexander for anything. But today he asked him to do something that, if proven true, would change their lives forever.

Alexander had no choice. Philip had taught him about duty and honor and responsibility. He grasped the old man's hand and squeezed. "I'll find her," he vowed. "I promise you."

~

"He all but threw me out on my ear," Francie muttered.

Bernard stroked his beard. "You said his name was Bishop?"

"Yes. Rude, insufferable man."

"There were Bishops at Drakemoor years ago. I believe the husband was a groomsman and the wife a scullery maid." He paused a second and added, "And there was a boy."

Francie let out a harsh laugh that sounded more like a bark. "It wouldn't be this Mr. Bishop, I assure you. He's the image of starched perfection. I doubt he's ever seen a stable, let alone cleaned one out."

"Hmmm."

"He did study the locket, I'll give him that," she said. "But then he thrust it back at me as though it might dirty his hands if he held it too long, and told me he saw no resemblance."

"Hmmm."

"He wouldn't even consider the possibility," Francie continued, frowning at her uncle who didn't seem to be listening.

"He was a scruff of a boy, dark and dirty." He shook his head. "Pathetic little urchin."

"There was nothing pathetic about this Mr. Bishop, except perhaps his behavior." Her eyes narrowed. "Not even a proper introduction."

"Used to hide in the stalls when the earl and I came for our morning ride."

That got Francie's attention. "You were friends with Lord Montrose?"

Uncle Bernard's gray eyes darkened. When he spoke, his voice grew distant, as though transported back all those years to those very stables. "We were friends. Good friends. Philip was one of the only ones who accepted me."

"Why wouldn't everyone accept you?" How could anyone possibly find fault with such a wonderful man?

He removed his spectacles and rubbed his eyes. "It was all very complicated," he said. "Very complicated indeed."

"I don't understand." There was something sad and wistful in the tone of his voice.

Her gaze swept over her uncle's face, noting the small grimace he made when she asked him. His eyes were closed, his gray head resting on the faded green squabs. Wrinkles weaved their way from the ends of his eyes like a patchwork quilt. His mouth was a fine straight line, only half-visible beneath his bushy beard. He looked tired and weary and suddenly every bit of his sixty years.

"I was your aunt's tutor."

"Yes?" It was no secret Uncle Bernard was brilliant. He'd taught Francie everything from Latin to mathematics.

He opened his eyes and held her gaze. "It's not acceptable for a tutor to fall in love with his pupil," he said in a flat voice.

Francie reached over and grasped one of his hands. "I think it's terribly romantic," she assured him.

He continued as though she hadn't spoken, "Especially when that pupil is the daughter of an earl."

His words struck her and she pulled back, staring at the man in front of her. Aunt Eleanor? The woman who buried her hands in piles of rich, dark earth and sewed her own clothes? Francie tried to find the words to speak, tried to push them out, but they lay lodged in her throat, like an extra dollop of thick fudge. If Aunt Eleanor were of noble birth...then her mother was, too.

"I know we should have told you before, child." Uncle Bernard's words filtered through her shock. "But how does one inform a young woman she is the daughter of an earl and a countess, without addressing deeper, darker secrets better left alone?" His voice lowered. "Secrets that serve no purpose save to hurt and bring pain, and once discovered, will mark her for the rest of her life?" He shook his head. "We couldn't do it. Not until that scoundrel, Crayton, threatened your safety and made it absolutely necessary."

"My mother..." Francie managed, formulating a half-thought in her jumbled brain.

"Was a countess, as well."

"And I..." she began, trying to acknowledge what her brain was telling her.

"Was born of love and not position." Francie met his gray gaze, willing him to tell her what she already guessed. His eyes misted when he spoke. "You were born of love. A forbidden love."

"What are you saying?" She held her breath, preparing for the blow.

"Your mother was another man's wife."

Of all the possibilities she'd considered growing up—and there'd been many—she'd never once thought she was the product of an illegitimate union.

"Philip and your mother were childhood sweethearts. He offered for your mother, but her father laughed at him, telling him he wasn't wealthy enough. Determined to win her hand, Philip set off for the Far East, gambling in everything to turn a quick profit: silk, lace, jewels, spices. When he returned eight months later, he'd tripled his wealth."

"Then why didn't he marry her?"

Uncle Bernard's voice dipped, filling with sadness. "Couldn't. She was on her honeymoon. Her father forced a match with an earl. One with deep pockets and a lot of land."

"Was she happy?"

"She was happy when she found out about you, child," he said, skirting the question.

"And the Earl of Montrose never knew?" There were so many unanswered questions swimming in her head. How had the earl and her mother gotten together again? What of her mother's husband? It seemed patterned after one of the old Greek plays she and Uncle Bernard read about, where everyone who loves anyone dies or ends up alone.

"No, he never knew."

Before Francie had time to ponder her uncle's words, the carriage jostled and rumbled to a halt and the sound of the driver's high-pitched whistle filled the air.

"What's happened?" Francie leaned over to pull aside a thin, dingy curtain.

Through the small window, she could just make out a horse and rider. Both were silhouetted against a brilliant golden backdrop, both were huge, and both made Francie shiver. The rider dismounted and turned toward the carriage. She flipped the curtain back in place and scurried to the other end of the cushion, as far away from the door as possible.

Seconds later, the door flung open and a deep voice filled the carriage. "Miss Jordan?"

It was Mr. Bishop! Another shiver ran along her spine, though she couldn't say why. It wasn't as though she feared him, though his huge body dwarfed the opening of the carriage. It wasn't fear at all. It was just...just that she had never met anyone so intimidating.

"Yes?" Could that small voice really be hers?

He leaned into the carriage, pinning her with his silver-gray gaze. His hair was ruffled from the ride, a stray lock hanging over his forehead. "It seems I was in error. The earl requests your presence posthaste." His tone was clipped, his mouth firm and unsmiling.

"Of course."

He gave her a quick, almost imperceptible nod and turned toward Uncle Bernard. She heard the startled sound, low in his throat as though the sight of her uncle had caught him unawares. But how could that be? Surely he'd seen a second figure in the carriage when he opened the door. Very odd.

Even odder was Uncle Bernard's response. "Good day, young man." A hint of a smile peeked from beneath his bushy beard.

"Bishop," the other man corrected. "Alexander Bishop."

Uncle Bernard nodded. "Mr. Bishop. I'm Bernard Jordan." His smile broadened. "Miss Jordan's uncle."

The two men stared at one another like opponents on a dueling field. Mr. Bishop broke the silence first. "The earl tires easily these days. I'd like Miss Jordan to speak with him as soon as possible." With that, he turned and closed the carriage door.

They made the ride back to the earl's estate in silence. Francie kept thinking about the encounter between her uncle and Mr. Bishop. It helped keep her mind off the impending meeting with her father. Something passed between the two men, something more than casual interest.

"What did you think of Mr. Bishop?" she asked, keeping her voice light. If her uncle knew she were digging, he'd close up tighter than a pillbox. That was one thing about Uncle Bernard. He did not like to be pushed, pulled, or bullied into anything.

"Hmmm?" he asked. "Mr. Bishop?" He gave her a faint smile. "Fine young man."

"Why do you say such a thing?" Nothing she'd seen so far in Mr. Bishop's demeanor prompted her to think of him as fine. Bold, irascible, rash. Now those were words she'd tie to his name without a second's hesitation.

Uncle Bernard shrugged his bony shoulders. "He's got a way of commanding a presence I admire. And he knows what he's about."

"That adds up to arrogant in my book," Francie said.

Her uncle chuckled. "Give the poor boy a chance before you condemn him."

"Boy? I hardly think Mr. Bishop resembles a boy," she said, recalling his broad chest and cold eyes. "As a matter of fact, I don't think he was ever a boy."

"Now there's where you're wrong. Your Mr. Bishop was a child just like the rest of us, full of hopes and dreams. Perhaps his got trampled on when he was just a tot. But, no matter, just like the rest of us, that child is still in there, hidden beneath layers of refinement, no doubt." He stroked his beard. "But he's still in there."

Francie wanted to inform her uncle that even if Mr. Bishop had once been a child—and that was still open for serious debate—then he'd most likely never done anything that even bore a hint of resemblance to children's activities. She couldn't picture him climbing a tree or making mud pies or jumping in puddles. Or even hugging a dog.

Before she had a chance to voice her opinion, the carriage rolled to a halt. Drakemoor. Francie's breath caught in her throat. In a matter of minutes she'd meet the Earl of Montrose.

Her father.

Uncle Bernard leaned over and squeezed her hand. His kind gray eyes warmed her. "It will be all right, Francie," he whispered. "He'll love you as much as I do."

FRANCIE FOUND herself seated once again in the massive cream room with the burgundy sofa. She ran her fingers over her pale blue gown, smoothing first one wrinkle, then another and another until she'd worked a pattern along the fabric. When she reached the end, she started over on the other side.

She had just finished another round of smoothing wrinkles when the oak door opened and a giant of a man entered, leaning on a black cane. His eyes never left hers as he worked his way toward her, one hobbled step at a time. He had broad shoulders and a thick build with large, beefy hands. Despite his age and apparent infirmary, Philip Cardinger, the Earl of Montrose, commanded a powerful presence.

His light-red hair curled about his head with a dusting of white, and his blue eyes sparkled with unshed tears. Francie met his unwavering gaze, a single tear slipping along her own cheek.

"Francie," he breathed.

Her lips trembled as she offered a half-smile. She dug her fingers into the pocket of her gown and produced the locket. "I have this locket." She stood and opened her hand.

His blue eyes swept to the small gold object resting in her palm. He took another step toward her and reached for the locket. "May I?"

"Of course."

He took the locket, his long fingers brushing hers. His red head dipped low as he studied the picture. Then he reached into his vest pocket and pulled out a similar-shaped locket.

"I have its mate," he said, handing her the other half of the locket. His lips curved into a sad smile.

Francie took the locket and tried to still the clamoring in her chest. She looked down at the cameo, stared at the beautiful, smiling woman with the jet-black hair and emerald-green eyes. Her mother. Tears blurred her vision and she reached up to swipe at them.

A strong hand closed over hers. "I miss her still," her father whispered, reaching for her. Francie went to him, burying her head against the warmth of his chest where his heart beat steady and comforting.

Tears came for both of them then, pouring down like an afternoon shower. "I swear I never knew about you, child. If I had any idea you existed, I would've torn this country apart, village by village, to find you."

Francie sniffed and dabbed her eyes with the handkerchief her father tucked in her hand. "I know," she murmured against his chest. "I don't understand why my aunt and uncle didn't tell you about me."

He tensed at the mention of Aunt Eleanor and Uncle Bernard. "Things were very complicated. Perhaps they had their reasons."

Francie wanted to ask more, but the underlying firmness in her father's voice stopped her. Whatever his suspicions, he wasn't going to reveal them to her. At least not yet.

The earl loosened his grip and held her at arm's length. "You're beautiful, Francie. Your mother would be so proud of you."

"I wish I had known her."

"As do I." He fingered one of her curls. "But we can't change the past. All we can do now is forge a future." His smile broadened. "And it will be a great future for you here at Drakemoor."

Drakemoor. Francie never considered staying. She'd only wanted to press the earl for assistance and then head back home in her rickety carriage. But now, after meeting him, after crying in his arms, she realized she wanted very much to get to know this man.

But living in such a grand place, larger than any she'd ever seen? Her whole house could fit in the two rooms she'd visited today.

"I..." she hesitated, "...am not accustomed to living in a place like Drakemoor. I fear I might not adapt well."

The earl ignored her blustering. "We need to sit down before this old man topples over."

"Yes, of course." Francie moved to the side, allowing him

easy access to the nearest chair. She sat in its mate, a comfortable burgundy brocade.

"Now, what's wrong with Drakemoor?"

Heat seeped into her cheeks. "*Nothing.* Nothing at all. It's absolutely beautiful."

"Then why don't you want to live here?" He coughed and cleared his throat.

How could she explain? She clasped her hands in her lap and searched for the words. "I'm not used to such grandeur. I've spent my whole life in a little cottage, helping my aunt grow herbs and wearing homemade clothes. I wouldn't know how to act in a place like this."

"Bah! We'll buy you all the clothes you want. And if tending a garden strikes your fancy, so be it. You can design your own here."

Francie shook her head. "It's not just that. In Amberden, I have freedom. No societal expectations. I can act as I like, dress as I like. Even run barefoot down the street if I please."

The earl let out a laugh that ended in a coughing fit. He held up his hand when she started to get up. "I'm fine. As for running barefoot, that sounds like a splendid idea. I can just see Alex's face the first time you present yourself without slippers or stockings."

"Alex?"

"Yes, Alex. Actually, he prefers Alexander. I'm the only one who can get away with calling him Alex."

Francie's heart skipped three beats. "Oh. Are you referring to Mr. Bishop?"

He nodded, a broad grin spreading across his face. "Old stuffed shirt himself."

"Does he live here?" No. *Please say no.* "Sure does. Alex's like the son I never had."

"Well," Francie said, averting her gaze. "That could be a

problem. You see, Mr. Bishop doesn't like me very well." *And the feeling is mutual.*

"Why on earth would you say such a thing?"

"It's a feeling I have. Our initial meeting didn't go very well." What a serious understatement. The man had all but thrown her out of this house.

"Once you get underneath that tough hide of his, Alex is nothing but a pussycat."

Pussycat? Perhaps *roaring lion* would be a more apt term.

She shook her head. "I don't think so. We seem to rub one another the wrong way."

The earl wasn't listening. "How lucky can one man be? A son and a daughter." His eyes shone as they settled on her. "That means you two are like brother and sister."

She held her smile until she thought her face might shatter. Brother? Alexander Bishop? Not likely.

6

"What the hell's going on, Bernard?" Philip Cardinger demanded, his face red with emotion.

Bernard ignored his friend's outburst. "Would you like a cup of tea?" He pointed to the silver service in front of them.

"I'd prefer a whiskey."

"I'll make two." Bernard rose and walked to the side table where he poured two glasses.

"Bring the bottle. It'll save you another trip."

"You always were the practical one." Bernard steadied the drinks in one hand and grabbed the crystal decanter in the other. He walked to Philip and handed him his glass, then set the decanter on the table in front of them.

Bernard sank into a camel-colored chair and smiled. "I haven't been in your library in a good many years," he said, swirling the amber liquid in his glass.

Philip nodded. "Not since you were a frustrated tutor in love with one of your pupils. And I..." he paused a moment and when he spoke again his voice clogged with emotion, "I was in love with the most beautiful woman in the world."

"And she was in love with you."

"Love didn't matter to that bastard father of hers. He traded money for Catherine's happiness. Damn him. It gnaws at me still when I think of it."

"But now you have Francie."

Philip's gaze swung to Bernard, piercing him with keen blue eyes. "She is my child." It was a statement mingled with a question.

Bernard nodded. "She *is* your child."

Philip let out a long breath. "Then who in God's name is the girl living at Glenhaven? She's not Catherine and Edgar's daughter?"

"No, she's not," Bernard said in a soft voice. Philip took a healthy swallow of whiskey. "She's your daughter, too."

And promptly spat half of it out. "What did you say?"

"Catherine gave birth to twins. Girls. She made Eleanor promise if the child looked like you, she was to say it died and take it away. She didn't trust Belmont. Thought he'd try to harm the child when he figured out it wasn't his."

"Where the hell did you go and why didn't you try to contact me?" Philip asked, his voice filled with more pain than anger.

"I promised Eleanor," Bernard said simply. "She was petrified Belmont would find us. When she left Glenhaven, she left everything behind: her title, her money. We fled to Amberden, a small village two hours south of here. I worked as a tutor for the neighboring estates."

"Good God, man, had I only known." Philip ran a large hand over his face. "Here I was, probably tossing more food in the rubbish bin than you had on your table."

"We made do. We were very happy. I would change nothing."

"I would change everything," Philip said. "I would have demanded Catherine leave that bastard."

"The past is the past," Bernard said. "It can't be changed and no amount of regret will bring Catherine back. Now all we can do is see Francie is kept safe."

"No one will harm her," Philip vowed. "Not if he values his life."

The threat hung over the room, wrapping both men in a shroud of dark contemplation.

Philip broke the silence with a loud sigh. "I hear Belmont dotes excessively on the girl. Claire's her name." He rubbed his jaw. "I've heard she's beautiful. And more spoiled than week-old cooked cabbage."

"Not surprising if Belmont raised her."

Philip sighed again. "Two daughters. I can't believe I have two daughters."

"But you can only claim one, Philip. Belmont must never know the daughter he's raised since birth is another man's child."

Philip's eyes misted with overwhelming sadness. "I know. Nor can Francie or Claire know. Tragic that blood must ignore blood."

"It must be that way," Bernard warned. "It's a matter of survival."

❧

FRANCIE STIRRED her tea for the tenth time, listening to the tiny clicking sound her spoon made as it hit the sides of the cup. She looked once more at the large green room around her, decorated in pink and gold florals. Mr. Bishop cleared his throat. Again.

Of course, he was annoyed. He had to entertain her while

her uncle and father chatted. Entertain was too loose a word for what that rude excuse for a man was doing. If by *entertain*, her father meant escort her into this room, order tea and scones, and then deposit himself in a chair, and proceed to read his paper, then Mr. Bishop was doing an excellent job. There hadn't been five seconds of conversation in the last fifteen minutes. Francie slid him a sideways glance. Time to change that. She cleared her throat. "The earl seems like a wonderful man."

Silence.

"I'm sure you quite enjoy his company." Nothing.

"Drakemoor is beautiful, though a little overwhelming, I must say."

More silence.

"Of course, once I'm living here, I'm certain I'll grow accustomed to it."

Mr. Bishop crushed his paper beneath his large hands. "What did you say?" His silver eyes narrowed, making the scar on his face stick out in white anger.

He would not intimidate her, even if his horrid scar did. "I said," she repeated with careful precision, "once I'm living here—"

He slashed his hand in the air and leaned forward, dwarfing his chair. "You, Miss Jordan, will not be staying here."

"In truth, I would much prefer my small cottage to this...," she paused and took in her surroundings, "...overdone grandeur, but the earl insists I stay."

"Oh?"

She nodded. "He insists."

"How convenient for you."

Francie ignored the sarcasm in his voice. If they were going to live under the same roof, it was time to open his eyes about a few things. "I would prefer to stay at Amberden. Everything I've heard or read about the upper class reeks of constrictive breeding, loveless marriages, and grudging duty, woven with lies and deceit."

Mr. Bishop raised a dark brow in her direction. "If you've read about the shortcomings of our society, then you've also read of the unlimited jewels, fancy gowns, and personal maids?"

Francie nodded. "Of course."

His gaze swept her old blue gown as though she were a common beggar. "You have no interest in availing yourself of these things?"

"No."

His lips twitched in what could almost be considered a smile. He thought she was lying. His next words were soft, controlled, and biting. "You have no interest in the earl's vast wealth? No desire to sink your hands, elbow-deep into his coffers?" He rested a hand under his chin and waited for her answer.

"Of course not!" This man wasn't interested in the truth. He'd already drawn his conclusions about her and they were not complimentary. "Regardless of what you may think my motives are, Mr. Bishop, my main desire was to enlist the aid of someone who could help protect our village from being terrorized by a madman."

"And finding out about your true heritage was secondary?" he inquired. "Or merely inconsequential?"

Her gaze locked with his. "It was not imperative. At first, I was angry my real father did not seek me out, nor try to find out about me." Her voice softened. "Then I learned he couldn't because he never knew I existed."

"I see."

"You don't," Francie said, setting her teacup on the table. "You think I'm after my father's money." She stood up and grabbed her cloak. "You think I'm looking to make a good match in your polite society." She jammed her fingers into her gloves. "Silk and satins." She flung her bonnet on her head and tied the ribbons with quick, jerky movements. "Diamonds and rubies."

He stared at her, his expression blank.

Francie took three steps toward him, stopping a foot from his polished shoe. She looked down at him, anger and disgust thrumming in her veins. "People like you are why I want no part of your society. You always think the worst, never imagining anyone could possibly have a good intention, let alone harbor selfless deeds."

"It's been my experience, Miss Jordan, people always have motives, usually very selfish ones, for everything they do," he drawled. "You, I am certain, are no different."

What a cruel, miserable beast. "That's where you're wrong, Mr. Bishop." She turned and headed toward the door.

"Where do you think you're going?"

"I find myself in sudden need of fresh air," she replied, clutching the doorknob. She refused to turn and face him, refused to give him the satisfaction of seeing how upset he'd made her.

"It's raining outside. You'll catch your death."

"Then you needn't worry about me anymore."

She opened the door and slipped through before he offered any more arguments. Francie hurried across the marble floor, eyeing the great double door leading outside. To freedom. As she approached, the odd little butler tapped his foot, sniffed, and opened the huge oak door for her.

She ran down the brick steps, past the main drive, onto the well-manicured lawn. Francie ignored the rain pelting her gown and followed the tall privet, losing herself in a tangle of glossy green. Spotting a stone bench several feet away, she headed for it, and sank down onto the hard surface. She had a new father and a new home. And a new tormenter in her life. If she were to enjoy any measure of happiness with the first two, she'd have to do something about the latter.

~

"HE'S NOT YOUR TYPE," Jared Crayton whispered, planting a kiss on Claire Ashcroft's bare shoulder.

She shrugged him off, annoyed with his words. "You have no idea what my type is."

He nipped her neck, sucking and drawing her sensitive flesh into his mouth. Claire pulled away, wrapping the sheet around her. She still tingled with the aftermath of their love-making. Jared Crayton lay before her, naked, bronzed, and beautiful. He was an exhilarating lover, enticing and adventurous.

But he was not Alexander Bishop.

Jared's fingers worked a slow path down her spine.

"Stop." She turned to face him, well aware the sheet dipped to reveal a generous expanse of bosom. Soft, creamy breasts...Jared's favorite.

He chuckled, his green eyes heating at the sight of her. "I doubt you've ever told anyone to stop in your life."

Claire flung her long, black hair behind her and tried to look offended. A small smile tugged at the corners of his mouth. He was right, of course. She'd been hard pressed to say no to anyone since her fifteenth summer of sensual exploration with Oliver Milton, her tutor. What could she say? She enjoyed sexual adventure, enjoyed the forbidden attraction, the complete power she wielded over men. Claire traced tiny circles over Jared's chest, working her way toward his navel. He groaned and she smiled.

"Bishop isn't even one of our kind," Jared said, arching his hips to meet her roaming hand. "Underneath all the starch and manners, he's still a stable boy."

"I know," she said, running her tongue along her lower lip.

"Probably nothing better than an animal." He grunted as her finger touched the tip of his manhood.

"I hope not," she whispered in a low, throaty voice. Claire closed her fingers around him and Jared pumped into her hand.

"And just how will you explain your wedding night?" he bit out through clenched teeth. "No virgin's blood?"

She threw back her head and laughed. "Men have always been so gullible. A little chicken blood hidden under the bed will take care of that."

He groaned again and grabbed her hips, pulling her atop him. Claire reached out and braced herself against his chest, working her body along his thick hardness.

"Bishop's no fool." He lifted her and impaled her on his shaft.

"Neither am I," she whispered on a moan of pleasure. She rode him, slow and easy, teasing and tempting him with the feel of her.

Jared bucked hard and fast, almost dislodging her. "Enough," he growled, flipping her over and burying himself in her heat. He pounded into her like a wild man. Just the way she liked it.

Alexander Bishop would be like this. And more. So much more.

He was different from the men she knew, the ones who granted her every wish, doted on her excessively, and told her no less than three times a day how utterly beautiful she was. Alexander Bishop appeared immune to her many charms, which made him all the more desirable.

He'd rescued her twice. The first time, she'd fallen from her horse and sprained her ankle after a silly attempt to ride bareback. Alexander emerged from the early morning mist on horseback like a gallant knight in search of his maiden. He dismounted and knelt over her, smelling of man and fresh air, the scar on his cheek, stark, the silver bright in his eyes. Claire's belly twisted and shivered when his strong fingers touched her ankle. But he remained ever the gentleman, and though she hated to admit it, he appeared quite indifferent to her beauty and curves as he lifted her to his horse and returned her home.

The second rescue was not a rescue at all, though Alexander believed it to be and Claire encouraged the misconception. She'd been trysting with the stable boy in the far fields of the estate when Alexander once again appeared on horseback. Upon seeing her state of dishabille, he assumed the boy had been about to press himself upon her. Poor boy. Alexander punched him square in the face and then twice in the stomach. But again, Alexander himself remained immune to her, even when she permitted him an ample view of cleavage and calf. That's when Claire vowed she would have him.

And she would. *Soon*.

"Claire." Jared's moan filled the room. Seconds later, both exploded in a heated frenzy of slick sweat and sensual fantasy.

"What about *your* girl?" Claire asked when she had the breath to speak again. "Have you caught *her* yet?"

"No. But I will. Even if I have to pursue her day and night, I will."

Jared was not the most discriminating lover. How well she knew that. Their first tryst had been in a carriage scant hours after they'd been introduced. She shivered at the thought. There was something to be said for spontaneity.

"She's just a girl. Can't you settle on another?"

Jared smiled and traced the tip of her breast. "Oh, but she's not just a girl. Not Francie Jordan."

"Are you saying she's more beautiful than I am?"

Claire had known of her beauty since the age of three when her father filled her with tales of her boundless beauty and the advantages it would provide. He promised her she'd have everything her heart desired. Men loved her long, black hair, curling well past her shoulders. Some even wrote poems about her, saying she possessed the "face of an angel with eyes the color of a morning sky, skin as soft as rose petals and a smile to rival the sun." Oh, yes, she'd heard it all.

And that was years before any of them glimpsed her naked body.

"No, not more beautiful," Jared answered, deep in thought. "Just different. There's something about her, something wild and innocent that makes me hard just thinking about her."

"She's a commoner," Claire huffed, annoyed he would compare another woman's beauty to hers. He could sleep with as many women as he wanted, as long as he knew she was the most beautiful.

Jared turned to her, running a finger from her breast to her woman's heat. "You'll go after Bishop and I'll find Francie," he said. "But in the meantime," he whispered, stroking her, "let's just enjoy each other."

Claire moaned. "I'll miss this, Jared. You play me like a finely tuned instrument."

He threw her a cocky half-smile. "Who says you have to miss anything? Maybe we'll make it a foursome?"

～

FRANCIE WANTED to strangle Alexander Bishop with her bare hands. It was an odd wish coming from someone who protected field mice and had never squashed so much as a centipede in her life. They were all miracles of God, deserving compassion and respect.

All except Alexander Bishop. He must have come from the other end of God's rainbow—the dark side, where rude arrogance snuffed out good deeds and kindness.

Francie still seethed over the conversation she'd had with him earlier. She'd just returned from her walk, calmed by the fresh air and gentle rain. Unfortunately, the first person she encountered as she entered Drakemoor was the very person who'd necessitated the walk in the first place. Alexander Bishop pounced on her like a sleek cat, informing her he'd just spoken to the earl about a Lord Jared Crayton, Francie's would-be abductor, and now he had a few questions of his own.

She'd followed him into the same room she'd vacated an hour earlier, sat in the same rose-colored chair, pulled off her gloves, and waited. It didn't take long for him to make his point.

"The earl relayed your story to me about Crayton." He paced the room, shoulders straight, hands clasped behind his back. When he reached the fireplace, he turned and headed toward her, his muscular legs moving in slow, even strides. He stopped two feet from the hem of her gown.

Francie kept her eyes trained on the wallpaper behind his left ear. It was a floral pattern. Pink roses dusted with gold. Soothing. Peaceful. She took a deep breath and waited.

"I've met the man," he said. "Actually, he's not much more than a boy, but a very wealthy boy," he added and continued pacing. "From one of the wealthiest families in the area."

"What are you insinuating?"

"I think Jared Crayton's only harm is being the son of a duke."

Francie gasped and bound out of her chair. "You think," she

tried to keep her voice from shaking, "those young girls *asked* to be seduced?"

The odious man shrugged. "I'm not saying they asked him."

Her shoulders slumped forward a bit and she let out a breath. At least they agreed upon that.

"But I'm not saying they objected either."

"They did not welcome his advances," she bit out. "He took advantage of them. Preyed on their innocence. Stalked their naiveté. Threatened their family's livelihoods."

"Did he *force* any of them?" Alexander asked, shoving his hands in his pockets.

"Force them? Well...no, not in that manner of speaking. But he twisted—"

"My point," he replied. "Crayton took advantage of a *situation*, not a person. He didn't force any of those girls. If they believed he'd marry them, then they were foolish."

"Foolish? And me? What am I?" Francie's voice rose as she threw out the questions. "Am I foolish for believing his threat to ruin my aunt's livelihood? Am I foolish for running when he chased me through the woods and fields, stalking me?" She trembled. "Am I foolish to believe one of these days when he realizes his sweet words and ready smile won't win me over, he'll try something else?" She tried to control the near-hysteria in her voice, but the reality of her words gripped her, threatening to suffocate her with fear.

He stared at her a long while, saying nothing. When he finally spoke, his voice was low and soft. "No, Miss Jordan, I don't think you're foolish. Not at all. As a matter of fact, I think you're very smart." He stepped closer. "Very smart, indeed. You've got the earl fooled with your stories. He believes you." He leaned in close enough for Francie to see flecks of gold in his silver eyes. "But I don't," he whispered. "Not one word."

"I *am* his daughter!"

"Perhaps," he replied in a bland voice. "I concede, it would appear you may well be the earl's offspring. But the rest?" He shook his head and frowned. "What better way to obtain your father's affection and his sympathy than by placing yourself in danger? And at the hands of a duke's son?" He let out a short laugh. "It's nothing short of brilliant, actually."

"It's the truth!"

The beast of a man ignored her outrage. "If I were interested in bettering my position and found I was the daughter of an earl, I might well fabricate such a story myself. The earl, being the kind of man he is, would protect you and see that you'd want for nothing. You could travel in society dressed as a lady in the finest of silk. And perhaps, with the earl's power and wealth behind you, make a very fine match." His lips curved upward but bore not even the slightest resemblance to a smile. "But that's what you're anticipating, isn't it, Miss Jordan?"

"Of course not!" *The nerve of the man.* "I care nothing for such things. I do care about the girls of Amberden. That's why I came." Her voice dipped, faltered. "And...I wanted to meet my father."

"Ah, yes, of course. There is that. And not just any father, but one equipped to elevate a simple village girl to a position of true importance. A lady. And a little story about the Duke of Worthington's son would ensure the earl's sympathies."

"You're wrong!" Francie spat out. "I did no such thing."

"Did anyone see Lord Jared *stalking* you?"

"Of course not. He made certain I was alone."

"I see."

"No, Mr. Bishop, you don't see. You don't see at all," she said, pointing her finger at him. "You've got your mind made up I'm trying to trick my father and nothing I say or do will change that. I'm not even going to try."

"Good, because I won't fall victim to your antics." He folded his arms over his broad chest, staring down at her in all of his superior arrogance. "I don't like when a woman uses her charm and beauty and misguided circumstance to manipulate a man's heart. It won't work on me."

"It couldn't," she shot back. "You don't have a heart."

"Touché." He eyed her a moment longer. "I'll tolerate you for Philip's sake. Nothing more."

Then he turned and walked out of the room as though they hadn't just launched a private war against one another.

Francie didn't see Bishop for the rest of the afternoon until a short while ago, when he entered the dining room and she cast the object of her ire a quick, sideways glance. He sat at the end of the table, lifting his fork with methodical precision to his mouth. She bet if she counted the peas on his fork they would number the same each time.

Of course, her father placed her right next to him. Just close enough to catch a whiff of his spicy cologne and see the faint puckering of skin on the jagged scar running down his cheek. Just close enough to make her very aware of his presence.

"Alex, my boy, I'd like you to escort Francie and Bernard back to Amberden in the morning to collect her things," the earl said, stabbing a piece of pork. Two pink spots colored his cheeks. He'd made it through most of dinner without one of the coughing episodes she'd witnessed earlier.

Francie didn't want to upset her father, but she neither needed nor wanted Alexander Bishop to accompany her and Uncle Bernard. And from the tight lines around his mouth, *Alex* felt the same. Alex. She wanted to laugh at the absurdity. That name was reserved for men with quick smiles and charming dispositions who laughed a lot and were well schooled in the art of flirtation. Alexander Bishop fit none of those qualifications.

Setting down her fork, she met her father's blue-eyed gaze

and smiled. "That won't be necessary, Father. Uncle Bernard and I are quite capable of traveling to Amberden and packing up my belongings." She didn't want to feel beholden to Alexander Bishop for anything.

"I want Alex to go with you."

"I'm sure Mr. Bishop has more important things to do." *Like counting the number of peas he places on his fork.* "We can leave first thing in the morning and I'll be back the next day."

The earl shook his head. "Francie, I don't—"

"I'm going." Alexander Bishop's words sliced through the air, slashing any further objections.

Francie shot a look at him. His thick, black brows were drawn together in a straight line, the corners of his full lips turned down into a frown, and the scar running along his cheekbone was white. But it was his eyes that made her breath stick in her throat. They were cold, like a freezing rain, driving into her, battering at her defenses. A shiver ran through her with a warning. *This man is dangerous. Beware.*

She swallowed hard, pushing past her uneasiness. "That won't be necessary, Mr.—"

"Ten o'clock," he said, cutting through her words. He leveled one last cold look on her before setting his napkin aside and rising. "If you'll excuse me," he said, ignoring Francie and nodding to the earl and Uncle Bernard, "I have a previous commitment."

The earl chuckled. "Seeing Tess tonight, are we?"

Alexander Bishop shrugged.

The earl let out a hearty laugh. "Tell her hello for me."

"Tess?" The words were out before Francie realized she'd spoken. Heat flooded her cheeks. Tess? Who was Tess? Not that she cared if Mr. Bishop had a love interest, because she didn't. It was just that, try as she might, she couldn't visualize him being gentle with a woman, couldn't imagine him speaking tender words or holding her in his arms. The very idea made her light-headed.

"Tess is Lady Printon, widow of an old friend of mine," the earl said, sipping at his claret. "She lives down the road. They've been seeing each other for quite some time." He winked at Francie. "I've been hounding Alex to state his intentions, get moving, and start working on a passel of children before my time is up." He sighed. "But I might as well be talking to that door over there," he said, pointing a long finger at the thick, oak door leading to the hallway.

"Philip," Alexander's deep voice filled the room. "I doubt anyone is interested in my personal affairs."

"Just stating facts, son. You know I'd like to see a baby or two running around the house before I meet my Maker." His blue eyes twinkled. "But now that I have Francie here, who knows? Maybe she'll give me a little baby to spoil."

Francie felt the blood drain from her face. "I...don't think... so," she stammered.

The earl continued as though he hadn't heard her. "Who knows? Maybe Alex has been stalling with Tess because she's not the one for him. Maybe," he added, swinging his blue gaze from Francie to Alexander, "Alex has been waiting for someone else."

Her father's insinuation was quite clear. He meant Alexander had been waiting for *her*. How could he even think such a thing? Couldn't he tell they had difficulty being in the same room together?

Alexander cleared his throat. Twice. "I happen to like my single state, Philip. Very much." His eyes narrowed on the old man. "And I intend to keep it that way."

"I'm not saying you shouldn't. I'm merely suggesting a possibility. Isn't that right, Bernard?"

Uncle Bernard hadn't spoken more than three sentences

since dinner began. Every now and then, Francie caught his gray gaze swinging from her to Alexander Bishop. "Hmmm," he said, stroking his bushy beard and tilting his head to one side. "Hmmm. Francie and Mr. Bishop."

"This is ridiculous." Alexander shot the earl a murderous look. "Miss Jordan and I would never suit." His gaze settled on her. "Never."

Heat rushed to her cheeks and she blurted out, "Mr. Bishop is right. The whole notion is preposterous." Though he needn't be quite so adamant about it. For heaven's sake, you'd think she was a two-headed monster.

Her father smiled and shook his head. "One thing is for certain. You'll never get to know one another if you can't dispense with the Miss and Mister. Isn't that right, Bernard?"

All eyes flew to Uncle Bernard. "Usually, that's necessary at some point if an acquaintance is to develop into a relationship of any substance."

"Miss Jordan and I—"

"Francie," the earl corrected.

"Francie," Alexander said through clenched teeth. He was on the verge of losing his temper. She knew it. His eyes narrowed to half-slits, his mouth set in a firm line. And the jagged scar, the telltale sign, grew silver-white. "Francie and I," he began again, "are not in the least interested in developing a relationship of any kind." His gaze burned her with the heat of his anger. "Are we, *Francie*?"

"No, *Alexander*, we are not in the least interested," she forced herself to reply.

The earl raised his hands in the air. "Fine. Enough said on that subject. If you can't be husband and wife, then we'll have to settle for brother and sister."

"I agree," Bernard said. "Brother and sister. That should suit the two of them just fine." He smiled then, a slow, lazy smile she'd grown accustomed to over the years. He reserved this smile for situations, usually in her studies, when Francie formed one conclusion and the correct answer was the exact opposite. The more impassioned she became while arguing her position, the broader her uncle's grin.

But this was real life. And she was not interested in one Mr. Alexander Bishop. No matter how broad her uncle's smile stretched, she was not interested. Most definitely not.

_____

7

"Where is she, you old witch? Where's Francie?" Jared Crayton advanced on the old woman as she bent over in the fields, cutting some kind of purple flowers. And *ignoring* him.

"Look at me!" he demanded, his fists clenching and unclenching. How he'd like to get his hands around her fat neck and squeeze until she talked. He'd teach her to show respect for someone of his position. He was the duke's son, for God's sake. He was somebody. Unlike the inhabitants of this little, run-down village who depended on the generosity of the heavens for sun and fertile soil to ply their trade. He'd show the old witch who wielded the real power.

And then she'd get down on her knees and beg for mercy.

"Where's Francie? Tell me now, or I swear by all that's holy, when I find her, I'll make her pay for your disrespectfulness."

The woman turned to him then, her eyes shaded by the large bonnet she wore. "You'll never find her." Her lips curved into a small smile. "She's gone. Forever. And soon your days of terrorizing the village will be over, too."

"Bitch!" he roared, slamming his right fist into her jaw. A crackling sound filled the air as bone connected with bone. The woman stumbled and fell to her knees, clutching her face and moaning.

Jared took a step forward, stopping when his booted foot touched the hem of her drab, brown gown. She lay at his feet, a crumpled mass of muslin and disgusting tears.

"Now tell me and I'll spare you worse."

He watched her try to lift her head. It seemed an eternity before she inched upward to meet his gaze. Her jaw was already swollen and red and he wondered if he'd broken it. He should have been more careful. Best not to leave a trail. But the woman had made him so angry, he'd forgotten to use discretion. Not that it really mattered. He was, after all, the son of the Duke of Worthington. And these people were nothing. Nothing at all.

"D...Da..." Blood splattered from her mouth when she tried to speak. He must have hit her mouth as well. His aim was off. Maybe he needed more practice.

Jared stooped down to catch her words. "Tell me, old woman. Tell me, and be spared."

"Daaa...Daaa," she started again, wincing when she spoke. Her hands reached up to cup her jaw.

"That's it. You can say it," Jared coaxed, his words soft and gentle, as though he were a friend and confidant, not the man who'd just pummeled the side of her face.

A small smile played about his lips. She was going to tell him. He knew he'd make her talk. Why hadn't she realized that before he hit her? It was all her fault. If she'd only been respectful of his position and treated him with the deference he deserved, this whole matter would have been settled and he'd be on his way to Francie.

Francie. She was in his blood now, pounding and throbbing, filling him with desire. He had to have her. And he would. Just as soon as the old woman spoke.

Jared watched blood ooze from her lower lip. He should have taken better aim. It would have saved so much time. He'd be lucky to get the words out of her by nightfall.

"DDD...Daaa..."

Or maybe not. Maybe he'd scared her enough that she'd force them out, despite her obvious pain. Smart woman. "That's it. Keep trying."

"DDD...Daaamn...yyy...you," she pushed the words out, "ttt...to...hhh...hell."

The words registered a second after she slurred them out. *Damn you to hell.* "Damn you to hell," Jared roared, smashing her mouth with his fist. Her head snapped back with a loud crack just before she fell onto the dirt with a thud.

"Bitch." He straightened and brushed off his clothes. That should teach her to speak to him in such a disrespectful manner. He looked down at her with casual disinterest, noting the fine stream of blood trickling from her swollen lips. His gaze swung to the fields of herbs and flowers. The old woman loved those weeds. Francie said they were her livelihood. He eyed the purple and yellow stalks. Next time he asked her a question, she'd answer him straightaway. Yes, she most certainly would.

"WE SHOULD BE THERE SOON," Bernard announced. He'd made general statements to no one in particular the entire trip. Alexander guessed Bernard was trying to assuage the tension he and Philip created last night during their matchmaking attempts. It wasn't working. Perhaps they'd been only jesting as they later confessed, but if that were the case, Alexander wasn't laughing.

Neither was Francie. He glanced at her from the corner of his eye. She sat across from him in a pathetic little pink gown. She stared out the window, shoulders back, head held high, like a lady of quality. Once the earl had her clothed and jeweled, it would be hard to tell her from a *real* lady of quality. Say, for example, Tess.

Alexander buried the thought before it germinated. He'd spent the better half of last evening comparing his new "sister" to the beautiful widow. Much to his utter dismay, Tess came up lacking most of the time. How could that be? Tess was exactly what he wanted: blonde-haired, blue-eyed, with a sweet disposition. She'd never shown a hint of anger or dissatisfaction. And she had every right to. They both knew Alexander wasn't going to marry her, yet she'd taken him to her bed, knowing this was as much of Alexander Bishop as she would ever have.

Except for last night. He'd ranted about Francie Jordan for hours as Tess sipped sherry and nodded her blonde head. When he was through, she kissed him, ran her fingers down his body, and still he felt no desire. It was all because of her. Damn the woman.

She was a witch, a beautiful one, with her fire-red hair and sky-blue eyes. What man would want someone like Francie Jordan? She was too bold, too outspoken, and too brash. How could Philip and Bernard have even entertained the idea of Francie and him together? It would be disastrous!

But there was a small piece of him that admired her strength and applauded her tenacity. Even if she had fabricated the story about Jared Crayton, and he intended to find out, she would have done it to protect herself or elevate her position. Alexander didn't agree with it, but in desperation, a village girl might invent a story or two to endear herself to her long-lost father.

Perhaps it was her situation that bothered him most and made Alexander want to avoid her at all costs. If not for Philip's generosity, he would have been a homeless orphan, in a far worse situation than Francie's. His parents had not been of noble blood or even of reputable standing. They were cast-offs of society, a drunken groomsman and his obsessive wife, who had the misfortune of giving birth to a child they didn't want. If Alexander had been in Francie's situation, he'd have done anything to get out of the world of depravity he called home—lie, steal, cheat—anything short of murder.

He tugged at his cravat. All the years at Oxford, the fancy clothes, and private tutors hadn't really changed him. No matter how hard he tried, he was still the gutter-rat offspring of Harry and Alice Bishop. There were only two ways to keep the demons of the past at bay: Practice the role of the perfect gentleman at all times, in every situation, and never associate with anyone beneath him, least of all, anyone who might evoke some form of emotion that would force him to deal with his own unfortunate childhood.

His gaze flitted over Francie Jordan again. She was dangerous. A woman like her could elicit all kinds of emotions, if permitted. He would make certain they were never permitted.

"At last, here we are," Bernard said, pointing to a little cottage around the bend. "Home."

Alexander glanced out the carriage window. Home was a small, cozy dwelling made of different sizes and shapes of stone in varying colors of gray. Clumps of meandering ivy covered several stones, creeping along in haphazard disarray from the pitch of the roof to the corner of the small windows. The vibrant colors surrounding the cottage overshadowed its drabness. Splotches of red, white, and yellow adorned the pathways.

They looked like roses, scattered about in an irregular pattern, but it was hard to tell from the distance.

To the side of the house were fields bathed in purples, pinks, yellows, and reds. Something struck Alexander as odd, and it took him a moment to realize the flowers were lying on the ground or dangling mid-air from half-cut stalks, as though they'd been hacked away without a care for beauty or preservation.

The look of horror on Bernard and Francie's faces told him something was indeed wrong.

"Eleanor," Bernard breathed as the carriage slowed. "I've got to find her."

Francie turned to Alexander. "It was him," she said, her voice little more than a whisper. "He was here." She scampered after her uncle, leaving Alexander to follow behind. He'd seen the fear in her eyes, heard it in her voice. Could the threat of Jared Crayton be real? Could he have misjudged Francie Jordan? The truth lay somewhere between the Jordan home and the mangled fields.

He was about to enter the cottage when Francie flung open the door and ran outside. "She's not inside," she said, her voice quivering. "We've got to find her."

"We'll find her, child," Bernard vowed.

Alexander followed behind as Francie raced toward the fields, her movements swift and graceful as she called out her aunt's name. His chest tightened. He knew pain. He knew despair. And he had a terrible feeling Francie was about to become acquainted with both of these quite intimately. Someone had ravaged these fields, carved them up with hatred and vengeance, until each stalk lay decimated, the very life ripped out of it. Had Francie's aunt suffered the same fate?

He wasn't a man of prayer, held little stock in it, believing each man created his own destiny. Now, as he traveled row after row of deliberate destruction, he prayed the woman had been spared.

Minutes later, Francie's blood-curdling scream told him his prayers were useless. Alexander ran toward her, the sound of her screams pounding through him like heartbeats. Bernard was several yards behind, walking with a quick shuffle gait, his arms swinging side to side as though that would get him to Francie faster.

Alexander spotted her through a clump of green stalks. She knelt on the ground, huddled over a body, her red hair draping the other person's chest. Her shoulders shook, her arms clutching the lifeless form of a woman whose face was beaten to a swollen, purplish blue. The left side of her jaw bore marks resembling someone's knuckles—a man's, judging from the size. Her lips were cut and covered with dried blood.

"Oh no," a voice moaned from behind him. "Dear God, not my Eleanor." Bernard pushed past him, falling to the ground to kneel over his wife. He ran his thin, bony fingers over her face in a soft caress.

Alexander looked away. Too much pain, too much gut-wrenching emotion turning him inside out, making him feel things he did not want to feel.

A low moan slid from the prone form on the ground. His gaze whipped back to the old woman. She was alive! One eye opened to little more than a slit. Her breathing came in shallow puffs. When she tried to open her mouth to speak, a whimper of pain escaped.

"Don't speak, Aunt Eleanor." Francie smoothed wisps of gray hair from her aunt's face. "It's all right now. You're safe."

The woman's eyes inched open. Her swollen lips moved a fraction, but no sound came out.

Alexander's gut twisted again. "Who, in God's name, would do such a thing?" To a woman, no less?

"Who did this, Eleanor?" Bernard clutched his wife's hand, his voice trembling.

Francie cast Alexander a quick glance. "It was him," she breathed. "I know it." She closed her eyes and took a deep breath. Then she turned to her aunt and spoke in soft, soothing tones. "Aunt Eleanor, the person who did this, was he a tall, blond-haired man? Well-dressed, like a nobleman?" The old woman's eyes grew large.

"If the answer is yes, you need only blink," Bernard murmured.

They watched as Eleanor Jordan met her husband's gaze. And blinked.

Francie looked up at Alexander. "You didn't believe me."

Guilt crept over him, smothering him until he found it hard to breathe. No, he hadn't believed her, hadn't believed she wasn't trying to take advantage of the earl by creating a monster in Amberden.

But the monster was real. And deadly.

His next words stuck in his throat like a foreign language, hiding behind his tongue, until he pushed them out with great effort. "I apologize for my misjudgment."

Francie stared at him, her blue eyes filled with sadness and tears. Her bottom lip quivered as she tried to speak. "Please..." She sniffed twice and swiped at her eyes. "Please make him pay."

Alexander stared at the beautiful young woman kneeling on the ground cradling her aunt, and in that instant, he wanted to be her prince, wanted to slay her dragons and dry her tears. He wanted her to believe in humankind's innate goodness, even when he himself did not. Knowing he'd regret it, he opened his mouth and let the words fall out.

"I'll make him pay. By God, I'll make him pay."

ALEXANDER HAD BEEN WATCHING her sleep for the past half hour. She lay perched in an old rocking chair, legs tucked underneath her gown, head tilted to one side. A pair of serviceable brown shoes rested on the floor a few feet from one another. No doubt, she'd kicked them off.

Beautiful. With her wild mass of sun-kissed red hair cascading about her shoulders, a few loose tendrils falling over one cheek, Francie was the vision of beauty and innocence. Long dark lashes lay in contrast against her creamy skin. Though he couldn't see them from where he sat, Alexander knew a light dusting of freckles covered the bridge of her nose. He'd been close enough yesterday, during one of their...*discussions*, to notice. And the mere fact that he *had* noticed bothered him. He pinched the bridge of his nose. He wouldn't notice anymore. Period.

He cursed himself for promising to deal with Jared Crayton. It was an irrational, impulsive decision, driven by one woman's tears. What was the matter with him? If there were two things he abhorred most and never displayed, they were irrational and impulsive behavior. Yet, he'd exhibited both this afternoon without a second's consideration.

Blast Francie Jordan! He should have turned his back on her tears, kept to a firm resolve, and simply refused. No one expected such things from him, such involvement where it was not his concern. But Francie Jordan did. Some sense of duty drove her, some commitment to righteousness rare in the world and almost nonexistent in polite society. And she was hell-bent on dragging him along on her crusade of good against evil.

She shifted in her chair and sighed, let out a low moan, and snuggled further into the chair, heaving another sigh. Alexander's groin tightened. *Damn!* He sprung from the chair, nearly toppling it over, grabbed his jacket, and headed for the door. Once outside, he sucked in the brisk, evening air and cursed the smallness of the cottage. That's why he'd noticed her. That was the only reason.

If he'd been at Drakemoor, he'd be working on his books right now, or visiting Tess, perhaps. Or maybe relaxing in his library with a good book and a glass of sherry. Any number of things from his evening routine. But not watching Francie Jordan sleep. And not being so depraved as to get an erection over an innocent sigh.

Alexander cursed under his breath. Circumstance. That's all it was. He needed to get back to Drakemoor and pay Tess a visit. Then he needed to take Baron out and run the hills. It was the only time he forgot to be a gentleman and was as wild as the animal he rode. In truth, it was the only time he felt alive.

The only time he felt free.

"I was hoping to find you alone."

Alexander spun around. Bernard stood several paces behind him.

"I needed some air." Alexander dug his hands in his pockets. "It was stifling inside."

Bernard nodded and pulled a pipe and tin of tobacco from his pocket and began filling it.

"I prefer cooler temperatures," Alexander said. *And anyplace your niece is not.* What was wrong with him? He was babbling like an idiot.

"I don't want Francie to blame herself for Eleanor's attack," Bernard said, lighting his pipe and taking a long drag. "If anyone's to blame, it's me. I should not have left her alone." His voice cracked. "But I never dreamed the monster capable of such violence. Word in the village was he seduced young girls with his good looks and easy smile. Not this," he faltered, "this..."

"He'll pay for his actions," Alexander cut in, uncomfortable with Bernard's raw emotions. He wasn't used to seeing a man cry over a woman or express feelings with the openness Bernard showed tonight.

"I'm counting on you, Alexander. The monster has to pay for what he's done."

"He will," Alexander vowed, though at present he wasn't certain how he'd keep this vow. Perhaps he should request a private audience with the duke himself? Or maybe a little visit to the perpetrator first would negate a meeting with the duke. No. That wouldn't work. Jared Crayton's word counted for less than nothing. He'd have to speak with the duke himself.

"I want to get Francie and Eleanor to Drakemoor as soon as possible," Bernard said. "They'll be safe there."

Alexander nodded. "And Eleanor can recuperate in peace. Thank God it looked worse than it was. Swelling and bruises and no broken bones."

"Thank God, indeed," Bernard returned, taking another long drag on his pipe. "Eleanor's a tough one. We'll do just what the doctor said. She can lie down and rest the entire trip."

Visions of the crowded carriage flitted through Alexander's mind. If Bernard and Eleanor shared one side of the carriage, then Alexander would spend the entire ride tormented by Francie's closeness, her lavender scent teasing his nostrils. If she shared the seat with her aunt, he'd be forced to look at her, tortured by her sky-blue eyes and red-gold curls. If his eyes dipped below her neck, well, then he'd be in true agony.

"Francie may have a hard time adjusting to life at Drakemoor," Bernard said, interrupting his thoughts. "She's quite content here in Amberden."

"I've gathered that," Alexander said in a dry voice. He thought of her sleeping in the chair, tucked in with a blue and green blanket. Warm, cozy, and content. More seductive than the most skilled mistress sprawled on a silk counterpane.

A hint of a smile peeked from under Bernard's mustache. "That's Francie. Content with everything. She never complained, even when she had to wear the same gowns three years in a row, all too short and too tight. She never said a word." His smile deepened. "And Eleanor, well, she never was the best seamstress."

Bernard puffed away a few moments, saying nothing more. Alexander figured he was most likely thinking of his injured wife and just when the silence stretched to the point of uneasiness, the older man pointed the end of his pipe at Alexander. "Francie deserves the best. She should have grown up wearing the finest silks and satins. Diamonds, rubies." His voice thickened. "She shouldn't have had to dig around in that blasted dirt, sewing and crafting into the night with a needle that made her fingers bleed, even if she claimed to love it."

No, she shouldn't have, Alexander thought, with a twist in his gut. She should not have been forced into a crude existence, dependent on the land and her own industriousness to survive, when he, a product of filth and depravity, enjoyed a comfortable existence at Drakemoor with her father.

"Why did you take her away?" It was a question he needed to ask. Alexander pulled a thin cigar from his pocket and waited.

"Eleanor and I had no choice. We promised Catherine, who was Francie's mother and Eleanor's sister, to protect any child who bore a resemblance to Philip." He met Alexander's gaze. "When Francie was born we had to take her away or risk her safety."

"Take her from whom?" Alexander tried to keep his voice casual, but he wanted to know and that desire changed his tone from indifferent to something short of desperate. He searched

Bernard's face, saw the hesitancy there, and plunged forward. "I can't protect Francie if I don't know everyone who might pose a threat to her."

The old man sighed, his shoulders slumping forward on his bony frame. "It was Belmont. The man everyone thought was her father."

Edgar Ashcroft, the Earl of Belmont. Ruthless, cunning, manipulative. Rumor had it he'd pick the pockets of a dead man if he thought there'd be profit in it. Alexander didn't like him much and trusted him even less. But harming a child?

"I know Belmont," Alexander said. "He's a bastard, I'll grant you, but do you really think he would have laid a hand on a child? A babe no less?"

"I know he would have," Bernard answered without hesitation. "The man's capable of anything. Even murder."

Alexander tried to make sense of everything he'd just heard. "Belmont's daughter, Claire. Is she not his real daughter?"

"No," Bernard shook his head. "She doesn't belong to him."

"But she looks just like him. Same hair, same eyes, same coloring."

"She would have to, wouldn't she? Belmont would accept no less."

He'd come to Claire Ashcroft's rescue twice and even considered paying her a call until he spied her with her head in some chap's lap in the garden at the Almsteds' soiree. Of course, she had no idea he'd spotted her.

He wondered at Claire Ashcroft's heritage. A commoner? Had to be. For a coin-filled purse, anything could be bought. Catherine must have had it all planned out. If her babe were a red-head, she'd substitute it for a black-haired one. The color of their hair sealed their fates. The black-haired girl would be gifted with jewels, the red-haired one, a trowel.

Alexander's chest tightened. Francie belonged in silks and satins, with maids braiding pearls in her hair and putting slippers on her feet. Yet she claimed to care nothing for that sort of frivolity, seemed more intent with her flowers and her reading. She'd packed two boxes of books to bring to Drakemoor and only one pathetic, half-full satchel.

"Does Francie know any of this?" How would she react if she discovered Belmont was her mother's husband?

"Very little. The only one who knows the truth is Philip." His voice grew thick with emotion. "And Eleanor. She loves Francie like her own daughter. She would do anything to protect her."

Even suffer a beating for her.

"You must protect her, Alexander." Bernard's voice turned shaky with grief and fear. "From Crayton and people like him."

"She'll be under Montrose protection. And mine." He owed Philip. The least he could do was see to his daughter's safety.

"I know you'll take care of her," Bernard said. "She'll be safe with you." He smiled. "You've turned into a fine young man."

Alexander's eyes narrowed. "Why would you say that? Should I know you?" When he saw the old man in the carriage yesterday, he thought there was something vaguely familiar about him.

"Perhaps. Perhaps not. But I remember you," Bernard said, stroking his beard. "You used to hide in the stables when Philip and I came for a ride. I brought you bits of peppermint. You were too shy to come out of your hiding place, so I left them in a handkerchief tied to a stall door."

Alexander showed no expression. He'd loved the peppermints, had guarded them like treasures, and savored the fresh, mint taste of the little candies. Until his father discovered them one morning and made him turn them over. From that day on, Alexander collected the candies from the stall door, but never opened the handkerchief. If he'd done so, a beating would follow. Instead, he deposited it on his father's night table, right next to his whiskey bottle.

So this was the man who'd shown him kindness when he believed none existed. This was the man who'd taken a moment of his time to make a frightened child smile.

"Thank you for the peppermints. They became one of my fondest childhood memories."

The older man's smile deepened. "You're very welcome. I see fortune has smiled upon you."

Alexander nodded. "Fortune, indeed, in the name of Philip Cardinger."

"Philip thinks of you as his son." Bernard puffed on his pipe. "He's very proud of you."

The unexpected words touched Alexander, transforming him into the little boy of long ago, waiting for the peppermints. Only instead of peppermints, he waited for praise. Alexander was a grown man, successful in trade and commerce. He did not need kind little words doled out to him by anyone, least of all Francie's uncle. He threw down his cigar and stamped it out with the heel of his shoe.

Because he could think of no other response, Alexander nodded and muttered, "Thank you."

Long after Bernard returned to the cozy warmth of the fire inside, Alexander remained in the cool, night air, contemplating his predicament. He was about to take a stand against the son of one of the most powerful men in the land, one who would not appreciate having his son's indiscretions thrown at him by a commoner. Despite the power of the Montrose name behind him, if the duke's reputation were true, he'd ignore Alexander's words and do nothing.

If that should happen, Alexander would pay a private visit to Jared Crayton and employ whatever means necessary to stop the man. He sighed. The whole situation could get quite messy. Did he really have a choice? Did he not owe Philip for giving him a privileged life? Was this not the perfect opportunity to repay a debt of gratitude?

The answers were simple. Alexander Bishop was a man of duty and honor, first, foremost, and always. He would do his duty and bring honor to his name.

He would protect Francie Jordan.

8

F rancie was a daydream away from falling headlong into an afternoon nap, when a quick, urgent tapping dragged her back to the present. What was that insistent noise? Her gaze moved toward the sound and settled on the door. Someone was knocking. A quite determined someone judging by the frequency of the knocks. She ran a quick hand through her curly hair and scurried out of the overstuffed chair.

"Yes?" Francie asked, opening the door a fraction. It was James, the butler. "Begging your pardon, Miss Jordan," he said, with a quick tap of his foot, "but Mr. Bishop would like to see you in his study." His nose twitched twice.

"Again?" She'd been called to Alexander's study three times in the last three hours. First, he'd summoned her to inform her animals were not permitted in the house. Fine. Perhaps it had been a little bold of George to climb upon Alexander's favorite chair. It was a huge, burgundy affair, with extra cushions that puffed out and sank in when a body sat in it. George would like that. And he did. Too much.

She'd shooed the poor animal outside, settled him in the

stables, and not more than one hour later, Alexander summoned her yet again. It was Mr. Pib this time. Wasn't he supposed to be outside? Alexander asked, pointing to the calico cat perched on top of the heavy brocade draperies. After much coaxing and a few little bribes, Francie convinced Mr. Pib that life outside proved more entertaining than watching a disagreeable crank thumb through papers.

And the third time...well, how George found his way back into the house without being noticed was a mystery. But there he'd been, curled up on that blasted chair as though it was made especially for him. Alexander had not been very happy.

So what could be the problem this time?

James couldn't look her in the eye. His dark gaze shot about the hallway, darting to the right, swinging to the left, everywhere but on her. That was the first hint Alexander was not calling on her for pleasant conversation.

It was all very strange. Very strange indeed. Until today, Alexander hadn't spoken more than five sentences to her, taking most of his meals out, presumably with Lady Printon. When he was home, he closeted himself in his study from early in the morning until late at night, with only a short break to ride Baron.

Not that Francie was keeping watch, because she wasn't. She could care less if he stayed the night at Lady Printon's, though she knew from the heavy footsteps trailing down the hall in the early hours of the morning, he did not. She'd grown accustomed to listening for him and found it quite a coincidence that she preferred to read into the night and usually didn't tire until after he walked past her door. Some nights, his steps paused outside for the briefest of moments, and then moved on. Francie held her breath each night, wondering if he'd stop and knock, but most of all wondering what she'd do if he did.

The strange awareness between them began in Amberden. Everything changed in the fields where they'd found Aunt Eleanor. Why did Alexander take such great pains to ignore her? Was he embarrassed or angered by what transpired in Amberden? Not, of course, by Aunt Eleanor's injuries, but rather, his reaction to Francie's request. She'd seen the pain in his silver eyes, but there'd been a hint of something else as well. Understanding. She had not imagined the protectiveness in his voice. It was there. But was it for her alone or the whole village?

And if it were for her alone? What then? Alexander became just as vulnerable as she, revealing emotions she was certain he'd later regret. But she'd seen them and that changed everything. Alexander Bishop did have a heart, a real one, beating with feelings and emotions, despite what he wanted others to believe. The knowledge made him more human. More of a man.

The kind of man who could steal a woman's heart if she weren't careful.

James and his tapping foot brought her out of her musings. His right foot jerked in rapid staccato, his eyes fixed on the floor. Francie followed his gaze but noted nothing out of the ordinary. Why was he staring at her stockinged feet?

"James?"

He twitched his nose. "Yes, Miss Jordan?" Three taps from his shiny black shoes. Little ones this time.

"Do you know why Mr. Bishop requires my presence?" If she kept him talking, he might concentrate on his speech and forget the tapping and twitching.

The butler cleared his throat and clasped his hands together. "I think perhaps it has something to do with," he hesitated, "your dog, Miss Jordan." James's face turned bright pink. "Mr. Bishop was not pleased to find him on his favorite chair again." His high voice dropped to a whisper. "Said he was going to take the animal and make a rug out of him."

"He did, did he?" Francie hid a smile. Alexander tried so hard to make everyone fear him, but just yesterday she'd spied him playing fetch with George when he thought no one was watching.

"He's in his study, I presume?" She pushed her door closed and headed down the hallway toward the spiral staircase. Her hand glided over the polished railing as she descended, the feel of mahogany smooth beneath her fingertips. The heavy puffing of the little butler followed close behind. Francie stopped before the study, took a deep breath, and knocked twice.

"Come in."

Stay calm. Stay calm. Francie opened the door and stepped inside.

"We seem to have a slight problem," Alexander said from across the room. He stood with his back to the fireplace, feet planted wide apart, arms crossed over his broad chest. As usual, his attire was perfect, from the carefully folded snow-white cravat to the high black gloss on his shoes. His jacket and trousers were a deep, dark blue that would make his eyes sparkle if he weren't so determined to hide behind a mask of cold indifference. Alexander Bishop, Master of Blank Expressions and Bland Comments, controlled every word he said and every gesture he made.

Unlike Francie, whose face revealed her thoughts before she could, and whose words said volumes more than intended.

She advanced into the room and stood beside George, who lay half-sprawled, half-curled on the large, overstuffed chair. He lifted his head to sniff the air a few seconds, opened one golden eye, and content with his findings, sank his big head back onto the soft cushion.

Of course, George remained oblivious to the major conflict

he'd created. His tail thumped against the arm of the chair as Francie ran her fingers through his thick coat and concentrated on her next words.

"Well," she said, clearing her throat, "George certainly is clever, isn't he?"

"Clever?" Alexander took a step toward her.

"Oh, yes, clever for finding his way inside the house three times."

"Onto my favorite chair," he added, taking another step.

Why didn't he seem angry? He should've been furious if he'd been spouting off tales of turning George into a rug. But the closer he got, the better Francie could see him. She didn't miss the slight flaring of his nose or the strong set of his jaw. And then there was the muscle that twitched on the right side of his cheek, just enough to indicate extreme agitation. And the scar. It was white.

Alexander Bishop may not show it, but he *was* furious.

Best to get George out of there. Fast. Francie let out a little laugh that sounded like a squeak. "Well, yes, there is that. I think I'll just take him with me now and get him settled in the barn." She turned her attention to George who had both eyes closed and was snoring. "Come along, George. Wake up. It's time to leave Mr. Bishop to his business." The dog opened one eye but didn't budge.

Alexander now stood so close she smelled his spicy cologne. Nevertheless, when he spoke, his voice mere inches from her ear, she jumped.

"You seem to be having a little problem, Francie." The way he said her name, a low velvet rumble wrapped in a whisper, made her go all hot and cold inside. She didn't like it when he lowered his voice. He was toying with her.

"No," she answered, avoiding his gaze. "I can control George." She slipped her fingers under his thick leather collar and pulled. "Come along, George." The dog didn't budge. "George!" She yanked and the dog rewarded her with an irritated grumble. Alexander cleared his throat. "You do indeed exhibit immense control."

Francie ignored his sarcastic tongue as she straightened and moved behind the chair to George's hindquarters. "I can control my dog, Mr. Bishop." She pushed at the animal's back legs. "It's just..." She gave another push. "He's not used to..." She tugged. "Sitting...on...furniture."

"I see."

Her head snapped up. She thought she heard a hint of laughter in his voice, but when she met his gaze it was blank, his face expressionless. She looked like a fool. George was her protector. Her best friend. Why then was he lying there, like twenty sacks of flour, all soft and half-dead?

"George!" She hooked both hands in his collar. "Down. Now!" Francie yanked with all her might. George yelped and leapt forward, barreling into her with the force of a horse. Francie's legs flew out from underneath her as she collided with Alexander, sending them both toppling to the ground.

She landed square on top of him, or more specifically, on his muscular legs and the region in men deemed unmentionable. Francie tried to roll off, but a sharp pain shot through her right shoulder and she groaned as she fell back, clutching her shoulder.

"Francie? Are you all right?"

Did she hear concern in his voice? No. If he had his way, he'd probably let George have another go at her.

Pushing a clump of hair out of her eyes, she turned to search for her assailant. George lay curled in front of the fire on the Aubusson rug, none the worse for their encounter.

Spice and tobacco filled her senses and she shivered.

"Cold?" Alexander asked in that too-low voice again.

"No," she snapped. "I'm fine." Embarrassed by the intimacy of the moment, Francie bit her lip and forced herself to roll over and away from him. She landed on her stomach and pushed into a sitting position. Her gaze settled on Alexander, his neckcloth slightly askew, his hair ruffled with a stray lock dangling over his left eyebrow, harsh lines bracketing both sides of his mouth.

He studied her with the intensity of a hunter stalking his prey. His silver eyes were gray-black with tiny flecks of gold. Mesmerizing, entrancing eyes.

"James said you were displeased with George."

"I was not displeased with George," he said. "I was displeased with you."

Her eyes narrowed a fraction. She would not let her control slip. If Mister "High and Mighty" Bishop could manage such calmness, then so could she. "I was unaware George escaped," she paused, "again."

Alexander shifted to a sitting position with a deftness belying his size. "One must be aware of one's responsibilities at all times."

So now he was implying she wasn't responsible? Francie dug her nails into her palms. "I *am* responsible at all times, Mr. Bishop!"

He did no more than cock a black eyebrow, but it threw Francie to the edge of proper decorum, where she dangled a moment before pulling herself back up to respectable civility.

"I am responsible at all times," she repeated in a more subdued manner.

"As is evidenced by your wardrobe ...or lack thereof." His gaze traveled the length of her pale blue gown, stopping at her stockinged feet, which she attempted to hide under the hem of her gown.

"I think shoes are vastly overrated," she said, tucking the fabric under her toes.

The corner of Alexander's mouth twitched. "You would."

She gestured to his clothing. "As is much of your attire. I cannot imagine a neckcloth being comfortable, unless one is inclined to use it as a bandage or a napkin." She tilted her head to one side and said, "Or both."

He tapped a finger to his chin and murmured, "An interesting possibility."

"Quite."

A dim silence enveloped them, closing out the rest of the world save George's gentle snoring.

Who would have thought Francie would find this sliver of peace and quiet harmony with Alexander Bishop on the floor of his study? A slight pang of guilt nested in the center of her stomach. Could he say the same about her? Since the day she'd arrived at Drakemoor, claiming the earl as her father, she'd thrown Alexander's life into turmoil. He'd been the one delegated to escort Francie back to Amberden to fetch Aunt Eleanor, the one whose quiet nights were interrupted with Francie's feeble attempts on the pianoforte. And he'd been the one who swore he'd deal with Lord Jared Crayton.

She met his gaze and said, "James said you were very angry."

"Hmmm." He reached for a fat curl resting just above her elbow.

"So angry, in fact, you threatened to turn George into a rug."

"James talks too much." He let her hair fall through his fingers, and then scooped it up again.

"So you're not going to turn him into a rug?"

"Of course not." There was that voice. Like a caress.

"I'll be certain he doesn't disturb you again."

"George doesn't disturb me half as much as you do, Francie."

She swallowed hard. "Excuse me?" It was much too hot all of a sudden.

"I said, George doesn't disturb me half as much as you do."

Francie looked up to meet his gaze. "I haven't seen you in days. Not since we returned from Amberden." How could she have possibly bothered him when she hadn't seen him?

"And that's what's disturbing me," he said, winding a piece of hair around his hand and pulling her toward him. "It disturbs me very much."

"Oh." Her eyes grew wide with understanding. Oh. His spicy cologne filled her senses. Her eyes fluttered shut.

A roaring growl burst the quiet moment as George leapt upon them, a huge mass of muscle and fur, knocking Alexander away from Francie and pinning him to the ground.

"Damn you, George!" Alexander bit out. "Get off of me, you beast. Now!"

The dog whimpered once, lifted his paws from Alexander's chest, and moved his huge frame to lie by Francie.

Alexander pushed himself up in three quick moves. Anger permeated the room and the man himself.

She heard it in the sound of his rapid, unsteady breathing, saw it in the controlled, jerky movements of his hands as he straightened his jacket and brushed at the tan hair covering his trousers.

Whatever was about to happen before George charged Alexander was over.

Francie couldn't be angry with George. He was only doing what he'd been trained to do—protect his mistress from danger.

Was she in danger from Mr. Bishop? She wished she knew.

"Come, George," Alexander's deep voice boomed from behind her. "Now!"

Francie watched in amazement as George sat up and, without a backward glance toward his mistress, followed Alexander out of the room.

9

"Why would you want to invite someone like Bishop to supper?"

Claire Ashcroft heard the annoyance in her father's voice. Edgar Ashcroft, Earl of Belmont, never associated with anyone lower than a viscount. It was his rule. A person beneath his rank couldn't possibly have anything interesting to say.

Alexander Bishop fell well below the rank of viscount. He was a commoner. A captivating, dark, arrogant commoner. And Claire wanted him. Had wanted him since the moment he'd touched her, pulled her into his arms, and carried her to his waiting horse. Never mind the reason for the touch—a gallant rescue—he'd touched her. She remembered still the sizzle of his fingers as they grazed bare flesh. Ah, but he would prove an exquisite lover.

She'd thought he might send his calling card the next day, or certainly, within the next three. Alexander Bishop did neither. The apparent indifference continued, even after their second encounter and another rescue. No man had ever possessed the strength or will to turn away Claire's advances.

Until Alexander. He became her challenge. Her desire. *Her obsession.*

She smoothed out the folds of her peach day gown, adjusting the lace at the cuffs. French lace, from Madame Druillard's, the finest modiste in London. Only the best. It was what her father bred her to expect these past eighteen years. He'd given her everything she'd ever asked for from the time she could point. A pony at five, two horses at thirteen. Silks, satins, rubies, diamonds, and more. So much more.

He'd give her Alexander Bishop, too.

Claire turned to her father and gave him a sweet smile. He never could resist her when she smiled at him and lowered her voice to just above a desperate whisper, as though she'd die if he didn't grant her request.

"Alexander Bishop has a fine reputation, Father."

"As what? A stable boy?" He grunted and grabbed his glass of port, his ice-blue eyes narrowing in disgust.

"As a gentleman," Claire countered. "I've had occasion to meet him and was quite impressed."

"That he managed to string two syllables together?" The earl took a healthy swallow of his drink. "Or that manure didn't cling to his boots?"

"Father, really!"

The earl's lips curved in a twisted smile. "The truth is not often a welcome bedfellow."

Truth. Claire wondered what her father would say, if, in the name of truth, she divulged her string of lovers, many of whom fell well below the station of baron? If she were to tell him about the cook's son and the groomsman? And what of her father, the mighty Earl of Belmont, who made weekly visits to a widow half his age? Though he had only a handful of gray hair on an otherwise black head, he was still sixty years of age.

Should she confront him with that bit of honesty? She thought not.

No, truth was best left buried somewhere between tarnished honesty and blatant lies.

She'd try another tactic. "Are you saying he is not welcome at Glenhaven?"

The earl rubbed his close-cropped beard and laughed. "That's my girl. Always clever. You could've been a strategist for the Crown." He lifted his right hand and motioned in all four directions. "If one ploy doesn't work, retreat and try a second. Plan B fails, there is always Plan C and even D."

She hid a smile. "Why, Father, whatever do you mean?"

"You're my daughter, Claire. Shrewd and cunning, just like me." He chuckled. "First you play the role of helpless female and when that doesn't work, you retreat to indignant diplomat. Should that fail, you no doubt have another option waiting."

"Demanding compromiser." She laughed. "There's usually no need to venture past that."

"Lucky for me, I think. You drive a hard bargain, girl."

She walked up to him and pecked him on the cheek. "I learned from my father."

That seemed to please him. Claire knew by the smile on his face he enjoyed their verbal sparring. Her father was a tough man. Hated by some, feared by most, and he'd never shown a moment's compassion for his fellow man, whether they be friend or foe.

Fair was fair, and business was business. Personal feelings must be left at the doorstep. If someone was late paying a debt or needed a favor, they may as well spare their vocal chords because Belmont would show them no mercy.

The only exception was Claire. For her, he would do anything.

"I hear there's a new guest at Drakemoor," he said, with casual nonchalance.

Straightening, she pinned her gaze on him. He was busy plucking a piece of lint from his jacket, his curly head bent to the task.

"Oh?" She hadn't heard about any guest.

"A woman." His icy gaze met hers and he smiled. "Montrose's bastard."

"No," she squealed, her face lighting up. Oh, but she did love a good bit of gossip. "Who is she?"

"Name's Francie Jordan."

Francie Jordan. Jared's obsession. The woman he'd compared her to, as though anyone could compare to Claire Ashcroft. Curiosity and an unfamiliar feeling that might well be envy crept through Claire's consciousness. More beautiful than she? Well, she'd see for herself.

"Let's invite her, too," she said, already thinking of what she'd wear for the occasion. The royal blue silk matched her eyes, but the pale green satin had a neckline that would hold Alexander Bishop's attention.

"I don't think so. She's a bastard," her father said, scrunching his nose as though he'd smelled rotten cabbage.

"Father, I want to meet her." And make her own comparisons.

The earl cleared his throat and downed the rest of his port. "There is one more thing."

"Yes?"

"I think she may be your cousin." Claire almost choked. "My what?"

"Your cousin, but I can't be certain." He closed his eyes and pinched the bridge of his nose. "Your mother had an older sister named Eleanor. Quiet, plain, always doting on Catherine. She married her tutor." He snorted. "I don't have to tell you what a scandal they created. They lived with us until your mother died. Then they just disappeared. I never cared for either one and was glad to be rid of them." He grinned and stroked his beard. "Eleanor left behind a tidy little sum of money. Now they've turned up at Montrose's home with a red-haired daughter." His grin spread across his face. "Eleanor's hair was black, and her husband's was brown."

"Father," Claire breathed. "What are you saying?"

"The woman cuckolded her husband. I'll bet Montrose is the father. That's why they're back, most likely attempting to convince him to launch his daughter into society."

Claire made a face. "How crude. Some people have no dignity. Will you acknowledge her?" And then, "Will I have to?"

"Of course not, child. We'll say nothing. Good manners and proper breeding will prohibit anyone else from mentioning it." He ran a hand over his face. "Good God. Can you imagine? Illegitimacy linked to the Ashcroft name?"

Claire shuddered. "No, nor do I want to. It's extremely distasteful."

"Some people have no respect for title or position."

"But you do, Father." Claire threw him another of her bright smiles. "You understand your responsibility. As do I."

The earl beamed and Claire touched his shoulder, murmuring, "Now, about the matter of Mr. Bishop and Miss Jordan. When may I invite them to Glenhaven?"

"You'll give me no peace until I agree." He let out a sigh and waved his hand. "Go ahead then, send the invitation. Four days hence."

She threw her arms about his neck and said, "Thank you, Father. Thank you so much."

"Good God, child, it's only a dinner invitation."

But with careful planning and a little scheming, it will turn into a wedding invitation. Claire closed her eyes and smiled, thinking of Alexander Bishop's strong thighs and broad chest.

~

"I DON'T THINK you should be in here, child," the old woman said, wringing her hands. "Mr. Bishop wouldn't approve. No, ma'am, he wouldn't."

Francie glanced up from the mountain of flour in her mixing bowl and gave the cook a warm smile. "Please don't worry, Mrs. Jenkins. I'll take full responsibility for my actions."

Her comment seemed to worry the poor old woman even more. "Mr. Bishop wouldn't approve," she said again, shaking her gray head until the thick braided coil on top flopped from side to side. She'd been standing at the other end of the table, but now she moved closer, her short, round figure waddling to within inches of Francie. "In all the years I've been here, I've never seen him as much as poke his head in the kitchen," she said in a low voice, her brown eyes darting toward the door.

"Good. Then there's no reason to think he'll 'poke his head' in here today, is there?" She leaned over and gave a good punch to the flour mixture. "Needs a bit more water, I think."

Mrs. Jenkins cleared her throat but didn't answer.

Francie glanced at the cook and saw the worry on her round face. "Don't be concerned, Mrs. Jenkins. I'm making a surprise for Mr. Bishop."

"A surprise?" The cook's bun wobbled again. "Mr. Bishop does not like surprises."

"Well, tonight he's going to get one." Francie said, adding a touch of water to the dough. For heaven's sake, why would anyone take issue with rosemary and thyme bread? It was a peace offering, a request to start anew, forget all the unkind words and insinuations that had flowed between them. And the kiss that almost happened. Yes, especially that.

She'd been plagued with that memory for two days: Alexander's silver gaze boring into her, making her all hot and cold at the same time, his warm breath fanning her cheek, his spicy cologne invading her senses. Now, whenever she looked at him, her gaze wandered to his mouth and she'd think of that afternoon in his study. Sometimes, she wondered how it would feel to be kissed by him, his mouth moving over hers, wanting, needing, possessing. It was crazy to speculate such a thing, crazier even to consider wanting to speculate, but in the dark of the night, with no one but her thoughts, she did just that.

"Mr. Bishop—" the cook began again.

"—will be fine," Francie said, cutting off her concerns. She punched the dough once, twice, three times, enjoying the springy softness beneath her hands. "Everyone who's ever tasted my rosemary and thyme bread loves it. It's my aunt's recipe. We used to make several loaves a week and send them to the neighbors."

Aunt Eleanor. She was doing so much better, even sitting up in a chair and moving about her room with Uncle Bernard's assistance. Her face remained swollen and bruised, but her spirits were high. A taste of homemade rosemary and thyme bread might just lift them even higher.

"The only kind of bread Mr. Bishop likes is plain white dinner rolls," Mrs. Jenkins said, a half-scared look skittering across her face. "Sometimes white bread with strawberry jam. Depends on the day."

Francie looked up from her kneading. "Depends on the day?"

The older woman nodded. "White dinner rolls on odd days, white bread with jam on even."

"What if Mr. Bishop should desire to have a white dinner

roll on an even day?" she asked, not believing what she'd just heard. "What would happen then?"

"He wouldn't," the cook said, a broad grin spreading over her face to reveal two deep dimples on either side of her mouth.

"Why not?"

"They're Mr. Bishop's rules." She folded her fleshy arms over her ample middle and said, "And Mr. Bishop always keeps to his rules."

"I see." But Francie didn't see. Not at all.

"So now you understand about your bread. He won't eat it. Even if it was plain white, it's not a roll."

"And today's an odd day," Francie murmured.

Odd indeed.

"Now you've got it. Odd days for rolls, even for bread. And white. Always and only white," the cook said with an air of authority.

Oh, she'd gotten it all right. White bread and white rolls. Even and odd. All Francie knew for certain was Alexander Bishop was the odd one here. Crazy was a more apt description. Good heavens, what kind of man organized his meals according to a number system?

What else did he organize in this manner? And why?

Obviously, Alexander Bishop needed help. He needed someone to teach him about spontaneity and chance. Impulsiveness and happenstance.

She could show him those things. Francie enjoyed an unfettered existence, roaming the fields and woods of Amberden, gathering new experiences with the same enthusiasm she showed when gathering the herbs and flowers she loved so much.

Perhaps that's what Alexander needed. New and different experiences. Or perhaps only a new and different way to experience the same thing. She smiled. What better way to start than with a taste of her delicious, mouth-watering rosemary and thyme bread?

"WHAT IS THIS?" Alexander said, staring at the plate in front of him.

"Roast beef," Francie answered. "With cauliflower and potatoes smothered in a light cream sauce, of course."

He threw her a disgusted look. "I know how to identify food. There should be pork and peas on this plate. The only thing right about it is the potatoes."

"Delicious," Philip said, around a mouthful of cauliflower.

"Excellent," Bernard agreed. "Roast beef is one of my favorites. Didn't have it near enough in Amberden. Eleanor will love this."

"Where's the pork?" Today was Wednesday. Alexander ate roast pork with peas and potatoes every Wednesday. Roast beef was Saturday's menu. And it was to be served with carrots, not cauliflower.

Francie cleared her throat. "The change in menu was my fault. Mrs. Jenkins told me about the silly little rule you had." She scooped up a forkful of cauliflower and laughed. "Honestly, Alexander. Pork on Wednesdays, roast beef on Saturdays? What if on Monday your mouth watered for a fine piece of roasted pork?"

"I'd wait until Wednesday," he bit out.

She shook her head and laughed again. "But you needn't. That's the point. You could have a loaf of bread and a hunk of cheese if you'd like."

He glared at her. "But I don't 'like'. What I would like is for you to not interfere with the hired help."

"But, Alexander," she said, pinning her blue gaze on him. "It's so..." her voice dropped to a whisper, "boring."

The earl and Bernard fell into coughing fits within seconds of each other.

"Father! Uncle Bernard!" She was half out of her chair when both men raised their hands to ward her off.

"Fine. I'm fine," Philip said, coughing one more time.

Bernard took a drink of water, his face red. "Me, too. Must've gotten something caught in my throat."

He coughed again.

"I've got something in the library to take care of that little tickle," Philip said. He pushed his chair away from the table and addressed Alexander and Francie. "If you'll excuse us for a few moments?"

"Of course." So the old men didn't want to wait around to hear him explode.

When they'd both left, Francie turned to Alexander and whispered, "Whiskey."

"Whiskey?" He cocked a brow.

"Whiskey," she repeated, nodding. "That's what they're going to use to take care of that little tickle."

He almost smiled but buried it with a frown. "Yes, I imagine they are." He set down his fork. "Whiskey has many purposes, some of them even medicinal."

"I can't believe Father is imbibing when he knows he shouldn't." She worried her lower lip. "He should refrain from all manner of alcohol—"

"Francie," Alexander cut in.

"Yes?"

Those clear blue eyes looked at him with such innocence, such honesty, it tugged at something deep inside, making him want to forget about his proper lifestyle, forget about eating pork on Wednesday and roast beef on Saturday. Forget about everything but wrapping himself in the warmth of her smile.

"Yes?" she repeated.

Was he imagining it or had her voice dropped an octave to a breathy whisper? His gaze fell to her lips. Full, pink lips. Lips he'd come close to tasting. So close. God, but he couldn't get that image from his mind. The memory of Francie leaning into him, waiting for his kiss, kept him awake many a night. A couple shots of whiskey usually served as a soothing balm. As he'd told Francie, whiskey had many purposes.

Alexander ran a hand over his face. What was he thinking? He and Francie were as different as...as...as pork and roast beef. They had nothing in common. She was too impulsive, too outspoken, and too brash for his subdued tastes. She was too much of everything he opposed. Good God, the woman didn't even know how to behave like a proper lady!

"Alexander?"

There it was again, that low, breathy voice tapping at the cool exterior he worked so hard to maintain.

"What?" he snapped. Where were Philip and Bernard? They'd had enough time to throw back *three* whiskeys.

"You interrupted me." She tilted her head to one side and tiny spirals of red hair brushed the swell of her breast.

Nothing in common, he reminded himself.

"You were about to say something," she said.

I think your breasts would fit very nicely in the palms of my hands.

"Alexander!"

My God, had he spoken aloud? "What?"

Francie leaned over and touched his coat sleeve. His senses exploded with lavender.

"What's wrong? Are you angry with me for changing the menu?"

He frowned. That was a safe subject. Much easier to tell her he'd been thinking about pork and roast beef than to admit he'd been fantasizing about her breasts and lips. He was truly depraved. "I don't like surprises," he said in a stern voice.

Her face fell. "That's what Mrs. Jenkins tried to tell me." She looked away and her lower lip quivered. "But I wanted to show you not all surprises are bad. Sometimes they can be very good." She sniffed. "I'm sorry. I won't do it again."

Her words hit him like a kick in the gut. What kind of cad was he, anyway? A heartless one, no doubt. The poor woman obviously went to great lengths to involve herself in his meal, only to have him berate her for the effort.

Before he had time to consider his thoughts, Alexander found himself saying, "Perhaps once in a while would be all right."

She looked up and he saw a glimmering of unshed tears in her crystalline gaze. Her lips curved into a brilliant smile, lighting her entire face.

He never wanted that smile to fade.

"All right," he blurted out. "You may interchange the vegetables, but leave the meats the same." Her smile broadened. "For now," he added.

"And the dinner rolls and bread?" He heard the teasing note in her voice. "May I interchange those as well?"

Alexander opened his mouth to answer but was interrupted by the maid bringing in a covered dish. She set it down halfway between Francie and himself, curtsied, and left.

"I'll be right back," Francie said, rising from the table and reaching for the covered dish. "I think she brought in the wrong dish."

"Wait." Alexander circled her wrist with his hand. "How do you know it's the wrong dish when you haven't even looked at it?"

"Oh, I just know." She tried to disengage her hand, but he held fast. "Now, if you'll excuse me, I'll return in a moment with your dinner rolls."

What was the little minx up to now? A moment ago, she almost burst into tears. Now she wanted to bolt with a dish of food. He tilted his head to one side and studied her. Why was she avoiding his gaze? She was hiding something and he'd bet it was under that covered dish. He reached out and pulled off the silver lid.

"What's this?" He stared at what looked like a loaf of bread speckled with small bits of green.

"That?" Her gaze slid to the bread. "Oh, it's rosemary and thyme bread."

Alexander cocked a brow. "Another surprise?"

She nodded and shot him a look from the corner of her eye.

"Did you make this, Francie?" He knew it wasn't the handiwork of Mrs. Jenkins. White dinner rolls and white bread with strawberry jam were all she made. He'd drilled it into her brain so many times, she'd never deviate. This little concoction had to be Francie's creation.

"Yes."

She looked so pitiful, standing there, like a child gifting a parent with a handful of wildflowers, uncertain if they'd be put in a vase or thrown in the rubbish bin.

Alexander glanced at the bread again. Rosemary and thyme? He recognized the names, knew some people used them for cooking and such, but that was the extent of his familiarity with them. Hmmm. They were awfully...green. And there was quite a lot of it sprinkled about. He glanced at Francie, who stood staring straight ahead, her full lips tight and unsmiling, her chin lifted a notch or two.

Waiting. No doubt, waiting for him to make a nasty remark about the food she'd prepared. For him.

"Well," he said, releasing her wrist, "let's have a taste."

She swung around, eyeing him with suspicion. "Why?"

"Why?" he remarked, reaching for the butter. "Why, what? Why are we going to have a taste?" He slathered butter on a chunk of bread, covering as much green as he could. "Perhaps because it's part of the meal."

"You only like white bread and white rolls," she accused, still standing.

He took a bite. Hmmm. It actually was quite tasty, once he got past the fact it wasn't his usual fare. "And now I like rosemary and thyme bread."

"You don't have to eat it," Francie said, reaching out to snatch the slice of bread from his hand.

He caught her by the wrist and pulled her forward. "Stop it." He turned and found himself staring straight at her breasts. His gaze traveled up to her full, pink lips. "I like it. I like it very much," he said in a low, rough voice and wondered if Francie knew he was talking about more than just her bread.

"Thank you, Alexander," she said, a small smile lighting her face. "You're very kind." She leaned over and planted a chaste kiss on his cheek.

Kind? Would she still think him kind if he told her right now all he could think about was tasting her lips, touching her breasts, feeling her bare skin? *Kind?* Hardly.

He cleared his throat and met her gaze. He had to set her straight before she started imagining all sorts of other crazy things about him. "Kind is not a term usually associated with me."

She laughed, a tinkling sound that ran through his body like fire. "Because you want everyone to think you are some sort of cruel beast. You even had me fooled for a while." Her voice dipped to a low purr. "But you aren't a beast, Alexander, not at all. No beast would eat my bread just so he wouldn't hurt my feelings."

He frowned, hoping his scar stuck out white and ugly. "You should be afraid of me." Men twice her size couldn't look him in the eye.

"How can I be afraid of you when you've got butter on the side of your mouth?" She brushed it away with her forefinger. "And all over your lips," she murmured, tracing her finger over his upper lip.

Alexander caught her hand. She was playing a dangerous game and didn't even know it. He opened his mouth and flicked his tongue along the tip of her finger and heard the small catch in her throat. His tongue traced another finger, and then another. Sweet Jesus, but he wanted her.

"Come to me, Francie," he whispered, planting a kiss on the inside of her palm. "Let me taste you."

10

Their gazes locked as she moved toward him, stopping just a breath away from touching his lips. Alexander cupped the back of her head, buried his hand in her curls, and guided her to his mouth. The kiss was sweet and gentle, tentative at first as he moved his lips over hers, learning the taste and feel of her. She responded in kind, moaning low in her throat.

But it wasn't nearly enough. Alexander deepened the kiss, running his tongue along the seam of her lips until she opened her mouth, and then he plunged inside, tasting, devouring, possessing. She was heaven and hell wrapped in silky skin and soft sighs. As much as he wanted her this moment, he knew he couldn't have her. Could never have her. Not without marriage and that was out of the question. And yet, he couldn't stop himself from sliding his hand down her back, cupping her sweet, firm curves, and urging her closer. He slid his chair back from the table and pulled her into his lap, never once breaking their kiss.

She'd never be his, he reminded himself as his tongue

plunged deeper, harder, into the velvety recesses of her mouth. But oh, how he wanted her.

Francie moaned again. Her tongue met his, innocent and unsure. Her hands sifted through his hair, working the curls at the nape of his neck, trailing to his shoulders. His erection strained against his trousers, throbbing with need as his fingers stroked a path from her jaw to her neck, and further still, to the swell of her breasts. She arched her back, straining toward him. She didn't know what she wanted, but he did. He brushed the tip of her breast and felt it harden beneath the thin fabric. He began working slow circles over the peak, imagining a pale pink nipple underneath, imagining himself laving the pink bud, sucking it until she groaned with pleasure and need.

"Alexander," she breathed, dragging her mouth from his. "What are you doing to me?"

Her words hit him like a bucket of cold water. He jerked away from her, lifted her off his lap, and set her several steps away. *What the hell was he thinking?* His gaze shot to Francie who stood alone, arms wrapped about her middle as she stared at him, lips red and swollen from his kisses, cheeks flushed, hair wild. But she stood proud, despite the shimmering of tears in her eyes.

He ran a hand through his hair. Three times. What had he done? He, Alexander Bishop, had all but seduced a young inno-cent in the dining room of his home. Practically on the table, for Christ's sake, which was where they would have ended up had things progressed much further. Francie spread out on the white linen tablecloth and him between her thighs. God, but he was depraved. Philip's daughter. This was how he repaid the man who'd taken him in and given him a new life?

He really was no better than a stable boy. No matter how fine his dress or how many invitations he received to the ton's affairs, he was still a stable boy. Just like his father, who'd given in to impulse every time he picked up a bottle. Alexander had succumbed to Francie's innocence and beauty, disregarding who she was and what his responsibilities were. He disgusted himself. Why hadn't he just stood up and walked away? Why hadn't he kept his hands shoved deep in his pockets?

He knew the answer, didn't even have to give it a second's thought. Because he'd *had* to touch her, had to feel the heat between them, to lose himself in the touch, the kiss, the need that smoldered between them. And now he'd have to deal with the consequences of his actions. *Pretend it didn't happen?* Hardly.

There was only one other possibility. The thought lay like cold roasted duck in the pit of his stomach. He'd lie. He'd tell her the taste of her mouth and the feel of her delectable body meant nothing to him. A diversion. That's what he'd call it. A simple diversion.

He ran a hand through his hair one more time and opened his mouth to speak. Alexander stared at the spot where Francie had been less than a minute ago. Empty. She was gone.

"I don't want Francie going," Philip said.

"Nor do I." Alexander stared out the window watching the subject of their discussion crawl around on her knees, digging in the dirt. He wished she'd dig her way back to Amberden.

"I don't want her going near Belmont. I don't trust the man."

"Fine." Why wasn't she wearing a hat? Her skin was too fair to be in the sun without one.

"Did you hear me, Alex?" Philip sounded puzzled. "I said I don't want Francie accepting Belmont's dinner invitation."

Alexander turned around. Fine. Let her burn. He could care less. "I heard you. You don't want Francie accepting Belmont's dinner invitation."

The older man nodded. "You aren't going to put up a fuss? Tell me when nobility invites someone of a lesser station, the proper thing to do is accept?"

"No. I'm not."

"Hmm. Now that's a change." The earl coughed. "Are you feeling all right, my boy?"

No, he wasn't feeling all right. Hadn't felt all right since he'd left the dining room last evening. He'd spent the better half of the night poring over his ledgers in a futile attempt to drown out the sound of Francie's soft moans, block out the feel of her satiny skin under his fingers, and bury the taste of her sweet lips. Whiskey helped.

But he'd woken this morning in a foul mood and even his ride with Baron hadn't tamed his temper. Damn the woman! She seemed none the worse from last evening's interlude. He'd heard her humming outside a little while ago, some jaunty tune he couldn't get out of his head. And when he'd spotted her grabbing a few pastries to stuff in her pocket this morning, she'd smiled a bright smile and bid him good morning.

"Alex," the earl repeated, coming to stand next to him. "Are you feeling all right?"

"Of course. Why wouldn't I be? I'm fine." The words came out a little sharper than intended.

Philip cocked a faded red eyebrow. "I'm glad. Now aren't you going to ask me why I don't want Francie to go?"

Alexander shrugged. "I'm sure you have your reasons." Right now, he didn't care why the earl was refusing Belmont as long as she didn't go. Bernard's tale of Francie's true heritage stuck in his head. Alexander would never subject her to Belmont's cold scrutiny. Nor would he subject himself to an extended carriage ride with Francie. It would be too uncomfortable. Too awkward. *Too damn tempting.*

"Well, I'll tell you, anyway," Philip said, rubbing his jaw.

"Belmont's a ruthless, cunning bastard who never does anything without a reason. If he's invited Francie to Glenhaven, he's got a motive and whatever it is, I don't want her involved."

If that were the case, Alexander didn't want her involved either. "And me," he asked, "why do you think he's extended an invitation to me?"

"Now there's a question," the earl said, nodding his head in thought. "Could be any number of reasons." He coughed and cleared his throat. "First, he's heard about your uncanny ability in the stock market and wants to elicit your advice. I told you the old bastard would fleece a dead man for an extra coin. Or, perhaps, he's got some other sort of business proposition for you."

"As I expected," Alexander said. He had personal reasons for accepting Edgar Ashcroft's invitation. Word had it Lord Jared Crayton spent quite a bit of time at Glenhaven in the company of Belmont and his daughter, Claire. Alexander wanted to conduct his own investigation of Crayton before he confronted the Duke of Worthington and accused his son of assaulting an old woman.

"Of course," the earl continued, "there is one other possible reason."

"Which is?"

"Belmont may be sizing you up for his daughter."

"*What?*"

Philip's blue eyes twinkled with mischief. "Face it, Alex. You wouldn't be the first prospective groom to get roped in by the bride's father."

"That's ridiculous." Alexander shot him a look of disgust. "I've never heard of anything so preposterous." He needed a drink. He walked to the side table, poured two fingers into a glass, and downed it in one swallow.

"I'll have one of those," Philip said.

Alexander poured a fresh glass and refilled his own. "Claire Ashcroft doesn't even know me. Not really." A short ride on his horse after she'd fallen from hers, with minimal conversation and only necessary contact, certainly wouldn't constitute interest on either side. Would it? Admittedly, he'd found her beautiful and his pulse tripped a bit faster when he checked her ankle for swelling, but finding her in one too many compromising situations since then killed any interest he may have permitted to develop.

"Maybe she's attracted to your charming personality."

Alexander handed Philip his drink and shrugged. "I'm hardly husband material for the daughter of an earl." *Especially one who sheds her clothes so willingly for other men.*

"You've got money. Lots of it. All your own, too." The earl took a healthy sip of whiskey. "And I suppose some women might even be attracted to that surly manner of yours. Who knows? Maybe the girl thinks there's a beating heart under all your properness."

You're so kind. Francie's words clamored in his brain.

Kind? A beating heart? No, he wasn't kind or he never would have touched Francie in the first place. As for a heart, the only one in his chest was made of stone.

Alexander turned to the window and spied Francie carrying two buckets toward the garden filled with something heavy, judging by the way she staggered. When she reached the edge of the garden, she set the buckets down and wiped her hands on her plain blue gown, leaving matching streaks of brown on either side of the fabric.

Her cheeks and nose were bright pink. "She needs a hat," Alexander muttered.

"She needs new clothes," Philip added.

"Only a fool would be outside in the heat of the day." *Was the woman daft?*

"Francie doesn't feel the heat," Philip said. "She's in heaven working with her flowers and such. Look at her," he said, pointing a thick finger. "Look how happy she is."

Alexander glanced at her face and wished he hadn't. She *was* happy, damn her. Blissfully happy. With a little smile on her lips, humming that ridiculous tune again. How could she be so happy when he was so miserable?

He turned away in disgust. "Old George's got more brains than his mistress," he said, glancing at the dog lying on the Aubusson rug. The animal had worked his way back to this room so many times in the last several days, Alexander had finally conceded and allowed him to stay. But only on the rug. Furniture was prohibited, specifically Alexander's favorite chair. For his part, George seemed satisfied with the arrangement.

Philip chuckled. "She's gotten to you, hasn't she, Alex?"

"Of course not," he shot back. "If Francie wants to behave in such a ridiculous manner, that's her business."

"She's gotten to you all right," the older man said, chuckling again. "I can hear it in your voice."

"She hasn't gotten to me, as you say. I just don't like to watch people make fools of themselves."

"Especially, when you're the fool, eh, old boy?" Philip squeezed Alexander's shoulder.

Alexander raised his left eyebrow. Had Philip just called him a fool?

"I wasn't going to bring this up," the earl said in a sympathetic tone, "but, have you looked in the mirror today?" The old man's eyes worked their way from the top of Alexander's head to the tip of his shoes.

"Yes, of course," Alexander said, running a hand down his jacket and trousers. "Why?"

"Your jacket is blue and your trousers are gray."

"Like hell they are." Alexander held out his arm to inspect the color of his jacket. Blue, a deep, dark midnight blue. He looked down at his leg. And his trousers were...gray. "Damn."

The earl crossed his arms over his broad chest. "Like I said, she's gotten to you."

Alexander swore under his breath. "Francie has nothing to do with this. It's Thomas, damn him. What good is a valet if he can't choose matching clothes?"

"Oh, no, don't blame this on Thomas," the earl said. "I have it on good authority you booted the poor man out this morning telling him you could 'goddamn well dress yourself'. Sound familiar?"

Heat stained Alexander's cheeks. "He was too bothersome this morning, chatting about some nonsense or other. I had no choice but to boot him out."

"Thomas has been a talker since the day he walked into Drakemoor three years ago. It never seemed to bother you before."

"A lot of things never bothered me before," Alexander retorted, shooting a quick glance toward the window.

"I see."

Alexander chose to ignore Philip's comment. "I'm going to change," he said, yanking at his cravat and heading for the door.

"Good luck," Philip called out. "Remember, blue with blue, gray with gray."

The door slammed shut, closing off Philip's laughter. Alexander swore again, cursing the day he ever laid eyes on Francie Jordan.

∾

"WELL, WHAT'S HAPPENING?" Bernard's quiet voice filled with curiosity and anticipation.

Philip grinned and offered Bernard a drink. "It's a little premature to celebrate their nuptials, but I'd say we're well on our way."

Bernard took a sip of his drink and asked, "Why? Did our little ploy during dinner work?"

"Hard to tell," Philip said. "But something happened, that's for certain. Both of them are acting mighty strange. First, there's Francie, up bright and early and running outside as though the devil were at her heels."

"Alexander, I presume?"

"That would be my guess. She's trying to avoid him, which makes me think something happened."

"A spat, perhaps?"

"Or a kiss," the earl said, smiling. "And you should see old Alex." He chuckled. "I've never seen him so flustered. Threw his valet out this morning and then put on a pair of gray trousers with a blue jacket. I didn't have the heart to tell him his cravat was cockeyed to the left."

"Good of you to spare him a little dignity. Alexander is such a proud man."

"That he is," Philip agreed. "But we both know there's no room for pride where love's concerned. And make no doubt, it will be a love match."

Bernard cast a doubtful look out the window. "How can you be so certain? From what you say, they're barely speaking to one another."

"Ah, but that's the beauty of it, my friend. Soon enough, they'll be doing more than just speaking." Philip followed Bernard's gaze and said, "What have we here?"

"It's James," Bernard said. "He's brought a hat for Francie. How very thoughtful of him."

"No, no, no. Don't you know anything about this love business? Think again," Philip said, as he watched Francie. "James wouldn't bring Francie a hat without someone telling him to do so. He wouldn't even know she wasn't wearing one. But someone else would. Someone who's been so distracted he can't think of anyone or anything else. Even when he tells himself he's not thinking of her, he's thinking of her."

"Alexander."

"Exactly. Alex sent James outside with the hat. Alex is the one who's concerned Francie will catch too much sun. Alex, my friend, is becoming thoroughly besotted."

Bernard thought a moment. "Hmmmm," he mused. "And Francie?"

"Why, can't you tell by the way she's looking at the windows, trying to catch a glimpse of someone, that she's wondering who sent the hat? And all the while, you can bet she's hoping it's Alex."

"You don't say."

"I do say," Philip declared, slapping Bernard on the back. "We'll have a wedding in this house by Christmas."

"What's your next plan?"

"A ball for Francie introducing her into society. Even without a title, there'll be a bevy of young bucks vying for her hand. Just wait and see. That will drive Alex insane. He'll be beside himself, torn between envy and a desire to protect her from them. And from himself."

"From himself?"

"Of course. Until he realizes marriage to Francie is what he wants, he'll torture himself trying to be noble." He laughed. "But that's a few plans down the road. First, we need to start throwing them together at every opportunity."

"I assume you have ideas on how to do that as well?"

"I do. Francie needs a new wardrobe. I'm sending her and Alex to Madame Druillard's."

"A carriage trip to London. Who will be chaperoning them?"

Philip threw Bernard a sly smile. "Mrs. Vandemeer, the widowed aunt from two estates over. I daresay, she's old as Croesus, blind as a bat, and deaf to boot."

"Do you think that wise?" Bernard's bushy brows drew together. "What if...?"

"He won't," Philip said in a firm voice. "But he'll be in hell for it, I'm sure. If my guess is correct, he'll be half-mad with wanting Francie by the time he returns from London."

"And then you'll throw the ball and have all of Francie's young suitors swarming about her skirts."

"Exactly. Quite clever, don't you think? Alex will be so jealous he'll demand to marry her posthaste."

"It's risky, Philip. If either one of them finds out you're plotting, they'll be very upset."

"That's why they won't find out, my friend. You and I are the only ones who know I'm giving them a little extra assistance." Philip glanced out the window again. Francie sat cross-legged on the ground, face turned and half-hidden by the broad brim of her hat. "What the hell is she doing?" Philip murmured.

Bernard pointed a long finger toward the far end of the estate. "There. She's looking out there."

Philip could just make out a horse and rider tearing across the back lawn toward the fields. There was only one black horse at Drakemoor and Alex was the only one who could ride him.

"See? What did I tell you?" Philip grinned. "They're made for each other."

"Unfortunately, they haven't been apprised of that fact," Bernard added, shaking his head.

"But they will be, soon enough." The earl's voice filled with emotion. "Francie's my daughter and I love Alex like a son. I'd never do anything to harm either one of them, but I don't want to see them throw away a chance at happiness because they're too proud to grab it." His voice cracked. "I loved Catherine. Loved her with every breath in me and I want Alex and Francie to know that kind of love, too."

~

"FATHER, are you sure you're feeling all right?" Francie asked, clutching the earl's large hand in hers. He was such a big man, towering was a better term, and yet at times like these, when he fell into coughing fits, he seemed more frail than James, a man half his size.

"Fine," the earl coughed, raising a hand. "I'll be fine."

She scanned his flushed face, noted the beads of perspiration on his upper lip, and thought him anything but fine. Alexander said he'd been having these coughing spells for months now, had even seen a doctor, but had thrown the man out when he pronounced leeches for treatment. He'd refused to see another doctor, declaring he'd sooner cut his own wrists than let them cover him with slimy creatures who'd suck him dead.

And that brought an end to the discussion regarding medical attention. Francie had taken to mixing up poultices every evening and placing them on his chest. The relief, though temporary, provided a quiet time for them to spend together. It was during these nights the earl shed his jovial, gruff manner and looked at her with a sad tenderness in his blue eyes.

"You have your mother's smile," he said, breaking the comfortable silence enveloping them.

She'd been waiting for days, hoping against hope he'd say

something about the woman he'd loved and lost. Francie's smile deepened and she squeezed his hand. "Tell me about her."

The earl heaved a sigh. "Oh, where to begin, child?" He closed his eyes and smiled. "She was the most beautiful woman I have ever seen. Eyes the color of emeralds, hair falling down her back in long black waves. I was mesmerized by her smile, captivated by her charm. I think I fell in love with her the first time I laid eyes on her. But it wasn't just her beauty that touched me. She was a good person, a kind person with a quick wit and a laugh that made my heart smile. And such an innocent. Catherine believed goodness and kindness would always prevail. I remembered this, even when I had no reason to hope any longer, even when I looked upon each day without her as a curse."

He opened his eyes and blinked the wetness away. "She was right. Goodness and kindness did prevail." He reached up to touch her cheek. "They brought me Alex." His voice softened. "And then they brought me you."

"Where did Alexander come from?" She'd always assumed he was the orphaned son of one of her father's friends.

"The stables," he said, simply.

"Stables?"

"Alex was the son of Harry and Alice Bishop, my groomsman and scullery maid."

"Servants?" she whispered. She'd sooner believe Alexander belonged to a descendant of the king.

The earl met her shocked look with his steady blue gaze. "It was all quite sad. His father was a no-good drunk, but I kept him on out of pity. One day he got himself killed trying to ride Baron's father. Alex's mother died within the month."

Francie pushed past the lump in her throat as she pictured

a young Alexander stripped of a father and mother. "And Alexander?" she breathed. "What happened to him?"

"He slept in the barn for weeks, no one to look after him, trying to carry on his father's duties, eating what scraps the cook sent his way. Barely thirteen and forced into a cruel, harsh world with not a soul to care about him."

Her heart ached for the little boy who had no home, no parents, no one to love him. She'd never known that kind of life. Her moments had always been filled with warm, nurturing swells of love and attention, plenty of food, fresh clothing, and a cozy bed. Alexander's bed had most likely been a scratchy mattress of hay, his pillow a balled-up shirt.

No wonder he'd become a staunch, proper perfectionist in his pristine cravat and elegant cutaway.

"That's why he dresses the way he does," she murmured. "Not a stitch out of place, not a wrinkle."

"Exactly. When I found him ,his clothes were so filthy I had to have them burned." The earl ran a large hand over his face. "Thank God for Alex. He gave me a reason to live after Catherine died. It was just the two of us, hurt and alone, him needing me as much as I needed him. I couldn't love him more if he were my own son."

"I think he feels the same about you." A servant's son. Orphaned and left to fend for himself. Her father's revelation into Alexander's childhood explained so many things. His clothes, his demeanor, his food. *His food*. Good gracious, his food! Now it all made sense.

"The meal the other night," she began, not certain how to broach the subject. "When I switched the roast beef and pork..."

Her father chuckled. "Almost sent him into a fit of apoplexy. I took great pleasure in seeing his discomfort. Well done, child. Well done." His tone grew serious. "Alex wants to control every detail of his life—his clothes, his food, his associations. He wants to remove all aspects of chance, deal only with the known. That's why he wants pork on Wednesday and roast beef on Saturday. Eliminates the element of chance. Makes him feel safer."

"It's only food. As long as it's well-prepared, why should he care?"

"Who knows? I've never gone hungry or lain awake at night wondering if I were going to be thrown in the street with the rubbish. I've never taken a beating from my father to spare my mother." He pinched the bridge of his nose. "That kind of fear claws at the most courageous of men, eats away at their core. I can't imagine what it would do to a boy."

"It turns him into a man who's afraid to trust, afraid to believe in anyone or anything but himself," Francie whispered, crying for the little boy who could not cry for himself.

"Perhaps," the earl agreed. "But the right person could gain his trust and make him believe again."

Francie listened but said nothing.

"I think you might be that person, child."

Her father's words hit her like a blast of frigid air on a frosty night, stealing her breath, making her heart skip a beat. "I...I don't think so." Alexander *trust* her? Look to her as something more than a nuisance he had no choice but to tolerate?

Memories of last evening darted before her, leaving her hot and cold all over. They'd been stealing into her thoughts, robbing her of sleep at night and common sense during the day. She couldn't get him out of her mind. Alexander's silver eyes burning into her, his strong, capable hands moving over her body, his lips searing hers in possession.

What had happened? They'd kissed. No, they'd done much more than kiss. Heat rose to her cheeks as she recalled the feel of his hands on her body, touching, exploring, pleasuring. And his mouth. She shivered. His mouth had stolen every sensible thought from her already addled brain every time his tongue dipped between her lips. And when he touched her breast, well, a whole new wealth of sensation started low in her belly and spread to the most private part of her body.

What would it be like to share those sensations with Alexander every night? To look into his silver eyes and see passion, desire, love. No, not love. He wasn't capable of that emotion. Francie's chest tightened. Love was a game of chance, a hope and dream at best, and Alexander Bishop was not one to wager on anything less than certainty.

What did it matter? Why should she care? The better question was why did she care? She didn't know, but the horrible, undeniable truth was she did.

11

"I hear you've a guest at Drakemoor," Edgar Ashcroft said, stroking his beard. Alexander felt the earl's beady little eyes studying him. He'd been doing it all evening, making bland, seemingly insignificant comments and then leaning back, one hand stroking his beard, waiting to see how Alexander responded. It was a game with Belmont, a test of wills requiring two people to participate.

Alexander refused to engage in the old man's cheap form of entertainment.

"Father," Claire Ashcroft whispered, a note of censure in her voice, "I'm sure Mr. Bishop does not care to speak of it." She turned to Alexander and bestowed another of her dazzling smiles on him, the third in as many minutes.

He studied the woman beside him. Claire Ashcroft was indeed beautiful, her rich black curls gathered atop her head with a blue satin ribbon, save a few stray tendrils escaping in random disarray. The effect was stunning, the errant curls accentuating the long, slender column of her neck and trailing to the swell of her full, creamy breasts. She played with a black curl, her fingers brushing her breast in a slow, even rhythm, so casual that had he been a less experienced man, he might have thought it all quite innocent.

There was nothing innocent about Claire Ashcroft. The look in her deep blue eyes as she murmured in soft, demure tones, spoke of passion and lust, just as her painted red lips did each time she ran her tongue along them. She might be beautiful and titled, a lady by all accounts, but Claire Ashcroft couldn't touch the bottoms of Francie's serviceable brown shoes.

Thank God he'd spared Francie this scene. He could hear her getting on her high horse, telling him the woman possessed no scruples and less honor than a pickpocket.

And for once, he'd have to agree.

"Well?" Belmont repeated, a note of impatience in his voice. "Are you going to tell us about the girl or not?"

Belmont was not a man to be kept waiting and from the sour look on his face, he wasn't pleased Alexander hadn't yet answered him.

"Her name is Francie Jordan," he said, toying with the curried rabbit on his plate. Today was Monday. Curried rabbit was always on the menu at Drakemoor. He didn't doubt Claire Ashcroft took special care to investigate his preferences.

Why had they invited him here? He'd been certain Belmont wanted to discuss the stock market or, at the very least, inquire about a partnership in one of Alexander's many enterprises. That would have been understood, even expected, as Alexander's opinion was much sought after and well respected among the ton.

But two clarets and a bowl of turtle soup later, Belmont still hadn't broached the subject of business. Rather, he'd sat back, stroked his beard with one hand, sipped his drink with the other, and let his daughter carry the conversation. They'd touched on all of the proper niceties and Alexander tolerated

Claire's coquettish remarks and sultry laughs, all the while waiting to glean the real reason for the invitation.

He had not expected Francie to be a subject of conversation, yet Belmont seemed determined to speak of her. Alexander cleared his throat and said in a guarded voice, "Miss Jordan will be staying on at Drakemoor, indefinitely."

That comment drew a laugh from the earl. "I should say. After all, she is Montrose's by-blow, is she not?"

"Father!" Claire Ashcroft chided. "How horribly indelicate."

"It's the truth. Everybody knows it, Claire. Bishop does, too. Whether he wants to admit it or not, he knows everybody's talking about Montrose's bastard daughter." The earl leaned forward on his elbows, his icy blue eyes filled with curiosity. "Tell us about her, Bishop."

"There's really not much to tell," Alexander hedged. "She came to Drakemoor a few weeks ago."

And I kicked her out.

"And?" The old man raised a black eyebrow.

"And she's brightened Philip's days." *And I don't know what she's done to me, but I can't think straight when I'm around her.* "He's thrilled to have his daughter with him."

"Father," Claire Ashcroft interrupted, "this is all very nice, but I really don't think we need to be discussing Lord Montrose's illegitimate daughter."

"But you see, my dear, I find this all very interesting," the earl said, sitting back in his chair. "Very interesting, indeed." He smiled at Alexander, a small twist of the lips that didn't quite reach his eyes. "I knew the girl's mother. Quite well, in fact."

"I see." *He knew about Philip and Catherine? How? And if he did, why the smug look?* Alexander wanted to end the conversation now before he reached across the table and grabbed the old man by his neckcloth.

Belmont took a healthy swallow of claret and pointed a

finger at Alexander. "I'll tell you all about her mother. Eleanor was her name."

Eleanor?

"Father! Enough!"

His daughter's warning had the desired effect, because Edgar Ashcroft scowled and downed the rest of his drink without another word.

So old Belmont thought he had it all figured out, did he? Thought Francie's Aunt Eleanor was her mother? Well, Alexander knew Philip's one and only love had a different name. Catherine. Belmont's dead wife. He'd sooner rip out his tongue than tell either one of these gossip-seeking vultures.

"Is she as beautiful as they say?" Belmont pried.

"How would Mr. Bishop know?" Claire asked her father and then shot Alexander yet another dazzling smile, more brilliant than all the others. "After all, they're practically brother and sister. Isn't that right, Mr. Bishop?"

He and Francie? Brother and sister? He had not one brotherly bone in his body where Francie was concerned.

"Mr. Bishop?" She arched a black brow just so and he wondered if she practiced that look in the mirror.

"Ah...yes...brother   and   sister."   The   words   almost choked him.

"See, Father? I told you, Mr. Bishop would have no knowledge of such things. Brothers never do." She lowered her lashes and gazed in Alexander's direction.

It was becoming damnably hot in this room. Alexander reached up to loosen his cravat a little. He wanted to get out of this blasted place. Now. Far away from this arrogant man and his lusty daughter. But he'd come with a purpose and he wasn't leaving until he knew the relationship between Crayton and Belmont, and Belmont's daughter, of course, though he had a feeling their association might well be of a more intimate nature.

"I think Lady Claire would prefer we change the topic of conversation," Alexander said, meeting the earl's icy gaze. "I'm curious about a young man who, word has it, is tormenting the village of Amberden, taking advantage of young girls, and leaving them with child."

Out of the corner of his eye, Alexander saw Claire Ashcroft straighten.

"Who is the lucky gent?" the earl asked, chuckling.

Bastard. "I believe he's an acquaintance of yours." He cocked a brow in the old man's direction. "Lord Jared Crayton."

"Jared?" Claire Ashcroft breathed.

"Young Crayton?" Belmont asked, a hint of a smile peeking out from under his beard.

"The Duke of Worthington's second son," Alexander said.

"I know him," the earl said. "Of course, I know him. He's a good friend of Claire's and I'm friends with his father. So he's getting girls with child?" Belmont asked.

Alexander nodded.

"A randy one, is he?" The old man shrugged. "They probably can't lift their skirts fast enough for him." He lifted his shoulders again. "Better some village girl than one of our young maidens."

"The girls are still being compromised," Alexander said. "Ruined, whether peasant or noble."

"It's not the same, and you know it, Bishop. I'll wager those village girls are swooning all around, hoping he'll marry one of them."

"And I'll wager he's promising every last one of them he'll do just that." Alexander didn't try to disguise the anger in his voice.

Belmont flicked a hand in the air. "So he tells a little untruth."

"A lie," Alexander corrected.

The earl shrugged again and smiled. "A lie, then. So, he tells a little lie. What of it? A woman of quality would never put herself in that position, would she, Claire?"

A dainty blush crept up his daughter's creamy cheeks. No doubt, she'd practiced that as well. "Oh, no, Father," she uttered, her blue eyes wide with shock. "Think of the disgrace."

"The disgrace?" Alexander echoed, not believing what he'd just heard. "Do you think a commoner is not subjected to disgrace?" Francie was right. A good deal of the ton consisted of liars, cheats, and faithless husbands and wives, who cared not for dignity or morality. For themselves or anyone else.

"Well... " she hesitated, toying with a long, black tendril. "Of course, most of them would feel a certain amount of disgrace, but in our society, a girl would be ruined." She drew in a deep breath. "She'd never be able to hold her head up in polite circles again." A shudder ran over her near-bare shoulders as she murmured, "It would be devastating."

"Claire's right," the earl added. "Admit it, Bishop. You've been on both sides of the marker, first as a stable boy and now as near a nobleman as one can get without the parentage." His beady gaze narrowed on Alexander. "If Crayton's got wild oats to sow, better he sow them with a village girl than a young lady of the ton."

Belmont's words filled Alexander with a mix of bile and disgust. This was the type of attitude he'd held in high esteem, hoping to emulate? The ton cared for no one but themselves and those who traveled in their circles. He'd known that, had even supported their actions, but hearing it applied in such callous terms to Francie and her village sickened him. He'd spent years wanting nothing more than to fit in, embraced by the ton, respected and well-liked. He'd achieved that status and more, yet now the association embarrassed him.

"Of course, he agrees with you, Father," Claire Ashcroft purred and rested her small hand on Alexander's coat sleeve. "He's just too much the gentleman to say anything that would imply his new sister fit into the lesser category." She smiled that brilliant smile of hers and said, "How noble of you, Alexander." Her voice dipped an octave as her fingers crept up to stroke the back of his hand. "How utterly noble."

FRANCIE PEEKED through half-closed lids at the man on the opposite seat of the carriage. Alexander Bishop's eyes were closed, his dark brows pulled into a straight line, his full lips turned down at the corners. He might look like he was sleeping but Francie guessed it was just a ploy to ignore her. *Again.*

She'd been the one who planned to ignore him, at least until she'd had time to sort out her feelings. But one couldn't ignore what one couldn't see, and Alexander had been absent or unavailable for the past seven days. Francie had tried to keep track of his whereabouts, but her heart sank every time she heard Lady Printon's name whispered with his. After the second day, she resigned herself to the fact that he was spending the evening and early morning hours with his lady love and given not the least thought to Francie and the kiss they'd shared.

She wanted to hurl angry words at him for abandoning her like a stale loaf of bread after awakening feelings she didn't know existed. But she couldn't. Somewhere beneath his cold exterior was a little, orphaned stable boy who'd slept in the straw for weeks, covered in filth, fearful of being discovered and booted out. She ached at the sight of the pale gray scar running down his cheek. A remembrance of his childhood days as well?

Francie shifted in her seat and stretched her arms. Alexander scowled, but his eyes remained closed.

She glanced at Mrs. Vandemeer who slept soundly next to her, eyes closed, mouth open, thin body propped against the burgundy squabs. Had the woman not let out the occasional snore, one might think her dead. Francie leaned forward and whispered, "How long are you going to continue ignoring me?" If he weren't going to attempt conversation, then she would.

"I'm not ignoring you," he muttered, his tone as low as hers. "I'm tired."

"As you should be. Any man who keeps the hours you do must be exhausted."

A silver eye popped open. "What are you implying?"

"Nothing." She ignored the edge in his voice. "What could I possibly be implying? Your business is your business."

"Exactly." He closed his eyes again.

"What you do and with whom is none of my business."

"Glad we agree," he mumbled.

"But if it were, then I would take it as my duty to inform you, your behavior has set the servants' tongues wagging."

Both eyes opened. "Behavior? *My* behavior has set them talking? What about *your* behavior? Running around Drakemoor barefoot, skirts hiked to your knees? Stealing a pair of my riding breeches? Digging in that infernal dirt all hours of the day and night? Spending hours in the kitchen, *cooking* with Mrs. Jenkins? For God's sake, you dare to tell me they're talking about *my* behavior?"

She picked at a loose thread on the sleeve of her gown. "I've always thought shoes too confining. I love the feel of grass between my toes. And marble is so refreshing on a hot summer's day. As for the breeches..." She shrugged. "Uncle Bernard never minded when I borrowed his on occasion."

"Well, I do mind. I mind very much." Alexander leaned toward her, close enough for her to see the gold flecks in his silver eyes. "Ladies do not wear breeches, and they do not immerse themselves in dirt or show the cook how to make rosemary bread," he said through clenched teeth.

"Rosemary and thyme bread," Francie corrected.

His face turned a deep shade of purple. "I swear to God, Francie, you're going to drive me to Bedlam," he said under his breath. His eyes narrowed as he studied her. "However, Newgate may have a certain appeal."

"Newgate's for criminals. People who do horrible things, like commit murder and the like."

"I know," he said, his lips curving at the edges.

Francie backed away until she hit the burgundy velvet squabs behind her. He was only tormenting her. Of course, Alexander would never harm her.

He glanced at Mrs. Vandemeer's sleeping form and then snagged the ribbons on Francie's bonnet, tugging them toward him. She had no choice but to follow. When he'd brought her within inches of his face, he stopped. His silver eyes glowed as he whispered, "But most of all, a lady never, ever kisses a man as you did the other night."

Francie tried to pull away, but Alexander wrapped the ribbon around his fist, bringing her closer still. He devoured her with his gaze that breath by breath settled on her lips. "Never, ever," he murmured.

How dare he accuse her of unladylike behavior when he was the cause of it? And what of him? "And a gentleman should never kiss one woman and court another," she hissed in an equally hushed tone.

He released her with such force she fell back against the

squabs and landed on her elbows. "Stay away from me, Francie. Just stay away."

"It was just a kiss," she said, trying to underplay that night.

Mrs. Vandemeer's body leaned sideways at an arresting angle, her rather large bonnet squashed against the carriage window. Quiet snores erupted from her thin lips.

"Just a kiss?" he growled. "How many other men have you kissed like that?" His eyes narrowed to silver slits. "How many have you allowed such intimacy?" He ran a hand through his perfect hair three times, making pieces stick out. "How many, Francie?" His words fell out in a low, furious tone. "How many have been inside your mouth, tasting you? Touching you?"

Her cheeks burned. "None."

"None," he repeated. "I shouldn't have either. You do realize that, don't you? Only your betrothed should be permitted such liberties. Only your betrothed should know you taste like honey and whimper when he touches your breast."

Oh, if only the carriage floor would open right now.

"And we both know," Alexander whispered, "I'm not your betrothed. I'll never be your betrothed."

Her heart splintered beneath his words. Why should she care he'd just declared he'd never marry her? Was there some part of her that hoped he would? Some part of her that wanted him to?

"And now I have to go on, seeing you every day, knowing what you taste like in my mouth, knowing what you feel like beneath my fingers, and try to forget." His voice grew rough. "I've been living in hell these last days. A hell of my own making."

"It wasn't your fault," she said, turning to face him. "It just happened."

"No, damn it, it did not *just* happen," he bit out. "You may not have known what to expect, but I knew exactly what I was doing." A tortured look crossed his face. "I knew," he repeated in a raspy voice. "And yet I didn't stop. I couldn't stop. Don't you understand? I wanted to kiss you. I wanted to touch you. I've wanted to since the moment I laid eyes on you."

Alexander wanted her? Goose bumps crept along her arms. *Alexander wanted her.*

Something wasn't right. He'd just admitted he wanted her, seconds after telling her he'd never marry her. "You want a mistress, not a wife."

He cursed under his breath. "I would never do that to you. Or Philip. I owe him my life. You deserve a husband who can love you and make you happy."

She stared at him.

"I'm not capable of that kind of love."

"I see." She turned from him and looked out the window.

"I doubt you do. Did you know I was a stable boy at Drakemoor before Philip took me in?" He let out a short, harsh laugh. "My parents both worked there. My father was a groomsman when he could keep his head out of a bottle. When he couldn't ,I tried my best to do his job. My mother was a scullery maid who lived her life plagued with one ailment or another. I only desired a normal life with two parents who loved me. But they were too consumed with their own demons to spare an ounce of attention on me. When they died, I couldn't cry. How can you cry over something you've never had?"

"Surely, they loved you in their own way."

"Of course they did. I've got the scar to prove it." Alexander pointed to the jagged white line running from his eyebrow to his cheek.

"What happened?" Once again, her heart ached for the child he once was.

He ran a finger along the scar, tracing the crooked path

down his face. "I tried to protect my mother from a beating. My father didn't like my interference."

"I'm so sorry."

He shrugged. "It was a long time ago."

"All families aren't like that. My aunt and uncle raised me and they loved each other very much."

"I'm sure they did," he said. "But I gave up on 'happily ever after' a long time ago. I'm a man of reality, not fairy tales."

"Then I'm sorry for you, Alexander." *Sorry you will never permit yourself to love or be loved.*

He met her gaze, his eyes dark and piercing. "So am I," he murmured. "More than you'll ever know." Then he closed his eyes, snuffing out their conversation and the small flame of hope in Francie's heart.

12

A little over an hour later, silent and withdrawn, Francie stepped away from the shiny black carriage and entered Madame Druillard's shop with a yawning Mrs. Vandemeer. Alexander fell in behind her, equally quiet and subdued.

She could care less about the latest fashions or the finest silks, but her father had been so eager to bestow this gift on her she couldn't refuse him.

Every time she thought of her conversation with Alexander, her head ached and her stomach lurched. He'd been honest with her and she'd tried her best in her most subtle way to persuade him to reconsider his position on marriage. How could she have been so bold? What must he think of her? She'd practically begged him to offer for her.

Why would she do such a thing when she and Alexander couldn't even agree on dinner selections? Yet, she couldn't deny the fire that flared between them when they were together. If opposites did indeed attract, then she and Alexander should be melded together.

Mrs. Vandemeer plunked in the nearest chair and busied herself with the tea and biscuits situated on the table before her. Francie glanced at Alexander out of the corner of her eye. Three other women in the shop watched him also, smiling and giggling in an effort to attract his attention. He ignored them all, working his way toward the back of the shop and a petite woman dressed in black who must be Madame Druillard.

Francie studied the older woman from a distance, curious as to what manner of person drew women from every corner of England, each as eager as the next to own one of the modiste's creations. Madame Druillard was a tiny woman, somewhere in her early fifties, with sharp features and coal-black hair pulled back in a bun. She reminded Francie of a little bird with her beak-like nose and pointed chin. Her skin was alabaster, her lips deep red. Francie couldn't discern the color of her eyes as they darted back and forth, from Alexander to the large book spread out on a table before her.

Francie moved closer, curious to hear what Alexander was saying to the older woman.

"And of course, she'll need ball gowns. Several, in fact." He rubbed his jaw. "I thought perhaps gold with a burgundy trim for one. Royal blue and silver, also. To match her eyes." He paused. "And green. When she wears green, her red hair shimmers with streaks of gold."

"Hmmm." Madame Druillard tapped a long fingernail against her chin. "Where is she, your mademoiselle? I must see her."

Alexander cleared his throat. "She's not my mademoiselle. She's..." he paused, "...she's my sister."

Madame Druillard lifted a sleek brow. "Sister? I see. Where is this *sister*, monsieur?"

Francie stepped around a bolt of dark green fabric.

"Madame Druillard?" She smiled at the stern-looking woman. "I am Francie."

The older woman turned. Her black eyes moved with great precision from the top of Francie's pale green bonnet to the tips of her scuffed cream shoes. Heat rushed to Francie's cheeks at the woman's bold scrutiny. The three young women in the corner of the shop turned to stare as well, assessing her as they would any rival.

Madame Druillard tilted her head one way and then the other, appraising, considering, assessing. After what seemed two eternities, a slow smile spread about her thin lips. "Sister, eh?" she repeated, threw back her head, and laughed.

"Yes," Francie managed. What was so amusing?

"If you say so, my children, then so be it. Come, dear, let me look at you closer." She motioned Francie forward with her tiny hand. Francie obeyed, stopping a few feet from her. "Now, Monsieur Bishop says you are in need of a wardrobe, yes?" She fingered the fabric of Francie's worn gown. "Yes," she murmured, "you are very beautiful. You should be draped in silks and satins, *non*, Monsieur Bishop?" she asked, sliding a gaze in his direction.

Alexander gave her a curt nod but said nothing.

"Yes, that is what you shall have. And the hair," she said, gesturing to the red curls peeking out from under Francie's bonnet. "Take the bonnet off." Francie untied the ribbons and slipped the bonnet off her head. "*Non!* As I guessed. You are not a schoolgirl. When you have silks and satins draping your body, you will be *magnifique*."

Francie blushed. "Thank you, Madame Druillard, but I have no need for silk or satin. Perhaps one would be fine. No more than two. I do need day gowns, but five should be sufficient."

"She needs everything," Alexander said as though Francie hadn't spoken. "From top to bottom. Inside and out."

Of course he was talking about her chemise and pantaloons. "Alexander!"

He threw her a quick, disgusted look and turned back to Madame Druillard. "Her father is an earl. We can't have her looking like a poor relation any longer. He wants her clothed in the finest garments you have."

The modiste smiled. "As you wish."

"Now let's talk about design." Alexander pulled out a chair and sat down beside Madame Druillard.

The modiste flicked a few pages of the book she'd been looking at and said, "I think we should begin here."

For the next hour, Alexander and Madame Druillard pored through the big black book, discussing everything from day gowns to cloaks and gloves. They ignored Francie unless they were debating a particular color or design. Then they scrutinized her person in great detail.

"I think this is the one," Madame Druillard murmured, draping a swath of pale pink material over Francie's shoulder and down the front of her. "Look at the way it brings color to her cheeks. A glow almost." Her black eyes narrowed. "And the red hair. Tsk. Tsk. It is like fire."

Alexander cleared his throat. "Fine."

"Yes, it is very fine," Madame Druillard murmured with a knowing smile.

Alexander looked away and busied himself with the black book. "These are the ball gowns?" He flipped through the next several pages. "Unacceptable. All of them."

"Why do you say this, Monsieur Bishop? They are beautiful gowns and they will look exquisite on mademoiselle."

"Absolutely not."

"May I see them?" Francie inched toward the intriguing

black book. She hadn't cared that Madame Druillard and Alexander chose her wardrobe as though she weren't there. She was only doing this to please her father. In truth, the selections were perfect for her. The sea-foam greens, sky-blues, pale pinks, vibrant yellows, soft lilacs, all of them were among her favorite colors.

"There's nothing to see," Alexander said, slamming the book shut.

Madame Druillard slid the book toward Francie and opened it. "Monsieur Bishop, perhaps you might tell me what is the problem?"

"The problem," he bit out, "is this." He jabbed a finger at the bust line of a yellow gown. "And this," he said, pointing to another on the opposite page. They were cut quite low.

"Yes? This is the style. It is the...rage...as you say."

"Not for Francie it isn't."

"It's not *that* revealing," Francie said, looking at the upside-down sketch. It was much lower than anything she'd ever worn, but it wasn't obscene.

He flashed her a cold look. "Stay out of this. I want to see something else. Something without a plunging neckline."

Madame Druillard smiled. "You are very protective of your sister, Monsieur Bishop."

Francie blushed. Alexander said nothing but the twitch on the left side of his jaw told Francie he was not one bit happy.

The older woman leaned over and flicked through several pages. She pointed to an elegant gown with a much less revealing neckline. "Perhaps this will be more to your liking."

"That's better."

"*Bon.* Good." Madame Druillard sat down again. "Now, let us discuss colors."

"Burgundy trimmed in gold, sapphire trimmed in silver,

and cream trimmed in burgundy." He rattled the color combinations off without a moment's hesitation.

"Ah, Monsieur Bishop, it would appear you have given this much thought. Yes." Madame Druillard nodded. "I agree. Mademoiselle will look *magnifique*."

"Fine." He pushed back his chair and stood.

"We are not finished yet, Monsieur. There are still more gowns. And the undergarments. We have not spoken of those."

Alexander shoved his hands in his pockets. "She can choose the rest." He met Francie's gaze. "I'll be outside." With that, he turned and quit the shop.

When he was gone, Madame Druillard turned to her with a smile and whispered, "He is not your brother."

"Is it that obvious?"

"To me it is," she said, her black eyes shining. "To one who knows what it looks like to see a man enchanted by a woman, as your Monsieur Bishop is with you."

"He barely tolerates me. And he told me nothing will ever come of the two of us."

"So, he has been considering this, no?" The modiste laughed. "That is a good sign. A very good sign."

"Of what?" Francie asked.

"You shall see. It will come clear soon enough. Now," Madame Druillard said, turning back to her black book, "we must find you undergarments."

"Yes. Undergarments," Francie repeated.

"And if I might make one very small suggestion. I think I know of a way to uncover Monsieur Bishop's true feelings."

"You do?" Francie stared at her. "How?"

"Change the gold and burgundy gown. Choose the design with the low neckline."

"Alexander will be furious," Francie breathed.

"Exactly." Madame Druillard smiled. "So furious perhaps he will forget himself in his anger and state his true feelings."

"It could be disastrous."

"Or wonderful. The choice is yours."

Francie smiled at Madame Druillard. "Let's do it."

"THE NEXT TIME you offer my services, I'd appreciate it if they did not include a trip to Madame Druillard's." Or a long carriage ride with Francie and an ancient chaperone who couldn't stay awake for longer than three blinks at a time.

"Why?" Philip set down his glass of sherry. "Madame Druillard is the best modiste in London, perhaps in all of England."

Alexander poured two fingers in a glass and took a healthy swallow. "Just the point. She is very talented and well aware of the latest fashion. Unfortunately, I found some of those fashions quite distasteful."

"Francie told me about the ball gown," Philip said, trying to hide a smile.

"I find no humor in a woman exposing her breasts to a bunch of mauling 'would-be suitors.'" Alexander glared at Philip. "And I would think, as her father, you would want Francie to display a bit more modesty."

"Indeed I do," Philip replied. "But I had *you* there, Alex. I knew I had nothing to be concerned about."

"A good thing, too. I think the little minx could have been persuaded to wear one of those gowns."

Philip laughed. "You sound like an outraged husband."

Alexander ignored that comment. "A few things will be sent next week. The ball gowns and the rest will follow in two weeks' time."

"Excellent," Philip said. "Now we can plan a ball to introduce Francie into society."

"You mean a husband-hunting party." Alexander poured another drink. Just the thought of all those men fawning over Francie put him in a mood. She wouldn't understand their true intent. She was too naïve, too trusting. She'd trusted him, hadn't she? Knowing her, she'd smile and converse with the worst of them, misinterpreting a touch on her person as a sign of clumsiness or awkward shyness. And all the while, the lechers would be groping for a hint of silk skin or a feel of satin curves.

The earl coughed. "I'll thank you not to mention the word *husband* in front of Francie. She's not thrilled with having this ball anyway and if you make her think she's going to be someone's prize, she'll never agree to it."

"Well, that's what it is, isn't it?" Alexander snapped. He'd been in a foul mood since he'd stalked out of Madame Druillard's yesterday afternoon. Francie's incessant cheerful chattering during the two-hour trip home had done nothing to improve his temper. By the time they arrived at Drakemoor, his head pounded and he wore a permanent scowl.

Blast the woman, she was driving him mad. He should never have let Philip talk him into escorting her to London. Like a besotted fool, he'd chosen most of her wardrobe, taking care each color was a perfect match; sky-blue to intensify her eyes, sea-foam green or lavender to offset her fiery mane. He must've sounded like an idiot.

Alexander cursed under his breath. He'd chosen rich fabrics and flattering styles to enhance Francie's natural beauty —and lure a bevy of young bucks and old lechers to the marriage market. Thank God he'd had the good sense to leave before Madame Druillard flipped to the section on undergarments.

"Alexander?"

"What?" He looked up from his whiskey and met the older man's blue gaze.

"Unless you tell me differently, I *am* going to plan a ball for Francie," the earl said. "And she will no doubt have numerous suitors lining Drakemoor the morning after."

Alexander pulled at his cravat. It was blasted hot outside and even hotter in here. "I'm well aware of that fact." He turned to look out the window. She was there, right in his line of vision, with her damnable rabbit, Miss Penelope. She was talking to the silly animal, making all sorts of gestures. And laughing. Did she know how ridiculous she looked out there, without a hat; his gaze shot to her feet, without shoes? Without a brain was more like it.

Did she know the sun illuminated her red hair, weaving a golden highlight through the tumble of curls? And her hands...the way she moved them, fingers spread wide over Miss Penelope, soft and stroking...her hands would make any man wish he were a rabbit? And her body...

"What's going on out there, Alex?" Philip called. "What's got you so engrossed?"

Alexander spun around so fast his whiskey sloshed to the rim of his glass. "Nothing," he said and moved to block the window. "I was just thinking."

Francie's sweet voice trickled through the window. "Thinking, eh?" the old man said, tilting his head to peek around Alexander.

"Yes," Alexander snapped. "Thinking. I was just thinking about taking a little trip, perhaps to the West Indies. I never did get to see our sugarcane crops and they're bringing in quite a nice profit."

"A trip," the earl repeated, taking another sip of sherry.

"Yes, I think I'll begin making preparations at once."

Alexander stepped away from the window and moved toward his desk, trying to ignore Francie's melodic tune drumming in his ears, seducing his senses. He pulled out a piece of paper and jotted a few notes to himself. "I should be able to leave within the week. The only pressing matter is a meeting with the Duke of Worthington. Once I am assured Jared Crayton poses no threat to Francie or Amberden, my services will no longer be required and I will depart."

"A trip," Philip said again, rolling the word around on his tongue as though it left a bitter aftertaste.

"Hmmmm." Francie's laughter swept over Alexander. His groin tightened and he wondered if there was any way he might leave tomorrow.

"Too bad you won't be here for the ball," Philip said.

"Yes, quite a pity." Alexander kept his eyes trained on the piece of paper in front of him. *I'd never survive the ball.*

"Francie will be very disappointed."

Alexander refused to meet the challenge in Philip's voice. He shrugged. "We all suffer disappointments in one form or another. She'll recover."

The earl coughed, a harsh, hacking sound that filled the room.

Alexander rushed to him. "Are you all right?" The coughing of late had grown more frequent and harsher.

Philip raised his hand, but another cough wracked his body, followed by five more, until he lay back in his chair, red-faced and huffing.

"Don't know...what came over me," he gasped. "It's usually not...that bad."

"I'll fetch you a glass of water." Alexander rushed to the sideboard and poured a tall glass from a crystal decanter. He returned to stand beside the earl. "Drink this. Don't talk."

The earl followed his command and when he'd finished

half the glass, he leaned back against the cushions and closed his eyes, his breath falling out in short little puffs.

"That... gave me a scare," Philip said, his eyes still closed.

"Not half as much as me."

"About your trip..." The earl coughed twice more.

"The trip can wait."

"Are you," Philip puffed, "certain?"

"I won't leave until I know you're all right." If something happened to the old man while Alexander was gone, he'd never forgive himself.

The earl gave him a little half-smile, his eyes still closed. "Thank you, my boy."

∽

"YOU'RE GOING STRAIGHT to the devil, Philip. You know that don't you?"

Philip opened one eye. He'd been ordered to bed, first by Alexander and then by Francie when she found out about his little coughing episode. "I really did have a coughing spell."

Bernard raised a bushy brow but said nothing. "Oh, all right," Philip muttered. "I made it sound worse than it was. But I couldn't let Alex take off to some godforsaken land right before the ball. We're close, Bernard. I can feel it." He grinned. "You should've heard old Alex talking about Madame Druillard's. Didn't want her wearing this gown. Too revealing. Didn't want her wearing that gown. Too revealing." He chuckled. "I think he'd prefer to have her wearing a sack to hide her shape."

"You're meddling, Philip. If either one of them catches wind of this, there's going to be a lot of trouble."

Philip turned on his side, both eyes open now. "They're made for each other. When they're in the same room, you can almost see the sparks flying." His eyes misted. "They belong together. I'm just helping them along a little."

"You're interfering," Bernard corrected.

"Bah! Once they're married, it won't matter how they got together."

"If either one finds out, there won't be a wedding. And it will be our fault."

"How would they possibly find out? Relax, Bernard." Philip leaned back against his pillow and smiled. "All will be well."

13

"I'm here to see His Grace." Alexander stood at the entrance of Strotham, the Duke of Worthington's residence. It took some negotiation to obtain an audience, but persistence paid off. Soon, he'd be face to face with Jared Crayton's father.

"Come in," the butler said. He was a tall, thin man with a shiny forehead and very large ears.

Alexander stepped over the threshold and into one of the most majestic dwellings he'd ever seen. Gold covered every surface. There was gold inlay on the ceiling, gold dripping from the chandeliers like raindrops, gold designs on vases, gold patterns woven into the wall coverings. A bit much for Alexander's taste, but it left no doubt as to the duke's financial situation. To identify him as simply "rich" would be a gross understatement. The duke belonged several leagues beyond rich.

"This way, sir." The butler gestured down a long hall illuminated by another gold chandelier. Alexander followed, eyeing a row of portraits hanging along the hall. Crayton ancestors, no doubt, framed in heavy gold, staring back at him with double chins hiked up a notch or two and smug little smiles on their round faces. It was hard to discern the males from the females. All wore wigs, all were plump, and all had the air of superiority stamped across their fleshy faces.

The butler stopped before a large mahogany door and rapped twice. Alexander heard someone giggle, a woman from the sound of the high note, followed by scuffling and a few more giggles. Then a man's hearty laugh filtered through the door. The butler cleared his throat, turned five shades of red, and knocked again.

The giggling and laughter turned to whispers. "Who is it?" a deep, gruff voice bellowed.

"Jones, Your Grace. A Mr. Alexander Bishop to see you."

Alexander heard the man curse. "Give me a moment." There were a few more giggles and a long, low growl. If he weren't so anxious to see the matter of Jared Crayton laid to rest, he'd have turned and walked out. But the safety of Francie and Amberden lay at the hands of the man behind the mahogany door. For that reason, Alexander stayed and tried to ignore the disgusting grunting and groaning seeping through the door.

After what seemed longer than eternity, the door burst open and a short, buxom woman dressed in servant's clothes stood before them. When she spotted Alexander, her full pink lips parted into a slow smile.

"Bishop? Come in," a male voice commanded. The woman slipped past Alexander, brushing against his coat sleeve as she headed down the hall.

Alexander entered the huge room decorated in burgundy velvet, cream brocade, and, of course, gold. A very large man sat in an overstuffed burgundy chair, fastening the last button on his bright blue breeches. His face was red, his gray eyes puffy, with a rheumy look about them. He had a small, round nose and the same double chin as the ancestors in the portraits hanging in the hall. There were more bare spots than gray hairs on his head, though he'd pulled the stragglers back into a pathetic-looking queue. The man possessed no neck. His body went from a double chin to shoulders with nothing in between. The white cravat made the duke look like a flower ready to blossom. Diamond and ruby rings covered his pudgy fingers.

This was the Duke of Worthington, a man reputed to sit at the right hand of the king. And he resembled a *flower*.

"Thank you for granting me an audience, Your Grace," Alexander said. A rose? Not with that pink jacket. A geranium, perhaps? No, geraniums had necks.

"State your business, Bishop," the duke said, eyeing him with a watery gaze.

Alexander cleared his throat. He would do this for Francie. "I've come to speak with you about a matter regarding your younger son."

"Jared?" The duke smiled, revealing a set of crooked, gray teeth. "Handsome boy, isn't he? Has all the girls after him." He chuckled. "Though he gives them a fair chase himself."

"Indeed. That's what I've come to speak with you about."

The duke pointed a fat finger at the chair next to him. "Sit."

The old man's insolence grated on Alexander like a day-old beard against a woman's skin. He almost turned on his heel and left. Duke or no, the man had the manners of a pig. His promise to Francie won out and he settled himself into the oversized chair next to the duke.

"Speak."

The old man enjoyed his power. Sit. Speak. Next he'd tell him to jump and roll over. That's when Alexander *would* walk out and hunt down Jared Crayton himself. Even though he didn't like to admit it, and certainly never acknowledged it, there was enough stable boy left in him to resort to his fists when necessary. And if this old piece of overcooked ham sitting in front of him dressed like a flower didn't stop issuing commands soon, he'd do just that.

Alexander tried for diplomacy. "Your son is indeed quite a nice-looking young man. But my reasons for seeking your assistance have nothing to do with his looks."

The duke raised a wiry, gray brow. "Insolence, Bishop?" One watery eye narrowed. "Speak."

At that moment, Alexander felt a kinship to George. Did the old man treat everyone as though they were animals and he their master? Or did he reserve that behavior for stable boys dressed in fine jackets and trousers?

Before he could respond, there was a soft rap on the door.

"Enter," the duke said.

It was the maid Alexander had seen earlier, laden with a tray of refreshments and a sultry smile. She set the gold-edged tray on the table in front of them and proceeded to fix the duke's tea. The old man's eyes centered on the jiggling mounds of flesh trapped in the confines of her bodice. His thick tongue darted out to lick his lips. Alexander looked away, but not fast enough to miss the old lecher's hand patting the maid's round bottom as she walked away.

When the door closed behind her, the duke turned to him, his mouth full of blueberry tart and said, "Nothing like pounding a bit of young flesh to keep a man young."

Alexander swallowed, gulping more tea than he intended. It scalded his throat. *Damn.*

"What do you think?" the duke asked.

"Your Grace?"

The old man chuckled and tore another piece of tart with his teeth. His double chin wobbled as he nodded toward the door. "Of Maude."

Alexander nodded, not certain what kind of response the duke expected. "She seems very nice."

"Hah! You should see how nice she is when she's got her lips wrapped around you. She's nice, all right." He stopped chewing. "You want to pound her yourself, don't you?" He laughed, his fat hand rubbing his stomach. "I could tell by the way you were looking at her. You'd like a go at her."

"No. No, I wouldn't."

"No?" He sounded insulted.

"No, thank you, Your Grace," Alexander responded. The old man looked offended by his refusal. "She's quite beautiful." *If you liked over-painted and over-used types.* "And it's quite obvious she's very much taken with you."

He smiled a huge, smug smile. "Right you are." He leaned closer to Alexander and murmured, "I just have to flick my finger, and I've got her wet and panting." He grinned and let out a loud belch.

"Indeed." *I have got to find a way out of this conversation.*

"She loves my touch." He made sucking sounds as he licked blueberry off of his fat fingers.

She loves your money and your power, Alexander amended.

"Pass me another tart," the duke commanded. "The cherry one."

Alexander picked up a silver utensil and placed a plump cherry tart on a white and gold plate. He passed it to the duke who plucked the pastry off the plate and sank his teeth into it. Red oozed down the sides of his mouth, trickling to his chin. He wiped his mouth with his fingers, then proceeded to lick each one.

"Well, Bishop, did you come for a reason or just to eat my food?" the duke asked, sucking on his little finger.

Thank God we didn't shake hands. Alexander shot a glance at his empty plate. The only one eating food in the room was the duke. He cleared his throat and said in an even voice, "It seems

Lord Jared has enamored himself with several of the young females in Amberden."

"And that's a concern?"

"He's gotten them pregnant."

The duke folded his hands over his protruding stomach and tilted his head to one side. "And that's a concern?" he repeated.

Alexander forced himself to remain calm. "It is to the young women and their parents who are left in disgrace."

"How can they consider being impregnated by a duke's son a disgrace?" A slow smile spread over his thick lips. "They should consider it an honor."

No wonder Jared Crayton scattered his seed like a farmer sowing his crop. "An honor, Your Grace?" He felt his heart racing in his chest. This pompous deviant thought these young girls should consider it an honor to carry his son's child? "They've been ruined."

"In what manner? We all know those peasant girls start rolling around in the fields with boys from the time they can lift their skirts." He chuckled. "Sweet young pieces of flesh, I'll wager."

"One of the girls your son is after," Alexander said, his left hand balling into a fist, "happens to be someone I know."

"Oh?" A grizzled eyebrow lifted. "Do tell."

"Her name is Francie Jordan. She's the Earl of Montrose's daughter. And she's my...sister." He hesitated. The word felt worse than dirt in his mouth but he pushed on. "Not my sister by blood, more by association."

"Are you pounding her, Bishop?" the duke asked, leaning forward a little, his rheumy eyes bright, his thick lips wet.

"No!" Alexander said, outraged to hear the old man utter such vileness about Francie. "No," he repeated in a calmer tone. "But I have a responsibility to her. And now to her village.

When Miss Jordan spurned your son's advances, he beat her aunt."

That caught the duke's attention. "The hell you say. Have you proof?"

"I have the aunt's word."

"Bah! A commoner's word is no better than a pile of manure."

"Please, Your Grace, I need your help."

"Hmmm," the duke murmured, his sausage-like fingers stroking the ruby and gold ring on the middle finger of his left hand. "What do you expect me to do?"

"Stop your son before he impregnates the whole village," Alexander said. "Keep him away from Francie."

"And if I do, Bishop? What's in it for me?"

"The knowledge you've saved the village. They will be forever indebted to you for your assistance."

The duke grunted. "I think I'd rather have a piece or two of young flesh. What about it, Bishop?" His lips pulled into a smile. "Bring me two young girls. If they're pregnant already, even better. Do that and I'll help you."

Alexander didn't know if he should twist the old man's cravat around his neck or just pummel his swollen face and be done with it. He clung to his last shreds of control. "I can't, Your Grace."

"Then I can't help you, Bishop," he said, steepling his fat fingers under his lips.

You won't help me. Alexander stood and bowed toward the worthless piece of flesh sprawled in the chair before him. "Thank you for granting me this audience, Your Grace."

The Duke of Worthington nodded. Alexander turned and headed toward the door, anxious to take his leave. He'd handle Jared Crayton himself. He had his hand on the knob when the duke's voice reached him. "Bishop."

"Your Grace?" He stopped but did not turn around.

The duke belched. "If you change your mind, I'll take a blonde...and a redhead."

The door slammed shut, closing out the duke's cackling laughter, but his crude remarks clung to Alexander, teasing and tormenting him with their depravity.

Only one thing remained certain. Alexander would take care of Jared Crayton. Wherever, whenever, however.

"YOU'RE A VISION, CHILD," Eleanor whispered, smiling up at her niece. "A true vision."

Francie fingered the gold silk of her ball gown. "It feels wonderful." She twirled around, watching her skirts swish about her ankles. "It's so soft against my skin."

"There's nothing like silk," her aunt said with a warm smile that deepened the dimples on both sides of her mouth. "But satin's a very close second."

Francie's own smile faded as she looked at the old woman's gray muslin gown. "Oh, Aunt Eleanor, didn't you ever miss this life?" She raised her hands in a helpless gesture. "You once lived in a grand house twenty times the size of ours with servants who called you Lady Eleanor." Her eyes misted. "You gave up so much. For me."

"And I'd do it all over again, child," Aunt Eleanor said, leaning forward in the overstuffed pink and gold floral chair she sat in. She reached for Francie's hand, her blue eyes serious. "You've given me more happiness than I ever could have imagined possible." Her voice quivered as she added, "You were the child Bernard and I never had."

"But didn't you miss this?" Francie waved her hand about

the room, indicating the deep, rich mahogany furniture, the heavy damask draperies, and the satin counterpane.

"How could I when I had you?" Her aunt squeezed her hand and pulled her closer. "You're the one who gave up this life, and you didn't even know it."

"I love my life in Amberden," Francie said, with a protective fierceness that surprised even her. "I wouldn't trade it for anything. Not one thing, Aunt Eleanor. Wearing these clothes is like a fairy tale." Her lips curved into a soft smile. "But I'd rather be running barefoot in a field of clover wearing breeches."

"Just so long as they're not Alexander's breeches," her aunt said.

Francie scrunched up her nose. "He's such an old spoilsport. I only borrowed them. Once."

Aunt Eleanor chuckled, her plump face rosy. "Once was more than enough for him, I daresay." She raised a gray brow. "Has he seen your gown yet, child?"

Heat rose from Francie's neck to the tip of her forehead. Her father and Uncle Bernard had both asked the same question. "Why do you ask?" She cast a glance at the oval mirror to her right. "There's absolutely nothing wrong with this gown."

It was beautiful. Anyone would agree. The gold silk fell in a gracious cascade, shimmering about her hips and legs. Burgundy trim accented the simple, elegant lines, dipping and curving to enhance the design. But to some, most notably, Alexander Bishop, there might be just a bit too much "dip" in the bust line. She eyed the pale flesh peeking out over the top of the bodice.

Perhaps she should not have taken Madame Druillard's suggestion to change the design from demure to daring. "*Is* there something wrong with it, Aunt Eleanor?" she asked.

"No, child," her aunt replied. "Trust me. It's perfect."

∾

"GET BACK UPSTAIRS, right now, and change," Alexander barked.

Francie took another step down the spiral staircase. "There's nothing wrong with my gown."

Nothing wrong, indeed. She was falling out of it, her full, ripe breasts pushing against the gold material, just begging for attention. She'd get it all right. She'd have every man aching to touch and fondle her before the night ended. Not himself ,of course; he wasn't aroused by such blatant displays of a woman's charms.

She took another step, closing the distance between them. Alexander didn't want to notice the way her red hair shimmered with seed pearls, gathered on top of her head and left to trail down in tiny ringlets, just so, in a most alluring fashion. He tried to ignore the sleek line of her neck. What would it be like to brush aside those ringlets and place a light, chaste kiss below her ear? She'd smell like lavender. That was her scent. Whenever she was near, it filled his senses, teased, and tormented him.

She was six steps away. Her silk dress rustled as she moved, swirling about her hips, cascading over her thighs, one constant motion, closing the gap between them. Closer, closer. His gaze inched from the gold satin slippers upward. To knees, thighs, hips, jumped over breasts and fled to her neck, chin, nose, eyes, hair. And back to her sky-blue eyes.

He would not look at her bodice again. "Francie," he said, annoyed she hadn't listened the first time. "Go upstairs and change that gown."

"No." She stepped onto the marble foyer.

Did she plan to defy him? Apparently so. "Fine. If you want to look like you work in a brothel, do not be surprised when the customers begin lining up."

He might as well have slapped her across the face. She stepped back, or maybe stumbled, her blue eyes wide with hurt, her full lips quivering.

He would not feel sorry for her. She'd brought this situation on herself. He turned and stalked off to his study, trying to block the muffled sound of her retreating slippers. Had he just heard a whimper or two? Blast the woman! He would not feel sorry for her. If she refused to change that damnable gown, well, then, she'd have to face a bevy of ogling, mauling men on her own. He wasn't going to help her. Not one bit. But even as he let the words flow through his brain, he knew they were lies. If anyone touched Francie, he'd smash his face in.

"Just look at those two, Bernard." Philip chuckled, shifting in his chair on the fringe of the ballroom. "They haven't been within twenty feet of each other since the ball began."

Bernard shook his head. "I fear your plan has backfired, my friend."

"Backfired?" the earl bellowed. "I couldn't be more pleased."

"They aren't speaking to one another," Bernard pointed out.

"I know," Philip said, smiling.

"They've stayed on opposite ends of the ballroom."

"I know." Philip's smile deepened.

"They've had numerous dance partners."

"I know."

"But not each other," Bernard added.

"I know."

"*Well, I don't know.*" Bernard scratched his gray head. "I don't know at all. What I do know is when a man and woman are interested in one another, they usually communicate in some form, spoken or unspoken."

"Oh, they're communicating all right," the earl said, sipping his sherry.

"What language might they be speaking?" Bernard inquired. "I know seven quite fluently and I don't recognize it as any one of those."

Philip leaned toward his friend and whispered, "It's the language of love."

Bernard raised a brow. "Language of love? You've gone off the deep end."

"Bah! You've had your head in those damnable books too many years." Philip pointed a large finger at the dance floor. "Observe. Alex is waltzing with that young lady, but every time he turns, his gaze shoots to Francie. Very subtle, but if you keep your eyes on him, you'll notice." Both men watched as Alexander took his partner through the steps, twirled her around, and swept his gaze over Francie and her partner.

"I'll be damned," Bernard whispered.

"Exactly," Philip said with a knowing look. "But she's been doing the same thing to him. Watch." They followed Francie this time, saw her smile at her partner, dance, one, two, three and turn, her gaze flitting over Alexander and then past, as though quite by accident.

"So, you see," Philip said, "they're mad for one another but both too stubborn to do anything about it."

"Well, by the way the young suitors are swarming around Francie, Alexander better make his intentions known quickly."

"Exactly," the earl said. "She'll have ten calling cards tomorrow if she has one. You'll see, Bernard," he said, taking another sip of sherry. "The next forty-eight hours will prove very interesting indeed."

14

"Who is the woman in the blue dress?" Francie asked the young man who'd fetched her punch. Lord Steven something or other. She couldn't quite remember but thought it had to do with some sort of bird. Pheasant? Peacock? Pigeon? No. None of those. There had been such a string of men for the past two hours, it was difficult to match faces and names.

"You mean the one standing by the punch bowl? The one who's been dancing with Alexander Bishop?" the young man asked.

"I hadn't noticed her partner," Francie said, sipping her punch. What a fib. She'd seen her in Alexander's arms half the evening. Gazing up into those silver eyes. Smiling. Laughing. Oh, and he'd been doing the same. Alexander Bishop laughing! She'd not have believed it if she hadn't witnessed it herself. Gone was the surly antagonist who never showed anything but censure toward her. He was a different man with this blonde-haired beauty. Quite different, indeed.

"Lady Printon," Lord Steven what's-his-name answered. "She and Mr. Bishop are an item, if you will."

Tess. "I see," Francie muttered, taking in the other woman's gold-blonde beauty. Even with her curls piled high on her head, she barely reached Alexander's shoulder. From a distance it was difficult to discern the color of her eyes, but Francie guessed they'd be some unique, mesmerizing color like aquamarine or emerald. Or maybe even dark topaz.

The woman's pale complexion sparkled with diamonds—chokers on her neck, teardrops dangling from her ears, even her fingers were covered in brilliance. Were any of those gifts from Alexander? As for neckline, good heavens, the woman's plunged much lower than Francie's! How did she stay tucked in? Had Alexander told Lady Printon she looked like she belonged in a brothel? Doubtful. She watched his full lips spread into a slow smile as he bent to whisper something in her ear. The woman laughed and tilted her head back just enough to expose her slender neck.

Francie turned away. No, she'd bet he hadn't lectured Lady Printon on her choice of clothing.

"Well, well, what an exquisite pleasure," a man's voice said from behind. It was a familiar, soft, honeyed voice. Francie turned and froze.

Jared Crayton stood before her, the picture of casual elegance in a black cutaway and trousers, his snow-white cravat darkening his bronze skin. Many a mother looked into those moss-green eyes and prayed to have him for a son-in-law, even though he was a second son. But Francie knew what evil pounded through his veins, just below the surface of civility.

She had to signal Alexander immediately so he'd take care of this beast before he took his next victim.

"So, you're Francie Jordan."

Francie turned to the woman beside Jared Crayton. She was beautiful, with rich, black hair, woven with tiny sapphire beads and gathered in ringlets atop her head. Eyes the color of a clear sky on a chilly morning stared back at her. A half-smile flitted across the woman's face, as though she couldn't quite bring herself to spread her lips wider. She wore a cream silk gown that clung to her small frame and matched the exact hue of her skin. It, too, dipped well below Alexander's standard of acceptable.

Sapphires dangled from her neck and ears.

"Allow me to make introductions," Jared Crayton said with a gallant sweep of his hand. "Lady Claire, this is indeed Miss Francie Jordan." His smile deepened as his gaze traveled from Francie's eyes to her bosom. "Francie, this is Lady Claire Ashcroft, the daughter of the Earl of Belmont."

Francie forced a smile and extended her hand, sliding a glance in Alexander's direction. *Blast the man!* He had his back turned to her. Lady Claire brushed her gloved fingertips against Francie's palm and withdrew. "You're Montrose's daughter," she said, her blue eyes narrowing a fraction.

"Yes, I am."

Lady Claire turned to her escort. "Jared, be a dear and fetch me some punch, please?"

"Certainly." He turned to Francie, his voice soft and intimate. "May I refill yours?"

"No." The word flew out of her mouth. "No, thank you," she repeated, in a more demure tone. She wanted him to be gone so she could slip over to Alexander.

Jared Crayton swept his gaze over her bosom once more, leaving no doubt he approved of her gown, before he turned and headed in the direction of the refreshments.

"I understand you're Alexander Bishop's sister," Lady Claire continued as though there hadn't been a break in the conversation.

Heat surged to Francie's cheeks. *Sister.* "Y...yes," she stumbled over the word.

The woman shifted her gaze to Alexander a moment before gliding back to Francie. "That's what Alexander told me." She gave Francie another quarter-smile. "He said you were like brother and sister. Actually," she added, dropping her voice to a whisper, "he told me he felt sorry for you."

"He felt sorry for me?"

"Well, yes. He said you were something of a poor relation, raised in a little village without proper education or social skills."

Alexander said that about her? "I see." Poor relation? Without proper education or social skills? When she got her hands on him, she'd yank his silly cravat so hard she'd make his eyes bulge.

Lady Claire's soft voice tinkled with laughter. "He likened you to a little country mouse journeying to the city. Quaint but quite backward."

"Quaint but backward?" She'd yank until his eyes popped out.

"Don't take offense, Miss Jordan. He meant no harm."

Meant no harm? She was going to cry...*after* she assaulted Alexander with his cravat. "I'm certain he didn't," she said, forcing out the truth. "You must have found it quite entertaining to think of a village girl like me living in a place like Drakemoor."

The black-haired beauty laughed again. This time, her smile spread in white magnificence across her face. "I must admit, it did give us a little chuckle. Drakemoor is one of the grandest estates for miles around. It needs a mistress of impeccable breeding who can bring dignity and honor to the position."

Impeccable breeding. Not a bastard child, even if she were the daughter of an earl. "Excuse me, Lady Claire, I'm not feeling very well."

"I understand." The other woman's words drifted to her. "I understand completely."

Francie sifted her way through the throng of guests and made her way outdoors, not stopping until she stood before her garden on the far side of the house. She closed her eyes and inhaled the scent of lilac and roses. It reminded her of Amberden, her own slice of heaven.

The tears came then. Great, gulping sobs wracked her body and fell in tiny paths down her cheeks. She tasted the salt of her anguish, her shoulders shaking with sorrow. She didn't belong at Drakemoor. No matter how much she loved her father, she couldn't stay here. Not with Alexander. Not when she had to see him every day, knowing he didn't want her here, knowing he and others like him ridiculed her for her simple ways.

"A beautiful rose in a rose garden," a soft voice called from behind.

Francie jumped, startled by the intrusion, but didn't turn around. "I'd like some privacy." She swiped at her eyes and sniffed.

"Soft and fragrant as a rose is sweet Francie," the voice continued as though she hadn't spoken.

"I want to be alone," she said with a little more force, sniffing again.

"Skin like velvet, tempting to touch, to kiss."

A chill crept up her spine, spreading through her body with slow, persistent intent. "Please go away."

"Such beauty blanketed in such sadness. Would that I could take away your pain."

A hand touched her shoulder and she spun around. "How dare you come here after what you did to my aunt."

Jared Crayton stared back at her, his handsome face cast in

a scrap of moonlight. "I have no idea what you mean." His charming smile made him look boyish and innocent.

"Don't try to deny it was you who assaulted my aunt."

He had the audacity to look affronted. "Why would I do such a thing? Do you think me some kind of beast?" He reached for a stray lock of hair that had fallen to her shoulder but she jerked back before he could touch her.

"You could have killed her, all because she wouldn't tell you my whereabouts."

The smile faded. "Insolence cannot be tolerated in the lower class. Your aunt shows no respect for those above her. She should consider herself fortunate to have suffered nothing more than a little blood and bruises."

Whether he came right out and said the words, she knew he'd been the one to attack Aunt Eleanor. She pushed past the anger and disgust swelling inside and said, "Any man who would strike a woman is not a man."

Jared Crayton's hand shot up so fast Francie thought he would strike her. But then he stilled, watching her shrink back, her arms shielding her head.

"No need to fear me, Francie," he said, lowering his hand toward her and turning his palm upward. "I'd never hurt you." He stepped closer.

"Get the hell away from her!"

Alexander. Francie turned and ran toward the shadowy figure approaching, mindless of the rose thorns snagging her gown and prickling her bare arms.

"Are you all right?" Alexander clutched her to him, his voice raw.

"I'm fine," she managed.

He reached out to touch her cheek, hesitated, then drew back and released her.

"Well, well." Jared Crayton approached them. "Isn't this a

charming little scene? Alexander Bishop saves the day." He smirked. "Rescuing his little sister from the clutches of evil. Your intentions toward Francie are as brotherly as mine, Bishop."

"Enough," Alexander bit out.

"Oh, enough, is it? I daresay it won't be enough until one of us gets between those creamy, white thighs of hers."

Alexander let out a low, feral growl and charged the other man, striking his left jaw, then his right, then his left again, with bone-chilling accuracy. Crayton stumbled backward and tried to escape but Alexander grabbed his cravat, yanked him forward, and delivered several blows to his midsection. Francie watched in horror and awe as the ever-proper Alexander Bishop proceeded to decimate the Duke of Worthington's second son.

"Stop," Crayton choked out, his words garbled with what Francie guessed to be a mouthful of blood. "Stop. I...beg you."

Alexander grabbed him by the lapels of his jacket and hauled him forward. "Keep away from her," he ground out. "Don't come near her again. And stay clear of Amberden." Crayton moaned in response. Alexander swore under his breath and threw him to the ground like so much rubbish. Then he turned and grabbed Francie by the arm. "Let's go," he said in a tone that brooked no argument. "He won't be bothering you again."

A sliver of moon lit the path as Francie followed Alexander toward the back of the house, accompanied by a chorus of crickets and a medley of night sounds. Nature's song drowned out the faint chords filtering from the open windows. She much preferred the rhythmic chirping in the darkness to a crowded room packed with eager young suitors begging a dance. It helped settle her jumbled nerves and her breathing slowed to even breaths, matching the cacophony around her.

When they reached a small copse of elm trees, Alexander stopped.

"Let me look at you." He released her arm and cupped her chin with his fingers. He moved closer, his breath fanning her face.

"I'm fine," she managed.

"Did he hurt you?" Alexander's fingers swept over her face.

"N...no," she stammered. He was much too close for her to formulate a single thought.

"Then why does it look like you've been crying?" he asked between clenched teeth. "What did he do?"

"No, that was...He didn't touch me."

After studying her a moment more, Alexander seemed to accept her words and let out a heavy sigh. "Thank God. He wasn't invited, you know."

"I assumed as much."

"He must've been determined to see you."

A shudder ran through her at the thought of what might have happened had Alexander not intervened. "How did you know where to find me?"

He shrugged. "I didn't. When you left the ballroom, I gave you a reasonable period of time to return. Then I started searching."

She let out a little half-laugh. "You were watching me? You seemed much too involved with Lady Printon to notice anything."

"I notice everything about you, Francie," he said in that low, gruff voice that made her insides quiver. "Sometimes too much." His fingers slipped from her chin to her shoulder.

Her heart skipped a beat, then pounded wildly. "Then you are quite the actor for I thought you were completely enamored of Lady Printon and unable to see anything but her." Once the words were out, she wished she hadn't said them. They made her sound petty and small, as though his love interest in another woman mattered to her.

"Jealous, Francie?" His fingers trailed down her arm, leaving little prickles of heat where he touched her.

She jerked away from him, angry he could affect her with the slightest touch. Angry also that she cared about his relationship with his paramour.

"Of course I'm not jealous! One would have to care in order to be jealous, would one not?"

"Yes," he agreed, in that too-low voice again.

"One would have to care."

"And since you and I obviously do not care for one another in anything other than a familial capacity," she said, careful to avoid his piercing gaze, "there's no reason to even consider jealousy as a viable emotion."

"Indeed."

"Indeed," she whispered, wishing she could make herself believe her own words.

Alexander cleared his throat. Twice. She waited for his sarcastic rebuttal. He had one, she was certain of it. After all, hadn't she read somewhere the one who cares the least or not at all, as in this case, possessed the most leverage in a situation? She waited for his quip. And waited.

"Look at me, Francie."

She inched her gaze to meet his, thankful darkness hid much of her face.

"I left for exactly five minutes this evening, during which time Crayton must have sought you out. Aside from that, let's see..." He tapped his chin with his forefinger. "You danced with James Trumane, Earl of Westhaven, first, followed by Adam Montale, Earl of Kilander, then Alex Drexel, Marquis of Rentworth." He paused. "You danced with him twice. Oh, I almost forgot Jason Gilian, the Marquis of Penton. And, last but certainly not least, that gangly fellow lapping along behind you all evening, Lord Steven Grosepeak, Earl of Starling. He also brought you punch."

Francie stared at him. He'd just named every partner on her dance card. In order. "How?" she asked, finding it difficult to breathe all of a sudden. "Why?"

Alexander gripped her arms with both hands, taking a step closer until not more than a breath separated them. "I wish to God I knew," he said on a ragged sigh. "Every time I saw one of them touching you, I wanted to tear him away."

"But you ignored me. Every time I turned to look at you, you were busy with..." She couldn't say the woman's name, not now, so she settled for, "Other things."

"A simple diversion that failed miserably." He ran his hands along her arms, making them tingle once again.

"A brother would not have such feelings of..." she held her breath a moment and then forced out the word *jealousy*.

He didn't deny it. "No, he would not. I behaved abominably this evening when you appeared in that gown. So beautiful. So alluring." His voice caressed her with such tenderness she could barely concentrate on his words. "I couldn't tolerate the thought of men flocking around you, vying for a touch, a taste perhaps." His fingers slid up her arms to stroke her neck.

His touch did strange things to her, making her long to feel his fingers on other parts of her body, doing what, she had no idea. But the need continued to build deep in the core of her.

"And a sister wouldn't want him to have those feelings," she murmured, resting her hands on his shoulders.

"No." His voice turned warm as the night air. "No, she most definitely would not."

He crushed her against his hard body. "I've waited so long to taste you again." His head lowered to take her mouth in a kiss that spoke of want and need and a desire that throbbed just below the surface of reason. She wrapped her arms around his neck and buried her hands in the silky curls at the nape.

His tongue plunged into her mouth, mating with hers. He tasted of tobacco and whiskey and she wanted more. Slowly, she sucked on his tongue, as he'd done the last time they'd kissed. Alexander groaned and cupped her, hauling her against him. Swirls of desire pulsed through her as the rigid length of him ground into her heat in the same rhythmic motion as her tongue. His hands played over the soft fabric of her gown to stroke the backs of her legs and the rounded flesh of her buttocks. Oh, but his touch proved exquisite, sending shivers through every part of her body. And oh, how she wanted more.

When he lifted her off the ground, she clung to him, mindless of where they were going or who might see them. Nothing mattered but getting closer to this man, pressing her body to his, skin to skin. She ignored the rough bark of the tree against her neck and shoulders, the tiny pieces of wood digging into her flesh. Everything faded except Alexander's hard body pressed against hers. And his touch. And his mouth. Oh, dear God, but she wanted more.

He worked his knee between her legs, urging them apart. Incredible heat rolled over her as he rubbed against her in the same slow, entrancing movement. His fingers traced the slender column of her neck, trailing to the top of her breasts. Francie's nipples turned to hard little peaks against the wisp of silk fabric. Alexander smoothed a finger over her breast, stroked the nipple through the material, and let out a low rumble deep in his throat. He inched the bodice down, exposing first one breast and then the other to the warm night air. When he broke the kiss, she moaned, her head falling back against the tree. A kiss that lasted forever with Alexander wouldn't be long enough.

She watched him through half-closed eyes and when his

fingertips brushed over her exposed flesh, she arched toward him.

He met her gaze, his silver eyes shimmering in the moonlight. He stroked her cheek and murmured, "So beautiful." His voice grew thick and hoarse. "So very beautiful."

Francie closed her hand over his. Then she turned it and spread his fingers wide, planting a kiss in the middle of his palm.

"And so..." He paused, taking her other hand and flicking his tongue in the center of her palm, "...responsive."

She shuddered, weak and dizzy from his touch. He traced her lips with his fingers and, lowering his head, took a nipple into his mouth.

She moaned, clutching his head with both hands. Such exquisite, incredible pleasure. Alexander sucked and laved her left breast while his fingers stroked her right. He pulled away and sank to his knees, lifting her gown to expose her legs. His fingers skimmed the expanse of silk hose, searching for bare flesh, inching closer to her woman's heat with each tiny touch. Francie held her breath as he hovered at the core of her. Wanton she may be, but she needed to feel his fingers on her. He cupped her with his large hand and she jerked against him, trying to control the scalding desire threatening to burn her up. He withdrew and worked open the slit of her pantaloons.

"Alexander, what are you doing to me?"

"Giving you pleasure, my sweet." She closed her eyes and waited for his fingers, crazy with anticipation and need. But when his tongue stroked her instead, she came undone, hips jerking wildly as she exploded against his mouth. If he hadn't clamped a hand over her lips, the whole of Drakemoor would have heard her release.

It wasn't possible to move or even consider moving. Her legs wobbled and she feared she'd topple if she tried. Alexander stood up and gently pulled the gown over her breasts.

"Francie," he whispered as he reached out to stroke her cheek. "I—"

"Alex! Alex!" her father's voice bellowed from several yards away. "Where are you, boy? Francie's missing!"

Alexander pulled his hand away and straightened his cravat. "I'm coming, Philip." He turned to Francie and raised a finger to his lips. "I'll sidetrack him and you sneak in through the servants' quarters." He gave her one fleeting glance and was gone.

15

"Stay where you are, Philip." He wanted to give Francie enough time to get away. "It's dark and you might hurt yourself."

"Bah! I'd know this land blindfolded upside down."

Philip was by the garden. Alexander hurried toward his voice, casting a quick glance behind him. No sign of Francie. He ran his hands through his hair and adjusted his cravat again.

"What in the devil are you doing out here?" the earl asked, his large arms folded over his stomach. "I need your help. Francie's missing."

"She's fine," Alexander said. "She's in her room. She just had a little upset." He cleared his throat. "Jared Crayton was here."

"Damn! How the hell did that happen?"

Alexander shrugged. "He was determined to see her. He just showed up."

"He's got to be stopped."

"I don't think we have to worry about Crayton anymore," Alexander said. "I handled the situation."

"Nailed him, did you?"

"He couldn't get a word out between all the moans and groans."

"Good boy." The earl chuckled and moved closer. His voice grew serious. "Thank you, Alex."

"It was the least I could do."

"I'm sure Francie is grateful. Thank you for protecting her."

Protecting her? Visions of Francie's soft, creamy thighs throbbed in his brain. He still heard her sweet moans of pleasure. *Protecting her?* Heat rose to his face and he was thankful for the darkness. "You're welcome," he muttered.

"But it looks as though your days of service will soon be over," Philip said, rubbing his chin.

"Excuse me?"

"I've had ten would-be suitors approach me already." He shook his head. "And one proposal."

"Proposal?" Alexander repeated, visions of red hair and whispered sighs flashing through his mind. He sucked in a breath of air. It was too damn hot all of a sudden. Yanking his cravat loose, he stared at the earl. "What proposal?"

The older man seemed amused by Alexander's reaction. "Absolutely entranced, the young man was."

"Who?"

"Young Grosepeak."

Alexander snorted. "He's no match for Francie. She'd have him tied in knots and stumbling all over himself."

"True," Philip agreed. "He is a little green. Perhaps she needs someone more experienced. Hmmm," he said, tapping his chin with his finger. "What do you think of Westhaven?"

"He's a little too experienced," Alexander said. He didn't want to tell Philip the ton placed bets on Westhaven's prowess. It was said he could bed any woman within a week. And the odds were always in his favor. No, Westhaven wouldn't do.

"Kilander, then. I think he's quite a handsome, polite young fellow. He and Francie would suit quite well."

Alexander shook his head. "They might. But what would Francie think about the mistress and three children he keeps?"

"Really?"

"Really."

"There was another young man. The one who came to see you for advice on the market last year. Penton, I believe. He seemed quite attentive to Francie."

"I'm certain he was," Alexander replied. "He's also probably quite attentive to the fact that Francie is now a very wealthy woman." He pulled out two cheroots, lit them, and offered one to Philip. "Penton was knee-deep in debt when he came to me. His father cut him off and he thought I might give him a loan."

"I see." The earl took a long drag on his cheroot. "And did you?"

"Absolutely not. I told him to give up his mistress and his gambling and then we'd talk about a loan."

"Scratch him."

"My sentiments exactly," Alexander replied, blowing a puff of smoke in the air.

"What about Rentworth?"

"Did his mother come with him tonight?" Alexander asked. "As long as Francie doesn't mind her tagging along, wiping his nose and telling him what to do, it should work out fine."

"What about you?"

Alexander bit down on his cheroot. He coughed, then choked, spitting out loose bits of tobacco.

"Alex? Are you all right?"

"No." He spit again. "I am not all right." He pulled out a handkerchief and wiped his mouth. "Don't ever do that to me again."

"What did I do?"

Alexander pointed a finger at him. "Don't try that innocent routine with me, Philip. I've known you for too many years." He spit out more tobacco shreds. "Why, I'll even wager you already knew what I just told you about Francie's would-be suitors, and you wanted me to object to every one of them."

Philip cleared his throat and looked away. "I have no idea what you're talking about."

"Don't you?" It all made sense now. Philip *wanted* him to see how unfit these men were. He wanted Alexander to be repulsed. And then he wanted him to play the mighty protector and rescue Francie from the clutches of the would-be villains. Very clever. The only question left was Francie's part in this little plan. Was she aware of it? Is that why she'd allowed him such liberties with her sweet body? Was she trying to trap him into marriage?

"Alex?" The earl's gruff voice interrupted his thoughts. "What are you talking about?"

"Just tell me one thing, Philip," he said, crossing his arms over his chest. "Does Francie know you've been scheming? Is she part of all this?"

"No!" He shook his head. "No," he repeated on a softer note. "And I'm not scheming," he added. "I was only trying to make you see the obvious."

"Which is?" Alexander asked, trying to control the anger in his voice.

"You and Francie belong together."

The words hit Alexander with the same force as the blows he'd delivered to Crayton earlier. He pushed back the image of Francie's tinkling laughter and sweet smile. He fought the vision of her pale breasts, full and ripe in his hands. *No*, he told himself. They did not belong together. They could not belong together.

"You know my opinion of marriage, Philip," he said, his words blunt and precise. "I've never pretended to want a wife."

"You're not your father."

Alexander ignored him. "I am responsible for myself. Period. I enjoy my life. I have no title so there is no pressure to find a wife and produce an heir."

The earl scoffed. "That is not the only reason to marry."

"Oh?" Alexander lifted a brow. "Do tell, Philip. Why *do* people marry? I've often wondered."

"For companionship. For stability." Philip cleared his throat. "To produce extensions of themselves through children." His voice lowered. "And for love."

"That's odd," Alexander said, letting out a harsh laugh. "Love didn't enter into most of the unions I've witnessed. Those couples married for quite different reasons." He held out a hand and ticked off his fingers as he spoke. "Land, money, titles, heirs, security. Perhaps, love of those things, but certainly not of each other."

"Why are you so jaded? Can't you just for a minute consider the possibility of marriage?"

"No."

"Why?" Philip's words were filled with sadness and a hint of disappointment.

"I can't." Alexander shoved his hands in his pockets. Why did they have to have this conversation now? Why couldn't Philip just accept his word and stop digging around, looking for answers that were only going to upset him? He sighed. Fine. If the old man wanted answers, he'd get them, but he wasn't going to like what he heard. "I won't take a wife because I don't ever want to look in someone else's eyes and see disillusionment or failure. And I won't bring children into this world to be at the mercy of two individuals who may or may not show common decency toward one another or their children."

Silence filled the night, wrapped itself around them, as he waited for Philip's response. When he spoke, his voice was soft, his words gentle. "You and Francie care for one another. She's full of love. Let her shower you with it. Let her teach you how to love."

Alexander shook his head. "Love? You're the only one who's ever shown me love. I wouldn't know how to love a woman. To care so much you think your life will end if you can't see her smile, hear her voice, feel her touch? I've never loved a woman like that." He drew in a deep breath. "Nor do I want to."

Philip swiped at his eyes. "Sometimes it happens whether you want it to or not. That's what living is all about, Alex. Cherishing those moments when she does smile, when her voice is filled with laughter. When love shines in her eyes and her touch is for you alone." He sniffed. "That makes it worth the risk."

"Not for me, it doesn't," Alexander said.

"Those are only words and they won't stop what's in your heart. You'll see, Alex. One day, you'll see exactly what I mean."

FRANCIE SAT cross-legged in the middle of the bed, staring at the door. It was half past two-o'clock in the morning and she still hadn't heard Alexander's footsteps traveling past her door on the way to his room. Where was he? Had he left with Lady Printon? Was he spending the night with her?

A sinking feeling settled in her stomach like a ball of dough that refuses to rise. She tucked her toes under her batiste nightgown, battling visions of Alexander's strong fingers moving over Lady Printon's well-endowed body. Was he touching her the way he'd touched Francie tonight? Giving her the same pleasure? Heat shot through her like a fire gone wild as she recalled every detail of their encounter. His hands pressing her to him, his manhood moving against her, his mouth at her breasts. She shuddered. And his tongue...oh, yes, his tongue... exploring, plundering her most private parts, shattering her into a million fragments of pleasure and ecstasy. She trembled again and wrapped her arms around herself.

Dear Lord, what happened out there this evening, in the blackness of night, against the rough bark of an old elm tree? And what would happen now? Her gaze darted to the crumpled gold and burgundy gown hanging in the corner, the jagged little snags and tears on the left side serving as a reminder of her narrow escape from Jared Crayton. She glanced at the bodice, which dipped low, even more so when it hung from a hanger with nothing to hold it up, and remembered Alexander pulling the fabric down, exposing her breasts, lowering his dark head.

Francie squeezed her eyes shut but memories of the evening still invaded her brain.

She heard a noise on the stairs and her eyes flew open. Alexander was coming. Francie stilled her ragged breathing and listened. Nothing but a quiet, insistent scratching on the door. She bounded off the cream counterpane and threw it open. Mr. Pib stared back at her, his wide gray eyes flecked with gold. He flicked his caramel tail in the air and walked past her, rubbing against her leg.

"You little devil," she whispered, closing the door behind him. "How did you get in here? You're supposed to be in the barn."

The cat jumped on the bed, turned around three times, and curled himself into a tight ball.

"If Alexander finds out about this, he'll string you up by your tail." She crawled onto the bed and rubbed Mr. Pib behind the ears. "But lucky for you, I believe he's not home tonight."

Saying the words out loud, even if only to her cat, made Francie miserable. He'd gone to his mistress. She'd tormented herself with those thoughts for the last three hours. Perhaps it was time to find out if they were true.

Before she could reconsider her actions, Francie grabbed her robe and headed for the door. If he were still at Drakemoor, he'd be in his study. Not with his mistress. Her heart skipped three beats as she hurried down the winding staircase, her bare feet padding a muted staccato. She reached the bottom of the stairs and slowed, turning toward Alexander's study.

What if she found him in there? What would she say? *I want to understand what happened tonight? Why did you pretend to ignore me at the ball and yet you knew my every move? Or perhaps, a confession of her own would be in order. My heart broke every time I saw you and Lady Printon in each other's arms. I want you to smile at me the way you smiled at her.*

I think I'm falling in love with you.

She gasped. *No.* She pushed the thought away. Loving a man like Alexander Bishop would bring nothing but heartache. Nothing at all, she reminded herself as she turned the knob of his study and peeked inside.

George barked twice, his golden eyes glowing in the semi-darkness. He lay in the middle of the Aubusson rug, his tan coat blending into it. Next to him was a long scrap of white cloth. When he saw the intruder was only Francie, his tail thumped three times and he plopped his head between his paws.

"What is it, boy?" Alexander's voice came to her from across the room. He sounded strange, as though he'd just woken up and was still groggy. "Nothing? Good boy." She heard a clunk. "Good...boy."

She slipped through the door and closed it behind her.

George's ears perked up at the click, but he settled again, his golden eyes following her.

"What a mess, George," Alexander said. Did she detect a slight slur in his words? "What a goddddd...damned mess."

Francie inched closer. Alexander lay sprawled in his chair, eyes closed, one hand clutching a decanter, the other a glass. His hair stuck straight up as though he'd run his hands through it several times. But it was his manner of dress, or lack thereof, that held her mesmerized. The ever-proper, ever-meticulous Alexander Bishop had discarded his cravat, which explained the white cloth at George's feet, and ripped his shirt open to reveal a mat of black, curly chest hair. A coil of heat sprang from deep inside Francie and wrapped itself around her tighter and tighter until she found it hard to breathe.

"Gooodddd damned mess," Alexander repeated, opening his eyes to tiny slits. He leaned forward and lifted the decanter, pouring a healthy swallow into the glass. Liquid sloshed over the sides and onto the desk and floor. "Hmmmph," he muttered, squinting at the glass. He lifted it and threw it back in one gulp.

Well, at least now she knew he hadn't gone to Lady Printon's. Francie inched backward. Perhaps she'd let him alone to his drink and his "goddamned mess."

"Philip doesn't know what he's talking about," he mumbled.

Philip? Francie crept forward three steps.

"It would never work." He shook his dark head. "Never, George. Not now." He lifted the decanter to his lips. "Not tomorrow." He took a drink. "Not ever." He wiped his mouth with the back of his hand. "But she's so damned beautiful."

Who?

"That hair. The color of..." He rubbed his jaw. "Of what? Hmmm, let me think."

Francie touched a stray curl. *Whose hair?* She held her breath, taking tiny steps closer.

Alexander's lips curved into a half-smile. "Of course, that's it," he said, his head resting against the back of his chair, his eyes still closed. "Hair the color of—"

"Ooooph!" Francie's foot hit the leg of the chair and she lost her balance, toppling head first onto the plump cushions of his favorite green chair.

"What the—" Alexander blurted out, his eyes flashing open. He darted around the desk so fast she thought she'd imagined his earlier inebriated state. "What the hell are you doing here?"

Alexander towered over her, hands on hips, the scar on his face white with anger. Francie pushed out of the chair in the most ladylike fashion she could muster.

"Answer me. What, may I ask, are you doing here, at this hour?" He pointed a finger at her robe. "Dressed like that?" His speech was perfect, enunciated with clarity and form. What had happened to the man who'd been slurring his words a few moments ago? She wished *he'd* come back. He seemed so much more approachable.

"I...was...worried about you," she managed, clutching her middle and training her eyes on George. Dogs were such fortunate creatures. They needn't get involved in things like relationships or worry about saying too much or too little. A couple of feisty barks, a little wag of the tail, and a spot by their master was all they required.

"Worried about me?" he repeated, crossing his arms over his broad chest. "How charming."

She tried not to notice the dark mat of hair or the tiny spiral ending in a V at his trousers. Her face heated with the thought of *not* thinking about it.

"Yes, well," Francie said. "I didn't hear you come up and I

thought perhaps you'd fallen asleep somewhere." *Like Lady Printon's.*

His dark brows pulled together in a straight line. "You were checking up on me?"

"No!" she said, denying the truth. "Why would I do such a thing?"

He cocked his head to one side and studied her, his silver eyes narrowed, his mouth turned down at the corners. "Why indeed?" he mused.

It was odd to see him in this state of undress and dishevelment, and yet, his mussed hair and open shirt seemed to fit him better than the starched, buttoned-up lifestyle he insisted upon.

Francie took a step backward. "Well, now that I know you're fine and not in danger of getting all crumpled..." She blushed, looking at his bare chest again. "I mean, now that I know you're here..." She shook her head. "No, that's not what I meant." She twisted her fingers in front of her. "Of course, you'd be here." Her gaze skirted around him, settling on George. "Where else would you be?" The next words flew out of her mouth so fast, she couldn't stop them. "Unless you were with Lady Printon."

She gasped and clamped her hand over her mouth.

"I see," Alexander said.

She inched her hand away from her mouth, one finger at a time. "And that would be none of my affair," she blurted out.

"No. It wouldn't be."

Heat rushed to her cheeks. She had to get away. Now, before she opened her mouth again and made some other totally ridiculous statement.

"Lady Printon is a very beautiful woman," Alexander said.

Francie pushed past the agony in her heart and murmured, "Yes, she is." Of course, she was beautiful. But did he have to announce it in front of her as though she couldn't discern the fact from a mere glance?

"She's a woman who presents herself well, as a true lady, regardless of title or distinction," he continued.

What he meant was she didn't run around barefoot or try to steal his breeches for riding.

"And she possesses a most agreeable temperament," he went on in an even tone.

She wouldn't dare disagree or raise her voice to him was more like it. Unlike herself, who spoke her mind at every turn.

"Who has no contrived expectations of what a relationship should be."

She would permit him other women.

"Any man would be proud to be with her."

She'd heard enough about Lady Printon, the perfect woman Francie would never be. The one Alexander really wanted. "Good," she bit out, meeting his silver gaze. "I hope you'll both be very happy." She had to get out of here before the tears started. And they would, once she accepted the fact that what happened under the elm tree tonight meant nothing to him. *She meant nothing to him.* Francie yanked the door open and ran down the hall.

Alexander stared at the spot where she'd stood just moments ago. "But that's the problem, Francie," he whispered, his voice ragged and filled with anguish. "I'm not happy. Not anymore." He ran a hand through his hair and closed his eyes. "Not without you."

16

Alexander heard the scream from somewhere deep in his brain, a piercing shriek that went on and on. No beginning. No end. He tried to rouse himself from his slumber, wanting to make it stop. *Dear God, make it stop.*

He blinked his eyes open. He was in his study, still dressed in evening clothes, shirt wide open, jacket discarded, trousers wrinkled, reeking of whiskey. And a head pounding almost loud enough to block out that infernal screaming.

He shot out of his chair. The high-pitched wailing that filled the air belonged to Francie. He bound out of the study and up the stairs, following the sound to Philip's room. Dread poured through him as he pushed open the door.

Francie knelt at Philip's feet, her slender fingers wrapped around one of her father's big hands, her cheek resting on it. Her eyes were closed, her face streaked with tears that fell unheeded onto her pale yellow gown. The screams tempered to a whimper, like a wounded animal alone in the wild with no hope for survival.

Alexander edged into the room, moving toward her and the man he'd thought of as father. His chest tightened, like someone squeezing hard with both hands, forcing every ounce of emotion from him. Pain ripped through him, gouging great holes in his heart.

The earl sat in a chair in full evening attire, eyes closed, a hint of a smile upon his pale face.

Alexander needn't touch his skin to know it would be colder than the first frost. And he needn't lay a hand on the old man's heart to know it no longer beat.

The Earl of Montrose was dead.

Alexander pinched the bridge of his nose and tried to gather his wits. He wished he was shaved and wearing fresh clothing instead of the rumpled, whiskey-soaked attire he had on. It reminded him of his father, of his heritage. Philip would have been disappointed if he knew the day Alexander found him dead, he looked and smelled like a drunk.

"Jesus."

Francie's head shot up, tears shining in her sky-blue eyes. "He's...dead," she blurted out.

"I know," he said, feeling stupid and inadequate.

"I...I...never got to say goodbye." More tears fell, trailing their way down her pale cheeks.

"I know," Alexander said again, thinking of the last time he and Philip were together. It was as close to a fight as they'd ever been. And it had all centered on Francie. Guilt tore at him, made him wish he hadn't been so damned harsh with the old man.

"Excuse me, sir, so sorry to interrupt." James stood in the doorway, white as paste, foot suspended as though he were too stunned to engage in that infernal tapping he insisted upon. His gaze darted from Philip to Francie and settled in the vicinity of Alexander's forehead. He cleared his throat twice and said, "Shall I call for Dr. Wellings?"

The bearded, bespectacled physician had guided Philip

through bouts of illness on many an occasion, but he would not achieve success this time. Still, the physician should attend him. Alexander nodded. "Yes. Instruct the rest of the staff we are to be left alone until Dr. Wellings's arrival."

"Yes, sir."

"And James, thank you."

"You are very welcome, sir." James backed up three steps and pulled the door shut. Alexander turned to Francie. "I'm so sorry."

"We'd only just started to know one another," Francie whispered. "After all this time. And now he's gone." She laid her head against her father's chair, still clutching his limp hand, her red-gold hair cascading about her like a blanket. He wanted to take her in his arms and promise her all would be well, she would never feel this kind of pain again. But he wouldn't because he knew he could never shield her from the agonizing heartache of loving and losing someone. The only protection was a wall of indifference, one she would never subscribe to but Alexander knew well.

He'd built his own wall out of grief and desolation one wretched brick at a time, and no one had ever breached it.

His chest tightened.

Except Philip.

≈

"FOR GOD'S SAKE, Claire, they just buried Montrose three weeks ago." Edgar Ashcroft frowned at his daughter. "At least, give the ground time to settle before you start after Bishop again."

Claire pulled at a long, black curl and released it, watching it spring out of her fingers. "I am not in the habit of waiting, as you well know, Father." She thought of Alexander Bishop's narrow hips and broad chest. "Besides, I might be just the diversion he needs after all the gloom circling Drakemoor."

The earl scratched his chin and mused, "Perhaps. Perhaps not." He leveled his ice-blue eyes on his daughter. "Bishop may already have a 'diversion'. Right under his own roof."

"What are you implying?" She knew, even before he said the name.

"Why, Francie Jordan, of course." He leaned back in his chair and crossed his hands over his stomach. "Quite cozy, I'd say. He can bid her goodnight like a proper gentleman and then sneak into her bed when the rest of the house is asleep."

"She's probably no better than a whore." Alexander would *never* do that.

"Claire! That is no language for a woman of your breeding. Besides, what could you possibly know of such things?"

She shifted in her chair, intent on smoothing out a wrinkle in her lavender gown. *Whore.* She knew the word well, had even been called it a few times by angry lovers. "I'm sorry, Father. I've heard the groomsmen use the word once or twice."

"I'll fire the lot of them," he snapped.

"No!" She didn't want to lose the sixteen-year-old boy she'd been sneaking out to see in the middle of the night. Nicholas. What he lacked in experience, he made up in other ways. Just a few flicks of her finger or tongue had him hard and throbbing three or four times in a row. She grew wet just thinking about him. No, she wouldn't let her father take him away. Not yet.

"Why such an allegiance to the hired help?" the earl asked, a thread of suspicion in his voice.

Claire cast him a furtive smile. "They meant no harm." Her smile widened. "They didn't even know of my presence." *Not until I lifted my skirts and slid out of my pantaloons.*

"Very well," he said, dismissing the subject with a wave of his hand. "But I want no more talk of that sort coming from your lips. You are a young lady of fine and proper breeding. An Ashcroft. With our name come certain duties and responsibilities."

"Yes, Father."

"Now, what is this infernal talk about Alexander Bishop?" he demanded. "And what do you think is going to come of it?"

"I'm going to marry him." *And ravish his delicious body.*

"What?"

Claire sat up in her chair, folded her hands in her lap, and met her father's cold stare. "I'm going to marry him," she said with the conviction of a saint confessing his belief in God.

"Have you gone mad?"

She shook her head, enjoying the feel of her thick hair swirling down her back. Alexander would like her hair, too. All the men did. "I'm not mad, Father," she said in a low, sweet voice. "Not at all. I am captivated by Alexander Bishop and I intend to marry him."

"He's a stable boy," her father bit out.

"He's a very wealthy man with more manners than most members of the ton," she countered. "And, he is very well respected in matters of business and finance." She tilted her head to one side. "The stock market is his specialty. Think of the possibilities, Father. He could help you triple your wealth." Talk of money would entice him. Everyone knew money was Edgar Ashcroft's grand mistress.

"Hmmm." The earl scratched his head. "Triple, you say?" His thin lips spread into a slow smile.

Claire giggled and bound out of her chair. "Thank you, Father. Thank you." She threw her arms around his neck and planted a big kiss on his cheek.

The earl's smiled broadened as he smoothed his hand over her hair. "If you really want this Bishop fellow for a husband," he whispered, "I'll get him for you. Trust me. I'll get him for you."

~

ALEXANDER STARED at the ledgers in front of him. He'd counted the same column five times and come up with five different answers. Damn. He pushed the book away, closed his eyes, and rested his head against the soft cushions of his chair.

What the hell was wrong with him? He couldn't think straight, couldn't concentrate, and couldn't sleep. Hadn't been able to for the past two days, ever since the solicitor paid him a visit.

He'd read the contents of the will several times, with and without benefit of whiskey. The words always came out the same, sometimes a little fuzzy or blurred, but always the same. Damn, Philip. What had he been trying to prove? What in the name of all that was holy was he going to do?

A soft rap on the door disturbed him from his thoughts. "Come in," he called in a weary voice.

He heard the click of the door closing, heard the footsteps shuffling across the room and stop beside his desk. "Hello, Bernard," he said, pinching the bridge of his nose. He was so damn tired.

"Alexander," Bernard's quiet voice soothed him. "You wanted to see me?"

Alexander opened his eyes and stared at the old man standing before him, so calm and peaceful. What he wouldn't give right now for a little slice of tranquility. Just one tiny sliver, like in the old days.

Before Francie.

"Sit down, Bernard. I need your help."

The old man sat in the chair across from Alexander's desk,

his eyes watchful from behind gold spectacles. "What can I do for you, my boy?"

"It seems Philip played a great joke on me. Unfortunately, I find no humor in the jest." He drummed his fingers on the desk and emphasized, "None at all."

Bernard stroked his beard. "Joke?" he repeated, and Alexander heard the wariness in his voice. "What sort of joke?"

"I had a visit from his solicitor the other day. A Mr. Barnes. Wiry little fellow with the personality of a pebble. He informed me one-half of Philip's estate is mine and the other half belongs to Francie."

"That seems fair."

"I thought so, too." Alexander pinned him with a cold stare and continued, "Until he told me the provisions under which I am to receive my share."

"Provisions?"

"I must marry Francie in order to get my half. Should I refuse, I lose all claim to Drakemoor."

"*What?*"

Apparently, the contents of the will proved as much a surprise to Bernard as they had to Alexander.

"Marry her or lose all hold to Drakemoor," Alexander bit out. His stomach churned just thinking about leaving.

"What are you going to do?"

Alexander shrugged. "I don't want to marry Francie. Or anyone," he added. "Nor do I want to give up Drakemoor."

"I see."

"Philip has left me in a damn fine predicament. Marry his daughter or get booted out of my home."

"It may not prove as simple as that."

Simple? The situation was anything but simple. "What are you talking about?"

Bernard cleared his throat and fixed his gaze on Alexander.

When the older man looked at him with his gray eyes narrowed to half-slits and his head tilted to the right at a slight angle, Alexander felt as though he were being studied, like an insect under a magnifying glass. Close careful scrutiny before systematic dismemberment for the express purpose of analysis. He tugged at his cravat and shifted in his chair.

"The choice may not be yours to make," Bernard said.

"Why not?" How could it not be his?

Bernard hesitated. "Eleanor wants to return to Amberden. She misses her home, her garden." He lifted his hands in an expansive gesture. "She misses her life. As do I."

"That's understandable," Alexander said.

"Francie wants to return with us."

The words struck him square in the gut, stealing his breath. Francie leave Drakemoor? He'd planned on both of them residing there, with Eleanor and Bernard present to keep the gossipmongers at bay.

He tried to suck in a gulp of air but only managed a few feeble gasps. "She can't leave." *If she leaves, I'll never see her again.*

"I agree," Bernard said. "She can't return to Amberden. She deserves better. Now that she's seen this world, the world she was born to, she can't go back," he said, sadness spilling from his voice. "I won't let her go back." His gray gaze pierced Alexander. "But I won't let her reputation be jeopardized by staying in this house with you."

"Well, I'm sure as hell not leaving," Alexander bit out.

"I don't expect you to leave." Bernard sat back in his chair and stroked his beard. "There were several very attentive young men at the ball. I understand at least fifteen calling cards arrived the next morning."

"Actually, seventeen."

"Better yet. Seventeen would-be suitors. Under the circumstances, it will be understood if Francie forgoes the usual mourning period and chooses a husband posthaste."

Alexander's jaw twitched. "You'd let her select a husband from that group of imbeciles?"

Bernard shrugged. "They're all well-bred young men."

"They're all misfits in evening clothes," Alexander spat out. "You're supposed to care about Francie, look out for her as a father. How could you even consider letting one of them get close to her, let alone put a slimy hand on her? If you do that, you may as well have turned her over to Jared Crayton. She'll suffer the same death with all of them, though some will be a little swifter than others."

The older man cocked a brow but said nothing.

"What?" Alexander demanded, annoyed with himself for revealing more than he'd intended. What had he just revealed anyway? He needed to clear his head and figure it out. Then he'd feel more in control. More like his old self.

"And you have no desire to wed Francie yourself?" Bernard asked.

"Of course not. Why?"

"You just gave a very passionate account of why Francie shouldn't marry any one of seventeen suitors. It does make me wonder if they are all as flawed as you say they are."

"They're worse."

"So you say. I'm wondering, though, Alexander, if there's not one possibility in seventeen young men, will there be any in twenty-seven or fifty-seven?" He smiled. "Somehow, I think not."

"That's not true." Alexander tried to deny what he was beginning to wonder himself. "If the right man presented himself, I'd consider his qualifications."

"Consider his qualifications?" Bernard repeated.

"Yes. And render my opinion on whether I felt him suitable or not."

"I see. Most judicious of you."

"I thought so."

"There is one other gentleman I had in mind. A well-respected young man of means. You know him. Name's Sebastian Trent."

"Sebastian?" Alexander said, leaning forward in his chair, fingers splayed wide on the smooth surface of his cherry desk. *"My neighbor?"*

Bernard nodded. "We had quite a nice little conversation the other day when he came to pay his respects. I'm not certain where you were, but since you weren't at home, Francie and I entertained him." The older man paused. "He was quite taken with her, apologized for not attending the ball. Seems he was away on business, but he looked as though he wished he hadn't been. He even asked if he might call on her after an appropriate fashion."

Alexander's jaw started twitching. "What did you say?" He tried to keep his voice even, as though Bernard hadn't just dumped a boulder on his chest.

"I told him the decision would be up to Francie, but I saw no reason why she wouldn't agree." He pushed his glasses up on his nose and stared at Alexander. "Do you?"

Alexander shifted in his chair. Sebastian Trent—tall, handsome, next in line for an earldom, with an easy smile and an even easier disposition. He'd worship Francie, give her everything she desired. He'd be the perfect husband. Alexander's fingers pressed into the hard wood of his desk.

Sebastian and Francie. *Husband and wife.*

"Alexander?"

"No." One word, powerful enough to change lives, alter destinies.

"No?"

"No," he repeated, his voice stronger. "He can't marry her."

"Marry her?" Bernard asked. "He only asked to call on her."

"Hah!" Alexander let out a harsh laugh. "But that's where this is headed, isn't it, Bernard?"

The older man gave him an odd look. "Yes, eventually, if they both suit. What would be wrong in that?"

What would be wrong in that? Everything. Every God-blessed thing would be wrong with that.

"Sebastian can't marry Francie." Alexander spoke with the firm authority of one who does not expect resistance.

"And why not?" Bernard asked, equally assertive in his demand for an answer.

Alexander glared at him. "Because," he began, his mouth flattening into a thin line, "she'd drive him to Bedlam within the week. What do you think will happen when she totes her entourage of animals with her? Do you think Sebastian will be as lenient as I've been when George deposits himself on his rug? And what about Mr. Pib and Miss Penelope? They spend as much time in this house as out and don't think I haven't noticed," he said, shaking a finger at Bernard. "I see the small, dark hairs on my chairs and I know it's that blasted cat. And that rabbit was hopping down the hall one morning when Francie thought I was out. Oh, yes, I saw him all right." He crossed his arms over his broad chest. "I chose not to say anything, because I didn't want to upset her so soon after Philip's death. But I've been watching."

"Perhaps the gentleman is an animal lover," Bernard offered.

Alexander snorted. "*I'm* an animal lover, but my love for them remains outside. It does not extend into the walls of my home."

"Francie does get attached to her animals," Bernard conceded.

"Attached? I'm surprised she hasn't snuck them to her room."

Bernard cleared his throat and shot a glance in George's direction.

"Bernard?" Alexander said. "She hasn't, has she?"

The older man shifted in his chair, re-crossed his right leg over his left, and coughed. "Only once or twice."

"So she brought the barnyard into her bedroom?"

Bernard shrugged. "She considers them family."

"I'm certain Sebastian will be impressed with her 'family'," Alexander said. "Especially when he finds out he'll be sharing a bed with them."

"Perhaps she'll have to reconsider."

Alexander grunted. "Perhaps," he said, making no effort to hide the sarcasm in his voice. "And what will happen when she prances through the hallway without stockings and slippers? And what do you think Sebastian will say when she steals a pair of his breeches to ride bareback?" He actually snorted again. "Do you think he'll be impressed? Intrigued? Understanding?" He didn't wait for an answer. "No, he'll be ready to wring her beautiful little neck. And then he'll send her right back here."

Bernard scratched his head and frowned. "That could pose quite a problem. Not to mention the disgrace."

"Exactly," Alexander said, his lips curving up at the ends. "The entire idea of Sebastian and Francie needs to die. Here." He jabbed a finger on his desk. "In this room."

"But what about Francie? She seemed quite taken with him."

"No," Alexander repeated, frowning. "She's not marrying him."

"And he seemed quite taken with her," Bernard said as though he hadn't heard Alexander. "If two people love each other, they can overcome great differences." He nodded, as though deep in thought. "Love is the key."

Alexander's heart jumped to his throat. He didn't want to hear any more of this rubbish about Francie and Sebastian Trent. Didn't want either of their names connected with the word *love*. They were not going to further their association with one another in any form, casual or otherwise. A vision of Francie and Sebastian in each other's arms, her head resting on his broad chest flitted through his mind, tearing his insides. Francie and Sebastian? Never.

Not if Alexander had anything to say about it.

"Once Sebastian discovers his love for Francie," Bernard continued, "I am quite positive he'll overlook her little peculiarities. He may even find them charming."

Alexander's jaw twitched. Twice. "Too bad he's not going to get the opportunity," he ground out.

"He's not?"

"No." Alexander leaned forward, resting his elbows on his desk. "Because *I'm* going to marry Francie."

"I see." The words seeped out in a single breath of understanding.

But he doubted Bernard understood. How could he, when Alexander didn't comprehend the reasons himself? He didn't know what force drove him to utter the words he'd vowed only moments ago never to speak.

All he knew was he couldn't bear the thought of Sebastian Trent's—or any other man's—hands on Francie. Bernard was right. Seventeen or fifty-seven suitors would still be unacceptable.

Alexander pushed back his chair. "I'm going to find Francie," he said, walking around to the side of his desk. "I want to tell her my decision." The sooner he talked to her, the sooner she'd get used to the idea.

A twinge of unrest settled over him. He hoped she wasn't going to give him a difficult time and insist on returning to Amberden, or worse yet, expect declarations of love or any other such nonsense.

"Good luck, Alexander," Bernard said, a hint of a smile peeking through his beard.

Alexander nodded, his expression grim and unsmiling. He was already thinking of his encounter with Francie as he strode toward the door, praying just this once she'd employ reason and not emotion.

Bernard waited until the door clicked back into place. Then he threw back his head and let the laughter roll through his body. "You would've been proud of me, Philip," he whispered. "You might have laid the groundwork, but I got him to propose."

17

Francie buried her face deeper into the soft blanket. The fresh smell of grass mingled with the heady fragrance of roses wrapped their scent around her, pulling her deeper into memories of her childhood. She'd spent many a summer day lying on a blanket with Aunt Eleanor and sometimes even Uncle Bernard, surrounded by solitude and flowers, daydreaming about a sea of tomorrows. All of them included a man who would duel for her and die to save her life and her honor. Kind, considerate, doting, and thoughtful, enamored not only of her physical beauty but of her spirit as well.

One who loved her beyond all reason.

Images of a tall, dark, brooding man more prone to caustic remarks than caresses filled her mind. In all of her childhood fantasies, she'd never once considered falling in love with a man like Alexander Bishop. Not even for a fleeting moment. She rolled onto her back and shielded her eyes from the hot sun. How had it happened? How had she been so foolish as to fall in love with him?

She'd stopped fooling herself the night of the ball, when Alexander all but admitted his feelings for Lady Printon. She remembered how his full lips moved as he spoke the words that cut her heart, made it bleed in pain and loss. *Lady Printon is a very beautiful woman...who has no contrived expectations of what a relationship should be...any man would be proud to be with her.*

She'd escaped to her room and cried until there were no tears left. She loved a man who would never love her. The next morning, when she found her father dead, she cried again and let love's anguish roll over her, blanketing her in its merciless embrace. To lose one's father and one's heart in the span of a sunset and a sunrise was almost unbearable. Yet she pushed through each day, finding solace in her garden as she toiled in the earth.

Thankfully, Aunt Eleanor and Uncle Bernard were there to comfort and protect, though she dared not disclose the pain caused by Alexander Bishop. It was humiliating enough to admit such a truth to herself but to share the disgrace with her aunt and uncle would be so much worse. Her feelings for Alexander must remain her secret, locked away until she left Drakemoor five days hence.

"Francie, wake up." It was *him.*

"Alexander?" She opened her eyes and shielded them with one hand as she stared at the tall figure before her.

"I need to speak with you."

She pushed herself to a sitting position and crossed her feet at the ankles. "Is something wrong?"

"Why isn't your hat on your head?" he demanded. "Your face is bright pink. And look at your arms. You'll be redder than those roses if you don't get out of this infernal heat."

"I love the sun," Francie said in a calm tone. Five more days of Drakemoor and Alexander and she'd be gone. She was not going to spend them arguing, no matter how much he tempted her.

"You'll see how much you love it when you're full of blisters and sick from too much heat," he ground out. "Your skin is too sensitive to be exposed to the sun."

"Do I hear concern in your voice, Alexander?"

He yanked at his cravat. "I just hate to see you make a fool of yourself. If you get sick, you'll make more work for Bernard and Eleanor. And," he added, "you might be ill on the carpets."

"What a touching thought."

"Let's go inside. I'm burning alive." He loosened his cravat a bit more.

Francie busied herself gathering up her things. "You wear too many clothes."

"Excuse me?"

The heat rushing to her face had nothing to do with the sun. "Wouldn't it be acceptable to forego the jacket and cravat on a blistering day like today?"

He shrugged. "I usually stay inside when it's this hot."

She stood and retrieved the blanket. "But you needn't," she said, her voice soft. "Even if you left those items inside, you'd still be a proper gentleman."

She watched his eyes narrow, his scar whiten. "I am well aware of what constitutes a proper gentleman."

Five more days, she reminded herself. *Hold onto your temper*. "Of course you are. I was merely suggesting from a woman's point of view."

Alexander shot her a sideways glance but said nothing. Tiny beads of sweat trickled along his brow, ran down the side of his cheeks. He grabbed the blanket from her and headed for the house. "Let's go."

Francie scampered after him, the grass warm and velvety between her toes. Did she really love this hard, implacable beast of a man? She sighed. Unfortunately, she did.

James opened the door, tapping and twitching as they passed.

"Good day, Miss Jordan, Mr. Bishop," he squeaked. "Quite warm weather we're having."

Alexander grunted and headed toward the study.

Francie smiled at the odd little man and stopped a moment. "Yes, James. It is quite hot." She leaned closer and whispered, "I think you'd be much more comfortable without your jacket. I'll speak with Mr. Bishop about it."

The butler's eyes widened, whether with fear or incredulity, she couldn't tell. She turned and hurried after Alexander. When she reached the study, he was already seated behind his desk. George held his usual position on the Aubusson rug. A dark tail peeking out from behind him indicated Mr. Pib had taken up residence on it as well. She shot a quick glance at Alexander. Had he seen the cat? He appeared preoccupied with the papers on his desk, so he might not have taken notice. Yet. But he would and she hoped to be long gone from this room when he did.

Why had he called her here? He seemed more serious than usual, if that were possible.

"A solicitor visited the other day regarding Philip's will," he began, picking up the papers he'd been studying a moment ago.

Francie remained silent. Her father had tried several times to discuss his wealth and what would happen to it in the event of his death, but she'd always managed to change the subject. He'd finally given up with a grunt and an assurance she'd never need worry about money again.

"You and I will each receive one half of Philip's estate." He took a deep breath and his jaw twitched a fraction before he added, "including Drakemoor."

She heard the words, understood the generosity behind her father's dictates, but all she felt was a big, empty gap where for a brief moment in time her life had entwined with his. She'd forfeit her entire inheritance if only she could see him one more time. But there would be no other opportunities, no second chances. Her father was dead and she was living in a house with a man who loved another woman. It was time to leave.

"Francie? Did you hear me?"

She nodded. "I'm leaving in five days." She lifted her gaze to meet his, expecting to see relief spread over his dark features.

"Like hell you are," Alexander growled. "You're not going anywhere."

That response she had not expected. "I plan to return to Amberden."

He bound out of his chair and shot around the desk.

Francie lowered her gaze. He would not see the pain in her eyes. "Aunt Eleanor and Uncle Bernard are going home." She picked at a speck of dirt on her gown. "I'm going with them."

"You're staying here," he said, towering over her.

Her head shot up. "I can't stay here."

He crossed his arms over his chest and studied her. "Philip wanted you here. You know that. How many times did he tell you that you belonged here?"

"I'm not a noblewoman," she whispered, shaking her head. "Nor do I have any desire to become one."

"Nobility isn't unique to bloodlines. You made Philip proud to call you his daughter." Alexander's voice dipped. "Honor his request and live in the society you were born to." His voice fell even lower. "It's what Philip wanted."

She squeezed her eyes shut. Her father asked too much. "Next you're going to tell me you've selected a husband for me, too." She let out a shaky laugh and opened her eyes to find him staring at her.

"As a matter of fact, I have."

How ironic. The man she loved had chosen a husband for her. "I don't want a husband."

He took a step toward her, closing the distance between them to less than two feet. Too close. "It doesn't matter," he said in a sharp voice. "You need one."

"I need one? That's the most ridiculous thing I've ever heard."

"You'll get used to the idea," he said, ignoring her remarks.

The man was mad. Truly mad. "Who, might I ask, is my intended? Do I know him?"

"Yes. You know him rather well."

"I do?" Curiosity got the better of her. "Do I like him?"

"No. Not particularly."

"You want me to marry a man I don't particularly like?" The man really was mad. "Why would I consent to such a thing?"

Alexander's lips twitched. He seemed to enjoy her aggravation. "Because you desire him."

Heat flooded her cheeks. "And how would you know that?"

He closed the distance between them and reached for her hands, pulling her to her feet. "Because I'm that man," he said, lowering his head to brush his lips against hers.

His words registered in her brain a second before she gave herself up to his kiss. "No!" She pulled from his grasp. "I can't marry you."

"Can't?" His mouth flattened into a thin line, the scar on his cheek white and puffy.

Francie backed away toward the door. How could she marry him, live with him, bear his children, knowing he loved another? "No," she said, shaking her head. "I can't." She took another step backward.

"Be reasonable, Francie. I'm the most logical choice."

"You...you're supposed to be my brother," she blurted out, grasping the first thought that popped into her head.

"We're no more brother and sister than Adam and Eve." He took a step toward her, and then another, and another until he was so close she smelled his spicy scent. "You know that, don't you, Francie?"

She stared at him, held by the soft, trance-like rhythm of his voice, moving over her, softer than a caress. It would be so easy to lose herself in his touch. So deliciously easy. He reached out to stroke her cheek.

But he loved another. "Aren't there any other suitors?"

His hand dropped to his side and he took several deep breaths before he spoke. "There were no others."

"No one called on me after the ball?" she asked. "Not even Lord Grosepeak?" She'd consider him as a marriage partner. After all, he couldn't break her heart and there was something to be said for that.

"No one."

"Oh." Her heart sank. "What about Sebastian Trent?"

His gaze narrowed. "No."

Her shoulders drooped forward in defeat. Now she'd be forced to marry Alexander and he was only asking her out of duty. He probably intended to keep Lady Printon as his mistress. Francie's stomach lurched at the thought.

"Is marriage to me so objectionable?" he asked, his nostrils flaring, his jaw set in a hard line. "Are you above marrying a stable boy?"

"No!" she said, horrified he'd think such a thing. "It's not that at all." Why not tell him the truth? Or at least part of the truth.

"I know you don't want to marry me," she said, her voice filled with sadness. "You're doing it out of duty to Philip." His jaw twitched and she knew it must be the truth. "I know you're in love with Lady Printon and I'm keeping you from her. I can't do that to you, Alexander."

She saw the surprise in his eyes and knew she'd done the right thing. Alexander was much too noble to put his personal desires above Philip's wishes.

"You incredible little fool," he murmured, cupping her face between his big hands. "Where on earth did you get such an idea?"

"It was obvious."

"Obviously untrue," he corrected.

She swallowed hard. "You mean you aren't in love with Lady Printon?" Her heart skipped two beats. She didn't want to breathe, didn't want to hope, and yet, she waited.

"No, Francie, I'm not in love with her. I've never been in love with Tess and I haven't been involved with her since a certain red-haired hoyden arrived at Drakemoor."

"But the night of the ball...the things you said about her..."

"Were all true," he finished. "She is a wonderful person, with beauty and breeding. And she'd make any man proud." He stroked her cheek. "But not this man."

His words sent shivers to her very fingertips. *Alexander didn't love Lady Printon!* But he'd certainly spent a lot of time with her. Doing what, she wondered. She probably didn't want to know, but something gnawed inside her, the need to know. "But what of all the nights you didn't come home until well past midnight." When she'd been watching the clock, waiting. "You weren't with her?"

He gifted her with a rare smile. "No, I wasn't with her. I was only trying to make you think I was. That blasted barn proved a most uncomfortable bedfellow."

A sliver of hope swelled inside her like a new bud reaching for the sun, waiting to burst forth into full bloom. But there was still one unanswered question, lurking in the dark corners of her mind, threatening to kill her newfound happiness. Her voice dipped to a painful whisper. "You said you'd never marry. Me or anyone. Are you certain this is what you want?"

A look very close to regret passed over his face for the briefest of seconds and then disappeared, making her wonder if she'd imagined it. When he spoke, his words were low and gentle. "I admit a short time ago marriage was not my first choice, but sometimes fate intervenes." His fingers traced the shape of her face, eased over her lips, and settled on her shoulders.

Fate! He'd trusted something other than logic and let it guide him to her. Her heart swelled with emotion and love for this most noble, most honorable man.

"What about my little habits? The ones that seem to annoy you so? Can you accept them?"

Alexander lifted a dark brow. "Are you talking about the fact you aren't wearing stockings and slippers? Or are we addressing the issue of the cat tucked under George?" He pulled her closer to him until they were almost touching. He bent his head to hers and whispered, "Or maybe we're talking about all of the undergarments you continue to forget to wear." He smiled when she gasped. "That, my dear Francie, is one quirky habit I could overlook." He planted a soft kiss on her neck. "I wouldn't mind if you wore even less under these gowns," he said, inching his fingers up her ribcage to the outline of her breasts.

Her skin tingled where he touched her through the fabric of her gown. "Oh, Alexander," she murmured, reaching up to loop her hands around his neck.

His silver gaze burned brighter than a million stars on a black night. Her heart skipped two beats as he bent his head and covered her mouth with his, his tongue probing the seam of her lips. She opened her mouth to welcome him and he pulled her closer. The ridge of his erection rested between her thighs, creating a slow, uncontrollable heat in her belly.

"You feel wonderful." Alexander plunged into her mouth again. His hands roamed her body in bold, arcing sweeps, touching, learning, possessing.

She moaned and clung to him, pressing her body into his, reveling in the sensations he aroused, sensations she didn't understand but craved like a person long starved.

Alexander inched the gown up her thigh, bunching the fabric in one hand and stroking her skin with the other. "Like velvet," he murmured against her lips. "So soft." His fingers circled the inside of her thigh. "And tantalizing," he whispered, working his way to her woman's heat. He cupped her, massaging her swollen flesh through the thin cotton of her pantaloons.

Her knees buckled and she grabbed Alexander's forearm, feeling as wobbly as a colt standing for the first time. He continued his tender assault with the flick of a finger over her nubbin. His tongue drove deep into her mouth, imitating the rhythm of his finger.

Pressure—deep, sweet, and dark—built inside her, threatening to erupt with the next stroke. Francie moaned again, torn between the pleasure of Alexander's touch and the dark, clawing agony demanding release. She reached out to cup his erection and he groaned. Encouraged, she rubbed her fingers along the hard ridge. He pushed against her hand and she felt the tip of his penis outlined against his trousers. Before she considered what she was doing, she started stroking that one little area, much as he was stroking her. *Hard, fast, flick, stroke.*

"Enough," he growled, tearing his mouth from hers. His free hand grabbed her wrist, stilling her fingers. His other hand found the opening of her pantaloons and slipped inside, one finger plunging into the very core of her womanhood. It was too much. She cried out Alexander's name as shimmering sensations tumbled over her, one jagged breath at a time, splitting her apart and hurling her into the white light of pure ecstasy.

Then she collapsed against his chest.

He held her in his arms, his gentle touch smoothing the damp hair from her face. When he picked her up and carried her to the chair, nestling her in his lap, she felt protected. When he planted soft kisses along her brow, she knew what it meant to be cherished.

"Francie?"

"Hmmm?" She curled deeper into his chest.

"I think it would be prudent to marry as soon as possible."

"Hmmm," she murmured.

"I'll arrange for a special license and post the banns," he continued. "Three weeks should work."

"Hmmm." He was speaking in that too-low voice again. The one that made her hot and cold and shivery.

"It would not be wise to wait longer than that."

A tiny smile played about her lips. She lifted her head and pushed a tangle of hair from her face. "It wouldn't?"

"No. Most definitely not. And stop squirming." She shifted once more, trying to get comfortable.

"I'm sorry. Am I hurting you?"

"Yes. No," he said in rapid-fire succession. "No. I'm fine. Just sit still."

And then she felt the reason for his discomfort throbbing against her thigh. "Oh."

"Yes. Oh."

They remained silent a minute but curiosity wagered with embarrassment and won. "Does..." She stumbled with the words, and tried again, "Does it do that often?"

"Only when I'm near you," he replied.

"Oh," she murmured, wondering if it had been doing that since the first day they met.

"Yes. Oh."

Good gracious. When would she learn some things were better left unknown or at the very least, unspoken? Eager to change the subject, she said, "Let's go tell Aunt Eleanor and Uncle Bernard the news. They'll be shocked to hear we're getting married."

"Something tells me they'll be expecting us," Alexander said in a wry voice. "And probably wondering what's taken us so long."

∿

"ALEXANDER BISHOP WON'T BE COMING to supper," Claire said, tapping a folded card in her hand. She stood in the center of the rose salon, her body rigid, her lips pulled down in a frown. It was a wonder she hadn't begun ripping the draperies from the windows. Or at least thrown a vase or two. Control and a clear head, that's what she needed right now, but oh, how she longed to screech her anger. And humiliation. No man had ever refused her attentions. Not until Alexander Bishop.

"Bishop's a busy man," Jared Crayton murmured, trailing a tanned finger along her collarbone and dipping into the creamy flesh above her bodice.

"Busy getting married," she bit out. Such a loathsome confession.

His finger stilled. "Married?" he choked out in a strangled whisper. "To whom?"

"Do you really need to ask?" She fought to keep her breathing even. Perhaps splintering one vase to the ground would provide a modicum of relief. The sound of glass hitting the floor, the explosion of color as the vase shattered into infinitesimal pieces of nothingness—like her heart—might be just what she needed.

Who was she fooling? She'd never be happy again unless she had Alexander all to herself.

"Francie." Jared breathed like a besotted fool.

"Yes, *Francie*," she snapped. "How dare he choose her over me?" She paced the room, growing more agitated with each step. "I'm much more beautiful. That's obvious." She ran a hand through her long, curly hair. "And *I'm* a lady. She's nothing but a bastard." The words rolled off her tongue like poison.

"Bishop and Francie. I don't understand. When did you find out?"

"It's all here in this tidy little note." She flung the white card in the air. "It's from Alexander himself. Seems he's too busy attending to his nuptial arrangements to dine with me."

"I knew Bishop was involved with her." Jared smacked his hand against his knee. "He tried to tell me they were like brother and sister, but one look at them together dispelled that notion."

She was not about to ask him what that meant. She didn't want to know. In the end, it wouldn't matter. "He's not going to marry her." Claire stared out the window. A garden blossomed before her, a veritable feast to the eyes. Roses in every color, red, pink, salmon, yellow, and white as well as a rainbow of gladiolas and carnations. But she saw nothing, save the white light of hatred and envy. Francie Jordan and Alexander as husband and wife? Not if she had her way.

And she always did.

Claire turned from the window, bracing her hands against the sill, and said, "We've got to stop them. Think, Jared. What can we do?"

"Abduction?"

"Too obvious. It must be something that will undermine their trust in one another, destroy the bond they've obviously forged, and rip them apart." *And then she could go to Alexander and pick up the pieces.*

Jared raised a golden eyebrow. "What about a physical assault?" He balled one hand into a fist. "I'd like to repay that bastard for what he did to me. I was so bruised and battered I couldn't stand straight for days."

"You're not to touch Alexander," Claire warned. "He's mine."

"I guess I'll have to settle for stealing Francie from him." His lips curved upward as he added, "That will have its own rewards."

Claire shot him a disgusted look. "No doubt. You can lust after Francie Jordan later. At the moment, we need to devise a plan." She walked to the silver tea service and sank onto one of the cream chairs. Surely there was a solution. If only she had a bit more time to consider the various possibilities. "Why such haste for a wedding? They're not even allowing for an appropriate mourning period." Claire poured tea into two china cups. "Alexander is a man of such form. It makes no sense." She spooned three heaping teaspoons of sugar into her cup and stirred.

"Perhaps she's pregnant."

The spoon clattered against the rim of her cup. *Pregnant.* That would crush any plan of severing Alexander and Francie's relationship. A child would bind the two for a lifetime. The very idea made her sick. "She can't be pregnant."

Jared sat down in the chair next to her and popped a butter cookie in his mouth. "Maybe the old man left everything to Francie and the only way Bishop can get his hands on it is to marry her."

Claire paused with the cup midway to her lips. She set it down slowly and turned to Jared. "What did you say?"

"Let's say Montrose left Francie everything," he repeated, biting into a blueberry tart. "She is, after all, his flesh and blood. The only way Bishop can lay claim to any of it would be through marriage. I'll lay odds he'd do anything to keep Drakemoor, even marry for it. Though," he said, licking his fingers, "marrying Francie Jordan is by no means a punishment."

"I'll thank you to keep that opinion to yourself." A glimmer of hope spread through her. What if Jared were right and Alexander was only marrying the woman to obtain Drakemoor? What if affection and love had nothing to do with the offer? Her heart swelled with possibility. And opportunity. Her father's estate was twice the size of Drakemoor. "Alexander may well have offered out of necessity and not choice," she murmured.

"Possibly. But it's only speculation."

"Hmmm." She must find out if there was truth to Jared's theory. But how? Perhaps Lord Montrose's solicitor?

"I don't like that look on your face," Jared said. "It usually means some sort of trouble."

Claire raised a brow. "Trouble?" A tinkle of laughter danced through her. "Not for us, Jared. If your theory is true, we have nothing to worry about. The wedding between Alexander and your little Francie will never take place."

"Exactly how do you plan to find out if he's marrying her to keep Drakemoor? Ask him?"

Claire ignored the sarcasm in his voice. Jared was not much of a forward thinker. "Don't be ridiculous. I'm my father's daughter, remember?" She eyed him over the rim of her cup. "I'll simply find out who the solicitor is and ask him."

Jared snorted. "I'm certain he'll be forthcoming with a wealth of information."

"Indeed, he will," she replied. "With the sum I'm offering

for his cooperation, he won't be able to refuse. Everyone has a price. It's just a matter of finding out what it is." Her voice dropped to a husky whisper. "And I'm very good at finding out people's secrets."

18

"Thank you for seeing me on such short notice." Lady Claire Ashcroft smiled at Francie over the rim of her teacup. "I've only just heard the wonderful news and couldn't wait to congratulate you myself."

Francie shifted in her chair. The woman's congratulations rang cold and untrue. The slight flare of her dainty nostrils made Francie think she meant quite the opposite of what she said. Claire Ashcroft grasped her teacup hard enough to turn the knuckles on her small hands white. Indeed, something was amiss.

Oh, why couldn't Alexander be here right now? He'd know how to handle this beautiful woman with the condescending smile. But he'd been called to an emergency meeting with a very important potential investor and would be gone most of the day.

"I must say, Francie, may I call you Francie?" Claire's silver laughter tinkled around her. "Thank you," she said, when Francie nodded. "And you must call me Claire. All of this business about titles and such. You're like one of us." Her voice dropped an octave and she leaned forward to add, "Even if your parents didn't have benefit of marriage. I'm certain they possessed great affection for one another."

"They were in love."

"Of course they were. I meant no disrespect. I want you to know I consider us equals, despite what society may dictate."

"Thank you." The words fell out stiff and awkward.

"And marrying Alexander, well... " She smiled. "That won't help your social status any, but I'm certain you have your reasons."

"We do." They did, didn't they? Of course they did. She was marrying Alexander because she loved him. And he was marrying her because...her thoughts scattered like leaves twirling in the wind, falling just beyond her grasp. She tried again. Alexander was marrying her because... he loved her? No, he hadn't said that. He needed her? Not exactly. Her shoulders slumped a fraction. He desired her. Obviously true, but not solid footing for marriage.

She gnawed on her lower lip. He'd said Philip wanted her to live at Drakemoor among his society, therefore returning to Amberden was out of the question. It was unsuitable for a young unmarried woman to reside in the same household as an unmarried man, without benefit of chaperone. She blinked hard. Alexander knew Drakemoor was the only household available. Because there'd been no suitors seeking Francie's presence. Not even pathetic Lord Grose-something or other. How humiliating. She blinked again.

"Francie?" Claire's too-sweet voice rolled over her. "Is something wrong?"

Francie blinked once more and rubbed her eyes. "I think I've got something in my eyes. Dust," she lied. "I'm allergic to it."

"You should fire the maid. I've no tolerance for incompetence."

"I'll be fine." Francie waved a hand in the air. "It must have been an oversight. Mrs. Jones is usually quite thorough."

Claire sniffed. "Nevertheless, people must learn they cannot take advantage of their employer. Perhaps, you need to make an example of her."

"No. It's nothing." And Mrs. Jones was innocent.

"You'll learn soon enough you must show the servants you are their master and as such, they are to obey you, despite personal opinions or objections. I once fired the cook for preparing fried eggs instead of poached."

"You fired her?"

"Of course. Threats never work as well as action."

"I see," Francie said, but she didn't. Was this what the ton concerned themselves with? Did they also believe action always replaced second chances? That there was no room for mistakes?

"Tell me how Alexander proposed." Claire lowered her voice to a whisper. "It must have been very romantic."

Romantic? Francie blushed. "He didn't actually propose."

"No? What did he do then?" Her blue eyes widened. "Or what did you do? Did you propose to him?"

"No!"

Claire raised a black brow. "Do tell."

Francie lifted her shoulders and said, "He just said...I couldn't return to Amberden...and I couldn't stay here alone without Uncle Bernard and Aunt Eleanor...so..."

"So he was going to marry you to save your respectability?" Claire finished.

"Yes," Francie said in a small voice. It sounded so cold and impersonal when Claire said it. Why hadn't it felt that way coming from Alexander's lips? Perhaps it was the way he said it or the silver gaze that blurred the true meaning. And when he touched her, well, she couldn't remember anything but the feel of him after that.

"Francie," Claire said, "I'd like to tell you something as a friend, and I do hope you will consider me a friend." She placed a dainty hand over Francie's. "I hate to even put the thought into words, but I must, for your sake." She took a deep breath and continued. "Is it possible Alexander is marrying you for his own reasons that have nothing to do with your honor or respectability?"

～

CLAIRE ASHCROFT'S words clung to Francie for the next several hours, dampening all thoughts of her upcoming nuptials. She would question Alexander the moment he returned and certainly he'd dispel her silly worries. But until then, her spirits remained gloomy. It was a relief when James located her in the library where she'd been pretending to read and informed her that her father's solicitor requested a meeting with her posthaste.

Francie frowned. "Is he aware Alexander isn't here?" Why would the solicitor require a meeting with her? She had no knowledge of her father's private matters. Alexander handled everything. James nodded and tapped his foot twice. He'd begun to relax the foot tapping around her and even hazarded occasional smiles. "He specifically asked for you, Miss Jordan." One small tap. "With no mention of Mr. Bishop."

"Oh. Well, see him in then, James." Perhaps there had been a complication of some sort or mayhap he merely desired to make her acquaintance. Curiosity often got the better of people and solicitors were no different.

The man who entered the library possessed the air of a nobleman. Tall, trim, and solemn, he appeared no more than a handful of years younger than her father. "Gerald Heath at your service, Miss Jordan." He bowed slightly and studied her through thick spectacles that distorted the shape of his eyes and made it difficult to discern their color.

"I'm pleased to make your acquaintance, Mr. Heath. May I call for refreshments?"

"Thank you, no. I won't be staying long."

So, the man had a very particular mission that it appeared would be delivered quickly, precisely, and without pretense. *Oh, Alexander, why did you have to pick today to be gone? I fear something is amiss.* Francie sank into the overstuffed chair by the fire and gestured for Mr. Heath to sit in the matching chair a few feet away. "I rather thought any business you had would be conducted with Mr. Bishop."

Mr. Heath coughed. Twice. "This visit is of a most delicate nature and as it concerns you directly, I thought it prudent to deliver the information myself." He paused, "At your residence."

In Alexander's absence? Curiosity warred with dread. Had this visit to do with her illegitimacy? Was Mr. Heath trying to spare her embarrassment by seeking her out instead of naming his concerns in Alexander's presence? If so, she should be most grateful to her father's solicitor for his discretion.

"Did Mr. Bishop explain the terms and conditions of your father's estate?"

"Yes. He told me my father's estate was to be divided between us."

Mr. Heath studied her from behind his thick spectacles. If only she could see his eyes. "Then he told you he would have to marry you in order to obtain Drakemoor and the other lands?"

"No." A horrible dread overtook Francie, spiraling from her head to her stomach in one gigantic plummet. "No." She shook her head. "He said I couldn't return to Amberden because my father wanted me at Drakemoor. And I couldn't reside here with Alexander as a single woman." She lifted her shoulders and let the rest of the sad truth spill out. "My father held a ball in hopes someone would express an interest in furthering my acquaintance, but there were no such offers." *Not even one.* "Alexander said the only way around the whole business of maintaining my reputation and keeping us both at Drakemoor was to marry."

How tawdry and unromantic it all sounded now. "Mr. Bishop is a good man. A very forceful man, but still a good man. You could do worse than marry him."

Marry a man who only wanted her for her property? Never. Even if the man was Alexander Bishop.

"Miss Jordan?"

Francie glanced up to find Mr. Heath standing next to his chair. In the span of a few minutes, the solicitor had crumbled her dreams. But he'd given her honesty, which was more than her future husband had done. "I thank you for your visit. I am most grateful."

"I've upset you. Please forgive me; that was not my intent." The man hesitated. "I've known Mr. Bishop a good many years and he's not a man to be forced into doing anything he doesn't want to do, no matter the stakes. Try to remember that."

Francie remained in the library a long while after Mr. Heath left. Alexander wanted to marry her for Drakemoor. For her father's land. She couldn't marry him now. She wouldn't marry him. The sooner she exposed his subterfuge to Uncle Bernard and Aunt Eleanor, the sooner they could leave for Amberden. However well intentioned her father had been in his desire to see her and Alexander wed, he should not have meddled. It had only proved disastrous and heartbreaking.

She found her uncle in her father's study reading; his spectacles perched on the end of his nose. Her fondest memories of her uncle were with his head in a book. He'd once told her words had the power to transcend time and place, to take one from a most miserable, desperate situation to a world of hope and possibility. She'd always believed and trusted him.

"Uncle Bernard?"

He lifted his gray head and pushed his spectacles to the bridge of his nose. A smile appeared beneath his mustache and beard. "Come in, my dear."

Francie stepped inside and closed the door. Her stomach jumped and quivered as she met his gaze. "I've come to deliver grave news. Father's solicitor just left."

"Oh?" He raised a bushy brow and waited.

She moved toward him and stopped before his chair. "Alexander is only marrying me to get Drakemoor and my father's lands."

She expected him to jump up in shock or, at the very least, frown in concern. He did neither. A horrible blush of guilt crept over his face, settled on his cheeks, slithered to his neck. "You knew?" The one man she'd trusted more than anyone had known and not told her.

"Francie," her uncle said, placing his hand on her shoulder, "your father believed you and Alexander belonged together and he was determined to give you the chance he never had. Please forgive him for his methods; his intent was pure. As for Alexander, he *wants* to marry you." He sighed. "Even if he doesn't realize it yet himself."

"Don't try to defend Alexander. There's no need." He'd never said he wanted to marry her. Rather, he'd implied he *had* to marry her because it was her father's wish she remain in his society. And there'd been no other suitors. Mustn't forget that humiliating fact. Alexander may well have felt it a fair trade— he'd marry Francie, a woman he desired but didn't love, and give her a place in society in exchange for Drakemoor, his one true love. All nice and tidy. Francie need never know. Or so he thought.

But thanks to Mr. Heath's conscience, she knew the truth. "Child—"

She cut him off. "Alexander never spoke of love or even undying affection. At least in that he was honest with me."

"He'll come around," Bernard soothed. "Once you're married, he'll realize how much he cares for you."

"I'm sure you're right," Francie said, forcing the words out. There was nothing left to be said. She turned to him and offered a wobbly smile. "I feel a horrible headache coming on. I'd like to rest a while."

"Do that, child." Her uncle pulled her into his embrace. "Don't worry, I won't say anything to Alexander," he whispered. "Not a word."

Francie squeezed her eyes shut. It didn't matter.

By the time Alexander returned, she'd be gone.

ALEXANDER STEPPED from the carriage and reached up to straighten his cravat. His fingers stilled as he recalled Francie's words. *You can dress as you like, or not.* The truth of those words struck him as he stood enveloped by darkness. The house slept. Not even James would greet him at this hour. Who would care whether he wore a coat or cravat? His hands dropped to his sides and he started up the old stone steps.

It would feel good to sit back in his chair and savor a whiskey or two. Maybe even kick off his shoes. Or rather, pull them off, and enjoy the cool surface of hard wood beneath his silk hose. She was starting to affect him, working her way under his skin and into his conscience, and there wasn't a damned thing he could do about it. Not that he really wanted to, other than enjoy the pure spontaneity of her presence.

The meeting had dragged on far too long.

Alexander had wanted to leave hours ago, anxious to reach home before Francie retired for the night. But the three gentlemen, two dukes and an earl, couldn't decide which of Alexander's three business ventures they should invest in. Before the meeting adjourned, they'd settled funds for two of them, with a commitment for the third in six months' time. Everybody had wanted his advice, cocking an ear to listen, hanging on his every word.

Too bad he couldn't get Francie to behave in a similar manner. He smiled and shook his head. Not very likely, he thought as he pushed open the oak door and stepped into the foyer. The hall was dark, save a small lantern casting dubious shadows from its perch on a marble table. He picked it up and headed for his study.

An overwhelming desire to see Francie struck him square between the shoulders. It was past midnight, but perhaps she was still awake, reading or maybe even listening for his arrival. She'd been in the habit of waiting up for him; she admitted as much the other night when they had the discussion about his relationship with Tess. If she were still awake, what harm would there be in popping his head in to say goodnight? They were, after all, betrothed.

Before he could consider his actions, he turned on his heel and headed up the spiral staircase. His heart pounded faster as he approached her door, rapped softly, and waited. Disappointment filled him when Francie didn't answer. He should leave now and wait until morning to see her. But he didn't want to wait, not another hour, or another minute, not even another second. He wanted to see her now and for once in his very organized, proper life, he let impulse take over and turned the knob.

Lavender smothered his senses as he slipped inside without a sound. His body jumped in response. The little witch was gaining control over him, more so every day. He lifted the lantern and pointed it toward the bed. *Empty.* The counterpane was in perfect order. Not a rumpled sheet or pillow. No one had slept in the bed this night.

A moment of panic gripped him. Where in the devil was she? Perhaps she'd been waiting for him in his study, as anxious to see him as he was to see her, and had fallen asleep. He might well find her tucked beside George and her blasted cat. He raced out of her room and down the stairs, unaware he held his breath until he let it out in a shaky rush and grasped the knob to the study.

A constant, steady droning greeted him, followed by a half-sigh. It was George, lost between sleep and dreams, no doubt salivating over one of Mrs. Jenkins's beef bones. Alexander stepped into the darkness and held the lantern in front of him. George lay curled upon the Aubusson rug, his tan coat blending into the rug's fibers, and the little nuisance, Mr. Pib, rested under his chest.

There was no sign of Francie. She wasn't sitting at his desk or lying on the sofa. The chairs were empty, too. *Where in the devil could she be?*

He turned to leave, thinking he'd check Philip's study next, when a faint glimmer from the lantern cast a shadow on his desk. Something lavender, something looking like an envelope lay there. He hoped it wasn't another blasted invitation from that bothersome Claire Ashcroft.

Alexander walked to his desk and picked up the envelope. His name was scrawled on the outside in a woman's bold handwriting. Curious, he opened it and pulled out a single sheet of paper. The scent of lavender filled his senses, telling him it was from Francie. Why would she leave him a note? Dread spread its nasty talons, digging into him, drawing blood. Before he read a single word, he knew. She was gone.

He forced himself to read the note anyway, to feel the pain her words would bring, like a knife piercing his heart, draining the life from him, one word at a time. There were three sentences. The first released him from any debt or obligation toward her. The second gifted Drakemoor to him, if not technically, then through forfeiture, for she did not intend to return to her father's estate. Ever. The third wished him well. Her signature was at the bottom of the page. Francie. Simple. Impersonal. *As though he were a stranger.* As though he hadn't touched her, or tasted her, or heard her soft moans as she reached her release in his arms.

Alexander balled up the note and threw it across the room. *Damn her!* Why did she have to leave now, when he'd just gotten used to the idea of marriage, even admitted to himself he looked forward to marrying her? Now she was gone with nothing more than a single sheet of lavender paper and three sentences.

Did she think she could just wish him well, as though he were a stranger she'd just met? Well, she wasn't rid of him yet. Not by far. He'd find her, damn it, and then he'd drag her back to Drakemoor. Francie was going to marry him, whether she liked it or not.

Alexander stalked from the room and headed down the hall, his boots resonating through the quiet of night. He didn't care whose sleep he disturbed, let the whole blessed household wake up. He stopped in front of Bernard's room and raised a fist, ready to pound on the door, but hesitated. Eleanor may not know of Francie's departure and there was no sense troubling her if she didn't, at least not yet. Bernard, on the other hand, probably knew everything about her "escape" plan, down to the last tiny detail. He rapped quietly on the door and waited.

Nothing. He lifted his hand again, preparing to knock louder. The door inched open and a slightly disheveled Bernard peered at him. "Alexander, what's wrong?"

"I thought you might be able to tell me." Amazing that he kept his voice low when all he wanted to do was shout out the words at the top of his lungs.

Bernard stepped into the dim hallway and closed the door behind him. "What do you mean? What's the matter?"

"Where is she?" Alexander was in no mood for games. He was tired and angry. And damn it, more than a little hurt.

"You mean Francie?"

"Who else would I be talking about?" Alexander snapped.

"At this hour, I imagine she's asleep."

Even an honest, straightforward person like Bernard could be persuaded to lie for the little witch. "Her bed's empty."

"What?" He seemed confused.

"I said her bed's empty and from the looks of things, she hasn't slept in it."

"That's impossible." Bernard turned and hurried down the hall, throwing open the door to Francie's room. Alexander stood behind him, his lantern offering a flickering illumination of the empty bed. The old man let out a long breath. "Where is she? She didn't feel well. She didn't even take supper with us. Complained of a headache after—" He halted mid-sentence. "Oh, no. Oh, no."

"What, Bernard? Tell me."

Bernard shook his head and turned to Alexander. "She came to me and asked if there was a provision in Philip's will that required you to marry her."

Alexander couldn't think, couldn't breathe. "You told her." It wasn't a question or a statement, not even an accusation.

Bernard let out a long sigh. "I had no choice. Philip's solicitor told her and I couldn't lie."

"Philip's solicitor?"

"He met with Francie today. Apparently, he explained the conditions of the will."

Alexander closed his eyes. "That makes no sense."

Bernard shrugged. "I tried to make her see, tried to make her understand her father meant no harm. He wanted the two of you together. That was all."

"He used us," Alexander said.

"He didn't use you. He loved you. He loved both of you. You were the two most important people in the world to him. Philip only wanted you to be happy."

"As he defined the word."

"That's not true." Bernard threw him a disapproving look. "He wanted you to know the happiness he never knew. He wanted that more than anything."

Alexander shook his head. "Somewhere along the way, he should have realized he was playing with real people, flesh and blood and feeling, not just whimsical fairy tales."

"Alexander—"

"Enough. It doesn't matter why Philip did what he did. At the moment, I only care about finding Francie. I have no idea where to start but Amberden, and I know she wouldn't be foolish enough to go there alone."

When Bernard didn't reply, Alexander narrowed his gaze on him. "Please tell me Francie didn't go there."

"I don't know where she went," the old man said. Alexander closed his eyes and pinched the bridge of his nose, praying for strength to get through this ordeal. When he got his hands on the little minx, he'd make certain she never tried anything like this again.

"...but if I had to guess, I'd say Amberden. She considers it home."

Alexander's eyes flew open. "What did you say?"

"It's the only place she knows. If she were troubled or upset, she'd head home."

"*This* is her home." Alexander fought to keep his voice down. "Drakemoor."

"I doubt she feels that way at the moment."

"Then I'll enlighten her," Alexander said. "But first I have to find her."

19

Alexander spotted the little cottage at the end of the village and prayed Francie was in it. He edged Baron closer, the sound of the horse's hooves on stone shattering the night air. If she were inside, lost in the safe embrace of slumber, he could breathe again.

He'd ridden as fast as the midnight road permitted, all the while wondering if she'd taken the same path hours before. Wondering, too, if she'd faced a dark road with all of its hidden treacheries. His chest tightened at the thought. A young woman traveling alone could meet a number of misfortunes, anything from a robber to a broken wheel on a carriage. Or worse.

An image of Jared Crayton raced through his head. The last time he'd seen the man, he'd smashed his pretty face and pummeled his body until Crayton fell to the ground in a lifeless heap. All for the sake of Francie. If the bastard were still preying on the innocents of Amberden, he may have come across Francie on her journey. And if he were bent on revenge or worse, still obsessed with her, he might have acted on those feelings. He might have—Alexander forced the possibilities from his brain.

He stopped in front of the cottage, dismounted, and tied Baron to a side post. There were no other signs of a horse or carriage, nothing to indicate anyone had traveled here. Alexander held his breath as he tried the doorknob. Locked. If Francie were inside, at least she'd had sense enough to lock the door behind her. If she weren't...he'd tear the countryside apart, village by village, estate by estate, until he found her.

He pounded on the door. Again and again he beat on the worn oak, but it was useless. "Francie! Francie!" Her name fell from his lips in a desperate litany. His shoulders slumped as he murmured her name one last time. "Francie." It was a plea whose only answer was silence. She wasn't inside and he had no idea where to look next. He turned and headed down the stone path toward Baron and a long night of what he feared would prove a futile search.

"Alexander?"

He swung around.

It was her. Soft and shimmering, cast in an ethereal glow from the candle's light flickering in her hand, red hair tumbling about her in a mass of curls.

"Alexander?" Uncertainty coated her voice, thick and heavy, smothered in doubt, laced with caution.

"Francie!" He moved toward her in trance-like steps. Once he reached her, Alexander lifted a trembling hand to her cheek. "Why did you leave?" He tried to hide the pain in his voice, tried not to let her see how her leaving ripped his world apart, but the words fell out in ragged breaths, each one more gripping than the last.

She gnawed and pulled on her lower lip, finally releasing it to tremble on its own. "You were only marrying me to get Drakemoor."

He wanted to tell her that this sort of arrangement happened all the time with the upper class. It was expected.

Properties were traded for titles or wealth or any number of things. Most times, the parties did not concern themselves with the eccentricities of the arrangement. It was merely accepted. Why then, at this moment, did he feel lower than when he'd mucked out stalls in Drakemoor?

The answer hit him square in the gut. Because he'd been dishonest with Francie. And with himself. He'd told her she needed his protection in marriage, told her there'd been no other suitors. Both lies. And he'd told himself he was only marrying her to obtain a hold on Drakemoor. Another lie.

He was marrying Francie because she was fresh and open and alive, and she made him feel that way. Something he hadn't felt in a very long time, if ever. She'd poured into his life like a tempest, raging on his perfect, proper existence, threatening to wash away everything familiar.

Yet, in its place, she'd left the promise of hope and possibility, wrapped in laughter and innocence. He'd tried to crush her freshness with restrictions and dictates and demands. Now he'd lied to her and jeopardized their chance for a future together. The only choice left was honesty.

He hoped it would be enough.

"I'm sorry." He forced the foreign words past his lips. Apologies were as unfamiliar to him as wide-mouthed grins and barefoot walks in the grass. "I should have told you about Philip's wild scheme to throw us together." He rubbed the back of his neck. "But I was furious with him for forcing me to choose when he knew I wouldn't be able to," he said, meeting her blue gaze. "I was the one who didn't know I needed you. I think I'd have figured it out, eventually." He pulled his lips into a faint smile. "Philip just helped me along a little."

"Are you saying you *want* to marry me?" she asked, her words soaked in doubt.

Alexander stroked her cheek. "I want to marry you." He cupped her chin in his hand and bent toward her.

Francie jerked back, eyeing him with suspicion. "Because you need me? I doubt you've ever let yourself need anyone. But you need Drakemoor, too, don't you? Then there's the duty you feel toward my father. Since no one expressed the slightest interest in me, you feel honor-bound to offer for me."

"Yes, no, and no." All that infernal blathering jumbled his thoughts. The woman would well and truly drive him to Bedlam. Only patience and a clear head would see him through this. "I do need you. More than I care to acknowledge." The confession pinched his brain and brought a slight smile to her lips. Damn, she'd never let him forget those words.

"And Drakemoor?"

"A want." He paused. "Not a need." The smile spread.

Double damn.

"My lack of suitors did not make you feel duty-bound?"

Alexander pulled at his neckcloth. If they were to begin anew, honesty must prevail. "It seems I was mistaken in regard to the presence of suitors."

"What?" Of course that piqued her interest. She peered at him as though he'd just sprouted horns. Or a second head. "I had a suitor?"

Alexander's jaw clenched. She needn't act so damn excited about it. All of her suitors were peacocks—with the exception of Sebastian Trent, but Francie needn't know about him. He cleared this throat, then mumbled, "Seventeen."

Francie stepped closer. Leaned toward him. "Excuse me?"

He cleared his throat. "Seventeen," he repeated.

"Seventeen calling cards?" Her mouth opened again but it took several seconds for her to produce sound. "Seventeen?"

"And none of them were acceptable."

"According to whom?"

He glared at her. "Me."

She didn't like that answer. Not one bit.

"If they were *my* suitors, should it not have been *my* choice?"

He shrugged.

Her gaze narrowed. "Should I not have been privileged to the knowledge that suitors existed? Even a single one?"

She had a point. "Perhaps. But it would have made no difference. You weren't marrying any of them."

"As I recall, you made it quite clear, the only one I wasn't marrying was you!"

"Enough!"

They glared at one another. The entire night had been a tumult of emotions. He had not expected Francie to claw him with questions and accusations. Alexander took a deep breath and forced out the next words. "There were seventeen calling cards. And a proposal from young Grosepeak. If you would like to consider any of them, I'll make the cards available."

She studied him as though looking for the fault in his words. "You would let me choose?"

He nodded. And then, because he wouldn't be able to live with himself if he didn't divulge the whole truth, he said, "Sebastian Trent paid a personal visit to your uncle."

"Sebastian did?"

She didn't have to sound so giddy, like a schoolgirl gawking over her first crush. Francie's excitement put Alexander in a foul mood. She'd certainly never gawked over him that way. Good God, that sounded an awful lot like jealousy.

"Alexander?"

"What?" She was going to make him deliver the blasted details. "Apparently, Mr. Trent was quite taken with you."

"He said so?"

Alexander scowled. Damned if he'd provide the details so

she could swoon and sigh. Honor could only push a man so far. "In so many words, yes." There. Duty fulfilled.

A tiny smile creased her lips. "He is a most handsome man."

Stabs of jealousy pricked at him. Only a fool would miss the wistfulness in her voice. "I couldn't say."

The smile deepened. "And intelligent." Handsome *and* intelligent. What was next? A tribute to the broadness of his shoulders? The elegant fit of his waistcoat? The line of his perfectly straight nose?

"And have you ever noticed the way his eyes twinkle when he laughs? Like stars on a dark night."

"No, I can't say that I have." Alexander's heart deflated. He was about to lose the only woman he ever truly wanted to a man with a perfectly straight nose and twinkling eyes.

"I daresay any girl would be delirious to catch Mr. Trent's eye."

Alexander settled his gaze on the shadowy interior of the cottage. He refused to watch Francie's face light with excitement and wonder as she expounded on the apparently limitless qualities of Sebastian Trent. When she finished, which he prayed would be soon, he'd force himself to look at her.

"Alexander?"

"Hmm?" He tried to ignore the sudden breathiness in her voice. It reminded him too much of the night in the garden, when he—

Francie touched his cheek. "Look at me."

She shouldn't touch him that way when she planned to marry another. They must forget everything that ever passed between them. Immediately. Especially anything involving bare flesh and tongues. Who was he kidding? He'd go to his grave with the feel of her skin burned into his memory. But she need never know that. He would give her what she wanted, even if it crushed his heart and scarred his soul.

He met her gaze. He longed to lift her into his arms and kiss her until she moaned his name. What he wouldn't give for one last kiss, one final touch, one—

"I don't want to marry Sebastian Trent."

"What did you say?"

"He's a very nice man. Handsome, intelligent, articulate, well mannered." She stroked his cheek. "But he's not you."

Hope pounded through Alexander. "No, I daresay he's not."

"For some inexplicable reason, I prefer a more complicated man. Serious to the point of sullen. Unsmiling. Unreadable. It makes for a greater challenge." She leaned up on tiptoe and whispered, "And he must absolutely possess a gaze that sends shivers through me. Mr. Trent does not possess such a gaze."

Alexander's lips twitched. "Of what importance are such shivers?"

Francie planted the softest kiss on his lips. "Of the greatest importance. Empires have been built upon them."

She was killing him, one breath at a time. The little witch had taken him from despair, to hope, to elation in the span of a light supper. "Do you know such a man?"

"I do," she murmured, her breath trailing along his neck.

"Do I?" he half-choked.

"Oh yes." She buried her head against his chest. "You most certainly do."

He waited. *Say it. Please.* "His name?"

She sighed. "Alexander Bishop."

Thank God. He scooped her in his arms and crushed her against his chest. "Then marry me, Francie."

"Yes," she whispered. "Oh, yes, Alexander."

He kissed her long and hard, his tongue filling her mouth, devouring her sweetness. Then he scooped her up and carried her into the cottage, kicking the door shut behind him.

"I want you, Francie." His words were thick with need and

longing. "I want you more than I've ever wanted anything in my life."

She smiled, a hesitant slow smile that shot through him in a wave of desire. The candle she held flickered over her face, and he saw the shimmer of tears in her eyes.

"Don't cry."

"I'm not crying," she said, swiping at her eyes.

Alexander leaned over and kissed the tip of her nose. "Of course not," he whispered. He shifted her weight in his arms and headed for the narrow stairwell in the back of the house. He climbed the steps to the second floor and stopped at the top of the landing. "Which room is yours?"

"The second one," she said. There was a catch in her voice that could mean only one of two things—anticipation or hesitation over what was to come. He prayed it was the first.

He strode down the hall and into a room so small he had to lower his head to avoid hitting the doorframe. His gaze took in the sparse furnishings. A single bed with a pink and green counterpane in some stitched design stood to his immediate right. In the far corner sat an old wicker rocker with a large basket filled with books. More books were stacked in a haphazard pile on the other side of the rocker. In another corner lay a rug and two oversized pillows, no doubt George and Mr. Pib's lair. The last three pieces of furniture were a simple chest of drawers in dark wood, a matching nightstand, and a white table with a wash basin. The only decorations in the room were bunches of dried flowers stuck in old jugs and lined against one another on the floor. Certainly not what one would expect for an earl's daughter, even an illegitimate one.

Alexander turned to Francie. Was she having second thoughts? Regrets? He released her and she slid to her feet. He took the candle from her and set it on the nightstand. The sliver of moon peeking through the solitary window cast its own small ray on them, warring with the candle for illumination.

"Perhaps I shouldn't have spoken in such a bold manner," he said. He was mere inches from her, the scent of lavender floating around him. But he didn't touch her. Coming to bed with him needed to be her decision.

When she remained silent, he cleared his throat and tried again. "Perhaps it would be best to wait until after the wedding." Three more weeks. He'd survive one way or another.

"Did you mean what you said?"

Twenty-one days. Five hundred and four hours.

"Alexander?"

"What?" He shook his head. "I'm sorry. You spoke?"

She gave a little huff. Obviously, she had spoken. And he'd missed it.

"I said," she repeated, "did you mean what you said?"

"I always mean what I say," he shot back.

"You do?"

"Or at least I did." He rubbed the back of his neck. "Until I met you, that is. Before, I only said what I meant. And meant what I said. But sometimes, you confuse me and I confuse myself so I have no idea what I'm thinking *or* saying."

"Really?" One of those tiny smiles that enchanted him so much crept over her lips.

"Really."

"Oh."

One little word, spoken with just the right emphasis, told him she was more than a little pleased with his answer. Thrilled actually. He scowled and shoved his hands in his pockets.

"You haven't answered my question," she said, a teasing little note in her voice.

"What?" he bit out, wondering if he were getting a glimpse of the next twenty-five years of married life with this woman.

She sighed and dropped her voice to a whisper, as though she thought someone else might hear. "When you said you wanted me more than you've ever wanted anything in your life, did you mean it?"

So that's what the smile was about. Damn him and his big mouth. He should never have let his damnable emotions run away with his senses. Now she'd want to analyze the devil out of those words, question the meaning behind them, and beat them to an early death.

"Make love to me, Alexander."

"Excuse me?" That response he had not expected.

"Make love to me," she repeated in a breathy whisper. "When you're near me, I can't think. My heart gets all fluttery like there's a giant butterfly inside." She placed her hand over her heart and drew in a shaky breath. "When you're away from me, I can't sleep for dreaming of you. Missing you. There's a gaping hole inside me only you can fill."

He stared at her, not daring to believe what she'd just said. For the second time in his life, he'd found something he wanted desperately to believe in. Philip was the only other person he'd trusted enough to bestow the same honor. His chest tightened. Could he believe in Francie and risk his heart?

He pushed the questions aside, refusing to think about them at the moment. He had time, at least a little, before he'd be forced to make a decision. And then, he prayed to God, he'd have the strength to make the right one.

"Alexander?"

He brushed his fingertips over her cheeks, tracing her lips, her chin, trailing them along her neck. "You are so beautiful." He worked his fingers through her hair, loving the touch and feel of it, like silk draped over his skin.

Standing on tiptoe, she planted a kiss on his mouth. So soft. So sweet. She gave him another and this time her tongue darted out to run along the seam of his lips. Alexander's groan of pleasure filled the room as he captured her tongue, sucking on it in a long, slow, even rhythm. Francie moaned and pressed her body into his.

He stroked her feminine curves through the thin batiste nightgown. How he wanted her. Now. He lifted her hips and pressed her into him, moving her against his erection. She moaned again and tightened her grip around his neck, rifling her fingers through his hair, mating her mouth with his. It was heaven and hell in a touch that lasted too long and ended too soon.

He ground his hips into hers. If he didn't have her soon, he would burst. "I need you, Francie," he said on a ragged breath. "I need you now." She answered with the slow, rhythmic movement of her hips against him. He grabbed a handful of her gown and with as much patience as he could muster, lifted the fabric over her head.

She stood before him, naked and beautiful, the candle flickering along her body in a silky, incandescent shimmer. If he touched her now, it wouldn't be with comforting hands to gentle her passage into womanhood. No, certainly not. If he touched her now, it would be with the passion of a man long deprived, one wanting nothing more than to bury himself between her silky thighs and slake his desire on her.

He inched backward and settled his gaze on a point just past her left ear. He couldn't look at her right now—not until he regained his composure— not that he hadn't memorized the exact shade of pink to her nipples, or the flare of her hips, or the pale red thatch of hair between her legs. They were burned in his brain, a torment that could not be erased.

Dear God, give me strength.

"Is something wrong, Alexander?"

He shook his head, narrowing his gaze on a crack in the middle of the white wall. It ran along a jagged path, dipping and disappearing behind her. He blinked hard.

"Why won't you look at me?"

"I will," he said. "I need a moment to collect myself."

"Collect yourself?"

"Only a moment." He closed his eyes against the temptation of her naked body mere inches from him. If he stretched out his hand, he could touch her soft silkiness.

"Don't you want me?"

His eyes flew open. "Want you?" he croaked. He let out a harsh laugh that held no humor. "That's the problem. I want you too much. I want you so much I'm afraid I won't be gentle enough and I don't want to hurt you." His gaze ran the length of her body. "I'm trying to 'collect' myself so I can behave like a proper lover should, with care and concern." He cleared his throat. "And restraint."

Francie closed the distance between them and touched his arm. "Perhaps I wouldn't mind so much if you weren't such a 'proper' lover," she said, her voice melting over him like warm honey. "Perhaps, I would rather enjoy an 'improper' lover. But I think what I would enjoy most of all," she said, her sky-blue eyes meeting his, "is making love with Alexander, the man, and not some image or expectation. Just the man," she whispered, rising up on tiptoe to brush her lips against his. "Just you."

That was it. He let out a growl and pulled her into his arms, plundering her mouth with his tongue. He wanted her so badly and she'd just offered him the greatest gift of all—herself. His hands were everywhere on her body, learning, possessing. He edged his way to the bed and eased her onto the counterpane, breaking the kiss only long enough to kick off his boots and untie his cravat. Skin to skin, that's what he needed.

His fingers trembled as he unbuttoned his shirt and tossed it aside.

"Let me feel you, Alexander." Francie reached up and urged him toward her. "Let me feel your skin against mine."

The most seasoned courtesan couldn't have spoken more sensual words. Heat shot through his body, burning his blood, pounding over him and into him. "I don't think you know what you're asking." A fine sheen of sweat broke out on his forehead as he fought for control. And lost.

"I'm on fire. Everywhere you touch me," she whispered. "I need...I need..."

"I know what you need," he murmured. He rolled to his side and laid a hand on her flat belly. She sucked in her breath as his fingers inched down, tracing the inside of her thighs.

"Oh, Alexander," she said on a sigh.

He stroked the swollen flesh of her nubbin, first fast, then slow, then fast again, delighting in the way her hips moved with the rhythm of his hand.

"Oh, no," he murmured, brushing a kiss against the slender column of her neck. "Not yet. We've only begun to explore." He trailed his hand to the opening of her woman's heat and inserted the tip of one finger.

She moved against him and moaned. He loved the soft little mewls she made when he touched her. In the dim glow of the candle, he watched her face flush with arousal. His wife-to-be would prove a most exhilarating bed partner. How very fortunate for him. Leaning over, he took a pale pink nipple in his mouth.

Francie cried out in unmistakable pleasure and buried her hands in his hair.

Alexander laved the peak, his tongue circling and flicking her flesh. She felt so good, so right. He wanted more. *He wanted all of her*. He worked his finger into the depth of her heat, so slick and hot. So ready for him. As he stretched her, his thumb stroked and circled the peak of her desire. Once. She let out a long moan. Twice. Her hands dug deeper into his hair. Three times. Her hips jerked off the bed. Four. She screamed and her whole body shook with tiny spasms.

Yes, he was very fortunate indeed.

He pulled Francie into his arms and cradled her, planting tender kisses along her brow and forehead.

"Was that what you needed, Francie?" She buried her head in his chest. "Look at me." He lifted her chin with his finger. "Never be embarrassed with me. I love giving you pleasure." One side of his mouth curved upwards as he added, "And I hope to give it to you every night, from our wedding night on."

"And what of you? I want to give you pleasure, too."

Spoken with such absolute innocence. Alexander cleared his throat.

"Let me give you pleasure." Her voice dipped to a husky whisper, and his erection jerked in response. "Teach me how. Will you do that, Alexander?" she asked, lifting a hand to stroke his cheek. "Will you teach me to give you pleasure every night as well?"

"Of course," he croaked. It was all he could manage. The notion of making love to Francie every night robbed him of all sensible thought.

"Thank you," she murmured, smiling at him. *Thank you?* She was thanking him for allowing her to make love to him? He blinked hard. If she didn't stop saying those things in that low, velvety voice of hers, the lesson would be over before it began and she'd have thanked him for nothing.

"I'm a little nervous," she confessed.

"I'll be gentle," he promised.

"Just be you, Alexander. That's all I want. That," she said, running her hand down his arm, "and a kiss. I love the feel of your lips against mine, your tongue in my—"

She got no further. Alexander devoured her with his mouth, his tongue plunging into the sweet recesses, mating with hers. Her fingers yanked at the waistband of his trousers, found the buttons and fumbled with them until they popped opened. He groaned when she slid the trousers from his hips and his erection sprang free. When her hands found his penis, he thought he'd explode.

He dragged his mouth from hers and said in a ragged voice, "For God's sake, Francie, I'm only a man. I can't take much more."

"You feel like velvet," she whispered, stroking the tip of him, "so hard...and yet so soft." Her fingers worked the length of him, circling his shaft until he thought he would die. Or explode. Or both.

When she tightened her grip, he growled and pulled her hand away. "I have to have you. Now. " He yanked off his trousers and settled over her, spreading her legs wide. He'd never wanted anyone as much as he wanted Francie. He grabbed her hips and pushed into her heat with slow, steady strokes until he reached her maiden's barrier. "I'll try to be gentle," he promised.

She smiled and touched the jagged trail of his scar. He pushed into her then, breaching her maidenhead with one deep plunge. Her face contorted in pain and she cried out. Alexander gathered her to him until the cry melded to a whimper and disappeared.

"I'm sorry," he whispered against her hair. "If I could have saved you from the pain, I would have."

"It...it's starting to ease," she murmured. "It doesn't hurt as much now."

Alexander brushed a tangle of red hair from her forehead and searched her face. "Next time will be better."

"Next time?" The disappointment in her eyes could not disguise the truth. She didn't want to share his bed again.

"Well, yes." He stumbled with the words, forced them out again, "Next time."

"Oh." She looked away, gnawed on her lower lip.

Alexander drew in a deep breath and sighed.

"Alexander?"

"Hmm?" He didn't trust himself to speak yet.

"When you said next time," she asked, her voice both shy and curious, "did you mean we're finished? Because I thought there'd be...more..." her voice trailed off.

His head shot up. "More what?"

She gave him a helpless look. "More. Just more."

Oh, thank God. Alexander threw back his head and laughed, something he didn't do very often and certainly never in bed with a woman. But the laughter rolled over him in gulping waves and soon Francie laughed, too.

"What did I say?"

He wiped his eyes with the back of his hand. "It was the way you said next time, as though you were dreading it. I thought you hated having me inside of you." He traced the swell of her breast. "And I thought you wouldn't want me there again for a very long time."

She lowered her voice and said, "I thought it was over and frankly, I was a little disappointed." She wriggled her hips. "As for not wanting you there, well, it's quite pleasant once one becomes accustomed to the sensation." She moved her hips again and laughed when she saw him clench his jaw. "Yes, I'd say *quite* pleasant."

"Witch," he growled, capturing her mouth in a fierce kiss as he drove into her. "My lovemaking is not pleasant." He nipped at her breasts. "Pleasant is a word used to describe Sunday afternoon rides in the park." His tongue rolled around a pale nipple. Francie gasped, as he grabbed her legs and lifted them over his back.

He thrust into her with long, steady strokes, deeper each time.

"No...not...pleasant..." Francie panted, trying to speak through her desire. "You're incredible. You...feel...incredible."

Alexander pulled out slowly and then plunged into her again. And again. She moaned and jerked her hips toward him, her face a vision of pure ecstasy.

He came undone, one delicious moan at a time. Francie scorched his very soul. Her silky skin under his fingertips teased him, the taste of her breasts tormented him, the sight of her wild and free in his arms pushed him past the boundaries of sensuality. He drove into her one last time and cried out her name as he spilled his seed deep inside her.

She jerked her hips and screamed his name in a release that made him hope half of Amberden hadn't heard her.

"Oh, Alexander," she murmured, snuggling into the shelter of his arms.

He sighed and buried his face in her hair. He'd never known such utter contentment in his entire life.

20

Francie raised her arms above her head and stretched, letting out a loud, unladylike yawn. Soon, Mr. Pib would inch toward her from the foot of the bed, eager for his "good morning" scratch behind the ears and rub on the stomach.

Her eyes flew open. Mr. Pib would not be coming for his morning scratch because she was *not* at Drakemoor. She was at Amberden. In her old room. In her old bed. She looked down. Naked. She pulled the covers up to her neck.

Visions of last night bombarded her in bright, bold, *intimate* detail. Heat poured over her, stealing her breath as she remembered how she'd given herself to Alexander. Several times. Several ways. He'd shown her things she never could have imagined possible. And then, when they were lying in each other's arms, exhausted and still trying to calm their breathing, desire would roll over them again. How could she ever have thought making love with Alexander as pleasant?

"Good morning."

She jerked her head toward the door and yanked the covers to her chin. The object of last night's pleasure stood in the doorway holding two steaming mugs. His black hair stuck out in places, though from the look of it, he'd tried to wet it down. He hadn't shaved either, which gave him an even darker, more brooding appearance than usual. His partially buttoned shirt bore several wrinkles and his trousers were just as unkempt. He looked wonderful.

"Good morning." Shyness overtook her as visions of last night flitted through her head. There was no way to act ladylike now, not after everything they'd done. He walked into the room and handed her a mug. She held out one hand while clutching the blanket with the other.

Alexander's mouth twitched when he saw her predicament. He leaned over and said in his too-low voice that made her hot and cold at the same time, "Francie, there's nothing under there I haven't already seen." His gaze swept the length of the blanket. "Or touched."

Her cheeks burned. Of course he knew she wore no clothes. He'd removed every stitch of them, hadn't he? But did he have to remind her?

"Or kissed," he continued. Yes. It seemed he did. He kissed the tip of her nose. "Don't be embarrassed. We shared something beautiful last night, beautiful and very rare."

That drew her attention. "You mean..." She darted a glance at him. "That's not what normally happens between a man and a woman?"

He lifted a black brow at her question. "No," he said, his lips curving into a faint smile. "Not normally."

"Oh."

"Yes. Oh," he repeated, raising the mug to her lips.

She took a sip of tea. "Thank you," she murmured, considering what he'd said. If what happened last night between them did not normally happen, then...what did? How was it different? Most of all, had Alexander ever experienced that same "not normally" feeling with Lady Printon?

"What happened last night between us…" She pushed past her embarrassment. "Has that ever happened to you with Lady Printon?"

He stared at her as though she'd asked him if he'd ever considered wearing a gown and pantaloons. "That is not something a gentleman discusses, especially with his betrothed."

Her shoulders slumped. Of course, he wasn't going to tell her. And she'd bet it wasn't just because of gentlemen's discretion. Lady Printon was a widow and she'd been Alexander's mistress. She knew much more about men than Francie's little thimble of knowledge. A woman like her knew about the "not normally" of intimacy. Had she thought he'd actually say, "No, Francie, I've never experienced anything like I did with you last night"? Well, she'd gotten her answer and he hadn't even uttered a word.

"Francie."

Did he have to speak to her in a voice that made her pulse beat triple time? She hid behind the shield of hair that fell over her face. "What?" she said in a tiny voice.

"Never," he said.

"Never what?" Maybe she could feign a stomachache or some other malady to divert his attention from her ridiculous question.

"I've never felt this way before."

His words hit her like a rush of wind. She peeked through a veil of red. "Never?"

He shook his head. "And right now," he said in a stern voice, "I'm wondering if it's a blessing or curse."

A smile inched across her face. *He said he's never felt this way before. Not even with "her."* Her smile deepened. "It's a blessing, of course," she said, pushing her hair from her face. "After all, I am the one you're marrying, so it's important we suit."

Alexander coughed and sputtered, almost choking on his tea. "That, I assure you, Francie, is not how men and women determine if they suit."

She blushed and looked away, remembering the heat and passion they'd shared last night.

"But don't be ashamed of what happened between us," he said. "Ever."

She shrugged. "It's just when I think of last night...of what we did..." She paused, trying to find the right words. "It wasn't very ladylike."

"No, it wasn't," he agreed.

She stiffened. "So I've decided I'll work on my behavior when we're...together."

"And exactly how do you intend to do that?"

She thought she heard humor in his voice. If he were laughing at her, she'd never speak to him again. "I intend to behave in a more...ladylike fashion."

"Oh?"

"Yes. I'll not thrash about like I did or call your name out."

"You screamed my name, Francie."

"I know," she said, shaking her head in disbelief. "I'll not do that again. Or make those funny little sounds. I think I'll be silent."

"Let me understand what you've just said. You're going to stop 'thrashing' about and eliminate all screaming, moaning, sighing, or other sounds that might be misinterpreted as pleasurable."

"Yes." She nodded. "That's exactly what I intend to do."

"Then I shall soon learn what it's like to make love to a corpse."

She swung her gaze around to meet his. "What do you mean?"

"Don't change a thing. I love it when you scream my name." He grabbed the edge of the covers and lowered them to her neck. His other hand reached out to stroke her shoulder. "You drive me mad when you moan in my arms and sigh when I give you pleasure." He inched the covers down to expose the top of her breasts. "And when I hear those choppy little breaths right before you reach your release, it makes me ache with wanting you."

Francie couldn't move, couldn't think about anything but the sound of his voice and the images he painted with his words. Heat pooled low in her belly and she felt a dampness between her legs.

"And when you lift your hips off the bed," he murmured, brushing his lips with hers, "I can think of nothing but being inside you." The covers fell in a heap between them. "But, it appears lately, being inside you is all I think about." His hand cupped her breast. "I want you, Francie." His tongue stroked the seam of her lips, begging entry. "As much as I did last night."

She shivered and threw her arms around his neck, pulling him down on the bed. "I want you, too," she whispered.

He groaned and reached for the buttons of his shirt. Aching need gripped her as he tore open his shirt and loosened his trousers. Grabbing her hips, he sank into her with a sigh. "This wanting, when will it be enough?" he growled, moving inside her with deep, heavy thrusts. "I fear it may never be."

Francie clung to him, her legs wrapped around his waist, her hips moving with his. Exquisite tension built as his body stroked her with pure sensation, lifting her to the height of desire, promising more pleasure with each thrust. Her release came, sudden and quick, with a force that shocked her. She screamed his name and he exploded inside her.

It was then she knew the answer to Alexander's tormented question, knew it with a clarity from the depth of her soul. The wanting would never stop.

~

"I WISH we could stay here a few more days," Francie said as she dried a dish and put it in the cupboard.

"That's impossible." Alexander leaned against the doorframe to the small kitchen. "I only have the clothes on my back and I'm itching to get out of them."

She shot him a quick glance, her cheeks blushing a most becoming pink.

"And into some fresh ones," he amended, though he found the thought of taking her back to bed quite appealing. They'd spent the better part of the morning there, arising only long enough to eat a bit of crackers with jam. His groin tightened as he recalled the intimacies they'd shared over the past several hours. If he didn't concentrate on something else, she'd find herself stretched out on the kitchen table with him on top of her.

This insatiable desire for his soon-to-be wife bothered him. It wasn't just the physical need; it was the way he found himself thinking about her at odd moments or anticipating her entry into a room. When she spoke, her soft voice rolled over him like a calming symphony. If she had this kind of control over him now, what would happen once they were married, when their time and intimacy increased tenfold? He jammed his hands in his pockets. It would only get worse. He might actually be in danger of falling in love with her.

That couldn't happen. Alexander had only loved one

woman in his life. His mother. But she hadn't even cared enough about him to live. He'd vowed long ago never to let a woman hurt him like that again. And he hadn't. But now Francie threatened to breach the carefully constructed wall separating indifference from caring, fondness from love. He had to stop her, and yet, a small part, deep inside his soul, didn't want to.

A banging at the door disrupted his thoughts and he was grateful for the intrusion. Thinking about Francie and his current predicament gave him a pounding headache.

"I'll get it." He turned on his heel and headed toward the incessant banging. There had never been such blatant disruption at Drakemoor. But this was the country and Francie was the most unconventional woman he'd ever met. Perhaps this was a common and acceptable greeting. He opened the door just as a young woman prepared to deliver another round of noise with her fisted hand.

She gasped when she saw him, her large brown eyes wide and guarded. She was a slip of a girl, much shorter than Francie, with a protruding belly. One of Crayton's conquests, he guessed. "Begging your pardon, sir," she said, inching her way back, "I...I was looking for Francie."

"Your name?" he asked. She looked like a scared rabbit about to bolt. Why was she afraid of him? He'd done no more than look at her.

"Sally," she murmured. "Sally Baines. I...I live down the street."

Alexander nodded. "Well, come in, Sally Baines, and I'll fetch Francie." He waved his hand toward the sitting room, but the young girl shook her pale blonde head and remained outside.

"No, thank you, sir," she said. "I'll wait here."

"As you wish." He turned and went in search of Francie, his

thoughts on the scared young woman outside. "Francie," he called, poking his head in the kitchen. "You have a visitor."

She was putting some green leaves into a small container. She looked up and smiled at him, sending a twinge to his groin. "Who?"

"She said her name is Sally Baines."

"Sally?" She set the leaves aside and wiped her hands on a towel. "Why didn't you invite her in?"

"I did," he said, his voice low. "She's worse than a scared rabbit. And swollen with child."

Francie's eyes filled with tears. "Poor Sally."

"Crayton, I presume?"

She nodded. "Sally was one of the first. Her parents blamed her. Called her all sorts of horrible names and almost threw her out of the house."

"I see." One's biological parents did not always guarantee safety or love.

"It's worse," she whispered. "They tried to force her to marry a man three times her age to save disgrace and when she refused, they threatened to disown her."

Alexander shook his head. "From the look on her face and the way she's acting, something's happened and I'd venture to guess it wasn't pleasant."

"Poor Sally," Francie murmured. "I'll be back." She reached up on tiptoe and gave him a peck on the cheek.

Then she was moving past him, a determined warrior on a mission, her red-gold hair flowing behind her. Alexander's chest tightened as he watched his betrothed, dressed as a commoner, in simple blue muslin and old slippers with her hair unbound and free. And yet, he thought her more beautiful than the grandest of ladies clothed in silk and jewels. It was then he understood the beauty of Francie was not in her face or her hair or even her well-curved body. Francie's beauty came from her soul.

He watched as she drew Sally into her arms, patted her back when the girl's shoulders shook and tears flowed from her pale face. All the while, Francie's lips moved, no doubt whispering soothing words. Alexander stood, mesmerized, as his future wife helped Sally Baines transform from a scared waif to a smiling young woman.

His breath stuck in his throat as she rested her hands on Sally's belly and he pictured Francie swollen with child. *His child.* He blinked and turned away. What was he thinking? He had no idea how to be a father. How could he even think about bringing a child into this world with a past like his? Francie's innocent naïveté was getting to him, making him want to believe in ridiculous impossibilities.

"Her family's disowned her."

Alexander looked at Francie, her blue eyes filled with concern for her friend, her full lips parted and waiting. He wished he believed in hopes and dreams and happily ever after. Just this once.

Francie was a gift, a summer's breeze blowing over him, touching him with her gentle caress. But summer didn't last forever and breezes gave way to harsh winds and bitter storms that smashed unsuspecting victims in their path. He would not be a victim, no matter how much she entranced him.

"Alexander?" her soft voice reached him. "She has nowhere to go."

He pushed aside his thoughts and said, "What do you want to do?" He knew she had a plan. She always did.

Her voice dropped to a whisper. "I'd like her to stay here."

He lifted a brow. "Alone?"

"I could stay—"

"No." He didn't give her a chance to finish the thought. "You are not staying here," he said. "It's not safe." He shook his head. "Besides, you're to be my wife. I want you back at Drakemoor."

"Sally has no place to go. I've got to help her." He glanced at the very pregnant girl standing just outside the doorway. Damn Jared Crayton and his noble blood. If he got his hands on him again, he'd make certain Crayton never fathered another child.

Alexander turned to Francie and said in a terse voice, "She can stay." It annoyed him how easily she could get him to do her bidding, as though his sole existence centered on pleasing her. He cleared his throat and continued, "I'll send someone to stay with her. She'll need help when her time comes."

"Thank you, Alexander."

His chest tightened further at her simple words. He looked away and busied himself with several large wrinkles in his trousers. "Make a list of food items and whatever other provisions she may require." His gaze darted to Sally once more. "And see that the child has plenty of blankets." He'd spent the first half of his life shivering under one threadbare blanket and too few clothes.

No child should have to live like that. Not even Jared Crayton's bastard.

"How can it be true?" Claire Ashcroft pulled the sheet around her breasts and stared at her lover. "How can it possibly be true?"

Jared Crayton folded his hands behind his head and cursed. "That bastard doesn't deserve to touch the hem of her gown."

"Rest assured, he's done more than touch that little whore's clothing." The very thought of Alexander's beautiful body entwined with Francie Jordan's enraged Claire. She wanted to destroy something—a vase, a glass, Francie's face.

"She told me she wasn't interested in the opposite sex. If she's no longer a virgin, Bishop forced her and he'll pay dearly for that."

Claire laughed. "That was her way of telling you she wasn't interested in *you*." She reached under the covers and slowly ran her hand down Jared's chest until she grasped his hardening shaft. "Trust me, she's no longer a virgin. But Alexander would never force her. He's too much the gentleman." Had she thought him capable of ruining a young woman, she would have orchestrated her own ruination ages ago. She'd been so patient, so calculating, so *good*, and that little bitch had merely opened her legs and stolen him from her. Well, she would steal him back. "I'll wager she threw herself at him just like her whore mother threw herself at Montrose."

Jared grabbed a hunk of her hair and pulled her close. "She wouldn't do that."

Claire slapped at his hand. "Let go. You're hurting me." When she began to exert pressure on him below the sheets, he released her.

"Blast it," he said, reaching over to encircle her breast. "Just the thought of his hands on her...I'll kill him." He squeezed her nipple until she gasped. "I told you this little scheme of yours would never work."

Claire turned toward him, offering him her other breast. She caressed the tip of his manhood and he shivered, relaxing a bit. "It should have. I gave it much thought and Mr. Heath assured me your little Francie practically swooned when he told her the terms of her father's will. I believe the man actually felt bad about it. Can you imagine?"

With both hands now teasing her, Jared murmured, "Francie does have a way about her, and I look forward to many hours of enjoying those ways."

Claire scowled. "Do not forget whose bed you're in now,

and who made you groan with indescribable pleasure only moments ago." How could he say such a thing? Francie Jordan wasn't fit to empty Claire's chamber pot. Perhaps Claire's scheme had been too subtle. She should have invited the chit to tea where she'd add a few drops of laudanum to her cup. Jared could have carried her off and had his way with her and Claire could have spent hours consoling Alexander.

"You set me on fire, Claire, I will not deny that." He traced her shoulder and planted a kiss along the hollow of her neck. "We understand each other. But we have other desires..." He licked a nipple. "One way or another, you'll have your Bishop and I'll have my Francie."

Claire tilted her head back and closed her eyes as Jared skimmed a hand along her belly. Soon it would be Alexander's hands touching her, Alexander's mouth exploring her curves, and Alexander's—

"You don't think they're in love with one another, do you?"

The question burst through Claire's brain, shattering all thoughts of Alexander. "Don't ever say that again." She shoved Jared away, bound off the bed, and scooped her chemise from the floor. Jared's hot gaze followed her around the room as she retrieved her clothing. He might think he was in love with Francie Jordan, but he still wanted her. *Every man wanted her.* Soon, Alexander would, too.

There was just the little matter of disposing of Francie Jordan. If Jared were not up to the task of removing the bitch from Alexander's life permanently, Claire would see to it herself. She would devise a more drastic plan and this time, she would not be so generous with the chit's welfare.

There had never been a man who did not desire Claire. Alexander would realize he desired her, too, once she stripped him of that little country mouse. Claire smiled and patted her hair in place. Nothing would keep her from the object of her affection. Soon, Alexander Bishop would be hers.

~

"SOMETIMES, I feel I can see right through to his very soul. And other times, he seems a stranger." Francie sat beside Aunt Eleanor in her bedroom, waiting for the carriage to arrive that would take them to St. Thomas's chapel and her husband-to-be.

Aunt Eleanor patted her hand and tried to soothe Francie's nerves. "It will be all right, child. You're feeling a case of wedding jitters, that's all."

"It's been like this for over a week." She shook her head, careful not to undo the magnificent pile of curls heaped atop her head and held in place with several tiny pearl pins. "When I'm too near him, I can't catch my breath. My stomach gets all quivery, and my heart beats too fast."

Her aunt merely smiled.

"And the most ridiculous things pop out of my mouth." She frowned. "Or rather, fly out."

Her aunt nodded.

"Of course, Alexander isn't afflicted with any of these conditions. If anything, he's more remote than ever." *Except when he thinks I'm not looking and he all but devours me with those silver eyes. That's when my heart jumps to my throat and I forget to breathe.*

It had been like this since they'd returned from Amberden almost three weeks ago. Francie had lain awake half the first night, wondering if he'd come to her bed. When she heard his footsteps on the carpet sometime after two in the morning, she'd held her breath. He'd paused for an eternity and then his footsteps trailed past her door, away from her.

He'd spoken little and smiled only once, a faint little half-smile when he spotted her rosemary bread on the table beside the basket of white rolls. He'd eaten one of each and told Francie to send his compliments to the cook, though from the look in his eyes, he knew she'd baked the bread herself.

That small little scrap of praise brightened her day and warmed her night. That was the pitiful part of the whole blasted situation. She'd been reduced to hanging on his every word, hoping for a smile, a gesture, or at least an acknowledgment. She wanted the man she'd seen in Amberden, if only a glimpse, but he'd buried himself so far under proper etiquette and a starched cravat, she wondered if she'd ever see him again.

She longed to feel his fingers stroking her senseless, hear her name on his lips as he entered her, smell the musky scent of their lovemaking clinging to her. "Francie?"

She jumped, startled by her aunt's voice. "Yes, Aunt Eleanor?"

"Often the most difficult men make the best husbands."

"They do?" Aunt Eleanor was right about so many things, but this?

"They most certainly do." Her aunt gave her a knowing look and nodded her gray head. "Your Uncle Bernard is a perfect example."

Francie laughed. "Uncle Bernard is the ideal husband. I can't imagine him ever being difficult."

"He was more than just difficult. Downright impossible was more like it."

"Uncle Bernard?" She pictured the kind, mild-mannered uncle who possessed the most diplomatic nature of anyone she'd ever met.

"Hmmm. Quiet. Temperamental. *Impossible*." Her aunt's eyes grew misty. "But only with me. You see, he was trying to deny the attraction he felt and the more his feelings grew, the worse his mood got."

"What happened?" Francie whispered, caught in a love story she never knew existed.

"My father betrothed me to an earl. Bernard was so miserable that one day he exploded and confessed his feelings." Her eyes twinkled. "Since that day, he's been the most wonderful, caring man alive."

"What did your father say?"

Her aunt's blue eyes clouded. "He believed wealth and power were the most important requirements in a marriage. Love, to him, was a useless waste of human emotion. He never forgave me for choosing Bernard."

Francie squeezed her aunt's plump hand. "I'm so very happy you did," she whispered.

"As am I, child." She sniffed and said, "But, enough about me. This is your wedding day and you should be smiling and thinking about that handsome groom of yours."

Francie blushed. If only her aunt knew she'd been thinking of little else these days.

"Your mother and father would be so proud of you," Aunt Eleanor murmured, her gaze settling on the locket around Francie's neck.

Their locket. Two ill-fated lovers. Her fingers closed around it. After her father's death, Bernard presented her with the other piece, the one with her mother's picture. Last evening, he'd handed her a small white box with a red ribbon tied around it. Inside, she found the locket fastened to a new gold chain.

"Aunt Eleanor, it was you and Uncle Bernard who raised me. I'm happy to have had a chance to know my father, but truly you are my parents."

Eleanor's eyes filled and she leaned in to squeeze Francie's free hand. Francie kissed her aunt's cheek and closed her eyes, willing her own tears not to flow.

Would she ever know a love as profound as her aunt and uncle's, or her parents'? She squeezed the locket, praying love would flow to her. This was her wedding day. She wore a beautiful cream silk gown covered with tiny seed pearls and adorned with French lace, the finest money could buy. Alexander had seen to that. Her stomach clenched as she thought of his wedding gift to her, an emerald necklace with a matching bracelet. He'd been most generous with her, in everything but the one thing she wanted most—his love.

21

Alexander shifted his weight for the tenth time in as many minutes and checked his timepiece. She was late. The left side of his jaw twitched. She should have been here twenty minutes ago. Where the devil was she? Bernard remained unperturbed by Francie's absence, his tall, slightly stooped form walking from one corner to the other, hands clasped behind his back. Only Father Braenton, the round little priest with the ruddy cheeks and bright blue eyes, commented on the absence of Alexander's bride.

"Perhaps Miss Jordan had a problem with her carriage," Father Braenton offered in a hushed tone.

Alexander shoved his hands in the pockets of his black trousers. "It's *my* carriage and it's in excellent condition."

"Hmmm. I see," the priest replied. "An illness then? Someone not feeling well? That might cause a delay."

Alexander shot him a dark look. "Miss Jordan and her aunt are in quite good health."

The priest coughed and cleared his throat. "She's only twenty minutes late."

"Twenty-two minutes."

"She'll be here."

"I know," Alexander ground out. But he didn't know. Not really. Not the deep-gut knowing he usually had about things. He had doubts, several of them. Small niggling tormentors reminding him he'd done nothing to engender Francie's affection since their return from Amberden. If anything, he'd been cool and evasive, trying to distance himself from her warm laughter and bright smiles. And he'd been very effective. All he need do was push his mind and body from the first ray of light peeking over the horizon until the house fell silent around the blackness of night. Then he could crawl to bed and sleep a few tortured hours until daylight beckoned him to repeat the ritual.

He ached to touch her, to bury his face in her lavender-scented hair, to taste her welcoming lips, to hear her moan his name. *Damn!* That was the problem. This obsession with her was driving him mad. He must get control, pull away a little, and detach before he trusted himself to be near her again. He'd shown her too much in Amberden, shown her a vulnerable side of himself even he didn't like to acknowledge existed. But she'd seen it. He could tell by the way she looked at him sometimes, as though she wanted to comfort him. As though she thought he needed it. He didn't want or need that kind of attention from anyone.

The sooner Francie learned that, the better. Of course, maybe she already had. She'd grown very quiet in the last couple of weeks. Not at all her usual self. Maybe that's why she was late. Maybe she wasn't coming. Maybe he'd succeeded at pushing her away.

"Praise be God," Father Braenton whispered. "She's here."

Alexander tensed, then looked up to see a flurry of white in the back of the church. He just made out the back of Francie's dress before she disappeared from his sight. His heart rammed against his chest; *she came*, it beat, in a bounding rhythm. *She came*.

Music filled the church and within minutes, Alexander found himself standing at the altar with Father Braenton at his side, waiting for Francie to walk down the aisle and join him.

And then she was there, filling the entrance, her arm laced through Bernard's. She glided toward him like an ethereal vision in a confection of cream silk and tiny pearls. When she reached the altar, she lifted her eyes to meet his.

He cleared his throat and swallowed hard. "Do you, Alexander Bishop, take this woman..." She wanted too much.

"...for richer, for poorer..."

He could never be what she wanted. Tiny beads of sweat broke out on his forehead.

"...in sickness and in health..."

Could never give what she demanded. "...until death do you part?"

Alexander opened his mouth to speak. He should set her free, let her find someone who could give her the love she deserved, without restriction or restraint. And yet he knew he wouldn't.

"I do," he said, with a fierceness that surprised him. Francie was his now. Until death do them part.

FRANCIE PULLED the silver brush through her hair one last time. Where was he? Where was her husband? She glanced at the door. The household had retired over an hour ago and she'd been waiting for him almost two hours. He *was* coming to her, wasn't he? She gnawed on her lower lip. Perhaps she was supposed to join him in his room. Had he mentioned something of that nature? No. She would have remembered.

After all, he'd spoken so few words since the ceremony, most of them were etched in her brain. She sighed. Would she ever understand the man? Probably not. But that didn't keep her from loving him or wanting to be with him.

She worked her wedding ring around her finger. Two rows of rubies surrounded by a row of diamonds—elegant and fashionable, like her husband. Her gaze dropped to her nightgown. It dipped low in a daring swirl of satin and lace that clung to her with each movement. Another gift from Alexander. Surely if he'd taken the time to pick it out himself, he meant to see her in it.

The minutes ticked by with Francie perched on the bed, staring at the door. Waiting. A half-hour later, she knew he wasn't coming. He must have changed his mind and decided to forgo his wedding night. How humiliating. Had he tired of her already? Perhaps her lack of skill bored him. Or had the reality of his wedding vows hit him square in the nose and he was already regretting his decision? It could be any of those things. In truth, it could be *all* of those things.

She bowed her head as self-pity closed in on her, squeezing tight. What worse humiliation than abandonment by one's husband on one's wedding night? It was preposterous. Horrible. Agonizing. Degrading.

Unacceptable.

The word crept into her brain, nudging aside the others. She lifted her head and stared at the door again. Her gaze narrowed on the knob. Unacceptable. He might not be coming to her this evening but that didn't prevent her from going to him. She deserved an explanation. And she would have one.

Scrambling off the bed, she grabbed her wrapper and belted it around her waist. If her husband were in this house, she'd find him. And then she'd find out if their marriage were real. If the words he'd spoken in Amberden about needing her and *wanting* to marry her were real or just another part of a grand scheme to inherit Drakemoor.

She snatched the candle from the bedside table and hurried from the room, her bare feet padding down the hall. When she reached the top of the stairs, she stopped to listen. There were no sounds below, nothing save the quiet tick of the clock in the foyer. Had she somehow missed him walking past her door to his room? No. Her new husband was downstairs, most likely in his study, unless he'd sneaked away somewhere in the darkness of night.

She moved down the spiral staircase and into the foyer. The tiles at the bottom of the stairs were cold and unwelcome beneath her feet. She held the candle before her as she crept toward the study, her gaze fixed on the eerie shadows flickering from the candle's flames onto the walls in front of her. She paused at the door of the study and listened. Nothing. Inching the door open, she slid inside.

He wasn't in his chair or on the sofa. The lantern on his desk burned low, which made it difficult to discern much past the illumination from her candle. Francie inched forward, holding the candle in front of her. She would have sworn he'd be in here.

Her heart sank to her bare feet as she realized he'd lied to her. About everything. She'd bet her half of Drakemoor he was spending the night in his mistress's bed instead of hers. He'd used her in Amberden to get what he wanted—Drakemoor. It had all seemed so real back there. So wonderfully real.

Damn him! It had all been a lie. She must face that knowledge and choose her destiny, though there really was no choice at all. She'd pack in the morning and this time she knew he would not come after her. There was no need for pretense, not when he had Drakemoor.

She turned to leave and the flame from her candle caught a

dark shadow on the Aubusson rug. George, no doubt. She held the candle closer. It was George all right. He opened one golden eye, blinked once, then closed it with a muffled growl. The animal hated to have his sleep disturbed. Poor George. He'd miss this rug. The house in Amberden boasted a few braided ones, but nothing as thick and luxurious as this.

She heard another growl that sounded more like a moan. George? The dog's huge head rested between his tan paws, his eyes still closed, his breathing slow and heavy. No, the noise hadn't come from him. Mr. Pib? No, it was definitely not a cat's mewling. She heard it again. A low groan that sounded like...Alexander?

Through the flickering flame she detected a man's shoe, and a long leg, clothed in black. Francie crept closer, careful to keep the light low. She inched the candle up his body, noting a broad chest with a half-buttoned white shirt, a too-square jaw, and a forearm shielding his eyes.

The first thought that bombarded her brain was that Alexander was not in Lady Printon's bed. The second was that he'd chosen to sleep on the floor next to a dog rather than with her. Before she could consider her actions, she drove her bare foot into his side.

"Ahhhh." He let out a cry of pain and clutched his side.

"Curse you, Alexander Bishop!" Francie gave him another boot. "Curse you to the devil."

He grabbed her foot and almost toppled her. "Stop it!" he growled, his fingers biting into her ankle.

She stilled, waiting for him to release his hold on her. The minute he did, she kicked him again. "Damn you!"

He grabbed the hem of her nightgown as she tried to escape.

"Let me go." She twisted and pulled to free herself from his grip.

Alexander yanked hard. The ripping sound of fabric filled the room and Francie shrieked as her robe tore open and her nightgown split a jagged path from her breasts to her stomach.

He was on his feet, quicker than a panther stalking its prey. "What are you doing here?" he demanded, moving in front of her to block any thought of escape.

She yanked the nightgown together with her free hand and met his gaze. He stood in the shadows, making it difficult to see his face, but she didn't need to look at him to know he was furious. Well, she was furious, too.

"I thought tonight was our wedding night."

He ran a hand through his hair and sighed. "I was detained."

Francie tried to laugh, a short harsh sound that came out like a hiccough. "*Detained?* Really? Did George detain you?"

"Of course not. I was doing some paperwork and I got sleepy, so I decided to close my eyes for a few minutes."

"On the floor? *With the dog?*"

He shrugged. "I needed to stretch out."

"There's a piece of furniture for that. It's called a bed."

"Sarcasm does not become you, Francie."

"No, it doesn't," she said, holding the candle higher so she could see his face. His brows were drawn together in a straight line, his lips turned in a frown. "And lying doesn't become you either, Alexander. So stop pretending. You spent the night devising every possible reason not to come to my bed. I waited for you, like a fool, listening and hoping you would come." Her voice shook. "But you didn't, because you had no intention of coming."

"I was—"

"No," she cut him off. "No more excuses. At least give me that." She took a deep breath and smothered the pain. "It won't work. This was all a big mistake. I actually thought you were with Lady Printon tonight. I almost wish you were. At least it would have made sense. Be honest with me and with yourself. You don't want a wife. All you really want is Drakemoor. That's all you've ever wanted. Well, you can have it. All of it. In the morning, I'm leaving for Amberden and when I do, please don't come after me."

"Francie—"

"Just let me go. Please."

"I can't," he breathed, a mere whisper filled with so much pain it startled her. "I can't," he said in a louder voice. He took a small step toward her and shook his head. "I wanted to come to you tonight, wanted it so badly I had to force down half a bottle of whiskey to keep myself in that chair," he said, pointing to the leather chair behind his desk. "Even then, I wanted you."

"Then why didn't you come?"

He blew out a ragged breath. "*I couldn't*. I have to fight these feelings, be stronger than this overwhelming need for you that consumes me. Day and night, I'm tortured with wanting you. Thinking of you. Needing you. It's hell."

"I know," she whispered, taking a step closer to him. As understanding dawned, relief unfurled the pain and tension that had built in her these past few weeks. In its place, love grew stronger.

"I have to distance myself, Francie. Until I get control again over these erratic thoughts. I must make sense of these feelings I can't understand much less anticipate."

He turned away, rubbing the back of his neck. "Alexander?" She touched his shoulder. "If you keep running from your feelings, you'll be a tortured man all of your life. Trust me." He turned toward her and she stroked his stubbled chin. "I won't betray you," she murmured, trailing her finger along the jagged path of his scar. "I love you. Let my love make you whole again."

He hesitated a second, then reached out and traced her lips with his finger. "I don't deserve you or your love."

She set the candle on the mantel and circled her arms around his neck. "I love you, Alexander. All I ask is you let me show you. Don't ignore me," she whispered, leaning up on tiptoe to brush a kiss against his scar. "Don't avoid me." Her lips trailed down his face to his chin. "And don't refuse me." She touched her mouth to his. "Just let me love you."

"Francie," Alexander groaned. "You bring me to my knees." He buried his hands in her hair and pulled her to him.

"Trust me," she whispered against his lips. "Trust me and my love will make you the strongest man in the world."

~

FRANCIE'S WORDS pounded in Alexander's brain, her promises coursing through every nerve in his body.

Trust me. Don't ignore me. Trust me. Don't avoid me. Trust me. Don't refuse me. Trust me. Just let me love you. Trust me.

He was so damned tired of waging this battle against himself and these feelings that clamored inside, begging for release. What if he did the unthinkable and opened himself up to her? Just a crack, giving her a sliver of trust? What then? Could he do that? Would she accept the meager offering or would she demand more?

There was only one way to find out. He released his hold on her and cupped her face in his hands. "Show me your love, Francie." He bent toward her, his voice thick with emotion. "Give me the strength to show you mine."

She smiled, a brilliant smile filled with love and desire. And hope. Her arms circled his middle and she met his mouth in a hot, hungry kiss that spoke of passion and promise. Alexander groaned and pulled her closer, nestling her hips between his thighs.

"I want you," he said, bunching her nightgown in his hand and dragging it up.

Her throaty laugh scorched him with need. "Then you shall have me, my husband," she murmured, pulling away. Her gown hung open, torn down the middle to reveal a generous expanse of creamy breast. A pink nipple peaked out from the edge of the fabric. His gaze followed the jagged edges of thin material ending just below her navel.

His fingers shook as he inched the nightgown from her shoulders and let it land in a white heap at her feet. The light from the candle flickered along her body, casting golden shadows over her naked skin. Her hair hung down her back in a red-gold display of fire and sunshine. His gaze drifted downward to the fiery nest of curls between her legs and he knew this goddess from heaven would indeed rescue him from his own private hell.

She moved toward him, hands outstretched, lips parted in a slight smile and held his gaze as she released the last three buttons on his shirt. She eased it from his shoulders, her hands splayed across his chest, her fingers curling in a mat of dark hair. When her fingers slid to the top of his trousers, Alexander forgot to breathe. Those damnable entrancing eyes never left his face as she worked the buttons, first one, then another, and another until she'd released them all.

The need to end this sensual torment warred with the desire to prolong the sweet anticipation. He clenched his teeth and prayed for strength when Francie pulled the trousers over his hips. He'd always been the dominant one, but not tonight. This night, his wife would explore his body and test her powers and he would let her, even if it killed him—which it might well do.

His penis sprang free—hard, ready, throbbing. When her hands circled him, it took every last ounce of control not to throw her over the sofa and dive into her like a madman. It's what he wanted to do. What he was dying to do. He blinked hard and tried not to think of those slender fingers stroking the length of him.

"Alexander?" Her soft voice drifted to him.

"Hmm?" he grunted. He couldn't speak, not now when he was fighting for his sanity.

"What's wrong? You're looking at me but I don't think you're seeing me."

If only those damn fingers would stop moving. "What?" He blinked again, bringing her back into focus. "I'm looking at you, Francie," he said, staring at her. "And I'm seeing you."

"You sound angry. Don't...don't you want me to touch you?"

Now there was a question. Her finger touched the tip of his penis and he jerked against her. He grabbed her wrist. "Stop." His words fell in short, raspy breaths. "Stop."

"You don't like it, do you? I'm sorry, I'm doing it all wrong."

"If you did it any more right, it would be over right now."

"Oh. Then you do like it," she whispered, a faint smile brushing her lips. "Perhaps overmuch."

"Not perhaps, Francie," he ground out. "Most definitely."

Her smile deepened and her eyes closed to a sultry slant. "What do you want to do?"

He swallowed and tried to force his addled brain into action. Her fingers pushed his hand aside and she stroked him again, this time concentrating on the tip, moving around it in slow circles. "What do you want to do, Alexander?" she repeated, her voice a breath of throaty sensuality.

He shook his head and reached for her wrist again.

"No," she said. "Trust me." Her finger found a bead of moisture and swirled it around until he thought he'd go mad. "Show me."

"I have to see to your pleasure," he said, sucking in a deep breath. *And in three more strokes it will be too late.*

"You will. And you are," she murmured, leaning forward to flick her tongue over his nipple. He jerked in response and she sighed. "It gives me great pleasure to know you're enjoying my touch."

"That's not what—"

"Trust me." She pulled away to meet his gaze. "For once in your life, for this moment in time, forget about shoulds and shouldn'ts, have to's and must nots." She stroked the jagged end of his scar. "Let yourself be free to act as you will. Without thought to situation or circumstance. Only feeling. Just let yourself feel. And trust me."

She'd offered him a gift he couldn't refuse. Didn't want to refuse. And hoped he wouldn't regret.

"Trust me," she whispered, with a smile. Alexander groaned and pulled her to him, plunging his tongue inside her mouth, unleashing all the passion burning inside him since Amberden. His hands moved over her body, kneading and molding her softness to his hard lines. He wanted to devour her, swallow her passion in a wild union, pound into her until he spilled his seed deep inside her. *Trust me,* she'd said. *Let yourself be free and act as you will.* Her words drove him as he lifted her in his arms, never breaking the kiss, and carried her to the edge of the sofa. Tearing his mouth from hers, he looked once more into the blue depths of her eyes and saw heat and fire. And love. It was the last that pushed him to do her bidding.

He turned her away from him, gently coaxing her over the arm of the green fabric, and spread her legs. Then he grabbed her hips and dove into her, hard and fast and deep. She cried out once, but the smile on her lips as she turned her head to look at his face told him it was a cry of pleasure, not pain. And then he let himself go, opening his heart as he thrust into her again and again as the freedom of love's trust carried him to his ultimate release.

A long while later, they lay snuggled on the Aubusson rug, Alexander's arm draped over Francie, his fingers brushing her stomach. Had he gotten her with child tonight? Part of him wanted it to be so. He pushed aside the thought, unable to deal with any more new feelings. Getting used to his new wife would be challenge enough. A faint smile played about his lips as he recalled her rather loud screams as she reached her own pleasure. Three times. He'd have to remember to kiss her next time just before, so she wouldn't alert the household.

He sighed. The things a husband did to protect his wife. His smile faded. He would do anything to protect Francie.

"I'm glad you've finally accepted the fact Bishop's got a bride," the Earl of Belmont said around a mouthful of roast pork. "From what I've heard, he's quite taken with her."

Claire stabbed a boiled potato with her fork. "Oh?" She tried to keep her voice calm. "I hadn't heard." That wasn't true. She'd been receiving daily reports from the young stable boy she'd hired to spy on the couple.

"That's all anyone's talking about," her father said, lifting his wine glass. "They've been seen walking together, hand in hand."

"You can't believe everything you see," she said, popping a piece of potato in her mouth.

Her father eyed her from above the rim of his glass. "Unless what you see and what you hear are the same things." He took a sip of wine. "Then, it's a fair conclusion that the truth is somewhere close by." The earl turned his attention to his other dinner guest. "Wouldn't you agree, Jared?"

Jared Crayton shot a quick glance in Claire's direction, cleared his throat, and worked up a smile. "So it would seem."

"Father, do we really need to discuss Alexander Bishop and his new bride?" She almost choked on the word *bride*.

"I don't want to see you suffer any more disappointment at the hands of someone not worthy to wipe your slippers. I told you from the beginning, Bishop wasn't one of our kind." He stroked his beard and eyed his daughter. "I would be much more pleased if you and Jared could find some source of mutual attraction. God knows, you spend enough time together."

Claire glanced at Jared who watched her with a faint smile on his full lips. She knew he was thinking of their most recent liaison a few short hours ago in the copse of trees on the far end of her father's property. She'd met him there with nothing but bare skin underneath her gown. He'd bent her over a fallen tree and taken her, without rumpling her hair or wrinkling her gown.

"Jared and I are good friends, but we don't think of each other in that light."

"But we are very good friends," Jared repeated, his smile deepening.

She kicked him under the table. He could be such an arrogant fool sometimes. If her father discovered her indiscretions, he'd send her to a convent. Or worse yet, he'd force her into marriage with one of her partners.

The only person she wanted to marry was Alexander Bishop. The fact that he already had a wife wouldn't stop her from pursuing him. Wedding rings meant nothing to her. She'd shared a bed with as many married men as single ones. They'd been nothing more than conquests.

Alexander was different.

He was her obsession. She'd wanted him from the first time she set eyes on him, dressed in dark cutaways, standing alone at the Dellwoods' soiree. Tall and devastating with his silver eyes and arrogant manner. Oh, and that wicked scar running along the side of his face. Unapproachable, that's what people called him. Which only made her want him more. The true obsession began when he refused her subtle overtures. She'd been perplexed at first. No man had ever been immune to her charms, not even the vicar, who personally delivered three baskets of strawberries last spring after she spotted them growing in his garden and commented on her love of the sweet berries.

She *would* have Alexander. Soon. Let her father think she'd given up on him. She sipped her wine and smiled at her father, then cast a sideways glance at Jared. She'd devised the perfect plan and very soon, she and Jared would have exactly what they wanted.

22

"Who would have ever believed things would work out like this?" Aunt Eleanor dabbed at her eyes with a lace handkerchief. "I had hopes for the two of you, but some days I thought you were going to kill each other." She shook her gray head and offered a teary smile.

Francie smiled back. She'd been doing that a lot these past three weeks. "I guess we were pretty impossible early on. Alexander's like a different man, now." She leaned toward her aunt and whispered, "I've almost convinced him to forgo the cravat and jacket at home and opt for something more comfortable, such as a lawn shirt with breeches." She didn't mention the fact that he was only considering the change in attire because it would prove less cumbersome to shed his clothes should the desire to make love to his wife suddenly arise...as it had yesterday in the meadow where they'd been picnicking. And the day before that in the stables. And the day before that in the carriage. And the day before that...

Of course, she'd had to agree to shed her underclothes this afternoon when they went for a late picnic.

"The way the boy looks at you is heartwarming, dear," Aunt

Eleanor said. "Just heartwarming. Your mother and father would be so pleased."

Francie touched the locket dangling from her neck. "When I wear this, I feel as though they're with me."

"They are." Aunt Eleanor lifted her teacup and took a sip. "Now, all they're waiting for are the babies." Her blue eyes twinkled over the rim of her cup. "As am I."

Heat rose to Francie's cheeks. "Perhaps one day."

"For as many times as the two of you are sneaking off together, I'd say it'll be sooner rather than later."

"Aunt Eleanor! What a thing to say."

Her aunt laughed. "It's only the truth." She sighed. "Young love. There's nothing more wonderful."

Each day, Francie's love for Alexander grew tenfold. But he'd yet to mention a word about loving her. *Could* he love her? Could he love a child of theirs? Or could she hope for no better than deep affection? If there were one wrinkle in her cloak of happiness, it was her uncertainty about her husband's feelings for her. No matter how intense their lovemaking, he never said the words she longed to hear. And yet, she said them to him daily, hoping one day he'd confess the same feelings.

A knock on the door disturbed her thoughts. "Come in," she called, wondering who would be intruding on them so early in the afternoon. Alexander had a meeting with a possible investor for one of his companies and wouldn't be back for at least a few hours. As for Uncle Bernard, Francie had last seen him napping in the library with a book folded over his stomach.

James entered, twitching and tapping. "So sorry to interrupt you, Mrs. Bishop, but an urgent message just arrived for you." He twitched his nose twice and handed her a white envelope.

"Who delivered it?" She glanced at the bold handwriting on the front.

The butler lifted his shoulders and tapped his foot. "I didn't recognize the man." He licked his lips. "He just said to see you received the envelope immediately."

Francie pondered James's word a second before she tore open the envelope and pulled out a single sheet of paper. She scanned the contents and her heart skipped two beats.

"It's Sally," she said, meeting her aunt's curious gaze. "It seems the baby's come, but...something's wrong. She's asking for me." Francie stood up and dropped the letter on the table. "I've got to go to her."

"Poor girl," Aunt Eleanor murmured. "Of course, you must go. Just as soon as Alexander returns, the two of you can set out."

"I can't wait for him," she said, hurrying toward the door. "Sally needs me now. I'll throw a few things together and leave." She turned back to her aunt. "Just have him meet me in Amberden when he returns."

"I don't think that's a wise idea, child."

"Jared Crayton's not going to harm me now, Aunt Eleanor. I'm a married woman."

Her aunt worried her bottom lip. "At least, have your Uncle Bernard go with you. Please," she said when Francie started to protest.

Francie sighed. "Very well, but you're interrupting his nap for no reason."

"It would give me comfort," her aunt repeated. "And your husband as well."

Francie nodded and ran down the hall and up the stairs. What could have happened? She knew despite the circumstances surrounding the baby, Sally wanted the child, thought it was the only family she had. Dear God, let them be all right. And what about the woman Alexander had hired to care for Sally? Where was she?

~

"We can't get there fast enough, Uncle Bernard." Francie had no sooner spoken the words when the carriage took a wide turn, and she almost tumbled out of her seat.

"I hope Jacob Graves is a better groomsman than he is a driver," her uncle remarked with a frown. "We'll be lucky to get there without any broken bones."

Francie bit her lower lip. "We had no choice. Mr. Graves said the usual driver had taken ill."

"Alexander doesn't like him."

"My husband tends to be quite critical, if you haven't noticed."

Bernard shook his head as they hit a rut in the road and fell back against the squabs. "Well, I daresay, he's not far off the mark with this one."

"Just a little longer," she said.

She'd no sooner uttered the words than the carriage jolted to a stop and tossed them from their seats. The door flew open and a man's deep, rich laughter penetrated the interior.

"Well, well, well. What we have here?"

Francie's stomach lurched at the sound of Jared Crayton's voice. She scooted closer to her uncle and waited for her nemesis to show his face. She'd not drawn her next full breath when the beast peered into the carriage and settled his gaze on Francie. "A sweet maiden and an old..." He paused, pulled a gun from his coat, and with deadly aim, pointed it at Bernard and fired. "...dead man."

Francie screamed as blood poured from her uncle's shoulder. "Uncle Bernard." She leaned over him and pressed her hands on the wound, oblivious to the hot liquid seeping between her fingers. She must stop the bleeding and get help.

"I think it's too late to help him," Jared said, "But I'll be honored to help *you*, Francie. Any way I can."

She ignored his crudeness and screamed for the driver, "Mr. Graves? Mr. Graves? Help me, please?" The lanky form of Jacob Graves bent over and peered inside the carriage. He had a bottle in one hand and a handful of coins in the other. "I got nothin' against ye, Mrs. Bishop. Surely, I don't. It's that bastard husban' o' yers I can' stand." He squinted rheumy brown eyes at her. "Always lookin' down on me fer beggin' a pint o' two. 'E's the one that's gotta pay."

"I don't understand."

"What Mr. Graves is trying to say in his less-than-eloquent manner is that he detests your husband and has agreed to help me with my little plan to take you from him."

"That's absurd. Please... " She looked from the driver to Jared. "You must help...*please*, my uncle could die."

He ignored her plea. "You're mine now, Francie," Jared Crayton said in a fierce voice. "And I won't give you back."

"I'm a married woman. You can't just *take* me."

He stepped in, pulled her uncle from her grasp, and rolled him from the carriage. The sickening thump of Uncle Bernard's body as he hit the ground made her light-headed. Jared Crayton tried to pull her toward him and when she resisted, he half-lifted, half-dragged her from the carriage. "I'll wipe every trace of that bastard's touch from your body," he growled, his green eyes full of dangerous promise.

"And Alexander will forget you ever existed," a woman said from behind them.

Francie swung around to find Lady Claire Ashcroft astride a chestnut mare. "Lady Claire," she begged, still fighting Jared's grasp. "Please, help me! This man's mad. And my uncle," she said, gesturing toward his prone form, "he's been shot and needs help."

The beautiful woman raised a well-sculpted black brow and smiled. "On the contrary, Francie. I think Jared makes perfect sense. He's waited so long to have you." She dismounted her horse and stood beside her. "Almost as long as I've waited for Alexander."

"What are you talking about?"

"Surprised?" Claire Ashcroft crossed her arms over her ample bust and pierced Francie with a cold blue gaze. "Not as surprised as I was when he wed you." Her voice turned icy with rage. "He's mine and no woman, bastard or otherwise, is going to take him from me."

"Alexander is my husband," Francie said with an authority she didn't feel.

The other woman shrugged. "A temporary inconvenience. What do you think he'll do when he finds out you've run off with Jared?"

"That's ridiculous. He'll never believe it."

"Trust me, he will," Claire Ashcroft said with a superior smile. "I can be very convincing, especially to a brooding husband." She took a step toward Francie. "Give me your wedding ring. Now."

Francie instinctively clenched her left hand into a fist but Claire simply turned her gaze to Jared and said, "Take it."

Jared slid his hand down Francie's arm and forced it toward him. With his other hand, he tore the ring from her finger, and with it, a bit of flesh. She cried out as blood dripped from the small wound.

"So sorry, my sweet. Let me make it better." The beast lifted her finger to his mouth and gently sucked the blood. She tried to jerk her hand away but his grip made it impossible.

Claire took the ring from him and smiled...an almost kind smile, and so full of madness Francie shivered. She was well and truly alone.

"He'll hate you for deserting him," Claire continued, speaking with a soft tone as if having a discussion over tea. "Hate you as much as he hated his parents for leaving him, and they died. What do you think he'll feel when he learns you left of your own free will?"

"But that's a lie!"

"He'll never know that, will he?" Claire's gaze narrowed on Francie's locket a second before she ripped the chain from her neck.

"No!" Francie lunged for Claire but Jared held her back. She tried to kick free of him, but his grasp tightened into a painful vise.

"Be still, sweet Francie," he warned. His breath fanned her ear, his voice whisper soft. "Or I'll take you in the woods and put something in your mouth that *will* quiet you down."

She squeezed her eyes shut, praying for an end to this horrible nightmare.

A piercing shriek brought her skidding back to reality. Claire Ashcroft's face burned with fury. "Where did you get this, you little witch?" She stalked closer holding out the locket. *"Where did you get this picture of my mother?"*

Francie couldn't have heard her right. "The locket is mine and the woman in the picture is my mother."

"Liar!" Claire Ashcroft slapped Francie across the face. "How dare you? That woman is *not* your mother. Your mother was a whore!"

"The woman...*is* Claire's...mother."

Uncle Bernard! He was alive and breathing despite the blood seeping through his jacket in a widening circle. But the blood loss must have made him confused for he knew Claire was not Catherine's daughter.

Claire Ashcroft beamed with superiority.

Bernard gasped for breath. "She's also Francie's mother."

Claire rounded on him, her beautiful face pinched white. "What did you say?"

"You...are sisters."

Enraged, Claire stalked over to Bernard, placed her boot on his shoulder, and forced him to the ground where he groaned and clutched his bleeding shoulder.

"Uncle Bernard!" Francie tried again to kick free of Jared Crayton's grip but he only held tighter.

"He's lying." Claire turned back to Francie. "I am of noble blood, not some wrong-side-of-the-blanket bastard." She clenched her fists and said, "My father is Edgar Ashcroft, Earl of Belmont."

"No," Uncle Bernard rasped. "Your father was Philip Cardinger, Earl of Montrose. You and Francie...are...sisters." Then his head fell back as he lost consciousness.

"No!" Francie screamed.

"I won't believe it. It can't be." Claire paced back and forth, ranting like a madwoman. "No. No. No!"

Tears streamed down Francie's face. *Claire Ashcroft was her sister?* As much as she wished it weren't so, her uncle wouldn't lie. Her gaze shot to his lifeless form. Had he died trying to save her?

"She's your sister," Jared Crayton said, his voice half-amazement, half-declaration.

"No," Claire barked. "She's *not* my sister."

Francie shook her head. "My uncle wouldn't lie."

"No one must hear this vile gossip," Claire said. "Where's that drunken groomsman?" Her gaze searched the woods until it settled on the old man, lying face down in the dirt with a pint in his left hand.

"Do you think your father, I mean, Belmont, knows?" Jared asked, curiosity flitting through his words.

"My father *is* the Earl of Belmont." Claire lifted her chin in a regal manner as her blue gaze narrowed on Francie. "He shall *never* learn of this conversation. If I have to personally destroy every individual here to secure that privacy, then so be it."

"I don't think that's necessary, Claire," Jared Crayton said. "Graves is too drunk to remember anything and Francie's uncle is half-dead. He won't make it through the night out here." His arm tightened around Francie. "And my little lovebird isn't going to see anyone but me."

Claire stared at Francie for several moments, then stuffed the ring and the broken locket into the pocket of her riding jacket, and headed for her mount.

"It's just you and me now, sweetheart," Jared Crayton murmured, brushing a kiss along Francie's temple.

"You'll never get away with this," Francie hissed. "Alexander will find me."

"He won't even know where to look. Besides," he added, trailing a finger through her hair, "Claire has been known to possess great powers of persuasion. Why, I've even been persuaded a time or two myself."

His insinuations disgusted her. She had to find a way to escape him.

Claire brought her mount around and said, "Proceed as planned."

"No need to worry. Everything's in order."

Francie watched her ride away, head held high, looking innocent and beautiful. No one would have guessed she'd just been involved in the kidnapping of her own sister.

～

"REMIND me to thank Sally one of these days," Jared Crayton murmured.

"Sally?" Francie tried to keep the alarm from her voice. "What about Sally?"

He laughed, a warm, rumbling sound that belied the evil running through his veins. "She's the reason we were able to lure you away from Drakemoor. And your husband. Quite clever, don't you think?"

"I don't understand," she answered, but huge weights of dread pulled her under to the dark side of truth.

"Of course you don't. That's why it was such a splendid plan." He released her and turned her toward him, his green eyes sparkling. "I knew Sally was staying at your cottage, knew she'd been tossed out with nothing but the clothes on her back." He smiled at her, a deep, warm smile that brought out the dimples in his cheeks. "That's when I decided to write the letter from Sally telling you something had happened to the baby."

"It was all a lie?"

He nodded, his blond hair swirling about him in the afternoon breeze. "Sally had the child this morning. A boy. I visited her. I thought that might please you," he paused, "it also afforded me the opportunity to step inside your home. Was your bed at the top of the stairs or further down the hallway?"

Her stomach lurched at the thought of Jared Crayton in her home, scouring out her bed like a lecher.

"Don't care to answer? Perhaps I'll boot them out and we'll try both beds. What say you to that?"

"How can you be so cruel?"

"Cruel? I'm not cruel, I'm clever," he boasted. "I know how to get what I want. Claire and I even took care of your husband. Didn't you wonder how it just so happened Bishop was gone when the note arrived? One of Claire's, ah, friends, an old gentleman who owed her a special favor, agreed to pretend interest in one of Bishop's companies."

"Why would you both go to such lengths to take me from the man I love?"

"Don't speak of such things! You only think you love that bastard. Soon you'll forget all about him. Once you've been with me, you won't remember anyone's touch but mine."

He grabbed her and bound her hands with a leather strap he pulled from his waistcoat. "Did I mention I love taming wild animals?" He trailed a finger along the back of her neck. "They kick. They buck." He paused. "They bite. Until they become accustomed to my touch. Then, even the fiercest, wildest creature turns to porridge. You're my wild animal, sweetest Francie, and I'm the master who will tame you."

"Never."

"Never? Did I not warn you against that word? I believe I did, shortly before your aunt suffered that unfortunate mishap in her weed patch." Before she could respond, he hoisted her in his arms and carried her to his waiting mount. "You may kick and even scream, but it will do you no good. Other than to arouse me, if that's your purpose. No one can help you now. Your fate is sealed and the sooner you accept it, the better for everyone."

He flung her across the saddle and mounted behind her. "You're mine now. And I'd like a bit of privacy, away from the drunk and dying." He chuckled and nudged his horse into a trot.

Francie tried to ignore the pressure of his thighs against hers and the all-too-frequent sweep of his hand over her person. She would sooner die than submit to the beast. Her wrists bled from attempts to free herself of the leather strap that bound her. Where was he taking her? Certainly, he couldn't just *keep* her. That was utter madness, and yet, everything about these last hours was madness.

She must escape. Blood seeped into the leather straps as she tried once more to free herself.

"Stop that," the beast hissed into her ear, "or by all that's holy, I'll stop right now and show you what happens when you disobey me." He stroked her hair. "I do so want our first time to be special, with me, the perfect lover. Don't force me to behave otherwise, my sweet."

Francie swallowed her revulsion and forced herself to breathe through the panic. "Where are you taking me?"

"Interested, are we?" He thrust a hand against her belly and pulled her closer. "There's a cottage on the far end of my father's property. It's clean, quaint, and secluded. My father used it to tryst with the more comely members of his staff while my mother was alive. More prudent, he said, and less likely to cause a scene, though my mother never uttered a complete phrase her entire life. She knew her station." His breath fanned her ear. "And you will learn yours soon enough. Under me. On top of me." He jerked his hips against her bottom and said on a ragged sigh, *"All over me."*

Francie squeezed her eyes shut and prayed Alexander would find her before it was too late.

When Jared finally stopped his mount, her body ached but her mind sought desperately for a way to escape. Mayhap she could locate a knife and drive it into the beast's heart. Or smash his head with a rock. Or shoot his private parts to bits. She, who had never so much as squashed a bug, had been reduced to the true contemplation of murder.

Could she do it?

To protect the love she and Alexander shared? The answer roared through her in a resounding *yes*.

He dismounted, hoisted her from the horse, and set her on her feet. "Charming, is it not?" he asked, gesturing toward the cottage.

Had she not known what atrocities occurred within the whitewashed walls of the structure, she would indeed have looked upon the cottage, with its daisies and asters clustered around the perimeter, as charming. Despite her revulsion, she forced an answer. "Yes, it is."

That seemed to please him, for he smiled and said in a gentle tone, "Come, I've a special surprise for you."

He let her enter first and inside she found roses of every color stuffed in vases, pitchers, and pots, their scent greeting her with familiarity and longing. Oh, to be back in the garden at Drakemoor with Alexander watching her from the library window.

"I know how you love your flowers. I had them brought here just for you." He smiled down at her, his eyes bright. "I can make you happy, Francie. If only you will let me." His lips brushed her cheek, trailed along her jaw, and hovered near her mouth.

She jerked her head away and for the first time in her life, she knew hate.

"Don't turn away from me," he spat out and grabbed her chin with two fingers, forcing her face toward him. "Don't ever turn away from me again." He clutched her arm and dragged her to the bed. "Why must you fight me so? Can you not see your efforts are futile? *I will have you.*" His voice dipped. "Often." He fingered the lace rimming the neckline of her gown. "I'll wipe out every memory of Bishop's touch until all you think about is mine."

Nothing could make her forget Alexander.

"Lie down." He towered over her, his fingers biting into her arm. "Now."

If she did as he requested, he would force himself on her. If she did not, judging by the maniacal expression on his face, he might well kill her.

She would rather die than submit to the monster. With that thought, she kicked out and almost broke free.

"Damn you," he said, grabbing her arm in a punishing grip. He shoved her onto the bed and yanked her bound hands above her head. "Why do you choose to anger me? Would you prefer I take you with force?" He tied her hands to the bedpost. "Make you bleed? Bruise you until you can't walk?" He removed his jacket and folded it over a nearby chair. "That would certainly not be my choice," he said in a conversational manner as he removed first one boot and then the other. "I would much rather a willing bed partner. One who possesses desire, creativity, and a willingness to please." He untied his neckcloth and tossed it aside. "Will you be that person, Francie?" He slid onto the bed and lay beside her. "Will you be my willing lover?"

Before she could answer, he pinned her head to the bed and assaulted her mouth, plunging his tongue inside until she gagged. "Stop feigning distaste and kiss me." He wrapped his hand around her hair and pulled until she cried out. "Let's try again. I shall lean over and offer you my mouth. You will run your tongue along my lips and tease me until I open them. Then you shall..."

A pounding on the door interrupted the monster. "Lord Crayton. Please, sir, I must speak with you immediately!"

"What the devil is going on?" Jared Crayton rolled off the bed and straightened his clothing. "Just a moment, my sweet," he murmured, trailing a finger from Francie's neck to her breast. He leaned closer to whisper, "Don't bother appealing to him for help. He's completely loyal to my family." Then he straightened and made his way to the door, which he thrust open with a growl. "Dunstin, what the devil are you doing? I'll have you shot for disturbing me."

A slight young man with spectacles and a fluff of red hair bowed and thrust a satchel at him. "So sorry, my lord. It's the duke. He commands you take this and leave at once. There's enough inside to see you to the property in Devonshire. Do not return until he sends for you."

"Blast, man, are you mad?" And then, "Is my father mad? Has he tumbled one too many scullery maids?"

The man named Dunstin shook his head and darted nervous eyes in Francie's direction. "No, sir." His face turned a mottled red. "There's quite a commotion in the green salon, and it would appear you're in the thick of it."

"Damnation, stop your blathering and speak sense. How could I possibly be in the thick of anything when I am here?"

"A Miss Sally Baines's uncle is in the salon." *Sally's uncle?* Francie listened with growing fascination. Sally had but one uncle. No one had ever seen him but tales of his exploits filled Amberden.

"Good God." Jared Crayton ran a hand through his hair and sighed. "I'm to pay court to a commoner because I lifted his niece's skirt and got her with child? Absurd. Tell my father I'll see him later." He turned away and smiled at Francie. "I'm rather busy at the moment."

Dunstin stepped inside the cottage and said, "Miss Baines is dead, my lord."

Dead? Francie whimpered. *Poor, dear Sally.*

Jared Crayton's smile slipped. He swung around. "Impossible. I saw her and the babe this morning. They were both well."

"She bled to death, according to her uncle. The man demands to see you."

"Does he not know who I am? Who my *father* is? Why does the duke not toss him out on his ear?"

Dunstin shook his head. "A man named Mad Jack is not the sort of man one tosses out, on his ear or elsewhere. Your father wishes you to take this money and flee at once."

"Mad Jack?"

It was him, the legend of Amberden!

"Yes, my lord. He threatened to dismantle your body, limb by limb, beginning with your, uh," he floundered and glanced at his master's breeches.

If the man were as true as the legend, he *would* find his prey and dismantle him, beginning with his private parts.

Jared Crayton needed no more convincing. "Give me a moment to gather my things." He glanced at Francie. "And my lady friend."

"No, my lord. You must travel alone and unencumbered. The duke insisted."

Francie's nemesis pulled on his boots and shrugged into his jacket. "How did my father know I was here?"

"Servant gossip, I believe. You must hurry, my lord. Mad Jack does not appear one to be trifled with."

Jared Crayton leaned over and kissed Francie softly on the forehead. "You're mine now," he breathed. "I won't leave without you."

"Follow the duke's instructions," Dunstin said, glancing once more at Francie. "He fears Mad Jack's men are scouring the countryside in search of you this very moment. Please leave now, my lord. Your safety and your life depend upon it."

Jared hazarded one last glance at Francie. "I'll send for you," he vowed, then closed the door softly behind him.

She must escape.

The beast would no doubt find a way to transport her to Devonshire. She yanked at the leather strap, mindless of the pain and blood as the leather tore into her wrists. Every second that passed lessened her chances of escape. Francie thrashed about on the bed and yanked the strap harder, begging for a miracle. She opened her mouth and screamed for Alexander, for their love, for the hopelessness closing in, but no one heard her. No one at all.

23

When Alexander bound up the steps to Drakemoor, George greeted him with a very enthusiastic, sloppy kiss. Alexander had hoped his wife would be the one bestowing the kisses, not her dog, but he was fast learning that one never quite knew what to expect with Francie.

"Where is she, George? Where's that mistress of yours?" He patted the animal's head and received yet another wet kiss—this one on his hand. "Enough. Any more of this and I'll require a bath." Mention of the word *bath* sent the monstrous animal scrambling down the steps toward the row of privets located in the front corner of the gardens. Alexander sighed and hid a smile. It wouldn't do to show his wife how much he liked George or how much he now considered slobbering kisses on the ordinary level at Drakemoor. Since Francie entered his life, routine had flown out the door along with ordinary and boring. Speaking of his wife, he couldn't wait to see her. They had an assignation this afternoon—picnicking in the far fields—*with* a basket of goodies and *without* undergarments. Could a man reach any higher level of contentment? He doubted it possible.

Unfortunately, such contentment often shed its fine coat when met with disappointment as Alexander discovered moments later when his wife was nowhere to be found. How could a wife simply go missing? For that matter, how could a house that heretofore had thrived on order and decorum appear dismal and boring during Francie's absence?

His wife had well and truly gotten to him, wormed her sweet innocence and laughter right into his heart. He'd only been gone a half-day and yet he missed her. Terribly. Couldn't wait to see her. Talk to her. Touch her.

Dear God, he was in love with her!

The very thought made him light-headed and sick to his stomach. He loved his wife. How could it have happened? When? Should he confess? Yes, of course. He must be honest and admit the truth. Then what? Hand her the power to reduce him to a ninny? No, he couldn't do that. He must maintain composure and a sense of order about things at all times. No loss of control, no weakness.

But this was Francie. His wife. With bright smiles, open laughs, and an honest heart.

And he loved her.

But he wouldn't tell her. Not yet.

"Alexander, is everything all right? You look rather pale." Eleanor straightened her ample figure and peered at him from beneath her oversized sunbonnet. The kind Francie should avail herself to on all occasions and usually did not.

He cleared his throat and pushed the love business back to its hiding place, deep in the darkest corner of his heart. "Yes, fine. But I seemed to have misplaced my wife."

Eleanor removed her gloves and specks of dirt and manure sprayed the ground; fortunately, none landed on his boots. "She went to look after Sally." Her mouth pulled down at the corners. "She received a missive this morning. Something went terribly wrong and Sally needed her."

"She traveled alone?"

"Good heavens, no. Bernard went with her."

This information brought a fine coat of sweat to Alexander's brow. Bernard offered no more protection than Mr. Pib. He drew in deep breaths, mindless of the manure concoction fermenting a step away. "When did they leave?" He calculated the time it would take to travel to Amberden and back, with an hour or two tending Sally and the babe.

"Right after breakfast. Eight o'clock, I believe."

"And the note? May I see it?"

"Inside. Come, I'll fetch it for you. "

As they walked toward the front lawn, Alexander pictured his wife cooing over Sally's babe as the hours passed and the sun set. Were that to happen, she would surely enlist prudence and remain the night rather than attempt to return home in the dark.

Wouldn't she?

As Alexander tortured himself over his wife's reasoning capabilities or lack thereof, a carriage bearing the Montrose crest clambered up the long drive. *Let Francie be inside.* Alexander squinted. Why was the driver doubled over in apparent pain?

When Eleanor spotted the driver, she let out a strangled cry. "Bernard!" Without a thought to decorum or her bad knees, she hiked her skirts and hurried toward the carriage as it jerked to an unsteady halt by a row of well-tailored privets. "Oh, Bernard, what on earth has happened?"

Fear choked Alexander as he took in the old man's blood-soaked jacket, the nasty gash above the left brow, the broken spectacles. The man's injuries were not the result of a mere accident. They were intentional and Alexander would wager his half of Drakemoor they'd been delivered at the hands of Jared Crayton.

Bernard squinted and clutched his left shoulder. "Crayton took her."

"Where?" Alexander asked, refusing to panic even as Bernard's words confirmed his worst fear.

"On the road...halfway..." Bernard gasped and fell forward, wincing in pain.

Alexander caught the old man and lifted him, striding toward the front entrance. He struggled to remain calm. His wife, the woman he loved more than his own life, needed him, and he would not disappoint her. *He would find her.*

"Oh, dear Lord, our poor girl." Eleanor touched the edge of her husband's jacket.

Alexander heard Bernard whispering and his gaze leapt to his face. The old man was trying to speak, desperately trying to stay conscious long enough to tell him something more.

"No, Bernard," Alexander said. "Don't try to speak. Just rest."

"We must stop the bleeding," Eleanor cried. "Did that brute beat you?"

"No more questions, now. We must send for the physician." Alexander spoke before Bernard had a chance to tell his wife he'd been shot. Such an admission might well send the poor woman to the edge of sanity. Better let her think her husband's shoulder had been pummeled with a fist.

"Yes. Of course, you are right." She swiped her eyes and touched her husband's pale cheek seconds before the old man lost consciousness. "All will be well, Bernard. The doctor will see to you and Alexander will find Francie."

God willing, Eleanor was right on both counts.

∾

ALEXANDER GRABBED his gloves and hat, anxious to begin the search for his wife. He'd wanted to leave immediately, but the large stain on Bernard's jacket and subsequent loss of consciousness held him back until Dr. Stockert's arrival. What must Francie be enduring at the hands of that bastard Crayton? The possibilities bombarded his mind with horrendous and unceasing visions.

If Crayton harmed Francie, Alexander would kill him—with his bare hands.

Dr. Stockert's examination confirmed Alexander's suspicions. Bernard had lost a large amount of blood. Fortunately, the bullet burst through the skin and didn't necessitate fishing around for it—one bit of very good news. If they could keep the wound from putrefying, he had a chance.

All was as settled as it could be at Drakemoor with a nurse at Bernard's bedside and the entire staff on the lookout for unwelcome guests. After Bernard's bloody entry, Alexander had no choice but to alert the staff of Francie's disappearance and Crayton's part in it. There had been a time when Alexander would have taken a vow of silence rather than involve the staff in personal affairs. But that was before Francie.

"You know what to do, James?"

The butler responded without a single foot tap. "Indeed I do, sir." He raised a pistol and said, "If Lord Crayton comes knocking, I shall keep him here at any cost."

"Exactly right." Alexander hesitated a second and then extended a hand. "Thank you, James."

The other man's foot lifted, halted, and settled back on the parquet floor without a sound. He stood taller, puffed out his chest, and accepted his master's hand. "Godspeed, sir."

Alexander nodded and turned on his heel. Given the opportunity, even the most ordinary of men would rise to the occasion. Perhaps he'd put too much on his abilities and too little on everyone else's. There was indeed a certain amount of comfort knowing James would do his very best to protect Drakemoor and its inhabitants. Of course, Alexander would prefer to take on both tasks but he couldn't search for his wife and protect his home. He had to accept assistance—a novel approach for someone accustomed to relying solely on himself.

He needed help if he were to find Francie, not only from those residing at Drakemoor, but those who might know the whereabouts of her abductor. Visions of black curls and a too-sultry smile flashed through his brain as he mounted Baron and sped down the lane.

∾

"ALEXANDER, what a true pleasure it is to see you." Claire rose and smiled at him from across the room. "Do come in and I'll order refreshments." He'd come to her! For comfort? Commiseration? *Affection?* She would most gladly provide all three and more.

The object of her obsession raked a hand through his disheveled hair and made his way toward her. "I've no time for refreshments. It's Francie," he said in a voice that sounded wild and desperate. "I can't find my wife."

Wife? Oh, how she abhorred that word when spoken in association with Alexander. She wanted to tell him his wife had vanished. *Poof*, all gone. If Jared possessed even a speck of common sense, he'd keep her well hidden, maybe venture to Italy or the West Indies for a time. She tilted her head to give Alexander a better glimpse of her long neck and tapped a finger to her chin as though thinking, which she was, but not about that chit. No, she was thinking of Alexander Bishop with his shirt off, muscles gleaming from the sun and sweat...

"Claire." He touched her sleeve. "She's gone missing. I've come to ask for help."

She blocked out the pain in his voice. He should bleed with worry for *her*, not Francie Jordan. She looked up into the silvery depths of his gaze that shone bright, perhaps a bit too bright. "How may I help you, Alexander?" She loved the sound of his name on her lips and couldn't wait to whisper it as he made love to her.

"I have reason to believe Crayton has kidnapped Francie."

Claire drew a hand to her lips in feigned surprise. "Kidnapped? Are you certain?"

"Reasonably, yes."

He must stop speaking as though someone had pummeled his chest. She clasped his hand and delighted as heat and desire shot through her. Soon she would be at liberty to touch his entire body. "How utterly barbaric. I'd not thought Jared capable of such a deed." In truth, he wasn't. The final plan had been her idea and it was working splendidly.

"The man is capable of more than you can imagine. You must help me find them."

Not very likely. She gently disengaged her hand and turned away for fear he'd see the hatred on her face. "How could I possibly help?" Pray, Jared had already ravaged the bitch.

"Do you know where he might have taken her?" She hid a smile. The velvet timbre in his voice stroked her senses as she envisioned his naked body. *She would have him.* Soon. The very thought made her bold and anxious. "She's not worthy of you, Alexander." She slipped a hand into the pocket of her gown and clutched Francie's locket and wedding ring. "She has no breeding, no grace, no refinement. You deserve much better." Claire turned to him and traced the scar on his face. "You deserve me."

His jaw twitched the tiniest bit. A sign of interest, to be

certain, though he was much too noble to state his desire at present—but he did desire her—all men did. He merely needed a bit of persuasion. She removed the locket and ring from her pocket and opened her hand so Alexander could understand well and truly that his wife was indeed gone. "She's not coming back."

"Those are Francie's. Where did you get them?" He took them from her, his gaze wild and frantic. "There's blood on the ring. Claire, where the hell did you find them?"

"Blood?" She inched closer and inhaled his spicy scent. "Hmm. So there is." She shrugged. "He'll never let her go. And now that I have you..." She offered him her most dazzling smile and just the tiniest hint of cleavage. "I'll not let you go either."

He took a step toward her. "Answer me."

She would not let him intimidate her. "I've wanted you from the moment I saw you, and yet I behaved as a lady should, with grace and proper decorum. And then *she* appeared like a bit of windblown baggage and you actually wed her. Have you no idea what an insult that was to me?" She sighed. "Drakemoor was the true object of your affection; we all knew that. I daresay even *she* knew it. Still, I was quite put off by the whole affair. But Jared has her now so you'll not need to feign affection for her in order to share your precious Drakemoor."

"Where is she, Claire?"

He could be quite frightening if he chose to. She liked this side of him. Perhaps he'd show her more. "How should I know?" That should stir him up a bit.

Alexander grabbed her arm and yanked her to within an inch of his face. "You know and you'll tell me."

Indeed, she quite desired the angry, more primitive aspect of Alexander Bishop. "Will you leave bruises on my arm for my father to wonder about?" She smiled up at him. "He'll not be pleased."

Alexander's silver gaze narrowed on her neck. "Do not tempt me."

Claire laughed and stroked his cheek. "I think you are the type of man who is only tempted when he wants to be." She leaned on tiptoe and whispered in his ear, "Do you want to be tempted, Alexander?"

He released her arm and stepped away, his face void of the emotion that possessed him moments ago. "I should like to speak with your father." He straightened his cravat and stood waiting like an impenetrable wall.

"My father? Whatever for?"

"I plan to inform him of your part in Francie's kidnapping."

"Hah! He'll never believe you and I've admitted to nothing."

His gaze sliced her. "But you have." He opened his large hand to expose the ring and locket. "By your possession of these."

She glanced at the revolting objects. "They prove nothing." Father would never believe him.

"I also plan to present him with a list of names."

"Names?"

Alexander's lips worked into a smile that chilled her. "You haven't always behaved as a lady should, have you? I have a list of the men and boys with whom you shed your 'grace and proper decorum'. Do you not think the stable boy with nary a hair on his chin is not as eager to spout his prowess as the widower with nary a hair on his head? Indeed, they will talk."

She feigned righteous anger. "How dare you imply that I have been less than—"

Before she could finish her tirade Alexander interrupted, "Very well then, you won't mind if I have a moment with your father." When she didn't respond, he continued. "I'm a businessman, Claire. I study the market and take calculated risks that bring huge rewards. Do not think I conduct my personal life or affiliations with any less stringent guidelines. If I say I have names, I have them, and I will use them if need be."

Cruel man. Vicious. Unworthy.

"Tell me where my wife is or by all that is holy, I'll expose your indiscretions, beginning with Pastor Hulings."

ALEXANDER SPED to the cottage on the far side of the duke's property. If Claire were lying, by God, he'd plaster her indiscretions in *The Times* for all of London and half of England to see. He'd called her bluff when he told her he had the names of the men and boys she'd dallied with, but as he'd warned her, he was quite good at calculating risk. Too many men owed him money and favors; the names could be easily gotten and then even more easily spread throughout the countryside.

He had to find Francie, had to save her from the beast who threatened her. Alexander crested a hill and spotted the cottage Claire described. He forced himself to remain calm as he neared, for if he lost his head, he might jeopardize his wife's safety.

Let her be well. Let her be safe.

Alexander approached the cottage quietly and dismounted. Where was Crayton's horse? Had they already left? Or had Claire lied to him? Dread seized his heart as he inched open the door.

The inside of the cottage was dim with late afternoon shadows and he had to adjust his eyes to make out objects. A chair. Vases of flowers. A bed. He squinted and drew near the latter.

"*Francie?*"

She shook her head and pulled on a leather strap binding her wrists to the headboard. "No. Please, I beg of you. Please."

The sight of his wife tied to a bed sickened him. Cursing, he rushed to her and knelt before her. "It's Alexander, my love."

She turned to him, a wild, near-hysteric look in her eyes. "Alexander?"

He touched her tear-stained cheek with great tenderness and even greater caution. "It's all right, Francie. He can't hurt you now."

"Alexander," she whispered. "He vowed to get me. I fear he'll be back."

"No, no, my love." With a bit of effort, he unbound her hands and pulled her against his chest. "You're safe now," he whispered into her hair. "On my life, no one will harm you." He closed his eyes for a brief moment and thanked God she was alive. "Where is Crayton now?"

"On his way to Devonshire, I think. A servant came hours ago with a message and he left. He has a gun, he shot Uncle Bernard...and Claire..." she broke off sobbing and Alexander pulled her closer.

"Your uncle is being tended by the physician at this very moment. He arrived at Drakemoor a short time ago." He paused, debating whether he should tell her the state Bernard had been in. He decided on the truth. "He lost quite a bit of blood."

"That evil man shot him."

"And he shall pay. Come, my love, I need to get you out of here." Alexander lifted her into his arms and carried her from the cottage. Her eyes fluttered shut and she went limp, her face pressed against his chest. He could have lost her today. His heart pounded so hard it hurt to breathe. *He could not lose her.* Alexander lifted Francie onto Baron, climbed behind her, and wrapped his arms around her. "I love you, Francie," he breathed into her hair.

He rode with as much speed as he thought she could tolerate. When they were still some distance away, he found an isolated area amidst the trees and stopped. They would rest awhile and then continue their journey to Drakemoor. Alexander dismounted and helped his wife down, then with great gentleness checked her for injuries. His rage grew with each abrasion, each cut, and when he'd completed his examination, he vowed, *"I will kill him."*

Francie pressed his hand against her cheek. Her lips trembled when she spoke. "I thought I might never see you again."

He placed a soft, reverent kiss on her lips. "I feared you were lost to me forever. My life would be worthless without you. I love you, Francie, with every ounce of breath I possess. I've been a fool. An utterly, ridiculous fool."

Her eyes glistened. "I'll never tire of hearing you say that."

He kissed her temple. "That I love you? Or that I've been a fool?"

"Both." Her voice fell to a husky whisper. "I thought I might die and never hear you speak of love. And now that you have, I fear once will never be enough."

His hand trembled as he caressed her cheek. "That is quite fortunate for me, for I fear I will need to profess it several times a day." He paused, then asked the question he dreaded most. "Did he hurt you? Did he...force you?"

She shook her head. "No, he did not."

Relief flooded through him. His wife was safe.

"There's something I must tell you," Francie said. "It's about Claire Ashcroft." She bit her lower lip, a habit she had when caught in a bout of uncertainty.

He would spare her further upset. "I know she was involved in your abduction. I'll see she pays for her choice of regrettable friends and ill pursuits."

Francie worried her lower lip with greater ferocity and blurted out, "She's my sister, Alexander."

"Sister?" Surely, he'd not heard right. He searched her face, looking for something, anything, that would claim this word false. Claire and Francie could *not* be sisters. They possessed no like qualities save they were both females. They were as different as...Belmont and Philip, evil and goodness, arrogance and humbleness. Hatred and love.

"Claire is my twin sister. I learned of this today from Uncle Bernard when she discovered my locket. It all makes sense if one thinks about it. She could pass as Lord Belmont's daughter with her black hair and fair skin. I, obviously, could not." She raised a hand and fingered a lock of her glorious curls.

"She knows you are sisters?" he asked, still reeling from this latest discovery.

Francie shrugged as though the matter were of little conse-quence but he didn't miss the fleeting pain in her eyes. "I thought she'd come to help me."

Alexander eased her chin between his fingers and placed a tender kiss on her lips. "She'll not bother you again. I promise." Sister or not, he had plans for Claire Ashcroft. What would her father say when he learned she lifted her skirts for men and boys of every station? He'd not take it well, Alexander guessed.

"And Jared Crayton?"

He tensed. Mention of the man made him want to beat the bastard with his bare fists. He forced himself to relax and provide a reasonable answer. "I shall find him and deal with him." He would not tell her of the unsavory characters he knew in London who could rearrange a man's body parts in exchange for a satchel of coins.

◦⁓◦

FRANCIE DREAMED SHE HEARD HOOFBEATS, soft and steady at first and then louder, more persistent. It was him! She must escape before he returned. She yanked at the leather strap that bound her to the bed but could not free herself. She was well and truly trapped.

Jared Crayton said he would send for her. He would abuse her body, scar her soul, steal all hope for a future with Alexander, employing vileness and cruelty until he broke her. She would rather die. The hoofbeats stopped.

"No!" She thrashed about the bed, kicking and screaming. "No!" She would not give in. "Leave me alone! Don't touch me, you horrible beast!"

"Francie. Wake up. Look at me, my love."

Alexander? Her eyes flew open. Her husband stared back at her, an expression of such concern and heartache on his face, it pained her. "Alexander," she breathed.

"You had a bad dream," he said, stroking her hair. "You're safe. No one will hurt you, I swear it."

She blinked and took in her surroundings—she was in Alexander's room, in his bed, and he lay beside her, freshly shaved and smelling of spice and mint. His silk robe hung open, revealing a chest that made her light-headed.

"Francie?"

His soothing tone coaxed the words from her. "The dream seemed so real," she whispered. "I was trying to escape but my hands were tied and no matter how hard I tried, I couldn't free myself."

Alexander's silver gaze burned into her as he lifted her hand and gently kissed each finger. "I swear, on my word and on my life, no one will harm you."

"I believe you." She stroked the jagged scar on his face, wishing she could have protected the little boy he'd once been. "And I swear on my word and on *my life*, no one will harm you."

His lips twitched. "You will protect me?"

She nodded, warming to the idea of protecting her

husband. "I will." She might require assistance, but there was always George, who could tackle and foil an intruder, as well as the other residents of Drakemoor. They held great allegiance to their master. She'd heard of James's vow to keep intruders at bay and Mrs. Jenkins's stockpile of pots and pans at the ready to hurl from windows at unsuspecting interlopers. Even Aunt Eleanor admitted to tucking a kitchen knife in her apron—in the event action became necessary.

The residents of Drakemoor were no weaklings. To be sure, they were ferocious, loyal, and determined. They would protect their lord and mistress from all manner of beast—royal or not. Francie let out a long, calming breath. Indeed, they were safe.

"We'll catch him and see that justice is done." Alexander spoke with a steely certainty that made her wonder if the man had already been caught and was at this very moment receiving his torturous due.

"Have you located him?" She pictured broken bones and bruises. And blood—lots of blood.

"Not yet. But soon."

"Are you certain?"

Alexander's eyes gleamed. "Very certain."

She knew that look in his eyes and was grateful it wasn't meant for her. Jared Crayton *would* be captured. "You aren't the only one in search of him. Sally's uncle is on the hunt as well."

"Sally's uncle? What the devil are you talking about?"

With all the goings-on of the past several hours, she'd completely forgotten about the uncle. "I'm sorry. Sally's uncle visited the duke and demanded to see his son. The man must have made a rather strong impression because a servant arrived at the cottage with money and a note for Jared Crayton to flee immediately."

Alexander sighed and rubbed the back of his neck. "Is there anything else you forgot to tell me?"

"Just one more thing. Sally's uncle is not just any uncle. He's the stuff of legends."

Alexander lifted a brow. "Indeed?"

"Sally loved to speak of her mysterious uncle and his gallant adventures." She lowered her voice. "He's a pirate."

"A pirate?"

"Oh, Alexander, why such a sour face? I have it on good authority; the man is a pirate, though not a bad one. He's what is known as a gentleman pirate."

"I was not aware there was a difference."

"Indeed there is." She pictured a dark and dangerous man with a golden earring and devilish good looks. And politeness, of course. Those looks, according to legend, had stolen women's hearts from England to the West Indies. "Have you any idea who I'm speaking of?"

Alexander rubbed his jaw and said, "I cannot begin to imagine."

"His name is Mad Jack."

"Mad Jack?" He said the name with equal amounts irritation and respect.

"You know of him?"

Pause. "Unfortunately, I do."

"I thought tales of the man only lived in Amberden. The way Sally spoke of her uncle's outlandish antics, I often wondered if he could possibly be real or merely the figment of a young girl's imagination."

Alexander frowned. "He's real enough."

"Truly? You met him?"

Her husband grew distracted at the question, which told Francie he did indeed know the man. But the look on his face suggested he'd rather not offer details.

"Alexander?"

His frown deepened and when he spoke, his voice

contained a hint of anger. "I had a run-in with him a few years back over stolen lace and a trunk of gold. *My* lace and *my* gold. I lost half a cargo ship to the blasted thief."

Francie peered into her husband's eyes. "Oh, Alexander. He didn't harm you, did he?"

He scowled. "Other than my pride? No, he didn't harm me. I fared much better than most. We struck a deal; I could keep half of my cargo if I agreed to invest a portion of his ill-gotten wealth for a time when he quit the seas."

Francie laughed. "Oh, but that's rich! Mad Jack must be quite a businessman." How many men could strike business deals with the very person they'd stolen from? "Was he terribly handsome?"

Alexander scowled again. "I assure you, I didn't notice."

Perhaps it was best not to discuss the physical attributes of a man who had stolen from her husband. "If legend is true, Mad Jack will do more than speak with him when he catches him." A smile lit her face. "In fact, he'll not speak at all."

Alexander's gaze darkened as it slid to her lips. "What a splendid idea."

That look never failed to ignite her insides, making her want him with a deep, endless burn. "What? Not speaking?"

"Exactly." He tucked a lock of hair behind her ear and trailed a finger along her throat.

Francie forgot about Mad Jack and his adventures as Alexander's hand toyed with the ribbon on her nightgown. She placed her hand atop his. "I need you, Alexander."

His gaze jumped to hers. "I don't want to hurt you."

She shook her head and lifted her hand to caress his cheek, then she sighed and said, "I am most happy, dear husband."

He undid the ribbon and the gown fell open. Alexander dipped a hand beneath the fabric and cupped a breast. "Why are you happy, dear wife?" he asked as he leaned over and kissed her nipple. His tongue circled until she moaned.

"I'm happy because you saved me. I prayed you would find me, and you did." She buried her hands in his hair and held him at her breast. "But most of all, I'm happy because you love me."

Alexander placed a soft kiss between the swell of her breasts and lifted his head to meet her gaze. How could she have ever thought him cold and incapable of emotion?

"I do indeed love you," he said, "with my whole heart. I shall endeavor to treat you with the love you deserve for the rest of our lives." He traced her lips with his tongue and whispered, "My one true love."

And then there were no more words as he proceeded to show her exactly how much he loved her.

EPILOGUE

"Would you like another strawberry?" Alexander held a plump berry to Francie's lips. It was late afternoon on a warm summer's day. They were lounging on a blanket in a secluded area of Drakemoor, under an old elm tree.

"Mmm," she murmured. "They're delicious." She opened her mouth and took a rather large bite. Juice streamed from the corners of her lips and ran down her chin. He reached out and swiped at the juice with his finger. She caught his hand and brought it to her mouth, flicking her tongue over his finger, tasting the sweetness.

Alexander sucked in a breath and pulled his hand away. "If you keep doing that, I shall be forced to summon your aunt and uncle back to Drakemoor at once. Imagine their surprise when they are called from Amberden much earlier than expected?"

"Oh, pooh. You would never do such a thing. Besides, am I not permitted to touch my husband?"

"You are, but if you continue to use your tongue for the touching, I won't be responsible for my actions." He tried to force a stern look on her but failed miserably.

Laughter tinkled through her. "Promise?"

"Be serious, Francie." His silver gaze dropped to her swollen belly. "I would never do anything to hurt you." He placed a large hand on her protruding middle. "Or the baby," he finished in a soft voice that shivered through her.

"There's no need to worry. I'm healthy as a horse." She touched the dark hair peeking out of his lawn shirt. "And I have a very healthy appetite."

A shadow of a smile played over his full lips as he turned to her. "You're a witch."

She ran her fingers down his shirt to the top of his breeches. "Then let me bewitch you."

Alexander's gaze darkened to a smoky gray as he unbuttoned his breeches. After all these months together, when he looked at her like that, it still made her heart skip three beats. She lifted her gown and smiled at the look of surprise on his face when he saw she wore no undergarments.

"You never cease to surprise me," he ground out as he lay on his back and helped her straddle him.

She sighed as he filled her completely, reveling in the look of pure bliss on her husband's face. He might sound fierce, but Alexander enjoyed her little surprises. Even anticipated them. And she so loved to surprise him.

"Francie," he said in a tight voice, "what are you doing to me?"

What was she doing to him? She might ask the same of him. Alexander need only look at her, and her body heated with desire. She craved his touch, his taste, his scent. Good Lord, even the sound of his voice made her insides thrum. She craved every part of the man. The yearning grew as Francie rode him with slow, even strokes, teasing him with her body, tormenting him with her words. "Don't you like it?"

His nostrils flared. "I like it overmuch. Put an end to this torment. Now."

She stroked the jagged scar on his face and stopped moving. "Is that a command, husband?"

His gaze narrowed as he reached for her. "A plea," he murmured, running a finger along her bottom lip. "A heartfelt plea from a thoroughly besotted husband in need of his wife."

For a man unfamiliar with expressing emotion, he was certainly coming along. "Oh, Alexander."

"You are my heart."

She quivered, overcome by his words. "I love you." She began moving over him again, slowly at first, and then quickening her pace until his expression turned dark and desperate. She loved that look. It came over him, right before he—

Alexander grabbed her hips and pumped into her with greedy abandon. Deeper and deeper, he pleasured her until she exploded with a lusty cry and a round of breath-stealing shivers. Alexander followed seconds later, his body tensing as he groaned her name and spilled his seed into her, hot, deep, and complete.

Afterward, they lay in each other's arms, basking in the warm rays of love and spent passion. It was always like this when they came together, intense and explosive, stealing conscious thought, wiping out everything but that finite moment in each other's arms.

"Something's digging into my back," Alexander said, pulling out a shiny black shoe and dangling it from two fingers. "If I'd left it on, I wouldn't have this problem."

Francie laughed. "No. If you hadn't insisted on setting them beside you in such a neat little pile, you wouldn't have this problem." She grabbed his shoe. "If you'd done as I'd suggested in the first place," she said, tossing the shoe in the grass, "we wouldn't be having this discussion."

"Francie! I like to keep things together."

She rolled her eyes. He really had eased up on his stuffy habits over the past several months. When they strolled on the lawns or picnicked, he left his cravat and jacket at home. And just last week, she'd convinced him to take off his shoes and run his bare feet over the plush grass. Now, if she could only teach him to fling his shoes across the lawn and resist the urge to chase after them, then she'd say they were making real progress.

She sighed and pretended annoyance. She reached behind him, grabbed the other shoe, and flung it in the air.

"Francie!"

She threw him an innocent look. "Now they're together."

He started to get up, but she grabbed his hand. "Lie with me. It's time for the baby's story."

Alexander glanced toward his shoes, lying several feet apart. Then he turned to his wife and placed his hand on her belly. "What shall we tell him about today?"

"You mean, what shall we tell *her* about today," she corrected.

"Very well." He kissed the middle of her belly. "Should we tell her about the villain who abducted her mother and found himself captive to one of the most notorious pirates on the sea?"

Francie shook her head. "I don't think stories of a pirate shipping an earl's son off to the Americas is what constitutes a fairy tale."

Alexander rubbed his jaw. "Even if the story is told in all of Amberden?"

"They talk of the man's private parts being eaten by a school of fish!"

Her husband shrugged. "Perhaps that is a bit harsh. We

could tell her of the daring heroics her father employed as he outwitted the woman who was deeply enamored with him."

Francie rolled her eyes. "She was obsessed with you but enamored with every breathing male."

"Unfortunately for her, there are no males, breathing or otherwise, in the convent her father sped her off to once he learned of her dalliances."

"Must *I* tell our daughter a story today?" Francie sighed her impatience. "You're much too interested in villains and seductresses."

Her husband's lips twitched as they did when he tried to hide a smile. "I think I've got it." He gazed into her eyes and began. "Once upon a time, there was a fiery young maiden who lived in a small village. She was very happy with her tiny cottage and the brilliant flowers that surrounded her. But one day she was taken from her small village and brought to a castle, where an ornery ruler lived. This ornery ruler never laughed and rarely smiled. Until he met the fiery young maiden..."

MANY THANKS for choosing to spend your time reading *A Taste of Seduction*. I'm truly grateful. If you enjoyed it, please consider writing a review on the site where you purchased it. (Short ones are fine and always welcome.)

If you'd like to be notified of my new releases, please sign up at my website: *http://www.marycampisi.com.*

ABOUT THE AUTHOR

Mary Campisi writes emotion-packed books about second chances. Whether contemporary romances, women's fiction, or Regency historicals, her books all center on belief in the beauty of that second chance. Her small town romances center around family life, friendship, and forgiveness as they explore the issues of today's contemporary women.

Mary should have known she'd become a writer when at age thirteen she began changing the ending to all the books she read. It took several years and a number of jobs, including registered nurse, receptionist in a swanky hair salon, accounts payable clerk, and practice manager in an OB/GYN office, for her to rediscover writing. Enter a mouse-less computer, a floppy disk, and a dream large enough to fill a zip drive. The rest of the story lives on in every book she writes.

When she's not working on her craft or following the lives of five adult children, Mary's digging in the dirt with her flowers and herbs, cooking, reading, walking her rescue lab mix, Henry, or, on the perfect day, riding off into the sunset with her very own hero/husband on his Harley Ultra Limited.

If you would like to be notified when Mary has a new release, please sign up at http://www.marycampisi.com/

For more information
https://www.marycampisi.com
mary@marycampisi.com

Made in the USA
San Bernardino,
CA